Kiss me...

Eli's fingers brushed Isa's satin soft skin. Her whiskey-colored eyes locked on his. Full lips parted as she pulled in a breath, and every ounce of man in him wanted to sample every drop of woman in her.

Before he could answer the question *why?* he'd leaned in and captured her waiting lips with his. It was like the entire warehouse caught fire. Heat climbed his torso, scorched his spine, incinerated his brain. Her pillowy lips gave and took until a sound like a high mew came from her throat.

She smelled like spice cake and tasted better, her own brand of fire and smoke and sex. It'd been months, damn near a *year* since he'd had a woman in his arms and this woman was all woman. From her high, high heels to legs that disappeared into a skirt, to the delicate blouse he'd wanted to cut every last button off of and see what she was hiding beneath it.

As soon as he could take his lips off hers...

"In Lemmon's latest her signature style of storytelling laced with emotion and grit will engage readers with each turn of the page."

—RT Book Reviews

A BAD BOY FOR CHRISTMAS

"Shopping for a hot holiday read? Look no further than *A Bad Boy for Christmas*...With charismatic characters, stirring situations, and enough sexy to fill an entire town's worth of stockings, this latest in Lemmon's Second Chance series is 400-plus pages of Christmas magic."

—USA Today, "Happy Ever After" blog

"Connor and Faith are strong and complement each other, and their chemistry is explosive. Lemmon is an expert at the modern-day romance."

—RT Book Reviews

"Sexy and well-constructed...Likable and realistic characters with believable emotions, and the right balance of fantasy fulfillment, make for some good holiday heat."

—Publishers Weekly (starred review)

RESCUING THE BAD BOY

"An amazing read and I can't wait for the next installment."

—TheBookNympho.com

"Nobody does a bad boy like Jessica Lemmon."

—HarlequinJunkie.com

HARD TO HANDLE

CAN'T LET GO

TEMPTING THE BILLIONAIRE

The
BASTARD
BILLIONAIRE

JESSICA LEMMON

FOREVER

NEW YORK BOSTON

Copyright © 2017 by Jessica Lemmon
Excerpt from *The Billionaire Bachelor* copyright © 2016 by Jessica Lemmon

Cover photography by Claudio Marinesco. Cover design by Elizabeth Turner.
Cover copyright © 2017 by Hachette Book Group, Inc.

Forever
Hachette Book Group
1290 Avenue of the Americas, New York, NY 10104
forever-romance.com
twitter.com/foreverromance

First Edition: February 2017

Forever is an imprint of Grand Central Publishing. The Forever name and logo are trademarks of Hachette Book Group, Inc.

The publisher is not responsible for websites (or their content) that are not owned by the publisher.

The Hachette Speakers Bureau provides a wide range of authors for speaking events. To find out more, go to www.hachettespeakersbureau.com or call (866) 376-6591.

ISBNs: 978-1-4555-6661-7 (mass market), 978-1-4555-6663-1 (ebook)

Printed in the United States of America

OPM

10 9 8 7 6 5 4 3 2 1

ATTENTION CORPORATIONS AND ORGANIZATIONS:

Most Hachette Book Group books are available at quantity discounts with bulk purchase for educational, business, or sales promotional use. For information, please call or write:

Special Markets Department, Hachette Book Group
1290 Avenue of the Americas, New York, NY 10104
Telephone: 1-800-222-6747 Fax: 1-800-477-5925

For Aunt Sherry and Uncle Bill

ACKNOWLEDGMENTS

Huge thanks to Tracey Slemker for talking at length with me about prosthetic limbs (any mistakes are mine), and to Gwen Harmon for the introduction. Thanks to Michele Bidelspach, Michelle Cashman, and the rest of the team at Forever. To Jonathan Cannaux for being on the cover—the only way it could be better is if we could see your gorgeous eyes!

As always, thanks to Nicole Resciniti, agent extraordinaire. Friends and fellow authors, Kate Meader, Lauren Layne, and Jules Bennett for your plotting help and friendship. And to my husband, John, who encourages me to live out my dreams each and every day.

Last but not least, huge hugs to my fellow romance authors who offer support and LOLs online and in real life, and to you, dear reader, for joining me on this journey. I couldn't do it without you.

The

BASTARD
BILLIONAIRE

CHAPTER 1

The flames in the fireplace were nearly extinguished, the curtains drawn on the high windows of Elijah Crane's office. Rain pattered on the glass, providing a soothing backdrop for his work. He pecked at his keyboard, his mind on the e-mail, when a mousy, quiet voice lifted in the darkness.

"Mr. . . . Crane?"

The desk lamp and a slice of natural light made its way past the doorless entry to his office. His newest temporary assistant stood blocking that light, her shadow a long, narrow wedge.

"Reese Crane called," she said as she walked into his office. "Your brother."

Like he needed that clarification?

"I know who Reese Crane is, Melanie."

"He asked me to . . ." Her small voice grew smaller until it vanished altogether. Reason being, Eli had taken a deep, rumbling breath and pushed himself up from the desk.

Slowly.

Let it never be said intimidation wasn't an art form.

He kept his eyes on the woman now standing at the other side of his desk. She was young, in her early twenties, and from what he'd gleaned in the last eight or so hours since she'd started this position, weak. He'd bet he could run this one off in record time. Not that he was keeping track, but maybe he should. He was getting good at it.

He blew out that same breath, keeping his lip curled, his expression hard. He let the breath end on a growl.

"What did I tell you this morning?" he asked, his voice lethal.

His latest temporary personal assistant currently putting a massive cramp in his style blinked her big, doelike eyes. "Not to interrupt you, but, Mr. Crane—"

"Not. To. Interrupt me." He made a show of pulling his shoulders straight and hobbling around the table. Her gaze trickled down to the prosthesis at the end of his right leg as he affected a limp. One he didn't have. One he'd trained himself *not* to have.

The help found him more intimidating when reminded he was an amputee. He'd used it to his advantage on more than one occasion. "Do I look like I need to be bothered with trivial questions, Melanie?"

"N-no, sir, but it's about Crane Hotels and I was hired to—"

"You answer to me," he told her point-blank. "I don't care if it's a memo from the Pope. I asked not to be interrupted. I *expect* not to be interrupted."

"But the board meeting..." Melanie trailed off, her eyes blinking faster as if staving off tears.

Tough shit, sweetheart.

The sooner word reached his brothers that the ninth—or was Melanie the tenth?—PA to set foot in Eli's warehouse left in tears, the better. He wasn't interested in resuming a position with Crane Hotels for a myriad of personal reasons, none of which he'd shared with them. The thickheaded men in his family didn't listen when he'd clearly and concisely said no to a pencil-pushing position at the Crane home base, so he'd resorted to showing not telling. The more assistants Reese had sent, the brasher Eli had become.

"Mr. Reese Crane said all you need to do is read this report and give your opinion. I can reiterate on the conference call for you," she squeaked.

Eli elevated his chin and stared her down. She didn't hold his gaze, hers jerking left then right and very purposefully avoiding dipping to his missing limb for a second time.

Sucking in a breath, he blew out one word. "Fine."

"Fine?" Melanie's eyebrows lifted, her expression infused with hope. She was sweet... and about to get a lesson in hard knocks. He hadn't always been this rigid, but change was inevitable after what had happened. She was about to be on the receiving end of the not-so-nice guy he'd become.

"You want my opinion? I'll give you my opinion." He lashed a hand around her wrist, removed the folder from her hand, and tossed it into the fireplace. There were mostly embers now, but a single flame crawled over the edge of the folder as it slid onto the concrete floor. The fire fizzled, smoking instead of igniting.

Well. That was unimpressive.

"You...you're..." Melanie's fists were balled at her sides, her eyes filling yet again as she visibly shook.

"Spit it out. I don't have all day."

"You're a monster!" She turned and ran—yes, ran—from his office, through his dining room and to the warehouse elevator. He stepped out from behind his office wall to watch the entire scene, arms folded over his chest. There were few doors and walls in this place, so not much hampered the sight of another victory won by Eli "Monster" Crane.

Back in his office, he stomped on the smoking file folder at his feet. Once he was sure he wouldn't burn down his house, he chucked the folder into the wastebasket at the side of his desk.

"Sorry, Reese," he said to thin air. "You'll have to manage without me."

They'd managed without him for the years he was stationed overseas. His brothers could put one foot in front of the next without him. God knew being away hadn't improved Eli's ability to weigh in on financials.

But that's not why they wanted him there. Reese and Tag, and their father, wanted Eli there because they believed Crane Hotels was part of Eli's future. A legacy, like CEO was for Reese. Like Guest and Restaurant Services was for Tag.

Eli's avoidance was in part because he had spearheaded a sizeable personal project and in larger part because wherever he went, unfortunate events unfurled. He wasn't *quite* ready to topple the company his father had grown into an empire.

His cell phone buzzed with a text from an old friend

he'd contacted earlier this week. He lifted the phone and walked smoothly from his desk to the kitchen, reading the text.

Yep, still in business.

He tapped in a reply. *Let's talk more next week. Give me a choice of dates.*

He pocketed his phone, feeling a charge shoot down his arms. Since he'd come home, he'd been consumed with giving back. With changing the worlds of men and women who'd made sacrifices. For their country, for their families. Men and women who'd returned home with less than they had before they left and were expected to drop back into the flow of things.

Penance, some might argue, for everything in Eli's past. He wasn't above admitting that evening the scales for his failures was a big part of what drove his actions now.

Which meant he had no interest in stepping in as chief operations officer of the gargantuan Crane Hotels, no matter how many PAs his oldest brother sent over.

Keep 'em comin'.

Eli had become adept at running off PAs. In fact, he'd become even more creative about the ways he could get them to quit.

If poor Melanie had her way, he'd reside in a creepy mansion atop a hill. The gossip rags would murmur about the beastly Crane brother no one dared bother lest they suffer his wrath. He let out a dry laugh, amused by the bend of his thoughts.

After the year he'd had, that sounded a lot like heaven.

* * *

The phone was ringing off the hook today, which normally would be a good sign. But the caller on hold sent Isabella Sawyer's stomach on a one-way trip to her toes.

"Isa?" her assistant called again from her desk. "Do you want me to take a message?"

"No, Chloe, I'll take it." She didn't want to take it, but she'd take it. She shut her office door and in the minimizing crack watched as her friend's face morphed into concern. Isa gave Chloe a thumbs-up she didn't quite feel. Lifting the handset of her desk phone was like facing a firing squad.

"Bobbie, hello," she said to Reese Crane's secretary.

"Hold for Mr. Crane," Bobbie clipped in her usual curt manner.

She'd had similar conversations with Reese several times already. *Nine* other times, to be exact. One for each of the personal assistants she'd sent over to work with his brother. Isa was pretty sure this was the "you're fired" call she'd been expecting three assistants ago. At least she had a prepared response this time.

"Isa. Here we are again," came Reese's smooth voice.

She'd met him once in passing, at an event she'd attended on behalf of her personal assistant company, Sable Concierge. Reese Crane was tall, intimidating, handsome, and professional.

And married. Not that he was Isa's type. Business guys in suits for clients, yes. Business guys in suits for dating potential, no thanks. She'd been there, done that, and picked up the dry cleaning.

"Mr. Crane, I'm sorry we aren't speaking under better circumstances."

"So am I. You promised me you'd found the ideal PA for Eli this time around."

Melanie hadn't been second string, but Isa had already gone through her top choices. Elijah Crane had chased off every last one of them. They were down to her assistant Chloe, whom Isa needed here in the office, or a new hire named Joey. No way would he last thirty seconds.

Isa refused to pull her other PAs off current assignments to cater to Elijah Crane. If she lost the Crane business, she'd need her current roster of clients or they'd all starve.

"Solve my problem." Reese's commanding tone brooked no argument, nor should it. Isa was at his beck and call for one simple reason: his seal of approval would help her budding business advance to the next level, or, if she continued failing to provide a suitable assistant for his brother, could tank it. She wanted to wedge a foot in the door with the elite in Chicago, and since her parents weren't supportive of her choice in vocation, Reese Crane held the key to that door.

"I have a solution. A PA who has over three years experience at my company and a decade prior working as right-hand woman to Sawyer Financial Group. I can guarantee your brother will absolutely *not* scare her away."

"Who is this maven?" he asked, but the lilt of his voice suggested he'd already figured out.

"Me."

A quiet grunt that could have been a laugh came through the phone. "I take it you're not much of a wilter."

"No. I'm tenacious and stubborn."

"An exact match for Eli."

"Once I convince him to get more involved in Crane Hotels, I'm sure I can place one of our many qualified assistants in my stead. I do have a company to run."

Afraid she'd overstepped boundaries with her confidence, she cleared her throat, her mother's scolding voice in the back of her mind whispering, *Be polite, Isabella. No man appreciates a woman who disrespects him.*

"My foray as his assistant will be brief," she continued. "But there's no need for him to know I'm top brass."

"Right. Let's not give him a challenge he'll embrace," Reese muttered.

"Exactly. I'll act as if the company sent me. Like I'm a nameless number eleven. But trust me when I say, I'll exceed your expectations."

"Eleven," Reese muttered.

She could have kicked herself for reminding him how many assistants they'd run through already.

"I apologize for the lack of professionalism you've seen so far. I appreciate you giving Sable Concierge another chance. My company is one I want you to lean on any time you're in need of help."

"Your company came highly recommended, Ms. Sawyer." Reese said, his voice taking on a gentle quality. His voice did that whenever the topic of his wife came up.

"Thank Merina for me again," Isa told him.

"I will. Your success is imminent, I presume."

"You can bank on it." She said her goodbyes and hung up the phone, pulling in a steady breath. One more shot. She had one more shot to pull this off. No, Reese hadn't said it, but he hadn't needed to. She'd fire her if she were he. Wife-recommended or not.

Last fall, Isa randomly scored a position for one of her assistants at the Van Heusen Hotel with Merina. The other woman had suggested Isa's company for Elijah's transition from Marine to Crane COO. In comparison to what Merina's brother-in-law had been through serving his country, placing a PA was supposed to be easy. Eli had been through the physical hoops to regain his mobility using a prosthetic leg, and his warehouse home was equipped to accommodate his working from there as well.

The assistant's job was to help Eli field Crane Hotels's conference calls, answer and forward e-mails, and tend to the light load of work Reese had handed down to Eli to oversee.

Eli had done none of it.

Isa sent in seasoned help, and a startling number of her employees left either in tears or so angry Isa nearly lost them altogether. Elijah Crane, regardless of the team's sensitivity training and the day they'd spent with a rehabilitation expert for amputees, was not an easy guy to feel sorry for.

He was "mean," according to one of her employees, "miserable" according to another, and poor Melanie, who unfortunately had turned in her notice after her first and only day at Eli's, had referred to him as a "monster" on her way out the door.

Well. The scourge of Eli Crane ended here. Isa wasn't accustomed to buckling under pressure. If Eli was determined to be miserable, he could ruin his own life, but she wouldn't allow him to tank her company's future. Despite the reassurance she'd given Reese, Isa had expected Melanie to last two or three days. She'd lasted one.

Chloe had been trained to run the office in case Isa was away, so Isa had no doubts she could handle Eli during the day, then tend to Sable Concierge after hours. Answering e-mails could be done at any time of night, and she could return phone calls during lunch or early in the morning.

As owner and operator, Isa was willing to do whatever it took to make her business a success in Chicago. If she had to work two jobs for the short term, so be it.

Elijah Crane hadn't given her a choice.

* * *

Eli sat at the kitchen table and watched the hubbub in front of him, face resting in his hand, scowl on his face. His sister-in-law, Merina, was bustling around setting the table. She paused in front of him.

"You look like your brother when you do that." Her mouth flinched into a teasing smile.

"The one you married or Tarzan?"

"I heard that." Tag loped into the room with three to-go bags from Chow Main, the best Chinese food joint in town. Eli's mouth watered at the sight of the generic paper-inside-a-plastic bag with the happy face on it that read HAVE A NICE DAY!

Tag's girlfriend, Rachel, followed him in, a bottle of wine in each hand.

"Hey, Rach," Merina greeted, setting the last place. She accepted one of the bottles and spun the label around. "Ooh, good choice."

"It's a customer favorite. Or was, when I bartended." Rachel flashed Eli a quick glance, then looked away. She wasn't sure about him yet, and for good reason. They hadn't spent a lot of time together. He hadn't exactly been warm and fuzzy since he'd returned home.

Reese filtered in behind them, still wearing his suit from

work. Merina reached up and tugged the knot in his tie loose, standing on her toes to press a lengthy kiss to his lips.

"Sexy man," she murmured.

"Vixen," Reese commented, cupping her ass in one hand.

Patience shot, Eli gestured at the dishes on the table and bellowed, "Can someone please explain why we can't eat Chow Main out of the containers like normal human beings instead of dealing with this bullshit?"

He crossed his arms over his chest and glared at his family, all of whom had glued their eyes on him. Merina clucked her tongue. Reese's lip curled in mild irritation. Rachel bit her bottom lip and stepped closer to Tag, who wrapped an arm around her, opened his mouth, and let out a hearty laugh.

At that laugh, the tone of the room shifted back to light and fluffy, and the chattering continued as Rachel and Tag unloaded the food onto the table.

It seemed the only person Eli was capable of scaring off were assistants. His family was entirely immune to him.

"We're here," came a call from across the warehouse. Eli's father, Alex, and his assistant for years, Rhona, filed in together, her hand linked in his. It'd been recently discovered that Alex and Rhona were partnering in more than business, and since Eli's old man was retired and had been for some time, Eli guessed that Alex and Rhona were partnering more often than not on a personal front.

Love was in the fucking air, he thought with an eye roll.

"Hey, Eli." Rhona pulled her scarf from her neck—it was only September, so he had no idea why the scarf—and smiled brightly at him.

He lifted a hand and gave a brief wave. Rhona filed into the fray, cooing over the wine as Merina apologized about not knowing she was coming and pulled an extra set of dishes from the cabinet. A low sigh worked its way through Eli's chest.

Happy. Every last goddamn one of them. Surrounded by this much love caused a heavy streak of loneliness to course through him. Damned if he could understand why. He'd been a miserable bastard lately.

"Beer, bro?" Tag asked, collapsing next to him into a chair. His brother's hair was down in golden-brown waves, his beard full like Eli's but neatly trimmed, *not* like Eli's. He'd let the facial hair and the hair on his head grow and he resembled a homeless dog some days. Meanwhile, Mr. Pantene Hair next to him...

Eli swiped the bottle. "What, no frosted glass? Shouldn't we have coasters?"

He gestured to the set table, in the center of which rested a bowl filled with oranges his last assistant had brought over. She'd probably been instructed by Reese to monitor his vitamin C intake. That was another thing—since he'd been back, he'd been tended to, coddled, and overly cared for. He'd busted his ass getting himself up and moving so he was dependent on no one. As a completely independent and capable man, he resented the fussing.

"It's been half a year, E," Tag said, leaning back in the chair and sucking down some of his own beer. "You're going to have to get used to us being in your face. We missed you."

That last bit paired with an elbow jab and Eli grunted. He knew they'd missed him. Hell, *he'd* missed *them*.

His brothers and father had found happiness, which Eli admittedly found soul-sucking, but it didn't mean Eli wasn't happy for them. He just wished they would go be adorably coupled off somewhere far, far away from his sanctuary.

"I can go out into public, you know," he grumbled, setting the beer bottle next to his plate—on the table, no coaster, *thank you very much*. "You guys don't have to come in here and serve me."

He was skilled at his new role of miserable bastard, and since everyone expected it now, he was determined to excel.

"Oh but we do, Lord Crane." Merina smiled demurely as she leaned over and handed him a glass. "We know you don't want to be seen out and about yet. Trust me, I spent enough time with the media breathing down my neck. I don't blame you."

Wasn't that the truth? Other than a brief article in the *Trib* that had mentioned him as a war hero and a quote he'd said over the phone taken completely out of context, Eli had successfully avoided the limelight. Reese and Merina had not, but that'd been the plan. And it had worked out well for both of them, despite their initial dislike for one another.

Eli liked Merina. She was tough. She was bold and clearly had enough forearm strength to pull the stick out of Reese's ass. At least partway. Eli had never seen his oldest brother this...at peace. And now that Reese was living a utopic existence with his biggest dreams coming true, he wanted Eli on board to tiptoe in the tulips alongside him.

No, Reese wasn't through pressuring Eli into coming back on at Crane Hotels full-time, but he had lightened up some. As evidenced by him strolling back into the dining room area sans tie and jacket. Unlike Tag, Reese was always suited. Tag was the opposite, typically in cargo pants and a skintight Henley to show off biceps he was always pumping into ridiculous sizes.

Eli was as comfortable in a suit as out of one. He could don fatigues, jeans and a tee, or a three-piece Armani and feel like himself. The clothes, in his case, did not make the man. Even his body didn't make the man, though he worked his ass off to maintain his. He couldn't do all the things he used to be able to do, but the better shape he was in, the better he felt about the leg.

"The media doesn't give a shit about me," Eli said, and that was the way he liked it.

"They will when we name you COO," Reese piped up.

Eli sent him a death glare. Reese, the oldest, didn't flinch. Even with a sleeve of tattoos and a surly attitude, Eli didn't intimidate his oldest brother. Reese had known Eli when he'd sleepwalked to the neighbor's house, so Reese wasn't about to be intimated by a grumpy Marine.

"We found you a new PA," Reese announced.

"No."

"She starts next week," he continued as if Eli hadn't spoken.

"Well done, Reese." Alex took his seat across from Eli. He folded his fingers at his chin and smiled through a snow-white goatee, looking very Dos Equis's "Most Interesting Man in the World" in that position.

"You're wasting your time," Eli said to the collective masses. "I've told you repeatedly, I'm not interested in Chief Pencil Pusher, but if you insist, *Clip*..."

Tag barked another laugh, proud to hear his nickname

for Reese (Clip, short for Paperclip) used by someone other than himself.

"You're the most like me, Eli," Alex said, starting the familiar speech.

Because Eli had heard it about a dozen times over the last nine months, his vision began blurring at the edges. Talk of legacy and history would follow.

"Reese has my business savvy," Alex said, a proud smile stretching his goatee. "He was made for CEO." On that Eli couldn't disagree. Reese bled Crane Hotels's black and white. "Tag is my free spirit, perfect for the entertainment sector of Crane. He's always winning hearts."

"He won mine." Rachel slid onto Tag's lap instead of sitting in her own chair. Eli looked past lowered eyebrows to see her nuzzle Tag, who smiled like a lovesick fool.

Must be nice.

"But you, Elijah," his father continued. "You have my sense of duty. You have a lion's heart. That same sense is what propelled me into the service." Alex pushed up a sleeve, revealing a faded tattoo reading *semper fidelis*. Eli turned his arm to show off his matching tattoo. They did have that in common. What they didn't have in common was that his father was a war hero who saved people, and Eli, though he'd been lauded as one, had saved no one.

"But now your duty lies elsewhere, son."

Here it came. *Don't say it. Don't say it.*

"It's time to be the man Crane Hotels needs you to be."

Next to Eli, Tag snorted. Reese even cracked a smile.

Eli referred to this as Dad's "Batman" speech. It always ended with that same ode.

"I'm busy, Dad," Eli skirted. Because *cursed* would have sounded maudlin.

"We'll see."

He and his father met eyes for a few beats before their stare-down was interrupted.

"Okay, food!" Merina gestured to the spread. Typically, Tag ate three entrees on his own, but Merina preferred to have a bite of everything on the table. If Eli wasn't fast, she'd dig into his without asking. "Ooh, Eli. Your shrimp pad Thai looks amazing."

He pointed. "You have to give me an extra crab rangoon if you steal my food."

She slid a glance at Reese. "Did he used to be nicer?"

"No," Reese deadpanned.

Eli and Reese exchanged what could be construed as brief smiles. Reese knew better. Eli used to wield affable charm like a weapon. Before war had hardened him. Before his friends had died because he hadn't been able to save them.

But that was in the past, and this was now. His new normal was his family's presence every other Friday since he'd returned after leaving parts of himself in Afghanistan. Yes, his leg, but also two very good men. While he was away, a lot had happened to him, and as much had happened to his brothers. Reese was married, for the second time to the same woman; Tag was practically married; and Dad... whatever was going on there.

Eli understood how everyone assumed he'd slip into the slot bookmarked for him at Crane Hotels the moment he was well. For him, things weren't that simple. He loved them too much to fail them.

Reese dished out some of his Mongolian beef onto Merina's plate while she stole a sip of his wine.

Rachel slid off Tag's lap with a smile and Tag lifted her hand and kissed her fingers.

Rhona unwrapped a pair of chopsticks and handed them to Alex, who beamed at her, the happiest he'd been since Lunette Crane's death.

Eli reminded himself again that he didn't want what they had. He refused to want something he couldn't have. Life had spoken. He was listening.

CHAPTER 2

Instead of going downstairs to Sable Concierge's offices via her apartment overhead, the next morning Isabella drove to Elijah Crane's warehouse downtown. The building featured its own parking area, fenced and locked. Reese had given her the passcode—a passcode that didn't work as he'd predicted.

"He changes it all the time," he'd told her when she'd stopped by the Crane Hotel yesterday to pick up a key. "You can bypass it with this. He knows you're coming."

She locked the gate behind her and let herself into the warehouse. Eli lived upstairs, and the downstairs was empty, a huge sprawling area not set up for anything in particular. Shame. It was a great space.

Shaking the early autumn rain from her coat, Isa ran a hand through her hair and pressed a button on the freight elevator to Eli's lair. Upstairs, she slid open a heavy, metal elevator door and stepped inside, shutting it behind her. No doubt Eli was aware of her entrance. The metal scrape had echoed off high ceilings and tall windows she had no idea how he kept clean. They were, though. Rain pattered the cobweb-free panes as she stepped into the apartment, her mouth gaping in awe. She'd never seen anything like this place.

Stylish exposed brick walls dotted with windows; concrete floors with rugs separating rooms. A long, wooden table encircled by mismatched cloth chairs took up most of the dining room. A leather couch, chair, and coffee table (no TV) marked the living room area. Fat concrete pillars were interspersed with a few dividing walls—like the one hiding the area behind the dining room table. A bed peeked around a doorway at the end of the corridor, and a room she guessed was a bathroom bisected the hall. To her right was the kitchen, divided by a long countertop and a half wall over the sink.

"Don't get comfortable," came a low, male warning from behind the wall that must be hiding Eli's office.

Heels clicking, then muting when she stepped onto the rug, Isa made her way into the bowels of Eli's sanctuary, her heart hammering. She wasn't typically the nervous type, but the dim light inside the warehouse and somber rain pecking the windows gave the space an eerie quality. As she paced closer to the room where the voice had come from, she heard the distinct crackle of a fire.

In the air there was a different kind of crackle entirely, a low buzz of premonition in her bones.

She'd owned her confidence on the phone with Reese, but now that the air in Eli's home was pressing down on her, she was less sure of her promise to reform the middle

Crane brother. Standing in Eli's hallway was like hovering at the mouth of a cave where a hibernating grizzly bear hid. And she was unarmed.

But you are armed, she reminded herself. She hadn't been lying when she'd told Reese she could handle this situation. As a woman who had walked away from her family's money, expectations, and the man they'd chosen for her, Isabella Sawyer was nothing if not capable of overcoming challenge.

She was a woman who'd branched out on her own and had taken control of her life, without her family's blessing. One surly ex-soldier with a chip on his shoulder wasn't going to scare her away.

Squaring her shoulders, she stepped around the wall to find no door separating her from Eli's office space. The dark-haired man in question jotted notes on a paper, his head down, a lamp on his desk lighting his way. In the dim glow, she made out the edge of a beard and a trail of tattoos decorating one arm. Squinting didn't help her discern the inky images.

Without looking up, he spoke again. "You can leave."

Bite me, Crane.

She was tempted to say it aloud, but she wasn't positive he wouldn't bite her. In his case, his bite could be worse than his bark, and his bark was downright intimidating. It wouldn't be the first time Isa had stood up to a man who believed he held the cards, but she was playing a long game. Best not to push too hard just yet.

She stepped into his office and introduced herself. Or, well, the version of herself she wanted him to know.

"Hello, Mr. Crane. My name is Isabella. Sable Concierge sent me to serve as your personal helper. I've already been brought up to date by your brother about Crane Hotels's latest—"

"Isabella." He tossed the pen onto his desk. Lifted his head and met her eyes.

Her tongue stuck to the roof of her mouth, the remainder of her speech glued to it. Dark hair ruffled like he'd repeatedly pushed his fingers through it, an equally dark, thick beard lining a strong jaw, Eli Crane commanded attention. Deep blue eyes narrowed as he tracked down to her stilettos and up her professional—and, yes, a little tight at the thighs—dress she'd worn for this appointment. There was nothing overtly sexual about the dress, but no matter what she wore, her curves tested the limits of the seams. She was a woman and refused to hide her femininity—or mute it— especially for this man.

He shifted at the desk, pushing one palm into the wood, and his tattoos flexed, his muscles shifting temptingly.

Lord have mercy.

The crackle in the air this time wasn't a buzz of warning but of something else. Something heavy and weighted.

Unwanted attraction.

The kind you feel for a man when you know that you shouldn't. The kind packaged to be tempting, but when you get close, learn that the enticing beauty is laced with deadly poison.

The feeling was so strong, the pull so palpable, Isa struggled not to advance a step.

"No," he said.

"No what?" She tightened her grip on her Kate Spade tote, wedging her heels to the floor.

"No to Isabella. Too ornamental." His lip curled with what appeared to be disgust and she tamped down the temptation to be offended. This was his game. She wasn't going to play. "Can't you go by something else?"

"Most people call me Isa."

He hummed. The rough and tumble sound snagged her chest and her heartbeat kicked up a few notches.

This was awful. Just awful. Attraction to the wrong man had happened to her twice in her life. Once with her second boyfriend, to whom she'd bequeathed her virginity, and once with the man her parents had picked for her, who had turned out to be king of the jackasses. Twice she'd lived to regret following her hormones. She'd make no such mistake a third time. Especially with her business on the line.

"As I was saying, Mr. Crane."

"Elijah."

"Elijah," she corrected, forcing a smile.

"No…" His eyebrows lowered and he cocked his head in thought. "Go back to Mr. Crane."

He was pushing her. She was supposed to react. Lash out. Start arguing. This was his pattern. A few more pokes and he'd expect her to turn and run out crying or shouting how she'd never return.

Too bad, buddy.

"Very well." She straightened her shoulders and tried again. "Mr. Crane. So, your brother tells me—"

"What if I call you Izzie?"

"Pardon?"

"Nah, that's no good. Oh." He snapped his fingers. "Bella."

"Absolutely not," she clipped, letting her control waver. Her ex had called her Bella and she'd hated it.

"No, you're right." Eli's mouth pulled into a frown. "That's worse. I don't like any of the short names for

Isabella. What if I call you..." He snaked a gaze over her dress, which was professional and a respectable length. His trickling assessment made her feel as if she wore next to nothing. "Bettie Page?"

He leaned back in his chair, his shirt molding to a very fit chest. "You sure you're from Sable Concierge? Not a call girl service?"

"Mr. Crane." Her voice held an authority demanding respect. Enough was enough. She refused to let him bully her, whether the air snapped with wayward attraction or not. Whether he thought she was a lowly PA or not. She was not his plaything. And her choice of dress, no matter how evocative this male chauvinist found it, was nothing to be ashamed of. "I will not allow..."

He pushed to standing, up, up until he loomed, and then he took one heavy step toward her, then another. He favored the leg with the prosthesis, clad in a shoe to match his other one, the metal-colored leg peeking out from a tear in his jeans.

"I changed my mind, Bettie." He tilted his head to one side, a rogue gleam in his eyes as he stared her down. "You can call me Eli."

* * *

This one promised to be fun.

Sable Concierge had sent over an assistant who was not only female, she was sex in stilettos. The second he laid eyes on her, half of him expected her to tear off her glasses, pull her hair down, and give him a lap dance. Only she wasn't wearing glasses, and her hair was already down.

Dark, nearly black locks flowed over her shoulders in thick waves. Her eyes were fringed with jet-black lashes, and even slitted with disgust, they were more of a whiskey hue than flat brown. Her curves didn't stop at her shoulders. The cream-colored dress she wore hugged every hairpin turn on her body, and hers was a body made for hugging.

Reese. That son of a bitch. He had to have known what he was doing when he had them send this assistant in particular. Eli shook his head. *Low blow, brother.*

"Listen, sweetheart—"

"Eli, you will respect me while I'm working for you. You've done a decent job of disrespecting my coworkers, and I will not suffer their same fate." She jutted her chin forward, pinning him with those whiskey eyes again. "I'm accustomed to being underestimated because I'm a woman."

Yeah, he'd noticed the woman part.

"I'm sure you've had your fair share of being undermined." She sent a glance down at his prosthetic leg and snapped it back to his face.

Confident. It was the only word that flitted through his startled brain. He looked deeper, beyond the high cheekbones, fantastic rack, and manicured eyebrows. Worry lines bisected her eyebrows, suggesting she wasn't bulletproof. She was a woman who fretted regardless of what she wanted him to believe. Over her work? Her home life? His eyes snapped to her full, red mouth, and he noted a small silver scar at one corner.

"I don't give anyone the opportunity to underestimate me," he answered, yet his thoughts returned to his family and the way they were trying to take over his life. Trying to force him into a mold of their making. Well meaning, maybe, but facts were facts.

"That's a luxury I've never been afforded, I'm afraid. I'm often underestimated before I open my mouth, as you've aptly proven."

Between them, the air hung thick with challenge, neither of them willing to back down first. She'd rendered him speechless. Eli sucked his tongue against his teeth. Isabella Sawyer was complex. Just what he didn't need in his life. A complex, confident woman who challenged him.

"Do you have another desk?" she asked, eyebrows lifted, her hand wrapped around a gargantuan orange leather tote.

"I already told you to go." He didn't like to repeat himself.

"Very well. I'll work at the dining room table," she said. Before he could repeat himself a third time, her ass was wiggling away from him, one hand rising to flip her hair. Over her shoulder, she slid him a thick-lashed glare.

As he'd played up his limp, Isabella was playing up that lithe wiggle.

Eli couldn't help but think that he'd just met his match.

* * *

Isa didn't feel the confidence she portrayed as she swished away from Eli en route to his dining room table, but *fake it till you make it* had become her motto when she'd started her business three years ago in her apartment's living room.

Old habits died hard.

The endgame was Sable Concierge earning a gold seal from the Cranes, but she'd be damned if she would allow another man to slot her into the category of brainless bimbo. She had a bark *and* a bite and wasn't afraid to use either.

Her company was born of the deep-seated desire *not* to climb the financial corporate ladder her family had so wanted her to scale. She'd named the company after herself, after writing Isabella Sawyer on a napkin in a coffee shop and trying to come up with a combination of letters that sounded both approachable and professional.

Sable won.

She'd started out with one employee: herself. After working nearly ten years for her parents' financial firm from the tender age of eighteen, Isa had learned plenty about what it took to be a good PA. She was organized, had a good memory, and knew the fastest way to execute any task. Her favorite part of buzzing around Sawyer Financial Group had been taking the stress from the executives' shoulders and granting them a moment of relief. She was good at what she did. She loved what she did.

And it had never been enough for her parents.

No, her father, Hugh, and mother, Helena, insisted Isa follow in their footsteps. For too many years, Isa kept quiet as they promoted her from assistant to manager. She'd stopped short of being brought into the upper echelon when her soul couldn't take any more pressure. The financial business was dry as toast. Numbers on spreadsheets and thirty-page forms filled with lawyer-speak so boring Isa's eyes had glazed over.

She'd hated it.

By her twenty-eighth birthday, she dreamt of a business where she could go back to doing what she loved: organizing everyone else's busy day onto a tidy planner page and executing tasks by checking off lists. She knew she was overqualified for a starting assistant position, and so her company was born. After a short while she'd grown from one to ten employees, then fifteen, now thirty-two.

She was doing what she loved, owned a business she loved, and there was absolutely no way she'd allow beastly, sexist Elijah Crane to inhibit her success.

An hour later, her planner in hand, she straightened her shoulders and walked back to Eli's office. Since there wasn't a door, she rapped on the wall instead. The rainy day cast muted light over the room, which, save the desk lamp and dying fire, was the only light in the room.

"Elijah, I have a few questions for you."

"It's Eli, and I'm busy," he said, not looking in her direction. His face was lit by his laptop's screen, turned at an angle so she couldn't see what he was doing. In the reflection of a pair of black-framed glasses, she saw what looked like an e-mail.

He finally frowned up at her when she walked in, grabbed a chair from the other side of the room, and dragged it—damn, it was heavy—to the front of his desk. She sat, crossing one leg over the other and readied her pen over her planner page.

"First item," she read. "Reese requests your attendance at the board meeting tomorrow afternoon at the Crane."

"Are you hard of hearing, Bettie?"

"It's Isabella, or Isa as you prefer, and, no, I'm not."

His scowl deepened.

"Will you be attending?" she asked.

"No. I will not be attending. Get out of my office." He tore his glasses off and dropped them on the keyboard.

"Very well." She struck through the item with a line. "I

said I'd phone in with your responses. I assume you ignored my e-mail."

"I hate e-mail."

"You're replying to one now."

He blinked. Isa swallowed a smile. This man had no
idea who he was dealing with and she sort of loved it.

"I kept the e-mail short and sweet, Eli. You can finish
it in ten minutes even with that blunt-fingered, caveman-
style, hunt-and-peck typing method you seem to favor."
She made a show of checking off the task box on her planner page. "Next: lunch. Will you be ordering out, or do you
have special dietary restrictions?"

"I can feed myself, *Bettie*. I've been doing it for years."

"It's Isa," she corrected calmly. "And feeding you is
now part of my job. Not literally, of course. I trust you can
maneuver a fork to your mouth if you can move around on
a prosthesis."

He blinked again. She'd been testing him. She'd bet
none of her employees had spoken of his injuries or prosthetic leg so garishly. But if he insisted on being blunt with
her, she figured turnabout was fair play. Especially since he
was content to insult her.

"I don't like Isa," he snarled.

"Well, then call me Isabella."

"What if I don't like Isabella?"

"Then you are welcome to call me Ms. Sawyer, but it's
rather formal, don't you think? I'd feel enticed to call you
Mr. Crane."

"Mr. Crane is my father." Eli crossed his arms over his
chest, leaning back in his chair. The stance could have appeared relaxed if every muscle in his upper half wasn't
flexed.

"Then I suggest you find a suitable name to call me so I don't accidentally age you thirty-five years."

His mouth compressed into a line, but a spark lit his eyes as if he were enjoying the banter. The dark blue flashed with a heat that consumed the room and stole her cheeks. She swallowed thickly, licking her bottom lip as she recrossed her legs. Rather than watch him, she pretended to write in her planner. She was enjoying the banter, too. Her knees weren't as strong as she'd like.

"Sable," she said, clearing her throat of the awareness that'd pooled there.

"Say again?" His handsome face contorted.

She lifted her head. "Like my company. That...I work for," she tacked on. "You can call me Sable if you don't prefer Isa or Isabella." It was her nickname after all.

"Sable," he muttered, and the heated air between them intensified. Eli's low voice raked along her spine, sending a zap of electricity to her brain stem. In spite of not wanting to feel anything for him, she felt all sorts of confusing things.

Intrigue.

Curiosity.

Want.

"There you go." She flashed him a quick smile, then went back to her list, ticking off three more boxes before she stood and moved for the exit. "I'll order for you, then. No preferences on what you eat?"

"No meat unless it's seafood," he said.

"You're a vegetarian?" It was out of her mouth before she'd thought about saying it. She never would have guessed Eli, clearly a man's man, didn't eat meat. *Now who's being sexist?*

"Sort of."

"Very well. I'll let you know when it arrives." She gave him a curt nod and turned to leave the room, mindful of each step she took and wondering if he watched her as she left.

* * *

For the second time today, Eli watched his assistant's ass sway and wondered at the chutzpah of this woman. Didn't she know who she was dealing with? It wasn't often, if ever, he trotted out his family crest to remind people to respect him, but maybe the reminder was overdue.

"Sable" behaved as if she had little to no respect for his billions in the bank, or maybe she'd worked for so many billionaires in the past, she was bored rather than impressed.

Not that he wanted to impress her.

She'd knocked him off center for sure, and there was no denying that the palpable snap of attraction in the air was as inconvenient as it was enthralling. Eli Crane wasn't easily enthralled.

She'd succeeded at getting him to fill out the e-mail for a conference call she'd handle later. For the first few minutes, he pecked away with a childlike scowl on his face, answering carefully and succinctly, before deciding he was behaving a tad melodramatically.

Reese would be thrilled at the participation, and his assistant was right—filling out her requests wasn't time-consuming. Still, Eli wasn't stepping into COO until he was ready—no matter how many tasks Isabella Sawyer conned him into doing.

He clicked SEND and leaned back in his chair, arms over his chest, mind lost in thought on the upcoming boardroom meeting.

Until a samurai sword blade sliced down his back.

He barely contained a surprised bleat, swallowing down the pain and putting both hands on the arms of his chair to ride it out. It would pass. It'd always passed before.

He counted to three, then back to one, then up to three again. A few low and slow breaths later, the spasm relaxed enough that he no longer saw spots. Used to be the phantom pains, tingles, and stabbing needles came from the part of his right leg he no longer had, but that had since ceased. He'd noticed back pain more and more often lately. He swiped his hand over his brow to find sweat beading there.

God. He hoped this wasn't a new thing. Or, worse, that the phantom pains were planning to return for an encore.

"Stupid fucking chair." He pushed himself up and rolled the chair several feet away from the desk. He walked across the room, stopping halfway to prop a hand on the wall and take another breath. The elevator door screeched open. Lunch delivery, he assumed. Sable was nothing less than efficient. She'd insisted on ordering lunch and he had no doubt she'd marched out there and checked it off her planner right away.

He hobbled from his office, straightening his back as he clenched his jaw. He'd made it a habit to limp around the other PAs like Frankenstein's monster, but with Isa he sensed it was more like being the lame antelope in a lioness's sights.

A wave of admiration crashed over him in spite of himself. She was seriously underutilized as an assistant. She

should be someone's boss. *And not mine,* he thought with
a frown.

Eli arrived at the table as Isa returned with a bag of takeout.

"You're making a face," she said. "Do you not like In-
dian food?"

"I like all food."

"Except for meat unless it's seafood."

"Right." She didn't ask him to expound and he was glad.
He was sick to death of qualifying his preferences since his
unwelcome trip home.

Honorably discharged was a shitty way to say goodbye.

"Do you eat a lot of takeout?" Her tone was conversational as she unloaded foam containers and plastic ware.
"I do. Too much. Probably I should cook more, but I'm
so busy at work." She paused to send him a glance as she
folded the paper bag neatly. "Lots of people need assistants."

He didn't respond.

Her full lips pursed as she set the bag aside. He watched
as she stacked her sleek laptop, planner, and phone and
pushed them to the side. Her pen rested flush against the
stack. It was like watching a live-action game of Tetris.

"You do this a lot?" he asked before he thought about it.
He was supposed to be running her off, not conversing.

"Do what?" When she tilted her head, her long, dark
hair hung at her side like a drawn curtain. He was momen-
tarily blinded by how damn gorgeous she was. He blinked
out of his stupor and waved a hand in her general direction.
"Assist."

"Oh, of course." She opened the lid to her food and
handed him a plastic fork.

A tantalizing, spicy scent curled into his nostrils and his mouth watered.

"This is my job, after all. I'm well versed in how to serve," she said.

Seemed an odd choice for someone who was so damned bossy. But maybe *that* was her specialty. Bossing around her boss.

"Well, this can be your last day. I don't need your help." He dug a fork into his food and scooped up a bite. Holy hell, it was like having a mouthful of fire ants. Sweat coated his forehead anew as tears pricked his eyes.

"I should have warned you, I had them make both our entrees the same heat level." She took a dainty bite and chewed, not reacting to the hellfire the way he had. "Today isn't my last day, Eli, but if you'd like, I can finish up after lunch. I have another assignment that needs my attention."

Mouth the temperature of Hades, he reached for the water bottles on the table, knocking one over to get to the other. By the time he'd drained one and caught his breath, Isa had finished half her food and was pecking into her phone at the same time.

"What's it going to take to get you out of here?" he croaked, cracking the lid on the other bottle.

She finished typing on her phone, shut off the screen, and set it aside. Before she answered, she ran a tongue over her teeth, pushing her lips out and making him curious if they tingled the way his did.

He hadn't lusted after a woman since the last woman he'd lived with. Clearly he needed to have a conversation with his dick, because this was not the one to start with.

"Start by telling me what had you cursing and grunting earlier. Did you hurt yourself?" She cocked her head.

"No," he lied.

Her eyebrows jumped briefly. "You don't have to tell me. I'm not your nurse."

"You didn't answer my question."

"You don't answer any of mine."

"Dammit, Sable."

Her nickname suited her. It was exotic like her eyes and matched the deep brown of her hair. Her steady gaze reminded him of the spice in the food. She was almost too hot for him to handle.

"Forget it." Rather than continue to argue, he pushed himself from the table and stalked back to his office, fists balled at his sides in frustration. Having a woman here—sharing a meal with her—reminded him of a time he couldn't get back. A time in his life when he'd opened up, but it hadn't been enough. The one time when everything blew up in his face.

In his office, he glanced down at his leg in consideration.

Correction. *Twice.*

Twice now life had blown up in his face.

CHAPTER 3

"Three of the longest days of my life," Isa told Chloe. She plunked her tote onto her desk, where her assistant sat tapping out an e-mail.

After completing her third day at Eli's beck and call, Isa realized she *wasn't* at his beck and call. He didn't "beckon" or "call" her to do anything. She'd been the one pushing and prodding him. This assignment was certainly different than any in her past experience. Eli wasn't piling to-dos on top of to-dos onto her shoulders—quite the opposite. She spent most of her day trying to keep busy and e-mailing Reese to ask what to do next.

That stopped tomorrow.

She understood the gist of what Reese wanted and refused to keep bugging the busy CEO for details. The man had plenty to do that had nothing to do with his stubborn mule of a brother. Though, she admired the way he be-

haved as if Eli *were* part of his job. Worrying over him
like a mother bird fretting while her baby attempted to leap
from the nest.

"And...done." Chloe tapped the keyboard with flair and
waggled her hands in front of her like she'd performed a
magic trick. "So you survived another day with Cranky
Crane?"

"I did survive." Isa smiled at her friend's nickname for
their latest client.

"If anyone can do it, you can." Chloe rolled the chair
away from the desk. "I answered all of the e-mails I could,
sent out letters to clients who haven't paid in thirty days or
more, sent invoices to collections for clients who haven't
paid in *sixty* days or more, and fielded your many, many
phone calls. The good news"—she stood and pulled a
manila file folder from Isa's inbox—"is that the items you
have to deal with are all in this folder. You can work from
home if you like."

"Bless you." Isa stuffed the folder into her tote. One reason why Chloe was her right-hand woman was her insane
efficiency. "I will work from home. After dinner with my
parents." She lifted an eyebrow sardonically.

"Ouch. Is this about...?"

"Probably."

Chloe knew the story since she'd been Isa's in-office PA
for over two years. Isa leaned on her more than anyone.

"Anyway," Isa told her, "I should go before I'm late. I'll
walk out with you."

Together they shut off lights and computers, set the
alarm, and walked to the private parking lot. Isa didn't
bother going to her upstairs apartment to change. Dinner
with her parents was going to be a formal, dry affair, and

what she was wearing—a slim skirt paired with a blouse—
would do nicely. Or so she'd thought.

When she arrived at Flaire fifteen minutes late for dinner, she wished she'd changed. "Fancy" didn't describe the
place. It was oppressive, the sweltering atmosphere drowning diners in an air of money and pompous righteousness.

She thought of Eli, this time with a measure of relief.
His environment was nothing like this one despite his
money—in fact, she wouldn't have guessed his monetary
status if she hadn't known his background. At least working for billionaire Elijah Crane didn't involve a massive
mansion with a house full of staff buzzing about. She
could handle grouchiness, but the privileged elite, not so
much.

She spotted her parents the moment she bypassed the
host stand, her mother's red dress and her father's height
standing out. Helena Sawyer's long hair was pulled into
a proper chignon, black with a few gray threads she insisted gave her "character." Her father, Hugh, had lighter
hair than her mother's and turned an affable smile to Isa the
instant he spotted her.

"Mom. Dad." Isa sat.

"You're fresh from work." Her mother frowned.

"Yes. Busy day."

"You could have taken the time to change, Isabella. You
know we prefer you dress for dinner."

"I'm here now, so let's just deal with that." Isa ordered
a glass of white wine from the waitress and lifted the menu
to review the a la carte selections. Her parents followed
suit and reviewed their own menus, chatting off to the side
about which entrees to share and which to skip.

Isa was glad they were occupied by something other

than what she did for a living. It was an exhausted topic, one she definitely didn't want to broach after a long, *long* week, half of which was spent in the company of Eli's bad attitude.

There she went thinking about him again. She guessed that wasn't atypical considering she often took her work home with her. She hadn't been a personal assistant since she'd hired enough staff to stop. It wasn't all that strange that she'd be caught up in her thoughts, turning over the last days she'd spent with him.

Or it could be electricity snapping in the air whenever you're in his presence.

Hmm.

They ordered and Isa lifted her wineglass and took a hearty swig. "So. Why the dinner invite? What's the occasion?"

"We don't need an occasion to see our daughter, Isabella," her mother said, lids lowered, brows raised.

"You don't need one, but I'm sure there is one." Isa finished her wine and tapped the rim of the glass when the waitress walked by.

"Two glasses before dinner. Is that necessary?" her mother asked.

"Yes. Now. Occasion? Is someone getting fired? Married? Who died?"

"We're promoting Josh to president of Sawyer Financial," her father said.

News of her ex's promotion settled in Isa's stomach like a rock. The waitress's timing on that second glass was impeccable. Isa accepted the wine and drank down a hearty gulp.

"We'd like you to attend the ceremony next month."

Isa opened her mouth to say no, or more aptly *hell, no*, but her father anticipated the answer and spoke first.

"Just because you two are no longer dating doesn't mean you can't support him."

"Isn't that exactly what not dating him means?" she asked.

"This is a very big win for Josh," her father said.

Isa replied drily. "Yes, it's everything he ever wanted."

Everything he'd ever dated her for. She'd always wondered if, when she broke things off with him, he was saddened because their relationship was ending or because he might not be able to secure a higher station at Sawyer Financial.

"He's a very driven man, darling. You can't fault him for that." Her mother moved her hands to her lap as the waitress brought a round of tapas.

No, and Isa didn't fault him for his drive. She faulted him for not loving her in a whole and genuine way. He appreciated her breeding more than her as a person.

"You are still a part of this family," Helena continued, "even though you've opted to go the servant route rather than take on the position we grew and pruned specifically for you."

Isa closed her eyes and counted to five. That was the farthest she made it before her father started in.

"Our families have decades of past business between us. It would be rude for you not to show up and support the Lindens over some petty breakup eons ago."

"It was not petty, Dad," Isa said, measuring her words carefully. This wasn't a new conversation. One day, they'd hear her. For now, she would let them think she was having a repeat of her teenage drama years. "Josh was more in love with Sawyer Financial Group than he ever was with me."

Her mother let out a disbelieving *pfft*.

"And we broke up three years ago, which, yes, was a while but definitely not *eons*."

"He's single," her mother said. "And so are you."

Okay, so this angle was new. Isa felt her forehead crease. "I'm not... we're not getting back together."

"He'd like to see you, though. He misses you." Her mother cut a scallop in half casually as if she wasn't trying to steer Isa into the arms of a man who barely liked her, who'd never loved her.

"He doesn't miss me," Isa said. How could he? He'd barely tolerated her and her big ideas to start a business outside of Sawyer Financial when they were dating.

"I'm a man, Isabella." Her father lifted his martini to illustrate his point. "I can see when another man is heartbroken."

"Is that why Josh has been dating vapid excuses for women lately?" Isa mumbled. She wasn't jealous, but it was frustrating to know that he'd carried out the plan he'd warned her about.

If you don't climb to the top of Sawyer Financial mountain with me, Bella, I can find someone who will.

"You can't blame him for drowning his sorrows," her mother interjected.

"Oh, please." Isa lifted her wine.

"We've already spoken to him about reputation. As upcoming president of our institution, we can't have another repeat of Reese Crane's issues."

Isa put down her glass without taking a sip. Her father was referring to Reese's reputation with women before he'd married Merina. *Twice*. Rumor had it he'd nearly missed out on being named CEO because of his philandering ways, but who knew what to believe?

"Renegades, those Cranes." Her mother sneered.

"What do you know of the Cranes?" Isa asked, because seriously, how random was it that they'd brought up the Crane family the very week she'd stepped in as Eli's assistant?

"We read the paper," her mother said, chin aloft.

The gossip rags, she meant.

"Those groups of wealthy misfits are known for their rogue behavior. Sawyer Financial doesn't need that type of attention." Her mother chewed a tiny bite of scallop and carved another.

Yes, wealthy people were to be well behaved, quiet, and pave paths only with the gold of their ancestors. Heaven forbid one of them start a rebellion.

"Well, I'm sorry to say I won't be getting back together with Josh to help repair his reputation. I'll thank you not to pimp me out to the highest bidder in the future."

"Isabella." Her father's fair skin went pink. "Don't use that language with us. You know our position on you and Sawyer Financial. You know we want what's best for you. You're essentially *pimping out* the kinds of people your mother and I casually hire and fire. Where is the commitment in your business? To excellence? To permanence?"

His words never failed to cut her to the quick. Several defenses sprang to mind, all well worn. Frankly, Isa was too tired to participate.

"We want better for you." Her father's temper cooled and he laid a hand over hers on the table. She knew he wanted the best for her. At their core, both her parents did. But she refused to bend to their will if it meant sacrificing her dreams for theirs. "You're our princess."

She snatched her hand away. She was not a princess, *refused* to be a princess. She wanted to rule the kingdom, but she'd do so following her own rules, not those set by the elitist few.

"Dad, I'm happy. I tell you this nonstop. I'm happy with what I do. I'm good at what I do. I have thirty-two, er, thirty-one"—since Melanie's exit—"employees to oversee and I won't leave them in a lurch."

Isa used to try to make her parents proud but soon found it impossible. Now she'd settle for *quiet*. If they'd stop harassing her about her lowly choice of vocation, she'd be eternally grateful.

"Anyway," Isa said, slicing into her own scallop, "even if I wanted to date Josh, I couldn't." She hated to lie, but they hadn't left her much choice. "I'm seeing someone."

"Since when?" her father asked.

"Who are you seeing?" Her mother's brow rose to its highest point.

"It's still very new." *Like as of ten seconds ago.* Isa redirected her eyes to her plate. "I don't want to jinx it."

Especially since it wasn't true. Isa had been single and just fine, thank you, since she and Josh had split. She'd had a dinner date here and there before then, but over the last eighteen months, she'd quit dating altogether. Her focus had been on building Sable Concierge to the next level. And now that she was so, so close to that goal, her parents wanted her to start dating Josh?

No friggin' way.

"Well, since this development is so *new*, you can plan

on attending Josh's ceremony," her father said, adding an unfriendly, "Your new beau might not be around by then."

"Is Josh going to be single then?" Isa snapped.

"Yes," her parents answered at the same time. *Damn.* Had they put his dating status into his contract or something?

"And if you happen to be single," her mother added with a smile, "I'm sure Josh will be overjoyed at the idea of your reconciliation."

"Splendid idea, Helena," her father said with a proud smile.

A perfect example of why talking with her parents was akin to talking to a wall. They had an agenda, and they'd see it through. The option of not showing up was tempting, but she also knew there would be many Chicago elite at that party. It wasn't a bad idea to rub elbows with them. But the matchmaker thing was *not* happening.

To be sure, she'd hatch a plan of her own, Isa thought smugly as she sat back so the waitress could take her plate and replace it with a salad. Isa would find a fake date for that night to be her arm candy while she worked the room.

Win-win.

* * *

At her dining-room-table desk at Eli's house, Isa jotted the afternoon's tasks onto a pretty pad of paper she'd picked up at a fancy stationery store. Orange and gold flowers decorated the corners, and every narrow, crisp line was preceded by a checkbox. Nothing made her happier than a checked list, unless it was a pretty one.

She'd grown accustomed to working in here and was

starting to favor Eli's high ceilings and windows over her cramped, piled office. Today, the sun shone brightly, the day a little warmer than usual for late September. Sunlight filtered through the paned glass windows, giving an ethereal feeling to the rugged space—the dust motes sparkling like glitter. For the third or fourth time today, she pulled in a cleansing breath.

Dinner with her parents had left her frustrated for several reasons. Mostly because they were trying to mash her and Josh together. Simply put, Josh had been a bad boyfriend, prioritizing his work over Isa. Toward the end when he rolled out an ultimatum, she'd had an epiphany. She refused to take second place in his life—or in her own. She found the strength to leave him and the strength to move forward with her business idea at once. In a way, she owed Josh a thank-you for paving that path, but she sure as hell wasn't going to date him.

Her phone rang and she hesitated answering since she was on Eli's clock, but then figured he wouldn't notice anyway. He spent every day entrenched in...something, rarely coming out of his office. This job had become like monitoring a wild animal. Feed it, stay out of its way, and try not to disrupt its normal and natural pattern.

"Chloe, hey." Isa stood from the table and half ran/half walked to the kitchen where there was an additional partial wall between her and Eli.

"Sorry, hon. No luck."

"Did you try Tracy?"

"Yeah, he's getting married that day."

"Oh. Wow."

"I know. Unlucky, right? I heard back from the other guys on your list." Chloe had started reaching out to Isa's professional and personal male friends last week to ask if they could attend a social event with her. Isa hadn't elaborated further.

"And the rest of them?"

"All nos." The sound of Chloe flipping through pages of notes accompanied the saddest checklist ever. "Brandon is out of town for work, and Nathan said his wife would kill him."

"My gosh, Nathan is married too?"

"Uh-huh. And Travis and"—more paper flipping— "Jacob and Antonio...No, wait, Antonio isn't married. He's gay and his partner's birthday is that weekend."

"Stop." Isa couldn't take any more. "I'll have to make a plan B."

"Escort service?" Chloe joked.

Isa groaned. She hoped it wouldn't come to that.

"What do you need a date for anyway?"

Isa would gladly have avoided this conversation altogether but found herself in need of a sympathetic ear. She lowered her voice and cupped her hand to the phone. "My parents are trying to get Josh and me back together."

There was a measured silence. "Why?"

"The usual." She dropped her hand. "Breeding of the strong bloods, world takeover, yada yada." Isa kept her voice down when she added, "I told them I was dating someone. I didn't think it'd be this hard to find a stand-in by the time of the banquet." Yet here she was: dateless, and the ceremony was next week.

"Crap."

"Yeah."

"What about my brother?" Chloe chirped. "He's twenty-three but very mature."

"Absolutely not."

"He looks older."

"The idea was to be discreet and keep everything professional. Plus, doesn't your brother live in Maryland with your family?"

"Good point."

"Thanks for trying." Isa walked from the kitchen to the living room, careful not to say anything too revealing. "I'll work it out on my end."

"You sound formal. Are you pretending to work in case you're overheard by Beast Crane?"

"Yes, ma'am."

"Would you settle for a pretend girlfriend? I look great in a cocktail dress."

Isa let loose a laugh as she paced back to the dining room table. "I'll consider it. There would be the added bonus of stealing Josh's thunder."

"Sable!" came a shout from Eli's office.

"He does *not* call you that." Chloe gasped.

"He does."

"It's kind of sexy, though. Don't you think?"

She did. For some reason, whenever he bellowed her nickname, shivers tracked down her spine. And not in a bad way.

"Don't be ridiculous. Gotta go." Isa hung up on her friend and dropped her phone on the table, straightening her outfit for maximum Bettie Pageness on her way to Eli's office.

* * *

Isabella was clacking around his warehouse—he could hear those spike heels every time she stepped off the carpeting onto the concrete. His concentration had been interrupted several times in the last hour. He looked away from the calendar reminder announcing his friend was arriving soon to shout her name. *Again*.

"Sable!" There was a pause in her steps; then those steps came his direction. The closer the clacking drew, the tighter his gut went. She'd been here, what, two weeks now? Every damn time he saw her, that tightness extended from his gut to his chest the moment she poked her head—

"Yes, Eli." She leaned in, wrapping her hand around the edge of the wall, her dark hair coasting over one shoulder, her nails pale and manicured, her eyes catlike as she gave him a slow blink. He absolutely did *not* look at her cleavage, on display in a ruffly white shirt she'd paired with a black skirt that ended demurely below her knees.

"Your shoes are irritating," he said through his teeth.

"These?" She pointed a toe in a pair of shiny black heels that led to delicate ankles and the tempting swell of her calves. He shifted his legs beneath the desk, because it was either that or bite his knuckle in sexual frustration.

"Yes. Wear something quieter. Those are disruptive." Each time he heard her clacking, he had to mentally restrain his imagination.

Oh, the places it could go...

"What, like Crocs?" she asked.

He gave her a bland look.

"Apologies, Eli, but I'm not changing my shoes." She came into his office, her hips swaying with each sure step she took toward him.

"Fine. Then you're fired."

"Oh, no, not again." She smiled, her lush mouth tipping

at both ends. She lifted his empty coffee cup from his desk. "Refill?"

He breathed in the spicy scent of her perfume. How was it that she smelled like exotic temptation? He'd be damned if he was going to tell her to change her perfume. Then she might ask why he didn't like it, which wasn't the case at all.

He liked it way too much.

"No," he said.

She started away from him.

"Wait."

She spun on that spindle of a heel and cocked her head. "Yeeees?"

"Sit."

"I'm not a dog, Eli."

He raked his teeth over his bottom lip and called up his patience. "Ms. Sawyer, won't you have a seat?"

"I'd love to," she chimed, sitting prettily after relinquishing his empty mug to one corner of his desk.

"I heard you on the phone. Personal call?"

"I don't think that's your business seeing as how you just fired me."

The moment her voice dropped on the call, Eli had strained to listen to what she was murmuring about. He'd heard a name, Tracy—could be a guy or a girl—but the following comment about Nathan being married tipped him off. Nathan was definitely a guy's name. He'd debated bringing it up, but if she was going to continue to stay here and be a thorn in his side, she needed to respect his time.

"You're looking for a date on my time, Sable. That is my business."

Her eyes rounded guiltily. Damn. He'd hoped he'd been

wrong about that. He didn't know much about her, but he never heard her talk of anyone else or dating anyone else. He assumed she was single.

"I . . . It's not what you think." Her eyes flitted to the side. "I'm attending a function requiring a plus-one, that's all. You know what?" She affected a perfectly poised smile. "It won't happen again."

"Good." He didn't particularly enjoy serving as a dating service hub for his PA. That was just what he needed: one more happily, annoyingly in-love person in his orbit.

Isa rose from her chair and snatched his coffee mug. "If we're done here, I'm calling it a day. You'll be glad to know my disruptive shoes and I can see ourselves out."

"Very funny."

She winked, one glittering eye closing and reopening as that distracting smile remained. He had the sudden longing for Melanie and her blatant lack of sex appeal. Isabella Sawyer was a lot to deal with for a man who didn't want to deal with anyone.

Fist wrapped tightly around his pen, he listened as her shoes swept the most gorgeous woman he'd ever laid eyes on out of his warehouse.

"Stubborn," he grumbled, unsure if he was talking about himself or her. It hadn't taken long for her to ensconce herself into his work life.

A few minutes later, his cell phone rang.

"Zach," Eli answered. Zachary Ferguson was a few years younger than him and a talented builder. He'd worked with Crane Hotels in the past and Eli was hoping he could help him out with a project.

"I'm outside. Can't get in." Zach's Southern accent sounded foreign in this city.

Right. The gate.

Eli followed the path Isabella took, her faint spicy scent leading him like a bloodhound. "Hang on. I'll be down in a second."

When he reached the elevator, Zach interrupted him.

"Wait. We're good. Some woman in a white car just... *damn*."

The expletive left on an appreciative breath, and Eli could guess why. He ground his molars together and envisioned Isa flashing Zach a warm smile, her hooded, black-lashed eyes blinking as she pulled past.

"Thanks, love," Zach called, and it wasn't hard to figure he wasn't addressing Eli. "*Day-um*."

She'd been looking for an eligible bachelor this afternoon and had come up empty-handed. Eli didn't want her to consider Zach, for God's sake. Just picturing her with another guy brought out a territorial side of him he hadn't exercised in too long.

"Come on up," Eli said, his voice full of gravel.

He punched the END button on his phone and waited by the elevator, arms crossed. When the doors opened and Zach appeared, he looked as dazed as if Cupid had shot him in the forehead.

"Who was that?" Zach asked with a crooked smile.

"My assistant. She's taken," Eli tacked on, annoyed at the interest in Zach's expression.

"Mercy. I guess." Zach's accent was thicker than before.

It might be shocking to learn that Isa was single if Eli didn't know her. Few men enjoyed being handed their own balls by a woman.

Sure, keep telling yourself that as you cordon her off from available men.

"Good to see you again." With a quick raise of his eyebrows, Zach let the topic drop. He extended a hand and Eli accepted it.

Zach and Eli had worked together on a new build during one of Eli's stints home from the military. They knew each other. He'd worked with Crane Hotels in other facets as well, so it came as no surprise when Zach didn't react to the sight of Eli's bare legs poking out of from beneath a long pair of cargo shorts. No doubt Zach had heard about the injury.

Eli cleared his throat. Seeing someone for the first time since it happened was always the hardest part. They either reacted apologetically, awkward, or casual. He'd heard everything from "Thank you for your service" to "Tough break, buddy."

He didn't have a preference of reaction, save for he'd rather not have one at all.

"I'm sorry for..." Zach gestured.

Eli threw a hand to end the awkward pause. "Yeah, thanks. Beer?"

"Sure."

There. They were through that.

Beer bottles uncapped, Eli handed over Zach's. "Nickel tour?"

"Hit me," Zach said, taking a swig.

Eli showed him around the warehouse. When he reached the front room again, he said, "Home gym equipped with rehabilitation equipment. You may have noticed I don't have to worry about widening the doorways since I'm not in a wheelchair, but if I did, I only have a few. The bedroom"—he pointed to the end of the hallway—"office and bathrooms. Other than that, I have no problem getting around in here. Some soldiers aren't as fortunate as I am."

Zach's gaze meandered down Eli's prosthetic leg like he was wondering how any man could consider himself fortunate after losing a part of his person.

The answer was easy.

"Like the two men who died from the grenade that blew my leg off," Eli said, his casual demeanor doing nothing to stop the flood of acid from pooling in his stomach.

Christopher. That stupid bastard. Two kids, a wife, and he was just twenty-five. Threw himself on the grenade at the same time Benji shoved Eli to the ground.

Eli swallowed down the bitter-as-vinegar memory before he continued.

"Injured men and women come home from the military to apartments and homes with narrow hallways, doorways, countertops that are too tall, and various other obstacles that make it difficult to feel like you'll ever return to normal."

But there wasn't a "normal," only the new normal. New normal was wily. Slippery. Harder to get a handle on than he ever would have dreamed. After spending time trying to relearn the basics and realign himself into his previous life, he'd accepted that there was no alignment possible. He'd simply have to wedge himself into a new life. One that was a shadow of his old one.

On good days it left him feeling bitter. On bad days… well, he didn't dwell on what the bad days did to him.

Zach's wheels were turning. Eli could tell by the way the guy's eyes narrowed in thought. Zach walked through the gym equipment lined along the wall and pointed to the upstairs loft.

"Don't get a lot of use out of that area, I'm guessing?"

"No." Eli used to have his bedroom up there, near the exit to the rooftop. He used to sit outside and take in the city. It was the perfect ending to an evening. Stars, tall buildings, and a cold beer. He hadn't been up there since he'd returned home permanently.

Where he'd tackled every physical barrier with fervor, the metal staircase and railings were a no-go zone. They used to be his favorite part of the warehouse, but now they represented loss. No longer did he wake in the morning to take in the entire apartment spread out below or roll over with a girl in his arms and offer to get her morning coffee. No reason to go up there now.

That memory stung the way memories of Crystal always did. His relationship with her was the last one he'd had before he shipped out. She'd been upset that he was rarely home and said she was moving out. He'd been angry but mostly hurt. When he returned home injured, he'd called her to see if what they'd had was beyond repair. She'd e-mailed him back rather than called, writing that she'd heard about his injuries and while she was sorry, she hadn't signed up for a life of complications.

Being abandoned twice by her had stung like a bitch.

"What do you need from me?" Zach, beer in hand, sat on the weight bench, his fit form suggesting he wasn't a stranger to the equipment.

Eli rested a palm on bars he'd used to learn how to walk again, the metal a cool reminder of how far he'd come.

"I'd like to provide a service for our soldiers who come home with less than they had when they left. You're a good contractor. You know good people. And if you give me a decent rate, we can help a lot of men and women acclimate."

Zach nodded once.

"What's in it for you is the free advertising," Eli said, answering Zach's unasked question. Eli was asking for a cut rate considerably less than what Zach usually pulled in. "I'll mention your company on the website, on the flyers, and at every event held to raise money. Ferguson Builders will be synonymous with reliable work and a golden heart."

"Golden heart." Zach's mouth hitched and he looked to the window, his messy dark blond hair, shaved face, and country-boy good looks hinting at just that. "I know a few girls who would argue that sentiment."

"Then leave them off your references."

Zach chuckled. "All right. I'll work up an estimate."

"You can think about it. I don't need an answer immediately."

"Nah. I do better when I go with my gut." Zach stood. "You have more to show me, or was this all the pitch you had?"

"I have more." Eli paced to his office, Zach following, and for the first time in a long time, felt a genuine smile of pride crest his mouth.

Finally, Eli had a purpose again.

CHAPTER 4

Monday morning when Isa strode into Eli's warehouse loft, she expected three things: no greeting, the muted sound of shuffling papers or tapping of the keyboard coming from Eli's office, and a clean dining room table for her to spread out her laptop and planner.

She closed the elevator door behind her, humming the last song she heard on the radio as she drove here, and stopped dead in her tracks. Eli wasn't in his office. He was on his back on a mat in the workout area, arms behind his head, earbuds in, doing sit-ups.

Shirtless, slightly sweaty, totally distracting sit-ups.

He hadn't heard her come in, as evidenced by his grunts as he pushed through another curl, eyes closed, strain in the pull of his lips.

Isa... *stared*.

Stared at the bumps of his abs, the flex of his biceps, the

very short black running shorts climbing high over a pair of the most muscular thighs she'd ever seen.

She had opened her mouth to announce herself, honest, but Eli with his eyes closed, dark lashes shadowing his cheeks was mesmerizing. His hair had fallen in damp tendrils over his forehead, his lips peeled back, parting a full, thick beard and revealing stunningly white teeth. Had she ever seen his teeth?

It wasn't like he made it a habit to grin at her. Him grinning wasn't easy to imagine.

So lost in that thought, her eyes wandering the length of his body, over his bare chest and down to his legs, it took her a beat too long to realize he'd caught her gawking, her mouth agape. When her gaze reached his face, his eyes were open—deep, dark, seaworthy blue beneath two angry eyebrows.

On a final sit-up, he adjusted his leg and his prosthesis, then rested his forearms on his knees and caught his breath.

"Good morning," she croaked, then cleared her throat as she tore her eyes away from what might be the most gorgeous male specimen she'd ever laid eyes on. "I, um, didn't expect you to be"—*mostly naked, this sexy, utterly distracting*—"out here. Slow day in the office?" She capped the question with a nervous titter of a laugh, an obvious ploy to change the subject.

She hastily set up her laptop and pulled out a folder with a few forms Reese had sent over to her office. Items that needed Eli's immediate attention. Well, maybe not *immediate*. She would require him to get dressed before she could remove her dry tongue from the roof of her mouth.

Out of the corner of her eye, she watched him push to standing, rub his taut abs with one palm, and reach for his water bottle. His every movement was fluid, even when he put weight on his prosthesis and walked to the kitchen.

She sneaked a peek over her shoulder to admire his chiseled ass moving in those shorts.

Blinking to reset her brain, she turned back to the business of unpacking her tote, which took all of ten seconds. She logged onto her computer and sat, then stood, deciding maybe a cup of coffee would help.

Of course to get said coffee she'd have to go into the kitchen, where her grouchy, hot-as-hell employer was now guzzling the contents of a sports drink.

So she sat back down and glued her eyes to the laptop's screen. She checked e-mail and jotted appointments into her planner for Sable Concierge while she waited for Hot Marine in Short Shorts to evacuate the premises.

A few minutes into her work, a mug of coffee appeared at her right wrist, steam curling, creamed to the perfect tan hue. Gaping, she turned to slowly look up at a shirtless Eli, who stood over her and was still frowning.

He'd brought her...coffee?

"I guess you think it's indecent of me to expose you to my workout routine," he grumbled. "If I were you, I'd quit."

Granted, his delivery could use some work. Then again, she thought as he turned and walked to the bathroom, his gorgeously muscled back shifting, the delivery around here was top-notch.

"Getting a shower while you're here. Also indecent," he called without turning to face her. He shut the bathroom door behind him. Isa grasped her coffee mug and listened as the water started, imagining Eli stripping off those shorts and sliding under the spray completely naked.

All those long, strong limbs drenched in water and masculine hairy legs and arms and beard...

Goodness.

It was so much of a distraction that she didn't get any work done in the twenty minutes Eli was in there. Simply sipped her coffee and let her imagination run amuck.

* * *

Isa had refused to look at him, had barely spoken to him when she'd walked in. He'd opened his eyes and met hers and hadn't missed that her gaze was pinned to his leg, before snapping back to his face.

He made her uncomfortable if he had to guess. His thoughts went to Crystal, evidently not the only woman who didn't want to "sign up" for what Eli had going on.

This morning had been an interesting experiment as to what reaction he'd get from the opposite sex if he decided to leap into the dating pool again.

Not good, as it turned out.

Eli used to be the guy with the swagger—one he'd traded for a measured stride since the leg incident—and that swagger had drawn many a woman to his lap and then to his bed.

Of all the adjustments he'd made in his life, he'd saved women for last. Learning to walk, getting back into peak shape, working on building the charity was child's play compared to the hurdle of dating.

He shook his head as he leaned the prosthesis against the wall, peeling the sock off his stump and resting it on the edge of the sink. What would she have done if she'd seen him without the leg?

Much as he wished he didn't care, he did. The idea of her mortification at seeing him as less than one hundred percent man registered in an ugly, dark part of him.

"Fuck it," he muttered to himself, pushing off the closed toilet lid to step into the shower. He'd outfitted it with a shower chair, which is why he chose to use this one rather than the tub in the master bath attached to his bedroom. He needed to replace the damn thing with a bench so it wasn't glaringly obvious that he had to sit down to take care of one of life's most basic duties.

It never bothered him before, but having Isa here ...

He soaped his hands and started cleaning his body, smoothing his palms over the part of his remaining leg. She knew about it, obviously, so she hadn't been shocked to see that a part of him wasn't there. But today, there was something about her seeing so much of it that caused typically bold Isa to blanch.

Most days, he was in his office, legs hidden beneath his desk. Maybe seeing him had driven home the idea that he was different than what she was used to.

What is she used to?

He didn't know. On the phone last week, she'd been desperately hunting for a date. It didn't add up. Isa didn't seem the type to desperately do anything. She was as sure as she was ballsy. Except for today when she couldn't look at him. To her credit, he hadn't been the least bit warm to her since she'd started working for him. That cup of delivered coffee a few minutes ago might be the first nice thing he'd done for her. He'd even made sure to douse it with the creamer she kept in his fridge.

Hazelnut.

He'd poured a splash in his coffee yesterday, surprised at how good it was. Sounded like a sissy thing to him, but a few nutty, sweet sips later, he was hooked. He'd added some to his grocery delivery service so she'd have plenty on hand since he'd been pilfering hers.

He doubted one delivered cup of coffee could make up for his being the belligerent, insulting, handicapped billionaire who was content to wall himself in his private warehouse.

What he couldn't get over was that it bothered him. He'd found himself wanting to be seen by her as...well, as old Eli. The Eli who had swaggered on both legs. The Eli who used to be quick to smile. His dad used to joke that he was a sensitive Marine "like your old man." But Eli's sensitivity had been buried in favor of hardening. Crystal had accused him of growing hard, distant. She had never understood that war required a hardness unlike anything else. He'd done what he needed to be a good soldier.

Now that he wasn't a soldier, he wasn't sure what it took to be a good man.

He pictured the guys in his unit and squeezed his eyes closed. The pain that had lanced his foot and seared up his calf when the grenade blew part of him to kingdom come was nothing compared to the pain he felt when his friends took their final breaths that day on the scorching hot earth.

And here he sat feeling sorry for himself like a pussy. Another reason he didn't indulge the rooftop view. Moments like this one unveiled a broken part of him and he feared he'd hurl himself over the edge.

"Whatever." He stood from the chair to finish washing and rinsing, balancing by holding on to the bar attached to the shower wall. Soapsuds swirled around his foot. A strong foot leading to a strong leg. Even his injured leg was strong. Thick, corded muscles leading up to thighs he'd worked through multiple pains to get that way.

He didn't need Isabella Sawyer to approve of him. He didn't need anyone's approval, and never had.

He turned off the water and climbed out, gripping bars on the wall to aid him as he sat on the toilet seat and dried off.

"No more of this shit, Eli," he muttered to himself as he rolled on the sock and attached his carbon-fiber leg. "You're a lucky son of a bitch."

He stood and wiped the mirror with the towel, looking long and hard at his face. Lines marred his forehead from frowning. He was sick of himself, sick of feeling trapped in his own broken body and filled with unjustified anger. He needed a change.

He ran a hand through his beard, which had grown thick and was now borderline unkempt. He scrubbed the towel over it to get the water out and pulled the trimmers from the closet.

About time he started looking like the man he used to know instead of the one he'd devolved into.

* * *

Eli was quieter than usual the rest of the morning and afternoon. Isa ordered lunch—Mexican—and opted to deliver it to him and let him eat in private. Plastic to-go container in hand, she stepped into the shadowed room, the only light sifting in through the windows courtesy of an overcast day. Eli didn't have his desk light on, only the computer screen. He was hunched, squinting, his posture abysmal.

She told him as much followed by, "If you can unkink yourself, I have your lunch."

He blinked over at her, frowning as per his usual, only now she could see more of his face and neck than she'd ever seen before. She'd heard the razor whirring away and she'd imagined a big reveal when he finally stepped out. He'd ducked into his room, then the office without stopping to show her. She'd resisted curiosity until now, when she had a justifiable excuse to come in here and face him. Because, seriously, could she have acted more like a hormone-fueled teenager staring at him the way she had earlier?

Eli sat up straight and pulled his shoulders back. His T-shirt molded over a chest and torso she could easily envision bare.

Purr.

"When is the last time you stood and stretched?" She handed over the container, a plastic fork, and a stack of napkins. She was determined to focus on her job, on anything other than the attraction vibrating in the air between them.

Did he feel it too?

His eyes went to his lunch, back to her, and then he asked in a low, rumbling voice she felt in her tummy, "When was the last time *you* stood and stretched?"

"I stretch once an hour." Sort of. When she remembered. "I move around a lot, as you noticed the other day when you lodged a complaint about my heels."

His deep blue eyes ran down her legs like a caress,

lingering at the red heels she'd worn today. Red heels and a slouchy pair of army-green pants paired with a white button-down shirt. Casual and cool was what she'd been going for. Even dressed slightly down and less professionally than usual, with the way he looked at her she felt like she wore a tiny scrap of a dress instead.

"You trimmed your beard," she said to get his eyes off her body.

His hand went to his face, blunt, wide fingers stroking his remaining facial hair. The back of his neck had a good trim as well, but he'd left his hair longish—the front falling rakishly over his forehead. The full beard and ruffled hair suited him, but this slightly cleaned-up version suited him as well. It was a weird thought to have since she didn't know him.

Okay. This one-sided conversation was fun.

She was turning to leave when he said her name—his name for her.

"Sable."

Anticipation bloomed in her chest at the rough sound of his voice. "Yes?"

She threaded her fingers together in front of her, waiting anxiously for what, she didn't know. Just having his attention was its own reward.

Eli's brows bent, sadness eking into his expression. His lips parted but no words fell out. His eyes flicked away, then to hers—holding her gaze with fierce intention.

"Did you order lunch for yourself?" he finally asked.

"No," she answered, a bit stunned by the question. "I was going to go out."

"Fine," he growled. His features morphed, anger chasing away the sadness. He pried the lid off his food and fisted the fork, digging in for a bite while she stood idly by. Had he wanted her to join him? She was about to offer when he lifted his face, swallowed the bite he took, and said, "Take off the rest of the day while you're at it."

There was that mile-wide mean streak she knew too well.

"*Fine.*" She left his office, making sure her heels clopped as loudly and as much as possible while she gathered her things and left.

* * *

"That's not the worst of it!" Isa said as she palmed her margarita. She'd planned to meet Chloe for a much-needed girls' lunch at the same Mexican restaurant where she'd ordered Eli's takeout today. "I've been fired at least five times."

Chloe lifted her glass of sangria. "I think you secretly love that he's a challenge."

"At first, yes." Isa held up a finger. "Now it's less about the challenge and more of a concern. Will I be able to replace myself with another assistant? Who would put up with him?"

Isa had a company to run and Chloe filling in during the daytime hours and Isa working all weekend and most evenings until midnight wasn't a good long-term plan.

"I don't know, Isa." Chloe grew serious, her nose crinkling. "If he's not going to cooperate, maybe you should give up on the Cranes altogether. They may have wealthy contacts in Chicago, but they're not the *only* rich people who live here."

True. Her own parents were rich people, but they

preferred to keep what Isa did quiet rather than share that their daughter was an indentured servant. Which was exactly why she'd opted to go to a most uncomfortable banquet. If she could introduce herself around, make a few high-end acquaintances, she might be able to let the Cranes go.

"You're right," Isa confirmed, her voice strong. "I can overcome adversity. I can't let myself believe that Elijah Crane could single-handedly tank my reputation."

"'Scuse me." A velvet male drawl sounded over Isa's ear. If Chloe's gobsmacked expression was anything to go by, the guy speaking wasn't unattractive.

Isa turned and was pegged with two very green eyes, shaggy, sandy-blond hair, and a full-lipped smile.

"Did I hear you mention Eli Crane?" he asked.

Oh no, oh crap. She was griping about a client in public, which was a huge no-no. And had been overheard by... Chicago's own Chris Hemsworth, evidently.

She blinked at the muscular blond. Who *was* this gorgeous creature? Wait... she'd seen him before. Her eyes narrowed at the same time his did.

"You. You're his PA." The dashing guy with the decidedly Southern accent shook his finger, his smile staying in place. "You let me in when I swung by to visit Eli. I thought you looked familiar."

Chloe shifted her attention from the man to Isa and back again like she was watching a slow-mo Ping-Pong match.

"Yes, right. It's nice to officially meet you." She called up her hard-won professionalism, put down her margarita, and extended a hand. "Isabella Sawyer."

"Zach Ferguson." He shook her hand. "Commercial builder."

She could tell. He had rough palms, a firm grip. He was sexy as hell to boot. *And working with Eli,* part of her wailed. She could only hope he hadn't heard her disparaging her wealthiest client.

"You know, it's funny, I wouldn't think of Chicago as being a small town," he said with a casual smile. "Yet here we are."

"Here we are," Chloe interjected.

"Do you know the Cranes well?" Isa asked, being conversational. Which was decidedly smarter than ogling the golden god in faded jeans and a plaid shirt.

"I have done some work for them in the past, yeah." A close-lipped smile popped one of his dimples and Isa swore she heard Chloe moan into her sangria. Isa sent her a warning look and Chloe snapped out of it midswoon.

"Thanks for saying hello," she said, then fished for intel. "I assume if you'll be working with Eli I'll see more of you?"

"I'd like that." His top teeth closed over his bottom lip, and this time it was Isa who had to work hard not to whimper. "Too bad you're taken, doll. Not to be overly forward but I'd have asked you out today if not."

"Taken?" Chloe squawked.

Zach sent her a confused look. "Uh, dating? Betrothed? Wed? Not sure what y'all say up here."

Wow. The "aw shucks" thing really worked for him.

"Eli broke the news to me. But, hey"—he held up his hands in a disarming, adorable way—"I know how to work with a lady I find distractingly attractive."

Isa felt her cheeks warm. She'd just bet. This guy emitted charm like a poisonous gas. She opened her mouth to say that either Eli was mistaken or Eli was a horse's ass, but no words came out.

"Eli has my contact info," he said. "He and I are just getting started on the project, so I'm sure he'll loop you in soon enough."

Project? Isa knew everything about Crane Hotels as it involved Eli. She didn't remember a project. At once, the fascination with coincidence and Zach faded into anger, and Elijah Crane was front and center.

"Yes, I'm sure he will," she said, her words clipped.

"Nice to meet you, Isabella Sawyer." With a wink for Isa and a wave goodbye for Chloe, Zach swaggered back to the bar in—yep—cowboy boots.

"Urban cowboy," Chloe whispered as her eyes snapped back to Isa's. "Good Lord, the testosterone...I'm not used to that much packed into one person."

Isa took a hearty drink of her margarita. She sure as hell was.

Zach may be everything Eli wasn't: charming, smiley, and suave, but the one thing he couldn't do was out-testosterone Eli Crane. Regardless of how attractive and tantalizing Zach seemed, Isa's thoughts returned to Eli and her outrage hit apocalyptic levels.

"What did Eli mean by you being taken?" Chloe asked belatedly. It was understandable, as her pistons were likely misfiring after Zach's brief visit.

"I don't know. But I'm going to find out." Isa stood and shouldered her purse, eating another chip with salsa for the road. "Use the company credit card for lunch."

"Wait! Don't leave me here! What if he comes back?" Chloe stole a glance over at Zach, who had already sidled up to a blond woman at the bar. Chloe's mouth twisted. "Never mind."

Isa would have finished her margarita and dished about

how men suck for a while longer, but at current, she had a bone to pick with Eli. Who gave him the right to tell anyone she was "taken"?

She bid Chloe adieu and clipped out of the restaurant to the parking garage. After she shut the door on her white Lexus, she made a beeline for Eli's house, though she could have walked and made good time. The fumes from her anger would have propelled her every bit as fast as her V-6.

She parked, rode up the elevator, and popped open the door with a clang.

Eli strode out of the kitchen, red apple and knife in hand. "Thought I told you to take the day off."

She threw her purse on the dining room table and swept over to him in a huff so quickly, a breeze lifted her hair. He cut a thin piece of apple with the oversized knife and laid the slice on his tongue, the slow sensuality of the action causing her steps to falter.

Why . . . was that sexy?

Focus, Isa.

She forced her attention back to the run-in with Eli's . . . whatever Zach was to him . . . and propped her hands on her hips. "Zach Ferguson."

Eli paused, the knife piercing the skin of the apple.

"I ran into him at Elsa's just now. Or, rather, he ran into me. He let me know he would have asked me out if I wasn't—and I quote—'taken.'"

"He shouldn't be asking you out." Eli's voice was calm but his expression turned to granite.

"That's not my problem." She offered an impatient smirk. "My problem is that someone told him I was *taken*."

Eli sucked his tongue against his teeth with a *tst*, a sure sign he was irritated. Well, too bad. *She* was irritated.

"You're not to date Crane employees while you're working for me," Eli growled.

"I'm not aware of any Crane business Mr. Ferguson is doing." She crossed her arms over her breasts in challenge.

"The answer is no, Sable."

"You don't have any right to tell me who I can and can't date."

"You're not dating Zach."

"I might!"

"You won't!" He took a step closer, his top lip curled. "Not while you work for me."

She had no interest in going out with Zach. He was good-looking, but he had trouble written all over him. But she was equally pissed that Eli thought he could control her personal life in the same way he held her business's reputation hostage.

"I can wait you out," she said. "Given our track record, it shouldn't be too much longer before you fire me again." She snatched the apple from his hand and took a bite.

He took another imposing step closer and Isa, mouth still chewing, set the fruit on the table behind her and stood her ground. Eli might like others to believe he was a bear, but she knew better. She held those deep blue eyes, seeing in their depths a flash of something she didn't like: *hurt*.

She recognized it instantly, having seen it enough in her own reflection after she left her parents' company and her former life. She'd defied them, and as justified as she was by doing it, sometimes felt badly for going against their wishes. As fast as her temper spiked, it fizzled.

"Why?" she asked, taking a step closer to him.

"Why what?"

"Why did you tell Zach I'm taken?"

He was as silent as an Easter Island statue. Looked like one, too, come to think of it.

"*Eli.*"

He skimmed his fingers over the open placket of her shirt, the warmth from his skin radiating through the material. He flipped his hand over, keeping his eyes trained on hers and running the backs of his fingers over her breast.

She didn't dare breathe.

He lifted the knife and in one quick motion, sliced, and a startled exhale left her lungs.

"String." He held up a white thread, then let it flutter to the floor. His eyes danced over her face before lingering on her lips, then to the pearl button he was brushing with his thumb.

Isa tried to regulate her breathing, but it was hard to inhale when the air between them hung thick with longing.

Another swirl of his thumb over the button and Eli's eyes flicked to hers again. "Am I scaring you?"

He made her feel lots of things, but scared wasn't one of them. Isa was often in control. Of everyone. Of everything. Rarely was there a part of her world she didn't own one hundred percent. Until Eli. He'd challenged her every step of the way. And like he knew she could handle him, she knew he could handle her.

"Are you trying to scare me?" she asked.

Uncertainty flooded his eyes. Until now, she was certain she was someone Eli tolerated. Now she felt like someone Eli wanted. As much as she wanted him.

He continued rolling the button between his forefinger

and thumb, the corners of his mouth turned down in thought. The pendulum hung in the balance between them and Isa was determined to let it swing.

"Do it." She whispered the challenge, her eyes on his. "I won't run."

The frown left, his eyes narrowing as he raised the knife. Isa lifted her chin, giving him space. With the flick of a wrist, the blade of the knife moved and another thread snapped. The pearl button hit the concrete floor of the warehouse with a *plink* and the gasp of air Isa sucked in now was laced with desire.

She offered an encouraging half-smile.

Eli sliced another thread. Then another. *And another.* Until her buttons were scattered on the floor and her shirt sagged open. Her breasts lifted and fell as she drew in ragged breaths, as shocked as she was confused. As turned on as she was intrigued.

"Eli," was the only word that made it from her parted lips as one repetitive thought banged against the front of her skull, an incantation she couldn't deny.

Kiss me.

Kiss me.

Kiss me...

* * *

He hadn't been trying to scare her. Then he found himself hovering over her, knife in hand, and had scared himself. But Isa wasn't afraid. She didn't see him as a monster but as a man. And right now, a woman he wanted stood before him.

He brushed his fingers along Isa's satin-soft skin,

between her breasts rising and falling in a white lace bra, down her flat, smooth stomach, and along the waistband of her pants.

Whiskey-colored eyes locked on his. Her full lips parted as she pulled in a breath, and every ounce of man in him wanted to sample every drop of woman in her.

He leaned closer, satisfaction coating his chest when Isa's eyelids slid shut and she leaned closer to him. He captured her waiting lips, gently, and heat engulfed him like the entire warehouse had caught fire. Desire singed his torso, scorched his spine, incinerated his brain. Her pillowy lips gave and took until a high mewl came from her throat.

She smelled like spice cake and tasted better, her own brand of fire and smoke and sex. It'd been too long since he'd had a woman in his arms and this woman was all woman. From her high, high heels to her long, long legs hiding beneath a pair of inconvenient pants, to the delicate blouse he cut every last button off of and still longed to see what was underneath.

He dropped the knife to the table behind her and locked his free arm around her waist. She dipped with him, allowing him to tip her back, her long hair tickling his forearm. When he righted them both, his hand went to her jaw and he held her lips to his.

She didn't balk.

She advanced one step, two, until her knees bumped his leg…and his prosthesis. Her lips disconnected from his with a subtle pop, her eyes going wide. The fire licking between them smothered in the hanging silence.

She'd touched the part of him that wasn't him and now those dark lust-filled eyes were filled with alarm. Like she'd forgotten she was kissing a man who wasn't complete.

"I thought you weren't scared," he said between clenched teeth.

He let her go, frustrated with himself for getting this far, for taking what he wanted when jealousy roared to life over Zachary Ferguson, for God's sake. Isa wasn't Eli's to have. Up until two seconds ago, he would've bet she didn't even like him.

He started away from her, feeling pissed or confused or maybe both in equal measure.

"Where are you going?" She snatched a palmful of his T-shirt and tugged, her eyes going to his legs as he shifted on his weight. This time the heat that lit within him was his temper.

He turned, not the least bit smoothly, and leaned in. "Why'd you kiss me?"

"You kissed me!"

"You kissed me back." He came so close his nose practically touched hers, to test if she'd back away. To see if the reminder of all he was—of all he wasn't—would scare her for good. She only moved enough to elevate her proud chin.

"So?"

"So?" he repeated, backing up to focus on her face. "Did you forget for a second I had a handicap? Is that why you kissed me back?"

"By handicap, I assume you mean your horrible attitude." She held his eyes with hers. "And don't do that teeth-sucking thing just because you're pissed."

"The what?"

"It's your tic when you don't know what to say."

His tongue was pressed to the back of his front teeth, poised to do just that. He wedged his jaw tight and Isa hoisted a triumphant eyebrow.

"You don't want me to date Zach because you want me for yourself. Is that it?"

Because she was right and he didn't want to admit it, he chuffed a dry laugh and looked to the windows. "Yeah, right."

She lifted her hand to his cheek. Her soft touch, her smell...there wasn't a thing about Isabella Sawyer he didn't want. He wanted her lips on his, her hands on him, her truncated sounds of steep pleasure saturating the air after an all-day marathon between the sheets.

He wanted to be the man to put a smile on her face, hear that moan of pleasure coming from her throat like when he kissed her a moment ago.

There was one piece of equipment standing between him and taking Isa to heaven and back again. The leg. Isa, with her to-die-for perfect body...God. He felt his shoulders wilt, his anger fade into a muted sadness.

What in the hell had he been thinking? The Eli he'd been looking for was gone. The only one left standing was in front of Isa, whose shirt gaped because he'd cut the buttons off it. What the fuck was wrong with him?

"I overstepped a boundary. It won't happen again." He lifted his hand and placed it over hers on his cheek. As much as he wanted to turn his face, kiss her palm, and enjoy her comfort, he resisted and brushed her aside instead. "I'll replace your shirt."

"You'll replace my shirt," she repeated, her tone flat.

"Yeah." He walked away and this time she let him. He went to his office, determined to wrestle back two things he had no right to have: the burgeoning erection pressing his fly and an image of naked Isabella in his bed, legs spread, his face buried between her shapely thighs.

Jesus, that sounded *fantastic*.

"You can leave," he called through a throat thick with lust. He wouldn't ask her to compromise. Isa should never be asked to compromise.

CHAPTER 5

It took every bit of resolve she possessed not to follow him when he stormed off. Something had happened just now. Something more than that explosive kiss.

Seriously, *explosive*. TNT, dynamite. C-4.

Ka-boom.

She bent to pick up one of the plastic pearl buttons from the floor and rolled it between her fingers. What . . . was that all about? One minute he was slicing an apple, the next about to shred her clothes. Her shoulders shivered thinking about it. Not shivers of fear, either. Shivers of *want*.

Where Eli was concerned, there was an instinctual, almost animal attraction. Isa wasn't comfortable with how easily he'd disconnected her good sense from her "do me, baby."

Getting back to work was the only way to get through the afternoon, so that's what she did. She found a tank top in the bottom of her tote and knotted her ruined shirt at her waist over it. Then she sat down, put her fingers on her keyboard, and checked her e-mail. There were thirty of them—the perfect distraction from the lip-lock that had left her hot and bothered to the nth degree.

She handled a few from Bobbie at the Crane office with ease. *Yes*, Eli would be attending the dinner at the Royale London, a fancy Chicagoan banquet hall where Reese had invited lots of corporate muckety-mucks to rub expensively suited elbows.

It was a few months out yet, so she didn't bother to run it by Eli. He'd go because she'd make him, or he'd have fired her for real by then and wouldn't go, and it wouldn't be her problem.

A few e-mails from Chloe showed she hadn't hung around Elsa's to hit on Zach some more, instead returning to the office to respond from Isa's main account. Thank God for her, Isa thought with a breath of relief. She answered a few of Chloe's questions, knowing her worries were over the moment she hit SEND. Chloe could handle the bigger issues without her.

Isa pulled in a deep breath of accomplishment, considering why she loved being a personal assistant. Lifting the weight from her clients' shoulders was simple for her but life-changing for them. Her parents may well have thought her destiny lay in becoming president at Sawyer Financial, but as Isa rolled that title around in her head, she felt her nose wrinkle.

She could be there now. Wearing a beige pantsuit and carrying a calculator. Sitting in her beige office with beige carpet and walls. Living a beige life. A wave of very real nausea swept over her whenever she imagined that plight.

She pulled her focus from the screen to look around Eli's pad. Exercise equipment, black and silver. Blue mat. Red and rust-colored exposed brick, yellow warning stickers on the warehouse elevator from whatever business had predated him. The dining room table where she sat now was surrounded by mismatched chairs, each rustic wooden frame adorned with a different tapestry-styled cushion seat.

Instead of beige, her life was vibrant color. She ran a finger over a knot in the wood of the table. And damn if that color hadn't exploded into a kaleidoscope of neon when Eli's lips touched hers.

Aaaand she was thinking about the kiss again.

With a sigh, she pressed a button to print the e-mail she'd been reading, realizing belatedly that she was *not* in her office.

"Shit, shit, shit!" she hissed, hitting the CANCEL button repeatedly. From Eli's cave, the printer hummed.

Too late.

Standing, she smoothed her hands down her pants and flipped her hair. She had planned to quietly finish her work and leave without seeing him again. No such luck. And no hiding that she was heading his way when her heels clicked along the concrete floor.

Well.

The kiss had happened. The button incident had happened. There was no taking it back. Regardless of how either of them felt about it, she was going to continue working here. So. She would deal with the here and now.

Since the sun was shining, Eli's lair was welcome instead of foreboding. No fire cracked in the hearth today.

Also unlike his usual, he wasn't at his desk. He was at the printer.

"This yours?" He offered a sheet of paper.

"Yes." She couldn't keep from explaining. "Pressed the Print button by accident."

"*Mi* printer *es su* printer."

Isa accepted the document and Eli sank his hands into his jeans pockets, his forearms flexing with the movement.

"I wasn't—"

"I shouldn't—" they said at the same time.

He pursed his lips and she looked at her shoes.

"Go ahead." She was going to say, *I wasn't offended when you kissed me,* but now that she'd had a millisecond to think it through, maybe she should pretend the kiss hadn't happened. Which was...impossible. Standing this close to him, it's all she could think about.

"I shouldn't have ruined your shirt," he said.

"I dared you to."

"Why?" His eyebrows compressed along with his lips.

"Because you have accepted the role of beast, but I don't believe that's who you are." She let her gaze linger on his face before tracking down his body. "And because I like a challenge."

"Do you?" He took a wide step toward her.

She matched his move and took one step closer to him. "Yes. I don't wilt easily."

He threaded her hair between his fingers, a look of longing and hurt mingling in his eyes. "I was about to lie and say I shouldn't have kissed you."

Shivers climbed her spine as she remembered how firm his lips felt against hers. "Maybe...you shouldn't have stopped."

His hands moved to grip her shoulders and he lowered his head, closer, closer...

With only a tingle of warm air between their parted mouths, the unmistakable clang of the elevator doors jolted her like a shock.

Eli looked as alarmed as she felt, jerking his head around to a wide-faced clock behind his desk.

"We're early!" came a woman's voice.

"Who is that?" Isa asked in a rush, the sound of an intruder sobering her like a bucket of ice water over her head.

"My sister-in-law, Merina."

Alarm shot through her limbs. *Fantastic.*

Isa licked her lips and backed away from Eli, who allowed his palm to slide down her arm before he gave a brief nod of *Everything is fine.*

Except for the fact that Isa was trying to win over Merina and Reese, everything was fine. She fluffed her hair and straightened her shirt, which was basically useless since strings poked out here and there from the missing buttons.

Maybe Merina wouldn't notice.

Chin up, Isa stepped from Eli's office, the paper in her hand helping her look as if she'd been in there on official business.

Merina blinked at Isa, recognition written on her face. Isa couldn't be sure Reese had let his wife know Isa was pretending to be an employee of Sable Concierge rather than its founder.

With a quick shake of her head she hoped communicated that, Isa moved forward, hand extended. "I'm Isabella, Elijah's personal assistant."

"Of course." Merina nodded a little too vigorously. She knew plenty. "You know my husband, Reese Crane."

"Reese, nice to see you." Isabella shook his hand next. Okay, this was bordering on silly, but Eli wouldn't appreciate any level of scheming, so she wasn't about to admit she'd been lying to him all along.

She would tell him she owned Sable Concierge. Eventually.

"I should get going. We're through for the day, aren't we?" She directed the question to Eli. His hands, now stuffed in his back pockets, broadened his delicious chest and muscular shoulders. Yeah, so she'd just focus on packing up her things rather than drool over him for all the Cranes to see.

"For the day," he said, his lingering gaze lighting with challenge. "Thank you, Isabella."

Her full name sounded foreign on his tongue, but then, he couldn't very well call her Sable, could he?

"You're welcome. Until next week." In two minutes, she was packed and ready to go. The elevator door opened as she was strolling to it, revealing a giant with long, elbow-length hair walking arm in arm with a petite, gorgeous blonde. The man had to be Tag Crane.

She dispensed introductions quickly, but since there was no need to lie (she'd never met Tag), those were much easier. Rachel, Tag's girlfriend, was instantly likable the moment she grinned and said, "I love your shoes."

"Thanks," Isa responded. "I'm sure Eli gets tired of me clomping around here all day, but they're a weakness."

"He'll be fine." Rachel gave her a conspiring wink before her eyes studied the strings poking out from the missing buttons on Isa's shirt.

"If you'll excuse me." Isa closed her shirt with one hand. "Enjoy your dinner."

* * *

Eli hadn't invited Isa to stay for dinner, which was for the best. Especially with Merina and Rachel chattering away about Tag and Reese like they weren't in the room.

Notably missing was their father and Rhona, but Alex didn't make every family dinner, so no one was surprised by this. Least of all Merina, who'd made it a point to call and ask if they wanted pasta and salad. "Alex and Rhona are in Amish country. Did you know that, Reese?"

Reese hadn't known that, and Tag and Eli exchanged equally puzzled glances. Why was their father in Amish country? Did he need a bureau? Cheese?

Merina dispatched dinner—Italian—with minimal fuss. She'd insisted on dishes but let Eli win the argument for paper napkins. Now everyone sat at the table, plates cleared and wineglasses refilled. Beers sat in front of Eli and Tag.

"She's working out, I guess," Reese said.

Pretending not to know what his brother was talking about, Eli only frowned.

"Isabella. The PA position." Reese lifted his glass of red. "When I saw you with her, you two seemed to be getting along."

"I'll say," Rachel put in.

Eli glanced over and Rachel sipped from her glass.

"I'd have thought you would have fired her by now," Reese said.

"I have," Eli grumbled. "Several times."

"I bet." Tag let out a chuckle and sent Eli a knowing

look. "Hard to make moves on the girl when she's on the payroll." He sent Rachel a warm look. "Right, Dimples?"

Rachel gave Eli a nod of approval. "She's very pretty, Eli."

"And feisty." Merina smiled.

"Takes one to know one." Rachel held up her glass and Merina clanged hers in a "cheers."

"What's going on?" Tag asked, his smile gone.

Reese's brow lowered. "They do this more than they used to."

"Oh, come on, guys," Merina said, setting her glass on the table. "It's obvious Isa and Eli had something going on other than work."

"Don't be ridiculous," Eli growled, then followed Merina's gaze as it settled on a stray button on the floor.

Dammit.

The last thing he needed was for his family to know he'd crossed a line.

"No shit?" Tag asked, his smile edging across his face. "You and the PA."

Eli sighed and drank his beer.

"I like her," Reese announced in that commanding, authoritative way he had. Even Merina and Rachel paused to listen. "Especially since she massaged you into RSVPing yes to the Royale London event in November."

His brain may have become hung up on the word *massaged* if not for what followed.

"What?" Eli barked.

"Nothing," Tag said quickly, amused as per his usual. "Just a Crane thing."

Eli sucked his tongue against his teeth. He'd take that RSVP up with Isa first thing Monday morning.

Then he'd fire her. Again.

"We should go out next time," Merina said, breaking off her conversation with Rachel to focus on Eli intently.

"Be my guest," Eli said. "I could use the break."

Tag's laughter shook the table.

"With you in tow," Merina said.

"The two of you," Rachel said, batting her lashes. She was braver when she sat next to Merina. "Wouldn't you like to get out more?" She cocked her head in genuine curiosity.

"Look around, Rach. This place is big enough to hold a three-ring circus. Where do I need to go?"

"It'd be good practice for the event," Tag said. "Like seeing how a formerly captive animal reacts to being in the wild."

Eli sent him a death glare.

"You should bring your PA," Merina sang, a smile on her face. "Your father always brings his PA." She capped that statement with a grin and Reese leaned over and wiped it off her face with a kiss. Rachel, too far from Tag to do the same, winked at him and he grinned like a moron.

"That's it. Everyone out." Eli stood and grabbed his beer. "Your love connections are very inspiring but I'm not hooking up with my"—*insanely gorgeous*—"personal assistant. Take your matchmaking abilities over to the local college campus and do some canvasing there. Leave me out of it."

He turned for the living room, but since it was attached to the dining room and there was no wall, it didn't offer much privacy. And none of his helpful family members bothered standing and leaving. Instead, they fell silent for the count of five while Eli stared down his couch and weighed his exit, before he gave up and returned to the table.

Merina and Rachel went back to chatting, and Reese asked Tag if he'd heard back on the Texas Crane Hotel's pool bar numbers yet.

Eli let the din fade to the background and tipped his beer to his lips.

For whatever reason, their being here didn't bother him as much as it used to.

* * *

Monday morning, Isa swept in with her tote and double-shot cappuccino, phone to her ear as she slid the elevator door open.

"Yes, Chloe, that's fine. Thanks." At the dining room table, she found Eli's laptop at her usual place. The screen was open to a document, one with a blinking cursor where he'd stopped typing. She poked her head down the hall. His office was dark. So was the kitchen.

"Eli?"

No answer.

She glanced back at the screen and saw the words *my leg* and was lured like Icarus to the sun. Prying could lead to her demise but she read the passage anyway.

I don't miss my leg as much as I miss Christopher and Benji. Dumb sons of bitches. If I could go back three seconds, I would. I'd haul them both up by the fatigues and throw myself on that grenade instead. They could be here with their families nursing a lost leg or a scarred face. I don't have a death wish, but dammit, I'd trade my life for both of theirs.

Benji's wife won't talk to me. I know Michelle misses him, but all I want for her is—

"Sable!"

Isa spun away from the computer to face the bedroom where Eli stood in the doorway. He wore jeans and a tee as per his usual, arms at his sides, hair damp like he'd just finished showering.

Shit.

"Help you find something?" He advanced with smooth strides, veins popping from his forearms and his forehead at the same time.

She had no idea what to say. Just no earthly idea. There was no spin to put on the fact he'd caught her snooping. She had no plausible excuse. *Gee, I thought that was my computer* wouldn't work and neither would *I was just stretching my back, not leaning over reading your private journal entry.*

Given that she couldn't lie, she'd have to say something else. So she went with the question rattling her brain since she'd read what she shouldn't have.

"Who are Christopher and Benji?"

He blinked in surprise like it pained him to hear their names out loud.

"Dead soldiers." He didn't move for the laptop to shut the lid or come any closer to her. He simply folded his arms over his chest, and stared her down.

"Oh." Her heart ached from what she'd read, but she guessed telling Eli as much would silence him before opening him up. She licked her parched lips and told him the other thought in her head. "I didn't realize your injury was caused by a grenade."

A beat, then two, passed before he spoke.

"We were lucky. Some guys drive by roadside bombs and none of them walk away from it." His voice betrayed his words.

"You don't sound like you feel lucky."

"Doesn't matter how I feel. I *am* lucky. Many men have lost a hell of a lot more than I have."

It was on the tip of her tongue to tell him it wasn't a contest, that pain was pain. But she bit back the retort.

"I shouldn't have—"

"No," he agreed. "You shouldn't have. What are you doing here so early?"

"I've been awake for two hours, so I thought I'd get a head start. You're always up early."

"Marine," he said in explanation, his voice stone cold.

"Are you going to fire me? Because if so, there's no reason to unpack my tote."

The corner of his mouth flinched into an almost-smile. *So close.* She'd give anything to see it, to hear a full-on belly laugh from him. To know what caused a man like him to smile or laugh. She wondered if he'd ever been the laughing or smiling type, or if he'd always been serious and quiet.

"I take it you don't need coffee." He dipped his chin at her paper cup.

"No, I...I should've called and offered to bring you one." She clucked her tongue. "No wonder you fire me all the time."

A sound came from Eli that made her snap her head up and look at him. She caught the tail end of a smile as he turned and strode into the kitchen, her chest lifting with pride. She'd made him *laugh*.

She grinned at his retreating back, wishing he hadn't robbed her of the full effect. Did the brief laugh light his eyes? Twist his lips? She put a hand on her belly where butterflies came to life.

Someday she'd find out.

* * *

Isa spent the rest of the afternoon half in work mode and half in wonder.

When she'd first taken on this assignment, she'd sent the handful of potential assistants to sensitivity training so they knew how to deal with a man who'd literally lost part of himself in war. And while Eli definitely had signs of mild PTSD, she could now see it wasn't the main motivation directing his life.

She would brew a pot of coffee to share with him this afternoon, and then she'd find out what that motivation was.

"Sent you an e-mail," he announced as he strolled into the kitchen.

"Okay. I'll check it in just a second." She finished measuring fresh grounds and pressed the button to start the brew. When she turned, she found him scowling—nothing new there—but he didn't look angry. He looked...worried?

"What's wrong?"

"I"—he pulled in a deep breath—"need help."

"Well, that's what I'm here for."

His frown didn't let up. "I wasn't going to ask for help but you're *you* and you're good at what you do and I need help."

Every bit of his request was said through his clenched teeth and she felt her eyebrows lift. He'd spoken like a man who asked for help...never. It was music to her ears. Handling tasks people dreaded had always given her a feeling of supreme satisfaction.

"It involves you contacting Zach." He cleared his throat and finished on a thick growl. "Who I trust you won't date since I've asked."

Scratch that. His tone was more petulant than growly.

"I don't recall you asking." She leaned a hip on the counter, enjoying Eli's fidgeting.

"He's an important piece of what I'm crafting and he doesn't need the distraction."

"Ha!" She folded her arms. It wasn't as if she were Poison Ivy. She couldn't do anything to Zach against his will. Men *did* possess self-control.

But then she thought of her buttons plinking off Eli's concrete floor. She hadn't exercised much control with him, but it was because she hadn't wanted to. Couldn't he see that?

"Fine." She held up her hand like she was taking an oath. "I swear not to seduce Zach with my potent, exotic wiles, so help me God."

Eli's mouth started to smile until she added a caveat.

"If you agree to one small favor."

It was impressive how many lines he could call forth from his forehead.

"Be my stand-in date next Saturday, so I'm not forced to ask Zach." She was desperate. Chloe had overturned every stone and besides her twenty-three-year-old brother from Maryland, Isa was out of options.

"Stand-in date for what?"

"Fancy function." Snobby bankers and carefully measured insults from her parents. But more importantly, a place where Eli would be recognized. Showing up with a Crane was as good as getting a Crane seal of approval in that group. She'd impress clients simply by being there with Eli.

"Forget it."

Which was exactly what she'd expected him to say.

"Okay." She shrugged and walked to the dining room, calling over her shoulder, "I'm sure Zach looks great in a tux."

"Sable." There, now, *that* was a growl. She ignored it, sitting down at her laptop and pecking in her password. He hovered while she opened and read the e-mail he'd sent.

"You need a website."

"And a FAQ page," he said, pointing at the bulleted list. "And a contact that is not me. Also, a way to accept donations online."

She let his requests soak in as she reviewed the list and the paragraphs of carefully prepared descriptions for something called Refurbs for Vets.

"You're working on a charity." She announced her epiphany to the screen.

"Yeah."

"*That's* what you were doing instead of COO for Crane Hotels." She looked up at him, seeing him differently than she had a moment ago. This man who had lost so much wanted to give back. It was like a light-blocking curtain had been lifted.

"Can you help me or not?"

Okay, the curtain had *parted*. Definitely not lifted.

"I am being paid by your brother to do Crane Hotels

work, so you may have to pick up the slack on COO duties while I work on this." She gestured to the screen, knowing she'd hand most of the items off to third parties rather than sweat over the details herself, but he didn't know that. "This is going to take time."

The sooner Eli was acclimated at Crane Hotels, the sooner she could resume her position at her own company. If she ever hoped to replace herself with another assistant, Eli taking the reins on Crane business was paramount.

"Fine," he gritted out, and she resisted punching the air in celebration.

"Perfect." She offered a folder. "Next week's meeting notes and numbers. Your brother wants your take on it and since I haven't read through them yet, I won't be able to summarize in five or ten questions like I normally do."

His eyes narrowed like he suspected foul play.

She smiled, doing her best to project innocence.

"I'll get to work on finding a webmaster, securing a home page, and"—*words . . . website-related words . . . think, think*—"um, figuring out the best metadata for your charity."

"No need to oversell it." He snatched the folder.

"And, Eli?"

He let out a sigh like he knew what was coming, stopping short of his office and rocking on his heels while he studied the ceiling.

"Next weekend. Are you in?"

"Sure." He didn't know it, but he was doing her a huge solid. "I'd hate to subject you to Zach."

She beamed. Eli raised one eyebrow.

"Do you have a tux," she asked, "or do I need to arrange a fitting?"

He turned, rolling the file in both hands like it was a tube. She tried not to fixate on the way he was curling the edges of the perfectly flat papers within.

"Both," he answered. "I have a tux, and I need a fitting." He watched her when he said, "Clothes don't fit now that I'm a different man."

She turned over the phrase *a different man* for longer than she should, wondering what, other than the obvious, had changed him. And whether he was trying to become who he used to be or create someone new altogether.

* * *

"It better not be a wedding," Eli told the white-haired man currently measuring his inseam.

Isa had arranged for the tailor to come to him, which Eli appreciated, since that meant he didn't have to go downtown and deal with people and traffic.

She wasn't there to oversee the process either, which he also appreciated.

"Or a charity event," he added. He didn't need recognition for helping others. It was enough just to do it.

The tailor continued working quietly and Eli gave up on voicing his litany of wishes. Whatever "fancy function" Isa had invited him to didn't matter. He'd be trussed and pressed and present much like he'd been at a number of formal events his father had dragged him and his brothers to over the years.

"I'll have it to you by Thursday afternoon," the tailor told him. "Be careful not to remove the pins when you take it off."

Eli went to his bedroom and carefully removed the suit,

changed into his jeans and T-shirt, and returned the chalked and pinned tuxedo to the older man.

"It's a lost art, tailoring," Eli said.

Suit in his grasp, the tailor's brow pinched and once again, he didn't reply.

This was why Eli didn't start conversations. Small talk had never been his forte. That gene had skipped over Reese and Eli and been given in triple measures to Tag.

"Good day, Mr. Crane."

Eli opened the elevator and ushered out his guest, then walked to the window and examined the street below. This was his favorite part of Chicago. An area where tall new-build skyscrapers shined like mirrors next to rustic, hundred-year-old churches. The warehouse had been an abandoned machine shop when he found it and he'd had it completely overhauled to live in. He'd left the downstairs empty, figuring he'd install huge garage doors and park his fleet of expensive automobiles in it. Thing was, he never did buy a "fleet" of anything.

He'd reported for duty in the Marines repeatedly over the last ten or so years, and material possessions took a backseat to the real world. In between being gone, he used his time home to chill, check in with his family, and hook up with girlfriends, old or new. It had only taken a few days to slip back into his prestationed self.

This bout of recouping was taking a lot more doing.

When he'd returned home last year, he'd planned on holing up at home and not going anywhere. At least, that'd been the case until recently.

He didn't know why things had changed. Autumn was edging closer, which meant colder nights and crisp days.

Soon it'd be icy and snowy, the wind blowing off the lake and frosting the entire town.

Perfect season to stay in, stay warm, and work on his pet project.

He had wanted to be left alone.

Had. That past tense was pushed farther into the past after his family refused to stop showing up with takeout and after he'd reached out to Zach.

After you kissed your personal assistant.

Yeah. About that.

He was intertwined with Isa, not only because he'd curled her close and tasted her mouth. He'd let her talk him into attending an unnamed event he was dressing like a penguin to attend.

He'd let her believe he'd agreed so she wouldn't ask Zach, but his needs ran deeper than a competing male. Being needed was a rare occasion in Eli's life. Being needed by a woman an even rarer one.

Eli slipped on his shoes and pocketed his keys, setting off for a destination he'd been putting off for weeks. *Months.*

To visit Benji's widow.

Eli had reconnected with Christopher's widow, Amie. He knew too well what it was like growing up without a parent—his own mother had died when Eli was a kid. He'd wanted to make it right with Amie, to help her and her sons in any way he could.

Amie had been polite and agreeable when he'd asked if he could honor Christopher by posting the picture of the three of them—Eli and Benji included—on the Refurbs for Vets website. She'd wished him well and mentioned she was seeing someone. "A great guy I used to date in high school. He loves my boys," she'd told him.

Knowing she was moving on, that she had someone who loved her—that Christopher's boys were loved—had made it easier for Eli to shed some of the guilt that had built up over his friend's death.

Benji's widow, Michelle, was another issue altogether. She'd been just twenty-two years old when he died. They'd been married a handful of months. Eli's stomach twisted every time he thought of her.

He started his car's engine and navigated the route he'd driven many times, only to fall short of Michelle's house. He wondered if he'd make it there today or stop at the edge of her neighborhood and go home instead.

Eli had been a lauded a hero, but after his injuries and surgeries and the realization he'd never measure up to the two men who'd saved his pathetic life, he didn't feel like one.

He felt like an invalid, and not because of the leg. He felt like an invalid because in the clutch, when he could have saved two men—one a father, both husbands—he hadn't done it. His counselor at the hospital reminded him repeatedly that he hadn't had a second to react, and she was right. He hadn't.

One second he'd been laughing at one of Benji's horribly uninventive limericks, and the next his ears were ringing and there was sand in his eyes. And then the pain.

God help him, the pain.

Searing hot like red pokers through his foot and leg. He'd had a hell of a bout with phantom pain after. The military doctor explained it was because his foot had been so severely damaged that his brain held on to the image Eli could to this day call up without trying too hard. Getting past it had required a lot of meditation and a brief stint with prism glasses to make him see two whole legs instead of one and a half.

But. He'd survived. He'd rehabilitated even though it broke him into a sweat simply to put pressure on his prosthesis. He'd learned to shower without it, was careful not to drink too much water before bed so he didn't have to get up to pee in the middle of the night and fuss with snapping it on. He'd learned to move without a stagger or a noticeable limp, his new walk a far cry from his formerly smooth, confident gait.

He hung a left when his GPS told him to, though he knew the route by heart. He'd traveled it the second he'd been able to drive.

The traffic blurred as he slipped into autopilot, his mind on Isa's curves and thick hips, perfect for a man's grip. To her molasses-colored hair and deep, dark eyes. He wanted to know the way she moved during sex. Hear if she moaned or mewled or was as quiet as a church mouse. He wanted to know what color nipples rested on the tips of her lush breasts.

A distant honk drew him from his imaginings. He raked a hand through his hair and blew out a harsh breath. If he played his cards right, maybe he'd find out exactly the sounds she made, her hot breaths in his ear.

He hadn't had to contend with women or sex for a long, long time. He'd compartmentalized his life into medications, diet, rehab, and then the charity, adding challenges as others became routine or fell away completely. Sex was just another challenge to check off his list.

Or that's what he kept telling himself.

At the mouth of Bay Street, Eli came to a stop. Michelle's house was two turns away. He'd thought he was ready to tackle this moment—to look her in the eyes and apologize for not saving her husband. To ask if he could honor Benji by posting his photo on the Refurbs for Vets website.

He sat at the stop sign, head turned to the right, watching as an elderly woman raked the leaves in her yard. Heart heavy, lead in the pit of his stomach, Eli popped a U-turn and drove toward home instead.

Looked like another challenge on his list wasn't getting a check mark today.

CHAPTER 6

Isa sat in front of her computer in Eli's dining room-slash-living room, staring over the laptop's screen at the blustery day beyond, her thoughts circling one undeniable fact.

Tomorrow night was a bad idea.

When she'd invited Eli, she'd thought she had the arm candy part handled, but as the days lurched on and they circled each other at a distance, she'd begun to lose her nerve.

Not that she could *un*-ask him. That would be rude. He might be A-okay with eschewing common decency in his world, but in hers there were rules and one was: don't renege an invitation. Plus, she needed him.

To thwart Josh, to be present and impress the suits. Lord knew she could use an "in," and "I'm sure you've heard of the Cranes" seemed as good an intro as any.

The tailor had brought the altered tux back yesterday and Eli had disappeared into the back bedroom to make sure it fit. Isa chatted with the man—or tried, as he wasn't

much of a conversationalist—before Eli opened the bedroom door and bellowed he was "good to go" with the
tuxedo.

He hadn't shown a single inch of himself wearing the
suit—not even a peek of an elbow at the doorway, and Isa
had been watching closely. She did know he was wearing
a white shirt with a black bow tie and the kerchief in his
jacket pocket was going to be bright, almost hot pink to
match her dress. The tailor had taken an inch off the length
of the skirt and had fashioned some of the material into a
matching kerchief. Short skirts were her signature, and she
planned on showing up at the banquet dressed to impress.

Eli hadn't asked for further details and she hadn't offered, like both of them were choosing to ignore the fact
they had a date at all. Which seemed safer considering
ignoring the date and the matching-kerchief-to-dress also
meant not bringing up the kiss that was so long ago it was
beginning to feel like a mirage.

She'd commissioned a webmaster for the Refurbs for
Vets website, and Eli had done the work for this week's
board of directors meeting, handing over the notes so Isa
could call in and be present in his place.

By five-thirty, she was finished with her work for the
week, and there was nothing to do save for leaving. Just get
up. Grab her jacket and go...

But she should say something to him first, right? Since
they would see each other in a little over twenty-four hours
and need to play the part of a couple who at the very least
liked each other. A lot.

Surely she knew him well enough to have a drink with
him at a fancy party. Did he drink?

Sigh.

Well, she knew he was vegetarian. Who ate seafood. That had a name, but she'd forgotten what it was. Presbyterian? Something like that. Isa chewed on the side of her finger for a few seconds before noticing and stopping. No need to ruin her manicure over the man.

She pushed away from the dining room table and stalled by packing her laptop, planner, and the rest of her office implements into her Kate Spade tote. Then she mentally pulled on her big girl panties and walked to Eli's office. No sense in acting like the girl who'd been asked to prom for the first time. It was a business arrangement, for goodness' sake.

With a guy whose kiss sears like a brand.

Before she breached the door, she started speaking, determined to say her goodbyes and leave with as little awkwardness as possible.

"That last e-mail marked the end of—" She cut herself off when she barged into his office to find his cell phone to his ear. He raised one finger into the air to signal her to wait a moment.

"Uh-huh," he said into the phone, casting her a glare.

She mouthed the word *sorry* because, *Seriously, Isa, rookie move!*

"How much?" he asked the caller, grabbing a pen to jot down the answer on a yellow legal pad.

While he wrote the figure, she followed the line of his strong forearm, dusted with dark hair, up to impressive biceps, and a rounded shoulder, every inch of his arm decorated in a myriad of tattoos. She allowed her gaze to trickle along his mussed hair, neatly trimmed facial hair, and down the thick column of his neck. Dark whorls of hair sat at the very edge of his V-neck T-shirt, and a memory of the way he'd looked out of it stung her brain like the snap of a rubber band.

Rippling abs and strong pecs, glistening with sweat as his chest expanded to take in oxygen...

"Earth to Sable," interrupted a silky, deep voice.

She blinked and noticed he'd put the phone down, his expression bordering on confusion.

"Sorry. I'm...tired."

And hopelessly attracted to a Marine with a beard and a complicated reasoning system.

"I came in to tell you I'm done for the day. I forwarded you a few questions I couldn't answer for the webmaster. Aesthetic stuff. He is asking whether you want this color or that, this font or that." Isa threw a hand, feeling more uncomfortable the more she talked but unable to stop.

Working with Eli was one thing, but the idea of being at his side, her arm in his, introducing him to her parents... She probably should broach that topic, but the more intensely he watched her, the more she lost her nerve.

"So...I'll see you tomorrow." She lifted her hand in an awkward wave.

"Sable."

At the soft pronunciation of her nickname, chills trickled along her arms under her sleeved blouse. She smoothed her damp palms down her slim skirt and turned to face him.

"Yes, Eli?"

His eyes warmed when she said his name. The air between them didn't crackle so much as hummed. She enjoyed the quiet, amicable moment of shared appreciation. It was rare and had been absent from her life for years. Even when she and Josh were dating, she hadn't felt this particular pull. With Eli, there had always been a buzz, hum, or crackle between them. Being near him was like slipping into a really warm bath.

Mmm.

"Where am I picking you up?" he asked.

"Oh no. That's not necessary." This wasn't a date so much as an arrangement. "I can meet you at the event. I e-mailed you the address. It's really easy. It's the Vancouver Hotel on—"

"I assumed you wanted me to pretend to be a romantic date, not a colleague." His face broadcasted sincere curiosity.

Her parents would assume he was a romantic date. Isa was hoping Eli would play the part of both boyfriend— thwarting Josh's advances—and colleague, acting as a go-between while she mingled with wealthy business owners. She hadn't told him that part yet. She hadn't really told him anything.

"A date would pick you up where you live." Eli hadn't let up in his assessing stare. "A date would know what you expected of him."

Right.

"We should talk about how the evening will go," he said. "Specifically what you need me to do."

She swallowed thickly, not wanting to admit she needed him to stand in the way of her ex.

"Is this supposed to look like a romantic coupling?" he sort of repeated.

"I guess so." Eli was to be the big ole scary buffer between her and her parents' machinations to get her and Josh back together. "But also a professional one."

Eli stood, walking toward her on steady legs, which was more than she could say for her own. "Then I'm arriving with you."

"It's not necessary."

"It is." He took a step closer to her. "Your place?"

It was like she'd been hypnotized by his dark blue gaze—the way he moved toward her with purpose and control. Before she knew what she was doing, she felt her head jerk up and down in a nod.

"I'll need your address," he said, his voice warm.

"I'll text it to you." She watched his tempting, contoured lips when he spoke next.

"And this is a...wedding? Dinner?"

"It's a business thing," she hedged, snapping out of her stupor.

"A business *thing*. Thanks for clearing that up for me." His dry joke caught her off guard and the heat between them bloomed into something friendlier.

"A...uh...former employer of mine is naming a new president of their company." She was fudging for a very good reason: she didn't want Eli to back out. Mentioning him meeting her parents might result in just that. Plus, picturing the look on Josh's face when she arrived on another man's arm was a pleasant thought. "It's pretty dry, really."

"And you need me because...?"

She couldn't tell Eli she was looking to him to help her schmooze. Not until he learned she wasn't an employee of Sable Concierge—she *was* Sable Concierge.

"Because if you're with me, I can avoid being hit on all night," she said.

"I'm not surprised." Eli said, then floored her with a compliment. "You're someone I would have hit on in a former life."

That made her giggle. "You kissed me, Eli. That was you in *this* life."

The moment it was out of her mouth the air between them shifted again—less friendly, sexier. Especially when his gaze snaked down to her mouth.

"Is kissing you in my marching orders for tomorrow night?" he asked, his eyes picking up a trace of heat.

She wasn't going to pass up this opportunity. No way. No how.

"Yes," she answered. "Need to practice?"

In one motion he wrapped an arm around her and tugged her close, resting his forehead on hers. "What do you think?"

"Couldn't hurt," she murmured, gripping his biceps and giving him the permission he'd never asked for.

He dipped his lips to hers for a brief taste. Nothing like the intense, fiery, button-slashing kiss, but a tender, gentle meeting of the mouths before he backed away...

Too soon.

He released her, leaving her with a husky farewell. "Be safe driving home."

She took an unsteady step backward before leaving his office. She didn't look over her shoulder as she gathered her tote and opened the elevator, but she did angle her head to the upstairs warehouse window when she unlocked her car.

Her billionaire employer was framed by the panes, one hand leaning on the wall as he watched her leave. His face was partially hidden by the reflection of the overcast sky.

She swiped her tongue along her bottom lip, his flavor lingering there, and found herself looking forward to more.

* * *

One of the first changes Eli had made once he could walk on his new carbon-fiber leg was to adapt his car so he could drive. Took some doing to learn how much pressure to apply to the pedals now that he operated the vehicle with his left foot. At first, he'd driven with a series of herky-jerky stops and gos, but eventually, he'd found his rhythm.

It'd been like that with the leg, too.

After kissing Isa again and feeling firsthand the fire between them, he knew sex was an eventuality. Tonight, specifically, could usher in the perfect excuse to invite her home with him. There was only one problem. He needed it to go off without a hitch the first time. "Herky-jerky" wasn't exactly the calling card of a good lover.

He didn't doubt Isa would be out the door if he failed at pleasing her. It wasn't like she was a girlfriend who would patiently wait until he found his new rhythm. Crystal hadn't stuck it out with him—though to be fair, she hadn't been a girlfriend when he'd returned. She'd already bailed.

Driving his black Mercedes-Maybach, he felt like a better version of himself: capable and independent. The car had been a splurge considering he'd taken it out for test runs alone and never had a passenger.

Until tonight.

There was no way he was letting Isa show up to the function alone. She hadn't offered details on the evening, but he had pried out of her that he was supposed to be her romantic interest. They wouldn't have a problem faking the charge between them—given his family's reaction, it was obvious they liked each other as more than boss and assistant.

And now he was considering having sex. With his PA. He'd never been in a position to mind his manners or the corporate handbook. As a soldier, even the smallest decisions were life and death and never anything less. In the professional realm sleeping with his assistant was considered taboo, but he couldn't get himself worked up about the dynamic. What bothered him was that he was woefully out of practice at wooing a woman.

Women were the final frontier. He'd rehabbed his physical body and he was well on his way to resolving the emotional hurdles of losing his friends. But dating? Even driving to a woman's house to pick her up for an event was as foreign as if he was navigating his prosthesis anew.

He felt like a clumsy, shaky-legged fawn...trying to *swim*.

But Isa didn't look at him like that, did she? She didn't pity him or censor herself or try to be gentle with him. Every PA he'd had prior to Isa had been female, save one, and every one of them reacted to him professionally and courteously, but there had always been a touch of pity in their eyes.

Until Sable Concierge sent Isabella.

She was strong-willed. Drop-dead gorgeous. Sharp and intelligent. But she didn't yield to his belligerence. She didn't wilt at his commands. Under his hands and lips, she became pliant, but never had she looked at him with an ounce of pity.

Not a single damn drop.

He didn't know much about her, but he guessed by her demeanor and her dress that she'd been raised in a middle-class home, with hardworking parents. Isa wasn't afraid to get her hands dirty, and he'd bet she was from a matriarchal family, considering she wasn't intimidated by a billionaire Marine with a short temper.

He'd bellowed and growled at her and was rewarded with a raised eyebrow that seemed to ask, *Is that all you got?*

Honestly? Yeah, it was all he had.

Isa knew about his injury—and now knew about the incident behind it since she'd found his journal entry. And yet, where he should have raged at her for spying and fired her immediately, he hadn't. He was glad she knew and touched when she'd asked who they were. She felt like a safe space in that intimate moment, and he'd opened up to her—definitely something he hadn't done in a long, long time.

Crystal had accused him of being "walled up," which he took responsibility for now—too late to save their relationship, but that dab of insight could save a future one. Eli and "open" weren't exactly synonyms.

Isa, though...she knew he was closed off and angry, that there was a part of him trying to spook her. The thing that killed him was she hadn't shied away. Even after she'd found the journal, she hadn't run away. He hadn't been "more than she signed up for," that was for damned sure.

His GPS took him to a business district and announced he'd arrived outside of Sable Concierge. A sign hung over the door, another in the window announcing, "Professional assistants for your every business need."

He pulled into the lot, noticing one other car there. Isa's. What the—

He climbed from his car and caught sight of her stepping from the office in a blindingly gorgeous short, bright dress. She turned to lock the doors behind her.

"You didn't have to get out," she said, dropping her keys into a small clutch.

Goddamn she looked gorgeous. She wore a hot pink strapless dress that matched the kerchief in his tux pocket. The dress stopped midthigh and hugged every one of her generous curves on the way down.

"That is a dress." His throat was almost too full to push the words out. He walked to her door and opened it and again she told him he didn't have to. Before she lowered into the seat, he caught her elbow and tugged her closer. "You deserve to be treated well. Let me do it and stop protesting."

Her lips curved, her long lashes dipping as she looked at her shoes. Tanned, smooth legs led to spiked heels the same shade of pink as her dress. His mouth literally watered.

He blinked out of his scattered thoughts. "You're going to need a coat."

"And hide this dress? Forget it. We're valet parking. I'll be fine."

"You can wear my jacket." The air had a crisp bite to it tonight. He wouldn't let her be cold.

"I never suspected you as the chivalrous type, Eli," she told him, her grin parting bright pink lips.

She settled into the seat and he closed the door and rounded the car, noticing he smiled during that short walk. When he angled himself into the driver's seat and caught sight of the building in front of them, the lust-fueled smog cleared from his brain.

"Why am I picking you up at work?" he asked, but he'd already started suspecting. Isa behaved like no other assistant he'd ever had. She acted more like a boss. Or a business owner.

"Oh. Um. Would you believe I was working overtime?"

"Maybe," he conceded. "If I hadn't seen you with keys to the building."

She bit on her lip and flashed him a guilty grimace. "There's something I have to tell you."

"You own this company, don't you?" Isabella. Sable. His brain shoved those two pieces together like twins separated at birth.

"Yes."

"And you kept it from me."

"I didn't want you to view me as a challenge. You'd only fight me harder."

His nostrils flared as he took in a frustrated breath—her spicy perfume tingling his senses.

"You would have," she said quietly.

He would've. Again it struck him how she knew him and how his normal reaction to her breaching his walls didn't occur. He didn't want to argue about this. He just wanted to be next to her.

"I thought it'd be simpler if you thought I was an employee who wouldn't stop showing up."

"You mean you thought I'd underestimate you."

Another shrug. "Happens all the time."

He gripped the steering wheel, half pissed at the truth in those words. When he'd first laid eyes on her, he'd assumed she'd give up faster than the last assistant. He'd completely underestimated her.

He nodded out the windshield to the apartment over Sable Concierge. A pumpkin sat on the stoop alongside a potted purple mum. "Who lives up there?"

"I do."

Just as he'd suspected.

"There's more."

A stunned, "Ha!" exited his lips, but when he turned to take her in, Isa looked chagrined. His smile vanished.

"What more?" he asked, the first hint of gruffness eking into his tone. He wasn't a fan of being left in the dark.

"Tonight." She licked her full, pink lips and he fought not to let the seductive move affect him. "It's my parents' function."

"Not your ex-employer?" He hoisted an eyebrow.

"Actually..." She screwed her lips to the side, chewing on the inside of her cheek. "Both. The event is for Sawyer Financial Group."

Sawyer. Financial. The institution was a Chicago treasure. They did planning of all kinds—taxes, retirement, business—and their roster of clients was among the most elite. Isa wasn't raised in a middle-class family, not even close. She'd grown up as rich as he had.

"It's not a long story," she continued. "I'll tell you while we drive to the Vancouver."

Isa liked to tell him what to do. Liked to be in charge. He wasn't inclined to let her call the shots tonight.

"You can tell me now," he said, taking his hands off the wheel and sitting back in his seat. To her credit, she did.

"My ex-boyfriend is going to be at this function. Because he's the one who is accepting the position of president." She regarded her hands. Her sounding and looking small was such a departure from what he knew of her. He didn't like her that way—not at all.

"I was groomed for running Sawyer Financial my entire life," she said. "My parents introduced me to Josh. We were to be the power couple that someday ran the company," she told him, meeting his eyes. "My parents knew I didn't want the future they'd laid out for me."

"Sounds like an arranged marriage."

"Felt like one," she said, a sad smile twitching her mouth. "But without the marriage part. Josh planned on taking the position of president, and he said I could be VP or run staffing. Whatever made me happy."

"How generous of him," Eli said through clenched teeth, hating the jackass already. It was so obvious that Isa was a leader. The only reason her ex would have slotted her into a position less than the top—at her family's own company no less—was his own moronic need for control.

"He's the son my parents never had. It broke their hearts when we split. They blamed my stubbornness and my obsession with going into business for myself for driving him away."

"They wanted you to fulfill their dreams, not yours." He could relate. His father and brothers wanted him to be a part of the Crane legacy. If Eli had felt he'd earned it, he'd have already suited up. But that wasn't the case with Isa. She'd earned it; she just didn't want it.

"My parents wouldn't care that Josh dated me only to climb the ladder. They care about appearances as much as he does. Whenever the topic of my running a firm for assistants comes up, I can see the embarrassment on their faces. I may as well have gone into trash collection or cleaning hotels."

"Both honorable positions," Eli said defensively. He didn't station anyone into categories of high or low. He'd been raised to see people as equal no matter their income.

Isa's cheeks pinked at his unintentional correction. "I'm . . . I didn't mean it like that."

"I know." He put his hand on hers, running his thumb over hers, feeling the softness of her skin and enjoying the

length of time she held his gaze. Yes, Isa was beautiful. She
was also complex and caring. She was more than the president of a bank, and her parents should have assessed that
years ago. He could see it already and had only known her
a few weeks.

"No other secrets about your vocation or parentage,
then?"

"No, I think that's it." She smiled prettily.

"All right." Eli reversed out of the parking lot, noting
that Isa watched as he maneuvered the gas and brake pedal
on the left side rather than his right. He pulled onto the
road, hitting the gas pedal and taking off a little too fast.
He wasn't used to being watched so closely. He regulated
his speed a second later.

"So this Josh? You want me there because of him? Or
were you serious about men, plural, hitting on you?"

"Ugh. That probably made me sound completely full of
myself."

"Not completely. Only a little." He turned right and
flashed her a grin. One she returned tenfold, her eyes
sparkling in the shadowed interior of the car.

"My mother believes if she can get Josh and me into the
same room, we'll fall into each other's arms."

"Because proximity is equal to attraction." He'd thought
he was joking but as soon as it was out of his mouth, he
realized that sometimes, proximity turned up the attraction
to eleven. *Million.*

"Sometimes," Isa said as she watched out the window.

Eli remained silent as he turned left, then pulled to a
stop in front of the Vancouver. He stepped out, but not before telling Isa, "Stay put. I'll get your door."

A valet with white gloves stepped forward to take the

car keys from him, and predictably, Isa's car door opened a second later. He offered a hand and helped her out, tucking her palm against his elbow.

"I see your point about the stubbornness," he murmured as they turned for the building.

"Takes one to know one." Her tone was teasing and he returned her smile with a narrowed gaze. Then he took one step forward and saw the staircase leading to the front doors of the Vancouver and his light mood disappeared into the ether.

"Fuck." His voice was just below a whisper, but Isa heard him, her grip tightening on his forearm.

"Wait."

CHAPTER 7

Eli heard her but didn't look at her directly. His eyes were focused on the stairs leading to the hotel's entrance. Isa took them in, trying to see through his eyes. They must look like they climbed the side of Machu Picchu.

"Can we use the side entrance?" She pointed to a set of double doors she'd used on more than one occasion to slip out of Sawyer Financial parties unnoticed. "These shoes and stairs don't go well together."

She delivered the suggestion with a smooth, nonchalant tone, but Eli didn't seem to buy it. His chest expanded and his entire body hummed with frustration.

His eyes flicked to her heels, then to her face, his expression stony. This strong, brave man didn't want anyone to think he was less than capable. She'd be damned if she put him through his paces. He didn't have to prove himself to her.

"Please?" she asked, her smile cautious.

She sensed he wanted to argue, to call her on her fib, but he didn't. He accepted her offer with a tight nod of acquiescence and Isa let him lead her to the side door, pride flooding her chest that he'd granted her his trust.

The side entrance opened to a long hallway leading to the front desk, beyond which was the grand ballroom named the Toronto, where a fancy sign with ornate letters announced the Sawyer Financial Group had the room for the evening.

"Invitation only," Eli read.

"Trust me. I'm on the list."

He halted just shy of the entrance to the ballroom. She turned to face him, noticing the rigid set of his shoulders and the flat line of his mouth beneath his neatly trimmed scruff.

"Don't tell me you're getting cold feet," she joked. "I need you in there."

He thumbed her chin, eyes moving to her mouth a fraction of a second before he placed a kiss on the center of her lips. He didn't explain, didn't say it was his way of thanking her, but somehow she felt it was. Inside this luxury hotel, Eli in his tux, he looked as if he belonged. She'd seen him in jeans and T-shirts and wearing only a pair of shorts. What she couldn't square was that no matter what he wore, he belonged.

Or maybe what she couldn't square was how he belonged with her.

Eli tucked her hand into the crook of his elbow and walked her to the door.

Before they crossed the threshold, Isa spotted her mother sweeping across the room in a sage green dress with delicate lace sleeves. Helena wore her skirts nearly as short as Isa did, and who could blame her? It'd be a shame to hide those legs. All the women on her mother's side of the family were blessed with great legs.

"I'm guessing that's your mother," Eli said. "Green dress, right?"

"Good eye. Helena Sawyer in the ageless flesh."

"You look like her." He dipped his chin, then cast her an approving glance.

"I'll take that as a compliment."

"You should."

"My height is from my father's side, though," she said to fill the gap that hovered when Eli complimented her. She knew how to handle surly Eli, but the charming version was throwing her way off.

Isa looked at her seating ticket again, hoping the number on it was a mistake. But nope, there was a number eleven and table eleven was up front, directly in front of the stage. So much for slipping out early and avoiding the Sawyer Financial Man of the Hour.

A few corporate brass were sitting at the table already. Her parents were likely placed next to her at the table near the entrance of the stage, since one or both of them were speaking tonight. And Josh, of course.

It was no accident that Isa would be within babysitting distance. She let out a vibrating exhale that would make any yoga teacher proud.

"Were you assigned to sit next to someone you don't like?" Eli murmured as they approached the table.

"Well, that's a long list." She smiled over at him and he put a comforting hand on the small of her back. "I was hoping for a table in the back so I could slip out."

"That's why you brought me, Sable. You don't have to

run or hide." Eli slid his palm up her back and to her neck and she thought of the brief, yet flooring kiss outside this room. Her hair was up, so his fingers brushing the bared skin of her neck sent shivers through her.

She could count on him. As a steady, constant force.

She watched his lips as they came the scantest bit closer... Then her mother's voice interrupted.

"Isabella?"

In the wake of her mother's hoisted brow, Isa realized she hadn't properly coached-slash-warned him of what to expect. Namely that her mother and father weren't big fans of the "renegade" Cranes.

"Are you going to introduce me to your date?" Her mother's smile was plastered on, but her eyes allowed her thoughts through clearly.

"Of course. Helena Sawyer, Eli Crane."

Her mother's expression slackened and her eyes traveled to Isa's.

"Oh, really." Rather than extend a hand for him to take, Helena brushed the pearl necklace at her throat. "I wasn't aware Isa knew the Cranes... intimately." Her hooded glare swept over to Isa as if to say, *Aren't we a little old for teenage rebellion?*

"We are acquainted *professionally* as well," Isa said, tucking herself closer to Eli.

"Josh will be disappointed"—her mother ran a judgmental gaze over Eli—"if you don't congratulate him personally before we get started." She took Isa's wrist and gave Eli another fake smile. "If you'll excuse us for a moment."

"No, I don't think I will," Eli replied. Helena froze, scandalized. "We came together, didn't we, Sable?"

Isa didn't miss the sneer her mother shot her at the nickname, but Isa only smiled as she freed her wrist from her mother's grasp and went to Eli. Since when had he become her safe space?

Helena's mouth settled into a dissatisfied moue.

"Thank you," Isa whispered to him as they followed Helena through the well-dressed crowd.

"You don't have to play nice, you know," he said as they followed.

"I do if I hope to blend with this crowd." Everywhere she looked there were CEOs and corporate brass—and not just from Sawyer Financial. "I was hoping to make a good impression."

"We will. But it doesn't mean you have to adhere to the rules they set before you left. And you *did* leave, Sable."

At the mention of the business she'd proudly built, she pulled her shoulders back.

"In fact, let's have a cocktail before introductions." Eli's mouth played at the corners. "He can wait."

"He can," she agreed. And she liked the idea of making Josh wait for as long as they decided.

Eli shot Isa a full-wattage grin, his eyes on hers as he called, "Helena."

When her mother turned, he announced, "We'll join you in a few."

Without clarifying or waiting for Helena's approval, Eli turned on his heel and led Isa to the bar. She followed, liking that she had him to lean on. She had no problem battling her parents and had done it for years. But having him on her side was as surprising as it was amazing.

* * *

"You need to brief me before I talk to this guy." Eli steered Isa away from her aghast mother, liking how he'd swept her out of there. What he didn't like was that Isa didn't tell him anything about Josh other than her parents wanted them back together.

"All you have to do is say 'Nice to meet you' and then we'll go back to our table," she said. "No briefing necessary."

"I promise you, I will not say 'Nice to meet you.'" He let out a noise halfway between a grunt and a snort. "How long did you date him?"

"What? Why?"

At the bar he released her to reach for his wallet.

"Champagne okay?" he asked.

"I guess."

Since when did she not know what she wanted? He gave her his full attention. "Wine? Beer?"

Her eyes brightened. "I'd love a beer but that's really inapprop—"

"Two Stella Artois," he ordered, stuffing a bill in the tip jar.

"Frosted glass?" the bartender asked.

"Bottles." A moment later, he turned and handed over her beer, a cocktail napkin wrapped around the iced-down bottle. "You don't strike me as the type to conform in a crowd, Isabella Sawyer."

"Being here...around my parents." She shook her head. "I feel like a child around them—a misbehaving one."

"So if I weren't here, you'd choke down champagne you don't want?"

"My mother says ladies drink champagne." Her pronouncement brought her closer to his ear, the scent of her perfume wafting over him. The musky spice reminded him of cinnamon or ginger or some exotic flower. Maybe all three.

Eli took her hand and held her at arm's length, encouraging her to spin in a circle, which she did. When she was facing him again, bright pink dress revealing legs a mile long, sweating beer in one hand, a glorious grin on her face, Eli couldn't help smiling back. He tugged her closer, his hand low on her back sliding over the silk of her dress.

"Trust me, Sable. No one will mistake you for anything less than a lady. Even holding a beer bottle." He felt eyes on them and noticed a few men watching her with bald appreciation. "I think you're more of a catch with it."

They parted and drank down a few swallows, their eyes locked.

"Now," he said. "Let's hear it."

"Hear what?"

"Whatever I need to know about this Josh guy." He regretted steering the conversation back to her ex the second he did it. Isa lost her loose composure and sucked in a deep breath that tensed her shoulders.

"What do you need to know?"

"Did you live with him?"

"No." She practically spat the word. "Thank God."

He'd second that motion. Living with Crystal had been a mistake. Especially when she'd announced she was leaving him when he shipped out. It was an added stress he hadn't needed to leave—or come home to.

"Were you engaged?" he asked.

"Definitely not."

"How long did you date him?"

"Are you writing a book?" she snapped.

"Journal entry, maybe," he said, his tone even.

"Sorry." She shifted, smoothing the skirt of her dress. "I'm beginning to regret coming here."

"Why did you?"

She shook her head, seemingly at a loss for a reason.

"I don't like going into enemy territory blind," Eli said when she didn't respond. It brought a smile to the edge of her lips, which he liked seeing there. "I've got your six, Sable."

The second it was out of his mouth, the words settled in his chest like a weight. Being here with her had become about way more than making sure Isa didn't date Zach. This wasn't a trade for favors from a boss/employee. Isa had been in his and his family's corner since the beginning—he wouldn't fail her when she needed him the most.

"Josh and I dated on and off for five years," she said. "We split around three years ago."

"Five *years*." He and Crystal had ended things around the two years and three months mark. It was a long time to be with someone, and Isa had more than doubled that with her ex. "And you want me here because..." She'd alluded to it, hinted at it, but never truly told him.

"Because I want both Josh and my parents to know I'm not going to date him again. He once delivered an ultimatum that I choose his dream or my own or we couldn't be together."

"So you left."

No missing the proud arch of one of Isa's dark eyebrows. "Actions speak louder than words."

"So you're saying you're looking for some action." Eli

pulled her in again, unable to resist all that unbridled confidence and strength.

Her hand landed on his tuxedo shirt where she toyed with a button rather than push him away. "That's not what I'm saying."

"Well that's what I heard."

She tipped her head and smiled up at him. He smiled back. He liked her in his arms. He liked her relying on him. He liked her, period.

Over her shoulder he spotted Isa's mother and the guy he guessed was Josh looking in their direction. He assumed he was her ex given the stiff posture and the look of complete disgust aimed directly at Isa.

He liked that, too. Liked Josh seeing what he could no longer have. Liked Josh knowing she wasn't in a position to be given an ultimatum. It was time to deliver that message in person.

"Okay, Sable," Eli said, hugging her against him with a possessive arm around her waist. "Let's you and I go see this ex of yours."

* * *

Isa inhaled a lungful of pure relief as Eli braced her against his firm, solid side. Having him here, and knowing he had her "six" was more than she'd asked for but exactly what she needed. She could face Josh alone. She just didn't want to.

She'd been away from Josh for years, but since her parents brought him up regularly, he still felt like a part of her life. She couldn't help wondering if they did the same with him—regaling Josh with Isa's successes, which they probably recounted as failures, and then delivering a pitch for getting the two of them back together.

Until tonight, Isa hadn't realized the way she fell into line in this environment. It was disheartening how the strong, sure businesswoman she'd become since she left Sawyer Financial and broke up with Josh receded behind her former accommodating self.

Eli had reminded her of who she was. She had the bottle of beer in hand to prove it.

Josh watched them approach, his eyes flicking between Isa and Eli. Josh recognized her date. She knew he did—Josh kept up with local gossip and the up-and-comers. He knew about the Cranes.

"Josh, look who's come to congratulate you." Her mother stepped in to gesticulate among the three of them.

"Hi, Bella," Josh said with a nod. "Nice to see you again."

His gaze settled on where her hand rested on Eli's sleeve.

"Accompanying her is Elijah Crane." Helena's tight smile morphed into a frown when she spotted beer bottles in both Eli's and Isa's grips.

"Mr. Crane," Josh said. "I read a piece in the *Trib* about you when you came home. Honorably discharged. Thank you for your service."

Isa bristled. She had no idea how Eli would take Josh's generic and borderline condescending greeting.

Eli gave Josh a chin-lift that could either be construed as a nod or a fuck-you, and Isa, in her own immature way, hoped Josh took it as the latter. He didn't of course. The jackass.

"If you'll excuse me," Helena interrupted. "I have to go say hello to the Kitchers." Like that, she was off, gliding through the crowd to torment another unsuspecting group of people.

"Bella, you look..." Josh paused, his eyebrows jumping slightly. "Very pink."

"*Gorgeous* is the word you're looking for," Eli said, his tone gravel and dust.

Josh flicked him a peeved look. "Seemed an inappropriate observation to make since you two are together." News he'd obviously just learned. Damn her parents. They'd primed Josh for Isa showing up as his date tonight. She'd bet her shoes on it.

"There was never a chance we'd get back together," she told him.

Josh lost his air of politeness and clenched his jaw. "Still enamored with serving others, are you? Do you serve him?"

"We're done here." Eli's voice, low and lethal, sent a shiver of pleasure down her spine.

With the hand resting on Eli's elbow, she squeezed his arm gently. "We've both known for years we didn't want the same things, Josh. Why would you want me back?"

"Your parents want you back, Bella. You left them high and dry. Their only child not taking over the business when they needed you most." To Eli he said, "I understand what the two of you have in common."

Eli's glare turned murderous, eyes honed in on Josh like a pair of heat-seeking missiles. "You have two seconds to get the fuck away from us."

Josh's eyes flitted left then right, visibly nervous, but he stood his ground. "We're in public, Crane. I'd hate to see you make the paper for an unbecoming reaction."

"One." Fists balled, Eli took a step closer and Isa felt

his biceps flex beneath her palm. Josh had a few inches of height on Eli, but nothing in the way of muscles on his upper half. Eli would mop the floor with him.

"Very well." Josh held up both hands in a surrendering gesture. He stepped back from an advancing Eli and straightened his tie. "Enjoy the party."

Josh turned and walked away, nothing in his demeanor suggesting he was riled.

"He's good at that," she told Eli. "Saying the right words to ignite your temper, then walking away cool as a cucumber."

"What did you see in that asshole?" Eli grumbled, his intense focus now on her.

"I wish I could remember. I was a different person when he and I dated. He'd rage and I'd step down."

"What kind of rage, Isa?" Eli's voice gentled as he lifted a palm to her jaw. He searched her face, his expression a mixture of hurt and concern. "Did he ever... Did he hit you?"

"Eli. No." She shook her head vehemently. Josh was a jerk but had never crossed a line. He was all show. "Nothing like that. He delivered an ultimatum when he wasn't successful at getting my compliance. That's it."

"That's enough." Eli swept his thumb over her lip. When his eyes returned to hers there was more concern swimming there. "This scar?"

"I fell out of a tree when I was eight." She smiled. He'd noticed that tiny silver mark on her lip. He cared. She liked how Eli's intensity had focused to a finite point—*her*.

"You don't want to be here, do you?" he asked.

She shook her head and then told him the truth. "The only good part about being here is being with you."

Eli dipped his head and covered her mouth with his,

a claiming, delicious kiss she hoped her mother and Josh and everyone in the room witnessed. She hummed, feeling warm and relaxed and happy.

Against her lips, he made her an offer she didn't want to refuse. "Then let's get the hell out of here."

* * *

As Eli pulled from the valet station, he had an uncomfortable realization. He'd put Isa in a similar situation at work as Josh had when she'd dated him. Eli had been the one pushing her and challenging her at every turn. Hell, he'd *fired her* several times.

For a second he'd worried that Josh had hit her. He'd never believed someone could actually see red until the crimson veil washed over his vision. Josh was lucky Eli believed her, because if he'd sensed that Isa was fudging the truth even a little, Eli would have beat the other man unidentifiable.

There was never an excuse to physically harm a woman, which made him wonder if he'd crossed a line of his own.

"I cut the buttons off your shirt," he said in the quiet air of the car, shame coating him.

"Uh. Yes. I remember."

"You weren't scared of me then?"

"Of course not," she said so easily, he turned and looked to where she lounged in the passenger seat. Elbow on the edge of the window, she twirled a loose piece of her hair, giving him a smug smile.

"Because I'm so cuddly?" he asked. She put a hand over his and the pressure in his chest eased. She didn't see him the way she saw her ex—as overpowering her. If anything, she'd overpowered Eli—and his sensibilities.

"When I was with Josh, I was different. I didn't know what I wanted. Now I do…"

She let her voice trail off and Eli wondered if she'd been about to admit she wanted him.

"Josh never loved me for me. He loved the idea of our partnership. Like my parents, he was enamored with the dollhouse style of our coupling."

Eli could relate. When he and Crystal had dated, she'd gone on and on about having a family and a house and a sizable yard. What she'd failed to see was that he wasn't the kind of man who wanted a house with a yard to mow every weekend.

"It's hard to be with someone who doesn't know you," he said in a rare moment of openness—again. She drew the truth from him without even trying.

Isa opened her mouth, maybe to ask more questions, but Eli cut her off before she compelled him to answer.

"Do your parents know the real story behind why you and Josh split?"

"No. They think I went rogue and dumped him along with Sawyer Financial. They thought it was a phase."

"Oh, right. The start-your-own-business phase." He let out a dry chuff, then thought of his own business he was starting. If his brothers knew what he was doing, would they think Eli was going through a phase? Hell, for all he knew he was. He hadn't shared with them yet, and as he thought about it now, the reason was probably so he wouldn't have to explain.

"My family and Josh's family go way back. The Lindens have been friends with the Sawyers for generations.

My parents fear ill will and a bad reputation over all else."

"So you show up to your ex-boyfriend's ceremony with Eli Crane?" He stopped at a traffic light.

"You were a last resort, so you can't possibly feel used."

"Thanks. That's touching," he said, humor in his tone.

Her mouth dropped open and her eyes widened. "I... That came out wrong."

"It's okay," he said. He thought he'd meant it, but the gaffe did sting. Just enough to remind him he hadn't earned her trust. Yet she'd been earning his for a while now.

Way to go, Crane.

He accelerated through the green light. After a few silent minutes, she spoke again.

"To Josh, I was a yellow-brick road leading to the wizard. Haven't you had someone date you because of who you were?"

He thought about that a moment, then shook his head.

"I guess that makes sense. You're not exactly using your family's name to advance, are you?"

"Neither are you," he pointed out. "Sable Concierge isn't tied to them in name, and I assume you didn't borrow a hefty loan from them to start it."

"Not from them. Not from Sawyer Financial." The strength in her voice was undeniable. Isa didn't want a handout. She took the hard road. She *chose* the hard road. Look at him. He wouldn't even know her if he hadn't gone through her staff like disposable cups.

"Isabella Sawyer." He turned off the main drag, an idea sparking. And it was a far better one than dropping her off at her place.

"Yes?"

"Would you join me for dinner?"

"At this time on a Saturday night? We'll wait two hours for a table." The streetlight overhead illuminated her smile of pure excitement. He hadn't earned her, but this could be a start.

"You underestimate my reach. Don't you know who I am?" he teased. Then he lifted his cell phone and punched in a number as he edged into heavy traffic. "This is Eli Crane," he said into the phone. "I have a standing reservation."

CHAPTER 8

Eli was full of surprises.

He drove them to Benicia's Italiano, located on the Magnificent Mile, a very small, very ritzy joint that wouldn't bat an eye if a couple walked in wearing their finest attires—which they were. Upon Isa's brief inventory of the place, she spotted two other men in tuxes. Candles behind amber-colored glass in the center of every table bespoke tradition, but the crisp white tablecloths and the sunny orange and yellow motif on the walls gave the restaurant a modern feel.

Eli spoke to the host briefly and the older, bald man nodded and collected two menus. He led them to a cozy booth at the back of the restaurant where a bottle of wine and a cup filled with slender, crisp breadsticks waited for them.

"Chianti as per your standing reservation," the host said, placing the menus on the table and pulling Isa's chair out for her. She sat, eyeing Eli as he unbuttoned his jacket and

lowered his tall, lean form into the seat across from her.
She wished she could snap a picture of him to preserve the
moment—the moment Eli Crane put on a tuxedo and took
her to dinner after telling her ex off.

Tonight was one for the books.

"Color me impressed." She bit her lip to hide a grin
as she inspected the elegant crowd. "How'd you get us in
here? Does the owner owe you a favor?"

"The owner's son was my rehabilitation guy," Eli said,
studying the menu. "Ex-military. We spent a lot of time
together while I was learning to walk on the leg and he
mentioned Benicia's over and over. Said once I get out and
about to stop by and he'd have a table and a bottle of Chianti waiting for me."

"Wow."

"He's a man of his word."

"As are you."

Eli gave her a dark blue wink and her stomach clenched
in anticipation of where the night might lead.

Their waiter stopped by to chat about the specials and
fill their glasses. They each ordered the chef's special—
linguine with homemade noodles and mussels. A thick
loaf of fragrant, freshly baked bread arrived a minute later,
steam curling. Isa's mouth watered.

"You have a knack for making friends in spite of your
trying hard not to," she observed, tearing off a corner of the
bread and dragging it through a shallow dish of seasoned
olive oil.

"Are we friends?" he asked.

She paused, the bread dripping oil onto the white plate
in front of her. Why did that question feel so intimate? "I
think so."

He lifted his wineglass and drank, saying nothing more about their friendship.

"Thank you for getting me out of the ceremony. I really didn't want to watch Josh take the reins of my parents' company."

"Tell me how you started Sable Concierge," Eli said, clearly not wanting to discuss Josh any more than she did.

"I'm organized. I'm bossy. I'm good at being an assistant."

He laughed and she found herself pausing between bites of the bread to admire the brief flash of levity. Eli Crane was gorgeous when he smiled. Well, he was gorgeous anyway, but especially when he smiled. His eyes crinkled at the corners, his dark scruff parting to reveal a flash of white teeth. Her eyes lingered on his lips for a beat too long to be appropriate. She couldn't help it. She knew what his mouth felt like on hers—the firmness of his lips, the confidence of his touch—and the experience wasn't one she'd soon forget.

"Sounds like an organized, bossy person would be perfect running your parents' company. Why didn't you?"

She took his teasing in stride, lifting her wineglass. "Sawyer Financial isn't exactly thrilling. Besides, you don't appear overly eager to take on COO for your parents."

"Father," he corrected, but his tone was gentle.

"Oh."

"My mother passed a day short of my fifteenth birthday."

"I'm so sorry." Her heart squeezed. She could easily picture Eli spending his fifteenth birthday quiet and angry at the world for taking one of his parents away.

Isa slid her plate to one side so she could put her elbows

on the table—anything to move closer to the man who'd shared a personal detail with her—a detail she hadn't found on his laptop.

"She wrecked on the highway on her way to buy my gift. The video game I wanted was in the passenger seat." He took a deep swallow of his Chianti.

"Eli…" She wanted to touch him, but his rigid posture suggested he wouldn't accept her comfort.

"I'm not the best person for COO of Crane Hotels, Sable."

She tried to make the connection from his losing his mother to him being unfit for COO of Crane Hotels, but wasn't sure how the two pieces fit together. Had his mother not wanted him to go into the family business? Or had she wanted him to and the idea of doing so made the pain of losing her fresh?

"Your father and brothers believe you're perfect for COO," she said. "They believe COO is your legacy—"

"Don't"—he held up a hand—"give me the Batman speech."

"The Batman speech?"

"About how I owe Gotham a debt that would be paid in full by my suiting up and fighting crime. Or, in this case, reporting for duty at the top floor of the Crane Hotel." His delivery was dry, but there was humor under his words.

"Ah, this is well-tread territory."

"You need mudding tires to go in there," he said.

In his own way, he'd asked that she didn't push him on this, and she respected him enough not to. Whatever reason Eli had for not showing up for work at the Crane, he hadn't told anyone. Not yet. She wasn't going to push him. Not when he'd let her leave her parents' event elegantly, simply because she hadn't wanted to be there.

At the delivery of their salads, she kept the conversation going. "What is Zach's role in the charity?"

She'd read the website to better understand what Eli was doing. Refurbs for Vets provided ex-military support so their homes worked around them, not the other way around. Many vets came home needing prosthetic limbs, wheelchairs, or both, and navigating their homes became a whole new ball game when it came to mobility. Eli's brainchild promised "top-notch craftsmanship, styled to the individual's needs." Remodels to kitchens, bathrooms, and any other part of the house that would allow the returning soldier to feel at home. It was admirable, and obvious that home and family were important to Eli—to all of the Cranes.

"Zach is a commercial contractor who has worked with Crane Hotels before," Eli answered, forgoing the salad dressing and digging into dry lettuce. "He can get ahold of great deals on materials and he's an honest, hardworking guy."

"I would have guessed him hardworking, but he's a tad too charming for me to brand him 'honest.'"

Eli narrowed one eye.

"I can't find him charming?" She raised her wineglass and sipped, enjoying Eli's mild jealousy.

"You can as long as you don't get that swoonlike sparkle in your eye when I mention him." Eli rested his elbow on the table and wiggled one finger accusatorially at her.

"Why, Eli Crane. I had no idea you were capable of this kind of flirting." She was having such an amazing evening with him. It was unexpected. *Exciting.*

"I used to be capable of a lot of things," he murmured. There was a hint of grief behind his comment she didn't like hearing.

The pasta arrived shortly after the salads and Benicia herself left the kitchen in a tomato-sauce-stained apron to introduce herself. She was small, gray-haired, with a large nose and a larger smile. She shook Eli's hand, then Isa's in a flour-dusted, bone-crushing grip.

She'd informed them that the tiramisu was on the house, then scuttled back to the kitchen to send it out. Eli and Isa ate in companionable silence much like they did at his house every weekday. They'd shared a lot of meals together, which made tonight feel less like a first date...if that's what it was.

Dessert and espresso followed, but before she dug into her tiramisu—layered with homemade ladyfingers—there was a question she had to know the answer to. Tonight, he was being open and honest. How much more would he tell her?

"Eli?"

"Yeah?" He didn't look up, piercing his dessert with his fork.

"Do you miss your leg?"

* * *

In typical Isabella Sawyer fashion, she crashed through the barriers of politeness. Rather than tiptoe around the topic, she'd busted in headfirst. It was a manner he could appreciate.

"Yes," he answered honestly. Then waited to see where she'd go with the conversation.

She ate a bite of her dessert and chewed thoughtfully. He watched her full lips, no less tempting without the bright pink lipstick, his own fork suspended over his plate.

"In your journal—"

"That you weren't supposed to read."

"I know. I'm sorry. I was so…intrigued. You wrote you didn't miss it. But I would think you'd have to."

"Well, it'd been with me my whole life."

She gave him a small smile he returned. Then he told her exactly the way he saw things.

"Battle is nothing new. Men have fought brutal battles to protect what is theirs, what they love, since the beginning of time. Whenever I shipped out, I had one clear mission: keep the men and women around me safe. That was the *only* mission." His throat tightened as he considered how he'd failed two men in particular. "I'd sacrifice a part of my body to protect others. God knows Benji and Chris gave the ultimate sacrifice to protect me."

She reached across the table and stroked his hand. The shock of being consoled over this matter in particular sent a drove of pins and needles up his forearm. Sure his family knew the details and had given him plenty of attention, but from a woman…a woman on a date. This was new. Unexpectedly welcome.

"They gave the way you would have, Eli. They protected you. You can't deny them the same right to protect their friend."

"They shouldn't have." His lip curled, that hollowed-out feeling returning to his chest whenever he thought of that day. "Christopher had children. Benji had a wife."

"That's heartbreaking."

"I know what it's like to grow up without a mom.

Christopher's kids won't ever see their father again—and Benji won't get the chance to have children." As much as he missed and longed for his mother, Eli had been blessed to have her around for most of his childhood. Reese had more time with her, Tag had less, but at least they could cling to years of memories.

"For what it's worth"—Isa gave his hand a light squeeze—"I'm glad your friends sacrificed for you to be here. If you'd have all been lost, I'd never have met you."

He soaked in her words like rays of sunshine on a chilly day. She held his eyes with hers, her gaze unyielding. Unwavering. As usual, he was caught in a web of her strength and her beauty.

"You don't dwell, I've noticed," she said.

"No reason to." He slipped his hand out from under hers and she sat back in her seat. He was as relieved as he was disappointed to lose the attention.

"Yes, but I think it's because you're simply *not* a dweller. It's like you said, men have been sacrificing parts of themselves as long as humans have been on the earth. You know that, you accept that. The same way you lost your leg and accepted it. The same way, ultimately, you accepted my help."

"Were you inevitable, Sable?" She was the one who'd danced around the topic of fate—so maybe that was why the word flashed onto the screen of his mind. He wasn't sure if he and Isa were fated to meet, but she definitely fit him in a way no other woman had. With Crystal, there had always been a push and pull to get along—so fierce he would practically sweat from the effort. With Isa, there was that same dynamic, but the push and pull felt natural. Like no matter what, she was never truly at odds with him.

"I admit"—she lifted her tiny espresso cup and peered at him over the rim, a vision with her dark hair up and dangling earrings twinkling in the candlelight—"you drew me in. I mean, I didn't have a choice. You unsheathed your claws and stomped off every assistant I sent you. It was either show up myself or let you ruin my hard-won reputation."

A surge of attraction hit him so hard he didn't know what to do with it. The restaurant's sights and sounds dissolved around her like an ethereal cloud until she was the only one in clear focus. Isa was a force he wouldn't avoid. Even in a bright pink dress offsetting her warm skin tone, she reminded him of a cold wind snapping off the lake, burning his face as he walked into it.

"Beauty is a rare thing in war," he said, his own lust-infused voice sounding foreign.

Her cocksure smile slipped as she rested the mug on the tablecloth.

"When I came home, I didn't find beauty here. Months of rehabilitation, keeping my head down and working on the Refurbs project became my focus. Then you..." He shook his head in wonder as the epiphany hit him. "You come along, Sable, and absolutely choke a room with it."

Her whiskey-colored eyes darkened, shadowed by thick black lashes. Her voice wasn't more than a stunned whisper when she said, "Thank you."

"I'm not talking about the way you look." Though, *God*, Isa was a vision in every way. "I mean your spirit. You're fierce. Strong."

She quieted and he wondered if she was working through what he'd said. No doubt this woman had been told she was beautiful—gorgeous—a million times. Her body alone had to have drawn men like moths doomed to incinerate in the flame. But there was more to her. Layer upon layer of trust and power, independence, and a healthy dose of snark.

He was intrigued by every layer.

"Come home with me." It was out of his mouth before he'd meant to say it.

"Um..." Her smile was nervous.

Shit. Why had he blurted that?

"Sorry." He lifted his own espresso for something to do with his hands. "I haven't done this in a while—a long while. Not since—"

"Eli."

He expected to meet a pair of sympathetic eyes and hear a well-versed excuse. Instead, Isa's eyes sparkled in the candlelight and a rich, velvet laugh echoed from her throat.

"I was going to suggest my place instead," she said. "It's closer."

If he'd had a mirror in front of him, he knew he would have seen a grin that matched hers.

* * *

This was it.

An unexpectedly romantic evening with wine and food and delectable dessert was about to be followed by her inviting Eli into her bedroom. So lost in the magic of their conversation and the subtle ways he shared his secrets, Isa hadn't considered, until Eli pulled into her parking lot, that she wasn't only asking him in...

She was asking him *up*.

Outside the windshield, she mentally counted the steps leading to her cozy top-floor apartment. Her heart sank. To Eli, the flight must look a mile long.

The engine died when Eli turned the key and the only sounds in the car were her own heartbeat and their quiet breaths.

"Sable."

"I know. I didn't even think about it when I suggested we come here." She hazarded a glance over at him to find his eyebrows lowered. "We can go to your place. I don't expect you to compromise."

"What are you talking about?"

"The stairs." She pointed needlessly. "There are a thousand stairs leading to my front door."

He glanced out the window, then back at her. "I see that."

"But you can't... or maybe you don't want to—"

"If you're having second thoughts, just say it." His tone was clipped.

Her heart hammered. From excitement or nerves? Isa hadn't had sex in three years. Three. *Years.* When she looked at Eli, there wasn't a single part of her that didn't want to explore what was between them.

Unless things went beyond sex.

She'd thought Josh had been emotionally unavailable— and he had—but Eli Crane took the proverbial cake. She'd had her first date in forever with a stubborn, closed-off Marine, for God's sake. Sex would be amazing if his kiss would be anything to go by, but what about after? How would she continue to see him or work for him? How messy would things get if she were dating the epitome of Mr. Emotionally Unavailable?

True, Isa was strong and brave. But a relationship with Eli would test both those limits. She didn't know if she was ready to put herself in a position of such vulnerability—not yet.

This was a mistake.

"Sable—"

"You know what? I'm going to go. I'll see you Monday." She flashed a quick smile and climbed from the car, shutting the door behind her before he could say another word. Not that he did. The last visual she had of him was his frowning mouth and crinkled brow. A peek back at his car from the staircase didn't reveal more than a dark, reflective windshield.

Who knew what he was thinking right now?

All she knew was that the timing was wrong. Or... not the timing, but something. *Something* was off.

She'd done the right thing.

For her future. For her heart.

CHAPTER 9

Mondays were for overachieving.

Eli loved the fresh possibility of the first morning of the workweek, unlike most people who treasured Garfield-style litanies about hating Mondays. To him, a new week was a fresh start. A chance to make up for a week that didn't go well or a weekend where he'd indulged.

Or a weekend where he'd been blown off.

He'd wanted to indulge—to overindulge—over and over with Isa, but at her apartment she'd balked. The stairs. The goddamn stairs. At the Vancouver, she'd rerouted him, and then at her apartment, she'd given up on him. She'd proven to him that she was a lot like everyone else—first by coddling him, then by feeling sorry for him.

The entire evening had left a sour taste in his mouth and a fresh ripple of loneliness swamped him when he'd returned home alone. He regretted getting swept up in the moment at dinner as much as he regretted driving back to his place without arguing with her further.

He wasn't a total pig. He would have understood if she balked because she'd changed her mind or because she simply didn't want to be intimate. He couldn't help thinking she'd balked because those stairs acted as a reminder that he was different from who she was used to dealing with—a special case. A man with a missing limb that she didn't know how to accommodate.

Emasculating? Yes. Frustrating? Hell yes.

Today was his clean slate—Eli could start over, get back into the swing of things. Regimens were nothing knew. He was accustomed to following a routine. In his former life as a Marine, his days had been regimented. Once he'd come home, his days were regimented in a different way— organized by rehabilitation and relearning the basics like walking and how to care for and clean his wound. Now he worked out to maintain strength and muscle, ate a healthy amount of protein, veggies, and fruits, and focused on launching Refurbs for Vets.

He'd learned repeatedly that life was anything but routine. Once he'd found a decent gallop, there'd be a hiccup that temporarily set him back. Lately, it was family dinners, assistants in his house and in his way, and the occasional swamping fatigue reminding him to slow down.

Those hiccups paled in comparison to the major upset of Isa.

The woman wasn't a hiccup; she was an *attack*—the kind requiring a rushed visit to the hospital for emergency surgery.

Today he was ready for her. He'd been up since five this

morning, had started with a protein shake and an aggressive workout that spent his muscles and left him panting and sweating on the mat in his exercise area.

Then it was shower, shave, prep his meals for the day. He wasn't going to have takeout lunch with his assistant any longer. He'd crossed more than one line with her. He blamed proximity and good old-fashioned lust. Isabella was a beautiful, beguiling, and intriguing woman. He was drawn to her, which meant either she needed to stay out of his way or he would have to fire her.

For good.

The elevator whined, signaling Isa's arrival. He had mentally prepared for a low-cut shirt, short, short skirt, and high, high heels. But when she slid the elevator door aside, she wasn't dressed like the Isa of his memory. She wore a navy blue dress with a collar. The sleeves went to her elbows, the front buttoned all the way up, and the skirt hit her knees. There wasn't a single sexy thing about the frock.

Except that she wore it.

She scuffed in wearing flats instead of clicking along the concrete in a pair of impractical high heels. He found her scuffling less appealing than the clomping he'd bitched about prior.

"Nice shoes," he grumbled. She'd done this on purpose. Trying to tone herself down so he wouldn't find her attractive? It was no use. Isa permeated the room with sensuality the instant she stepped in it. Good thing he was immune.

Mostly.

"Mr. Crane," she stated primly. She wore a pair of large-framed glasses on her nose, and her hair was pulled into a high ponytail.

His libido was panting for her. He couldn't *not* be attracted to her. If she'd breezed in here in a paper grocery bag he'd still want her.

Well, too bad.

Right. He had shit to do.

Since most of that "shit" was up to him to assign, he'd prepared ahead. He slapped a stack of file folders down on the dining room table—aka, her desk.

"Need you to dig into these for me."

"And what are 'these'?" She rested her bright orange, fancy-looking purse on one of the fabric chairs at the table.

"Candidates for Refurbs. I need estimates on what kind of upgrades each of them requires. Zach's estimations are in there, along with my budget. You can go through and tell me what fits and what doesn't."

Her mouth formed a little *O*.

"I also need you to schedule the construction."

"Schedule...the construction?" She picked up a folder and thumbed through it. "Eli, I know nothing about—"

"There is an estimate of man-hours and materials in the folder from Zach. If you have questions, call him. His phone number is in there."

She blinked, her long lashes brushing the lenses of her glasses, her eyes big and innocent. She was so damn sexy his mind muddled.

"Why are you wearing those?" he asked through clenched teeth.

"These?" She pushed the glasses up her nose. "I wear them when I drive. My eyes have been getting tired from staring at a computer day and night. I do have to actually *run* Sable Concierge in addition to working here doing"—

she closed the folder—"construction scheduling, apparently."

She was challenging him, but he wouldn't back down. She was the one who wanted to work for him so damn badly.

"You sure you want me to call Zach?" She propped a hand on her hip in challenge.

"Be my guest." He added a nonchalant shrug that felt forced because it was.

Yes, he'd asked her not to date Zach. And, yes, Eli had done it because he thought—for a few insane moments—that there was something between himself and Isa. After Saturday, it was clear there wasn't.

She doesn't want you. Let it go.

When regret filled his chest this time he did his best to ignore it. He didn't have to look far into his past to find proof that he wasn't good dating material, and he didn't have to look anywhere but down for a reminder that he was a challenge. Crystal hadn't signed up for him, and Isa didn't want to either.

"My lunch is prepared for the week, so I won't be needing takeout," he said, putting an end to his own personal pity party. He knew who he was. Knew what needed to be done. He didn't need Isa to validate him. "I have a coffeemaker in my office now, so you're off coffee duty. You have your orders, Sergeant. I suggest you get started."

He turned and marched to his office, head high, adrenaline spiked. Back in control. Of himself. Of his surroundings.

As long as he ignored that niggling in his gut telling him he was acting like an ass.

* * *

What on God's green earth...?

Isa, manila folder in hand, stood scowling in the direction Eli had vanished, shaking her head at the interaction. She knew absolutely nothing about the construction business, though Eli had given her enough information and forms to ensure she wouldn't be speaking to him all day.

Coffeemaker in his office. *Pfft.*

His lunch was prepared. *Double pfft.*

"Fine," she said to herself, dropping the folder and tightening her ponytail. She plopped into the seat and tore the glasses off her face. They were from the dollar store. She didn't need them. She hadn't fibbed about the eyestrain, but her main purpose in buying the frames was to try and look more like a professional assistant. After their awkward departure Saturday, when she'd tucked her tail between her legs and fled up the stairs, she hadn't been sure she'd be able to face him Monday morning. First, she'd insulted him by suggesting he couldn't scale the stairs to her apartment, *then* she'd delivered the felling blow. She'd left him sitting in the car without thanking him for dinner or for being there for her through the Josh debacle. Without telling him the real reason she no longer wanted him to come up to her apartment.

Cold feet was the reason. Come this morning she'd felt the embarrassment anew but was determined to face him. She had decided to be professional and polite and by the time she delivered him a second cup of coffee, she'd planned on saying something like, "Sorry I freaked out. Care to try again?"

Evidently, grumpy Eli was back and he wasn't interested

in trying again. No...disinterest didn't seem to be what drove him. More like his feelings were hurt and he had erected a great big wall too tall for her to scale.

Fine.

He wanted things to be this way, and she could accommodate him. If Isa was anything, she was professional. She could learn about the construction business. Google was her best friend.

She sat down, emptied her tote, and fired up her computer. Then she dug in to the files next to her and set her sights on success.

* * *

Hours later, Isa stretched her arms overhead, blinking her grainy eyes at the time on her computer. Three o'clock! She surveyed the damage around her laptop as if seeing it for the first time. A browning apple core, an empty yogurt cup, and a wrapper for a granola bar had been cast aside amid piles.

Piles. On her normally tidy workstation.

She'd researched and read and organized. She'd fashioned a clunky schedule and worked up a spreadsheet for the budget. The only thing left to do was hand it over to Eli for his approval. She stood, her back giving an unhappy *pop!* since she'd neglected to get up and move around.

Angling for his office, she reminded herself again that she was a professional. Who probably shouldn't make out with her boss or think of making out with her boss every time she looked at him.

Sucking in a steeling breath, she stepped up to the dividing wall that she'd come to think of as the Great Wall of Eli, prepared to confront him. This time there'd be no sexy distractions. No high heels, no short skirt, no revealed cleavage. She'd go in, hand him the file, and turn around and leave.

She poked her head around the corner, fist poised to knock. It took her mind a moment to wrap itself around what she was seeing.

Eli, doubled over, one hand grasping the edge of his desk, his lips peeled into a grimace. His other hand was wrapped around one knee, his knuckles white.

"Eli!"

She rushed to him and he spared her a surprised glance— he hadn't heard her coming—and his eyes radiated so much pain, she swore she felt it herself. She rushed to comfort him, placing a hand on one rock-hard shoulder, the muscles in his arm standing out and strung as tight as cables.

"Get out!" His growl was accompanied by a glare, but the glare melted into a mask of pain when another wave attacked.

"What happened?" Her voice was borderline hysterical when she knelt on the floor and put her hand over his.

"Go!" His voice was low, not as loud, the one word fading as his face contorted again.

She'd read about this.

Phantom pain. Most amputees experienced everything from searing hot spikes to tickling to electrically charged nerve pain in the limb that wasn't there. Meditation helped. Mirror therapy helped. And so did someone massaging the area that wasn't actually flesh and bone any longer.

"Is it your knee?" she asked.

He blew out a stuttered breath through his teeth rather than answer.

She grasped his cheeks, her hands brushing against his soft facial hair as she forced him to look at her. "Is it your knee?"

"Foot," he managed, his blue eyes watering.

She'd bet her bank account he was referring to the foot that wasn't there. She moved a hand to his knee but this time he didn't push her away. Then she moved down his prosthesis, which she could feel through the leg of his pants.

"No," he said on an exhale, but he didn't physically try to stop her.

"I'm going to help. Do you want to stop hurting or not?" She pegged him with a challenging glare of her own. Eli held her eyes for a few seconds before finally giving a small but reluctant nod of permission.

She kept sliding her hand down. When she reached his tennis shoe and untied the laces, Eli snatched her wrist.

"You have to trust me. It's nothing I haven't seen before." When he continued frowning, she explained. "The morning you were doing sit-ups?"

"You mean when you couldn't look at me?" He gritted the words out between his teeth, a sheen of sweat glistening on his temple.

This beautiful idiot. He thought she was what… disgusted by him? Turned off by him? Nothing could have been further from the truth.

She kept her eyes on his when she told him what he'd obviously overlooked. "I couldn't look at you that day because I was so attracted to you I couldn't breathe."

The pain in his eyes receded some as he puzzled out this newfound fact. His fingers once again flinched around her wrist.

"Eli. Let me go so I can help you."

He released her, jaw working as he watched her untie and slip off his shoe. She returned her attention to his leg, straightening the prosthesis and resting the foot on her thigh. She dug a finger into the arch through his sock. "Here?"

He winced, unable to look at her, or maybe unwilling.

"Here?" She tried again, sliding her fingers down.

"Higher."

She moved her fingers up and massaged the false foot, watching as the pain melted from his handsome face. He let out a deep breath with a whoosh but didn't close his eyes. He watched her touch him. He needed to in order to send his brain the memo that the pained area was getting tended to. Despite feeling unsure of herself, she continued massaging his prosthetic foot until Eli's shoulders visibly unknotted.

When his hand rested gently on her shoulder, she stopped. He pulled his foot from her thigh.

"I wasn't sure I was doing that right." She gave him a weak smile and noticed her hands were shaking. That was *intense*.

"It's stupid," he mumbled.

"It not stupid. You suffered a major injury. One that took the lives of two of your friends and literally took a part of you. There's nothing stupid about what happened to you, Eli."

His eyes went to where she sat on her knees in front of him, then flicked to her mouth and danced around her face. She had to explain. Had to tell him why she'd run out on him that night like Cinderella at the stroke of midnight.

"Saturday night, I—"

Without warning, he grabbed hold of her ponytail, tipped her head back, and lowered his lips to hers.

The meeting of their mouths was electric on contact, shooting sparks into her bloodstream and erasing her mind of the explanation she'd been ready to give. The same undeniable force saturated the air no matter what they did, where they were, or what she wore.

Pure, unadulterated attraction.

His tongue slipped along the seam of her mouth and she rested her hands on his thighs, opening her lips to let him in, to taste him. She dug her fingers into his leg muscles, being careful to ease the pressure when she worried she might be hurting him. He hauled her up by the waist to thoroughly explore her mouth.

"Tell me to stop," he said between kisses.

"Why?" She allowed her tongue to graze the soft hair of his returning beard. "Will you?"

"Yes." He cupped her ass and met her eyes. "But I don't want to stop, Sable. Not until you're naked and satisfied and out of breath."

She stroked his face with her hand. "Then I'd be a fool to ask you to stop."

"Agreed." His mouth twitched.

She'd amused him, and herself quite frankly.

Isa stood, bringing her breasts to eye level with him, but his gaze stayed locked on her face. Standing over him as he sat on his office chair, his chest expanding with each breath, she couldn't think of anything she wanted more than him.

So she'd have him.

She unbuttoned the first button on her dress, watching as Eli swallowed, his Adam's apple bobbing with the movement.

"If only you had your knife," she joked as she slipped another button free. "This process could be so much faster."

"Don't tempt me." His voice was choked with lust instead of pain, which she preferred.

Another button open, then another, and she untied the fabric belt at her waist. His fingers dug into his thighs as he watched her slip the upper half of the dress off her shoulders. She may have dressed plainly for work today, but underneath she wore a silk cami and panties—both navy to match her dress. Judging by Eli's shell-shocked reaction to seeing them, she'd chosen well. Not that she'd expected to strip for him, but now that she had...

May as well keep going.

She took a step forward to stand between his legs. He swept his hands up her skirt, to the backs of her thighs, his eyes following her fingers as she ran them down her neck and tucked her thumbs into the straps of the cami.

Then slowly, slowly slipped those straps aside...

* * *

Eli felt a bead of sweat trickle down his temple as he watched Isa strip for him. She had teased him by sliding the straps over her shoulders, and from the heated glint in her eyes, he could tell she wasn't done yet. The more skin she revealed, the more he wanted to see.

She kept teasing him, tucking her fingers into the cups and tugging the material down to expose her breasts. She ran the tips of her fingers over dusky nipples that pebbled beneath her touch. By the time she circled in the other direction, closing her eyes and dropping her head back, Eli's erection was full tilt. He was couldn't sit idly by a second longer.

Splaying one hand across her back, he tugged her to him, closing his lips over one waiting breast and cupping the other with his free palm. Her hands went to his hair, kneading his scalp. He laved his tongue over and over her nipple, reveling in the sounds she made—soft, sensual, keening moans he hadn't heard in far too long.

Sex. He needed it.

He needed *her*.

He dragged his mouth to her other breast as his hands went to work on the buttons remaining on her dress. Soon it was on the floor behind her, his hands roaming over her smooth-as-silk skin to a pair of scant panties.

Correction: thong.

He slipped his thumb around the tiny piece of material and skimmed along her bare bottom. Her fingers pushed and pulled through his hair, her breath sucking through her teeth as one magic word exited her lips.

"Yes."

"Yes to what?" His lips left her breast to snake down her torso, then he drew a line with his tongue along the waistband of her panties.

"Yes to you. Yes to right now." She kicked off her shoes. She put one knee on his chair, then the other. When she was straddling him, she sank slowly onto his lap as he held on to her plush body. "Yes to this."

She ground against his hard-on, and he bit down on his lip. Pure pleasure saturated his bloodstream. His hold on her tightened as she slipped over his cock, mimicking what they could be doing naked if she gave him the chance.

"What say you?" she asked, a naughty smile playing on her full mouth.

He stopped her, holding her over his erection as he reached for the lap drawer on his desk.

Her lips curved when she saw the scissors.

"In case of emergency." He lifted the string of her thong and snipped. "This is an emergency."

She bent to kiss him as he discarded her ruined thong and rummaged with one hand in the drawer again. It was in there somewhere—*aha*. She pulled her lips away from his when he dropped a condom on the desk. He shut the drawer with a slam.

"Do you always keep condoms in your office?"

"No." He'd put the condom in there Saturday night. He'd come in here to work, frustrated about how the evening had ended, and emptied his pockets into the lap drawer. He didn't want to explain. He just wanted to feel human. Wanted to feel her. Wanted to feel something other than pain and guilt and frustration.

She lifted his T-shirt and he undid his belt. By the time they were both fumbling with his zipper, he lost his concentration and kissed the breasts hovering in front of his face again. Isa tasted of heaven, her cinnamon-spice fragrance abrading his brain. Her light brown skin glimmered like gold in the firelight from the hearth behind him, a trick of the light that infused her hair with bands of copper.

"Been a while." She shook the condom packet in her hand.

"For me or for you?" He snatched it away and tore open the gold foil, working the latex over his length as quickly and carefully as he could.

"Me, definitely," she said. "You, probably."

"Maybe I've been waiting." Sheathed, he turned his attention back to the gorgeous woman hovering over his cock.

"For?"

"You." On the word, he slipped the tip along her smooth folds. "What were you waiting for?"

Had she been waiting for a prince charming, or any man who didn't treat her as a ticket to a free ride to her parents' company? Did she need sex or closeness or both?

She leaned close and licked her lips, hovering over him but never fully seating herself. "You," she breathed.

She sank down and he gripped her hips, breaching her entrance as both of them let out a long, satisfied sigh. Isa licked her full lips, scrunching her eyes closed. He brushed a few stray strands of her hair aside that had wrestled from her ponytail.

"Sable. Are you okay?"

Those whiskey eyes opened, focused on him, pupils dilated. A grin spread her lush mouth and she tilted her hips, taking him in until there wasn't any more of him to take.

"I'm better than okay, Eli." She placed her hands on his shoulders and began to move, her rhythmic motions syncing with his clumsier ones. With one shoe off, he had no leverage on his right side. His foot slipped on the floor.

"Fuck."

"Hey." Warm hands closed over his face as she rerouted his gaze to hers, knocking every frustrated thought from his brain. "We've got this."

Holding his cheeks with her palms, her dark eyes locked on his, she slid off his cock and then lowered slowly, impaling herself again. Lost in her eyes and the truncated breaths they shared, Eli's mind blanked.

Isa set the pace, an agonizing one, and he shifted his focus to her raspberry-tipped breasts and the feel of her tight channel as she rode him. Every rise and fall scooted the chair's wheels across the floor until they bumped into the edge of the hearth, her plush bottom cradled in his hands.

She picked up the pace, slamming down onto his lap. Riding him until he felt a lightning bolt strike his spine and streak to his balls.

He held fast, his arms wrapped around her back, his face against her breasts as he used his upper body to move her a few final pumps.

His release hit him so hard, spots appeared behind his eyelids, a primal growl tearing from his throat. It took him several blissed-out moments to settle, to catch his breath, to come to, for God's sake. When he did, he became aware of his surroundings one by one.

Isa's fingertips in his hair.

Her pillowy breasts pressing against the side of his face.

Her lips closing over his forehead as she caught her breath.

"Sorry." He shifted and placed a kiss on her chin. "I owe you one."

Her dark eyes blinked and as a relaxed—and yeah, satisfied—smile pulled her lips, he questioned his need to apologize.

"Maybe I'm not sorry." His lips quirked into what felt like a dopey smile, but hell if he cared. He hadn't felt this good in forever. *If* ever.

"No apologies necessary." She kissed him briefly, but

he held her head gently and finished the kiss the way he wanted.

Wet.

Deep.

Soft.

He was rewarded with another of her smiles, one he'd put there, which made him damn happy.

"It's understandable you didn't notice my enjoyment since I laid yours on pretty thick." She flicked her tongue over his top lip and whispered, "Emphasis on the *thick*."

Okay, *definitely* sporting a full-on dopey grin now.

"I like this." She touched the corner of his mouth. "I've been trying to get you to smile since I started working here."

"Well now you know how to do it." He hugged her closer, enjoying her warm laughter and the ease between them. This was what had been missing Saturday. They'd both been on edge, uncomfortable. The attraction had been there, but not like this. He raked his fingers into her hair, wrestled it from the elastic, and let her hair fall down her back and over her smooth shoulders.

She shifted and he moved to help, both of them talking in hushed tones.

"You should—"

"I should—"

They shared a nervous smile.

"Right," she said. "Do you need my help with…anything?"

"No." More importantly, he didn't want her to help. "I have it. If you could just…give me a minute."

"Oh, sure. I'll just…" She lifted off him and they took a moment to appreciate the slow slide of him leaving her body. "Be out there," she finished on a breath. Hastily, she gathered her clothes and trotted away from him.

He sat frozen on his chair watching her ass sway and her hair trickle like a black waterfall to the middle of her back. The way her golden skin seemed to shimmer as she stepped from his office into the interrupting daylight.

Best damn idea he'd had in a long time, he thought with a grin.

And it wasn't even his.

* * *

In the bathroom across the hall, Isa dressed—sans her panties since Eli had shredded them. She grinned at her reflection as she finished buttoning her dress. She knotted the fabric tie at her waist and fluffed her hair, admiring the hue of pink at the apples of her cheeks.

She looked damn satisfied. Felt it, too.

It'd been a long time since she'd looked at her reflection and saw anything but the hardworking, harried owner of Sable Concierge.

Sable.

She loved when Eli called her that. Sable was the name she'd chosen not only to set herself aside from her parents, but also to establish a new identity she could rely on. One that was separate from her parents, from Josh, from the financial industry.

Hearing that name tumble off Eli's tongue, especially when doing what they were doing, made her feel sexy and sinful, in charge and take charge.

And the sex just now? What carnal, hidden cave had *that* crawled from? She'd never been so bold. Had never taken a man on a chair or stripped and touched herself in front of him—and never, ever would she have imagined doing it for a client.

She put her fingertips to her mouth to hide another smile that faded and faded fast. Eli wasn't just a client. He was her friend. Now her lover.

She had a lover for the first time in three years who wasn't tied to her by a promise. Who she wasn't tied to her by familial obligation. It was...thrilling.

She stepped out of the bathroom and crossed to Eli's office. He stood at his desk, fully dressed, both shoes on. His hair was disheveled from her running her hands over it while they made love. The sight of him standing there sure and strong made her heart skip a few necessary beats.

"So." Granted, not the most inventive of conversation starters but she had to say something.

"So." He slipped those capable hands into his pockets and her gaze trickled down his body, remembering the fullness of him inside her, the pleasure that singed her veins when he had his hands on her. She shuddered and didn't even mean to.

He walked toward her and she met him in the center of the room. They didn't touch. Finally, he came to her, so close she had to tip her head to take in his height. He slanted his mouth over hers, rewarding her with the softest touch of his lips before pulling away too soon.

She expelled a sigh, her heart thundering as her pulse chased to her belly before settling between her thighs.

"Same time tomorrow?" she asked, her voice low and husky.

He grinned and she nearly had to grab on to him to stay standing. Eli's smile lit his blue eyes like the sun-dappled surface of the ocean. It lifted his cheeks and parted the longer scruff she found so sexy she couldn't think straight.

"We have a bit of an ethics problem, don't you think?" He gave her a teasing wink and she felt the firm press of his palm against her back.

"Next time fire me first."

His smile endured and beckoned another of hers. "Deal."

CHAPTER 10

Isa arrived at work the next morning, her tote on her shoulder, unsure what to expect.

After the sex and shared admiration for one another in Eli's office, she'd mentioned the construction schedule. Eli had followed her to her desk and they'd sat and reviewed it together. An hour later, she had a better grasp of the construction business as a whole. Eli had stuck a few Post-it notes onto the makeshift calendar, and *voila*.

Le schedule.

She'd teasingly asked if he'd like her to contact Zach and he'd said no without hesitation. "I'll do it." Then he kissed her and told her to pack up.

No wonder she didn't know what to expect today. Work? Kisses? Work *and* kisses?

She voted for option C.

The elevator came to a stop, but as she reached for the handle, the door slid aside for her. She was surrounded by the piney scent of Eli, who hooked a hand around her waist, pulled her close, and kissed her gruffly. Her hand went to his chest to steady herself as she rocked on her heels.

He pulled his lips from hers and swept a heated gaze down her body to the low-cut blouse, tight skirt, and stilettos.

"You look like you today," he said, his voice holding a hint of humor. "Morning."

Humor. In Eli Crane's voice. *Who'd have thunk?*

She wasn't sure she'd ever get used to the sexy twist of his half-smile or the way it moved the hairs on his face into a path she wanted to follow. A path she could skip down in search of hard, wet kisses and dirty promises.

"I wasn't sure what I'd walk into today," she told him, breathless. "Your lips, as it turns out."

Another kiss had her eyes sliding shut, her fist clutching his shirt. When they parted, he took her tote from her hand and carried it to the table for her. It was such an oddly gentlemanly thing to do she stood stock-still for a moment, watching him move across the room before she followed.

In her defense, it was hard to look away from the back muscles shifting beneath a long-sleeved black cotton shirt or his firm ass in a pair of worn denim...

Hot.

His gait, she noticed as she walked behind him, was less even than usual.

"Are you having any pain today?" she asked as he set her bag down.

"Some. Nothing I can't handle." His jaw went tight.

So...probably the wrong thing to ask. Before she could

change the subject, he turned and said, "But if you want to put your hands on me, feel free."

"Same to you." She accepted his offer, sweeping her hands onto his shoulders as he once again grasped her waist. His blue eyes warmed and Isa felt as if she had stumbled into an alternate realm. One where she was allowed to touch him.

"What's on the docket for you today?" he asked.

"I work for you, Eli. Shouldn't you be telling me?"

"You work for Reese, Sable. Do I really need to remind you?" Humor twinkled in his eyes before he gave her a quick smooch and released her.

"I have a few papers for you to review and sign off on. Plus there's a board meeting later this month and Reese has asked that you attend."

Eli let out a long, unhappy sigh and she regretted the change in the atmosphere.

"I think you should go to the meeting," she said.

"Oh, do you?" he asked, not really asking.

"I do." She crossed her arms defiantly, standing her ground. She sensed that Eli wanted to work for his family but he was worried he might be the monkey wrench in the entire operation. Which was ridiculous. He was no more a bad omen than a black cat or a broken mirror.

His gaze wandered to her cleavage, stayed there for a beat.

"Up here, Marine," she said.

He met her eyes, his demeanor already lighter. "We'll see."

Which was not a no. Progress.

"What are you up to today?" she asked as he started for his office.

"I have work to do on Refurbs, but I'll be done by this afternoon. Maybe"—he pushed his hands into his front pockets and shrugged—"you and I can *reconvene* then."

Chills chased down her legs, but she replied with a cool, "We'll see."

He sent one last glance over her before turning and walking to his office—though if she wasn't mistaken, that walk was more of a strut.

Isa blew out a breath, her shoulders slumping from the weight of…whatever this was. Lord. She was so ill equipped for this kind of affair. If that's what it was. She had no idea if they'd last a minute or a month. But one thing was certain.

Being with Eli was thrilling. The not knowing. The edge they danced along with each other. The bite of their retorts mixed with flirtatious smiles and veiled promises.

After a lifetime of her parents trying to line up her future for her, after pushing and fighting to build Sable Concierge into a known name, Isa was tired of toeing the line. She was ready to step off the map—to have a little uncharted fun.

That's what this had to be with Eli.

Anything more would mean she was overly involved with a billionaire businessman. She'd already attempted a relationship with a man in a suit chasing power. Not that Eli was in a suit. And not that he had to chase power…It found him and he had the ability to wield it effortlessly.

She unpacked her bag, disliking how she couldn't categorize Eli into the no-go zone. Soon, that dislike faded and her mind was turning over something other than her to-do list or her agenda. Her mind was on the slowly ticking clock...and how long she'd have to wait to see if he'd be up for some of that messy fun again today.

* * *

That woman.

Eli pulled his hands down his face and shook his head to dislodge the fuzz in his brain. Isa had lined his head with cotton batting. He sat at his desk, shifting in the seat as flashes of yesterday afternoon crashed into him. When his immediate vision had been filled with two perfect breasts, a slim stomach, and enough dark hair to blot out the sun.

This morning he'd woken feeling so much like his old self, he was surprised to find he hadn't traveled back in time. The doctor had said there could be a subtle or rapid shift into acceptance. Every person was different.

Eli hadn't believed it. The doctor may know what he was doing because he'd read a lot of books and had worked with amputees, but he also had four working limbs, so how could he really *know*?

This morning Eli considered maybe that doctor was right.

He'd climbed out of bed and into the shower and— *boom*—realization hit him like a Mack Truck. It wasn't like he was gone and now he was back, more like he'd crawled out of a dark hole into the sunlight. He didn't have to try to fake the confidence straightening his back and squaring his shoulders; it was just...*there*.

Because of sex.

Accompanying his getting dressed were thoughts of Isa and the way she'd tangled her fingers into his hair.

The sounds she'd made when he thrust inside her again and again. And now he could add the pleased smile he'd kissed onto her face when she'd arrived to his stock of memories.

In an odd way, making her smile was equal to the feeling he'd had after they'd had sex.

Like he'd fucking *won*.

"Damn," he muttered. What the hell was he supposed to do with *that*?

He pushed his deep thoughts aside and focused on answering his e-mails, which was horrific. He hated e-mail. Hated communicating via anything other than in person, which he didn't love that much either. Now that he'd started the business of being in business, he found working from home had its drawbacks. Or hell, maybe no one in an office bothered to walk in and talk to you there either.

He was arriving at an uncomfortable realization. He didn't want to run Refurbs for Vets. *At all.* Starting the charity had been rewarding. Creating it from nothing and moving Zach and his team into place, invigorating. But the day-to-day grind? The e-mails and phone calls and—God help him—text messages? No. He didn't like it. Not even a little.

So hand it off to Isa.

He chewed on that thought for a moment, but only for a moment. Isa was running a business of her own—one he was technically keeping her from running. She'd go back to running Sable Concierge soon enough. He didn't trust anyone else to have their hands in Refurbs. It was his house of cards and he was doing his damnedest not to let it topple.

Plus, he hated to ask for help.

Cue the leg. When he'd returned to Chicago, he had no choice but to accept help from everyone—family and strangers. It was humiliating and frustrating and damn sad to have to rely on someone after years of relying on himself.

Which reminded him of Crystal. Because how many times had she asked that he trust her? With his hopes and his dreams? With his unresolved feelings of loss about his mother? He didn't share those things—not ever.

Yet he had with Isa.

He'd sat at dinner in Benicia's and spilled his guts about his mom. He'd told her about Christopher and Benji when she'd asked.

And now that he'd shared the details of his past, he felt...uncomfortable?

Vulnerable.

Not a good feeling. As a soldier, he was trained to protect his men from vulnerabilities. Hell, to seek out vulnerabilities in the enemy. While he was aware he was no longer at war, it didn't change the trigger twitching in his chest telling him the more access Isa had to his heart, the more in danger he was.

No.

Fuck a bunch of that.

Isa was here for the same reason he was—they shared work hours, sure, but they also shared amazing, consensual, fantastic sex. Sex that made them both feel great and look better. Sex without future commitments or worrying about a picket fence, two kids, and a golden retriever.

His biggest worry with Isa was that he might fail her in bed—that once she learned there was some maneuvering he'd have to try for leverage reasons, she, too, might decide he wasn't what she'd signed up for. That niggle of doubt squirmed in his stomach and he felt his face pinch into a scowl.

"Or maybe you shouldn't fucking question it," he mumbled as he punched the SEND button on the e-mail he'd finished crafting.

"Hmm?" came a soft hum from the threshold of his office.

"Sable." He hadn't heard her walk in here in those tall, black, shiny shoes. A vision of her on top of him in bed, his hands wrapped around the spikes on those heels as he lifted his hips to meet hers throttled him. That vision was a hell of a lot better than the worry it replaced.

"Thought you might need a snack." She carried an apple.

"Is it lunchtime?"

"It's two o'clock."

"Oh." His stomach gave a loud rumble. Evidently, being reminded of lunch was all it took to make him hungry.

"I debated bringing this." She put the apple on his desk, a knife alongside it. "I really like this blouse."

He grinned. He liked this side of her—frank *and* cute. Before, it was irritating. Now he found it refreshing. And sexy as hell.

"I owe you a shirt and a thong." He spun and laced his hands together, elbows resting on the arms of his chair.

"I'm not worried since my underwear is safely ensconced in my lingerie drawer." She leaned over his chair, her spicy scent surrounding him. "I'm not wearing any."

Oh yeah. It was fucking *on*.

He stood so quickly, she lost her balance. He wrapped

an arm around her to keep her from toppling. "You think we're doing this in here again, you're wrong."

"You didn't like office-chair sex?" Her hand wandered to the neck of his shirt, where her fingers played along the seam.

"I liked it very much, but I believe you came in here to remind me of lunch." Her hands flinched as her hold tightened on him, so he laid it on even thicker. "I'm going to lay you down and have a taste of what you're not covering with underwear."

Her eyes bloomed, dark sienna flecked with bits of gold. "Like that, do you?"

"I..." She shrugged, an awkward lift of one delicate shoulder.

"What's the matter, Sable?" He leaned in so his lips brushed hers. "Pussy got your tongue?"

* * *

"Shimmy into the bedroom."

His gruff voice sparkled over her like carbonated water. She obeyed, too intrigued not to. He walked behind her at an even clip while she pulled her hair over one shoulder and twisted, a nervous habit when she didn't know what to do with her hands. Though, she knew what she wanted to do with her hands, didn't she? Put them all over his body. Run them through his hair. Hold on to his—

"Stop."

She halted at the doorway of his bedroom and he slipped past her, brushing her waist with one hand. His bed was unmade, a pair of discarded jeans and a few T-shirts on the floor. A massive window stood over the bed, slatted blinds open to let in the sun. His dresser was on the far side of the room, along with a chair, and two different prosthetics rested against the wall next to the closet. One was shaped like a large C, no foot at the bottom. They were for running, if memory served.

"Messy for a military man," she said, sweeping her eyes back to the bed.

"I'm not on duty." He grabbed the corner of his gray comforter and tossed it open to reveal gray rumpled sheets. "They're clean. I don't like making the bed. More comfortable to slide into it messy."

There was a euphemism there she didn't take the time to turn over.

He snagged her hand and pulled her to him. "You ready?"

"Yes." Her heart thundered in anticipation of what he'd promised. Him between her legs, turning her on. He ran his hand down her blouse, over her breast, and to her skirt, where he slipped his fingers under the material. Once he reached the bare skin of her thighs, he kept going, his hand cupping her sex.

"Completely bare," he said reverently, sliding a finger along her damp folds. "And ready for me."

She opened her mouth and a high-pitched whimper came out. His touch felt that good.

"That's going to be my tongue next." Another stroke and she grasped his shoulder for support. If he kept this up, he'd drop her where she stood. Her knees actually wobbled. "Do you like it fast or slow?"

It wasn't a rhetorical question, she guessed, given the way he watched and waited for an answer.

"I...I'm not sure."

He tilted his head, his eyes narrowing. He stroked her again—one long, wet glide. "But you've had experience with this."

"Not a lot." She let loose a nervous smile. Josh had always been in too much of a hurry. And frankly, he wasn't very good at it. "I mean, yeah...with...myself."

Did she seriously admit to Eli Crane that she masturbated? Her eyes widened in alarm, but his smile turned sinister.

"In that case, you know exactly what you like, don't you?"

She swallowed around the lump hardening in her throat, grateful when he kissed her so she didn't have to answer. He slipped his fingers away, unzipping her skirt and giving it a shove. It hit the floor and she kicked off her shoes.

"On the bed, Sable."

She sat on the edge of the mattress, pulling her legs up and wrapping her arms around them. His grin was penetrating and sent another warm surge through her. The anticipation of having him taste her—having him inside her—filled her with unfamiliar longing.

It'd been years since she'd been in a relationship, and when she had, it'd been weighed down by a mountain of obligation. With Eli, there were only the two of them and a physical awareness that rivaled any attraction in her past.

Eli sat at the end of the bed, his back to her as he took off his shoes. They met the floor with a couple of dull thuds. He stood and slid his pants down, revealing a tight, round ass in black boxer briefs and thighs so strong she'd bet he used them to open jars.

She rested her chin on her folded forearms to hide her smile.

He sat, and while she couldn't see what he was doing, she could hear him working his pants down his legs and the sound of a click as he removed the prosthetic leg.

The last to go was his shirt. He fisted the material at the back of his neck and peeled it over his head, tossing it to the floor inside out. Messy, indeed. She liked that as much as she liked everything else about him. Especially those rippling back muscles. Eli was beautiful and rugged. Like a sculpted rock face.

When he turned his head, she admired his profile; the line of his neck leading down his shoulder and his tattoo sleeve. Flowers and lettering, a cross and the sun, interwoven with patterns she hadn't taken the time to interpret.

"Sable, lie down," came his quiet command.

She scooted back onto the bed and stretched her legs out, reaching for the buttons on her blouse.

"I'll get that. Need your eyes on the ceiling, honey." Another soft request.

She obeyed, eyes on the white plaster ceiling overhead as she listened to him come to her, moving at an uneven pace up the bed. Then her vision was filled with his gorgeous face. Dark hair falling over his forehead, intense blue eyes that had witnessed the horrors of war. She brushed her palm along his beard, almost filled in, and ran her finger over his bottom lip.

"You're so handsome it hurts." She whispered her confession. It earned her a grin and a kiss that curled her toes.

"Trust me, Sable. This won't hurt a bit." His fingers worked the buttons of her blouse as he continued kissing her. Together they helped her out of her shirt and she tossed it to the floor as he slid her bra from her arms.

His lips hit her breasts and her back arched as intense pleasure rocked her. He moved his fingers between her legs again and her eyes sank shut, the orange from the daylight bright on the screens of her closed lids. His mouth kissed a trail over her ribs and down to her belly button, closer and closer to his exploring fingers.

Then his tongue replaced them and she nearly shot off the bed.

Hot.

Wet.

Each lick was a firm stroke applying pressure to her most sensitive part. She raised her head to steal a peek and he lifted her leg and rested her thigh on his shoulder, never pausing his assault. He lay flat on his belly, propped up on his other arm, shifting every so often to accommodate her body and his.

Waves of pleasure rolled over her as he continued, his hand wrapped tightly around her thigh as she bucked against his face. He didn't slow when she cried out, but instead sped up, intent on getting her up and over. Her release built to a crescendo and finally on a shout—his name. Her orgasm found her, slamming into her as her inner muscles tapped out an intoxicating rhythm.

Her body trembled from the aftershocks, and she closed her legs against his persistent mouth, unable to take any more of his mind-numbing ministrations. She rolled to one side, pressing her knees together, but Eli parted her legs and pushed her to her back again. He army-crawled up her body, pressing kisses here and there as he did.

He pushed up on one arm and reached for the nightstand, coming up short. He swore under his breath as he shifted and tried again.

"What do you need?" she asked.

"Condom," he growled.

"Let me." She kissed him sweetly, then rolled over to open the drawer to fish out a packet. "Next time we'll slide one under the pillow."

Eli reached for it, but she swatted his hand away.

"Haven't you learned yet, soldier," she asked as she pushed his chest, "that I like to be on top?"

* * *

This was a lot fucking harder than he'd expected. Being between her legs, trying to navigate in bed and keep things hot. He'd planned on finishing her off, snagging a condom, and sliding in before she stopped pulsing. Then, with her legs wrapped around his ass, he'd slam them both home to the satisfying sounds of slapping flesh and keening moans.

Shit.

He'd thought relearning to walk and shower had been difficult.

The snag had delivered a blow to his ego and was starting to affect the part of him that should be a hell of a lot harder right now.

Fucking brain.

Stupid fucking brain.

While his brain did a great service controlling the rest of his body, it was doing a horrible job of motor function where he needed it most. He pinched the bridge of his nose and grimaced when a hand rested on his chest.

"Eli." The silken, sensual voice preceded a firm grip on his cock. One stroke had blood rushing there anew, hardening him instantly. One more stroke, and his brain was no longer reeling. His cock went as rigid as rebar in her fist.

Isa, her breasts swaying, hair swinging, hovered over him as a smile parted her sensuous mouth. Her eyes wandered down to what her hand was doing and he grasped a handful of blankets and threw it over his stump in a rush.

She'd already seen it, but better late than never.

Her eyes went to the blankets where his clenched fist held on, her hand still turning his cock into a seven-and-a-half-inch steel rod. She jerked the sheet and exposed his leg and his temper flared.

"Dammit, Sable."

Her hand rested on his knee, her eyes drilling into his. "Focus."

"I don't want…" He swallowed thickly, feeling his lip curl as he eked out the rest of his confession. "I don't want you to have to see it."

Chin up, she peered down her adorable nose at him, her lips pursing. Then. She *looked*. Let his erection slap his belly and turned between his legs, putting both hands on his right thigh. Those hands moved along his kneecap, over flesh that had healed into thick bands of scar tissue. She moved up his thigh and massaged the muscle there.

He snatched her wrists, turning her toward him as he used his ab muscles to pull himself up. "What did I say?"

"Do you want this?" She thrust her breasts out and up, one eyebrow gently rising. "Do you want me?"

"You know I do." His cock bobbed in agreement.

"Then you have to trust me. We need to work around

this"—she freed one hand and touched his right leg again—"and I'm willing to learn." She blinked bedroom eyes at him. "And practice."

He held her wrist and her eyes for a protracted beat, his chest lifting with another inhalation. Isa didn't appear to mind touching him—she didn't run and hide when she saw him without the leg.

"You're okay?" he asked.

"Why wouldn't I be okay? You gave me the orgasms of my life."

He couldn't help smiling. "Orgasms...as in more than one?"

"You're a man of many talents, Eli Crane." She moved closer and kissed him and he let her go to push his fingers into her hair. She rerouted her mouth to his neck, giving him a shove so that he was once again on his back.

"Bossy," he grunted, holding a handful of her silky hair as she dragged her tongue over his chest.

"You know it," she said, sliding further south. He sucked in a breath through his teeth when her damp tongue flicked over his abdomen. Then he nearly passed out when, one hand on his thigh, the other wrapped around his cock, Isa delivered a teasing lick to the tip.

If there was a favorite in the bedroom, it was this. Watching her repeat the motion, this time suckling the head past her lips, made him forget he had any legs at all. Every last one of his muscles tightened to the point of pain as this incredible, unflappable woman went down on him.

Giving up control should feel compromising, but with Isa, it was oddly...*freeing*. She connected with him on more than one level. And whenever she didn't understand him, she made an effort to. After being left behind by

a woman who didn't want to take the time, it was...
humbling.

Eli's head crashed to the pillow as Isa took him deep.
Her cheeks closed around his shaft, her tongue raking the
veiny ridge. He slapped a hand over his eyes and ground
his teeth together in an effort not to blow early.

A few silky slides later, the heat of her mouth was replaced with the cool tip of the condom. He moved his hand
to watch as she rolled the latex down and climbed over
him, her thighs hugging his hips. Hands on his chest, she
rose, then sank onto him. His head lifted off the pillow, his
hands tightening around her hips.

"Relax," she said, hands on his chest.

He relaxed but kept his hands on her as she moved. She
rocked, she slipped, she pounded. All the while her breasts
bouncing, her face contorting into pleasure-ridden pleats.
He tweaked her nipples, watching her mouth drop open.
Her breathless cries saturated the room as her movements
slowed.

"Keep going," he urged, because he was so incredibly
close.

"Trying," she gasped.

"Try harder." He thumbed her nipples and she grinned.

"Yes, sir." She pushed her hair off her face and picked
up the pace.

When she slowed, he clamped onto her full hips and
lifted his pelvis to meet hers, watching with a healthy dose
of male pride as she orgasmed yet again. This time he
joined her and they came, her final descent striking him
like flint to stone. They burned together, Isa continuing to
move as Eli's release tore through him on a loud shout of
carnal pleasure.

When his back hit the bed, she didn't have to tell him to relax. Every muscle in his body uncoiled, a buzz tingling through him like he'd been plugged into a socket. And his pesky brain, which kept failing him at the most inopportune moments, went blissfully silent.

Isa draped over him, her hair tickling his face, her lips brushing his cheek. He caught her head and kissed her lips, her heady flavor an elixir for everything that ailed him.

Eyes closed, he wrapped his arms around her, letting the feeling of intense satisfaction hang around awhile longer.

His heart pounded so hard, he might never recover.

He might never want to.

CHAPTER 11

I t occurs to me I don't have a life," Chloe said as she unpacked a bottle of wine from a paper grocery bag onto Isa's
countertop. "You get to have sex with this completely glorious billionaire Marine, and I..." She lifted the bottle of
cabernet. "Well, I have wine?"

"I appreciate that you have wine. It's been a long day."
After working late, Isa invited Chloe up to her apartment
for a drink. She needed a girlfriend and when she thought
of who she had to talk to, the only friends who came to
mind were work friends.

Plus, Isa liked Chloe. She trusted her, too.

Isa pulled open a cabinet and put the glasses on her
breakfast bar.

Wordlessly, Chloe uncorked the bottle and poured two
glasses. When Isa grabbed hers, her friend said, "Cheers to
us getting laid."

Isa lowered her glass away from her mouth. "Us?"

"I meant cheers to you because you've gotten laid, and cheers to me for getting laid in the future. I hope." Chloe twisted a finger around one of her curls.

"It could happen." Isa gave up and took a drink, letting the cabernet wash over her tongue in a fruity wave.

"Yeah, right. Do you think that hot blond from the Mexican restaurant swung in here and dropped off his number or something?"

"I do know him now. Sort of. I could introduce you."

"Huh-uh, sister." Chloe waggled a finger back and forth. "We're not talking about that hunk of man."

"His name's Zach." Isa batted her lashes.

"Elijah Crane." Chloe pointed a finger. "Spill it."

"All right, fine." Isa pulled out a stool at the counter and sat.

Chloe clapped her hands together and eagerly followed suit.

"You can stop dancing like a loon now. Eli and I did the deed. A few times," she added. Chloe had already busted her this afternoon and to be fair, Isa hadn't bothered fixing what Eli called her "JBF" hair.

"JBF?" she'd asked, resting her chin on his bare chest as they lay in his bed.

"Just been fucked."

She'd slapped his chest in reprimand, but it'd only earned her a dry, rough laugh that made her heart patter. She had *such* a thing for him.

"Please tell me some details—like what put that wistful twinkle in your eye. Let me live vicariously." Chloe spread her fingers over her collarbone and did her best Scarlett O'Hara impression. "I'm but a poor assistant with no social life."

"Hmm. This isn't a ploy for a raise, is it?" Isa teased.

"Not...immediately." Another grin from her friend.

"It happened on Monday—"

Chloe muzzled a sharp squeal with her hands covering her mouth. Then she reclaimed her composure and waved a "go on" motion.

"And Tuesday..." No interruption this time, so Isa told her more. "He's...intense. There is a battle he's fighting and I haven't figured out who it's with yet. His family? An ex who did a number on him?"

"His leg?" Chloe guessed, not totally wrong.

"Yes and no. Other than his hesitation over the stairs at the Vancouver, I've never seen him unsure. He walks, works out, drives...but when it came time for us to be intimate, he was uncomfortable." She stabbed her lip with her teeth before she said too much. "I don't want to share his secrets."

"Oh, I know. I mean, I can imagine."

But then she shared them anyway. "It's like with me, he isn't sure who to be. He's trying to protect me from this physical side of him, the part that is different and doesn't work the way it used to. But he's opened up about his past and his injury. He's a riddle."

"How do you feel when he opens up to you?" Chloe asked.

"Special," Isa answered frankly. "The first time we met I didn't dream he was the kind of man to share any personal details. I knew we were compatible after that first kiss, but I had no idea it could be deeper than a physical connection."

Which was exactly why she'd chickened out after the dinner at Benicia's.

"And here I thought I only needed Eli to secure my reputation in this city," Isa said with a small laugh. They'd moved so far past that point, it was hard to believe that's where she'd started with him.

"You've built your own reputation, Isa." Chloe shook her head as if it should be obvious. "You're an easy person to talk to. That's why clients love you. I receive a lot of calls from clients who only want to talk to you. You *are* Sable Concierge. Your empathy and honesty made this company what it is today."

"Thank you," Isa said, sincerely humbled.

"I believe in this company. I believe in you. No matter what happens with Eli Crane down the road, I have faith Sable Concierge will thrive because you're the person running it."

Isa's heart swelled—with pride and gratitude. The kind of approval her hardworking associate had poetically delivered was what Isa had sought for years but had never received.

"To Sable Concierge." Chloe raised her wineglass.

"Sable Concierge," Isa agreed, clinking their glasses and taking a sip. She cocked her head to one side in thought.

"What?" Chloe asked with a wide-eyed blink.

"You know, with your kind of passion, you'd be a great partner."

Chloe's mouth dropped open and her cheeks went rosy. "Partner?"

"Have you ever considered going into management with Sable Concierge? Our expanding company is currently in need of an additional supervisor."

"Are you interviewing me?" Chloe lifted her glass. "Over cabernet?"

"And chocolate." Isa stood and went to the fridge. She unwrapped the foil on a 72 percent dark chocolate bar with almonds and sea salt.

"Now," Isa said, handing a square to Chloe. "Tell me your number one strength."

"Easy. Dedication." Chloe ate the chocolate, then asked, "What about you?"

"Me? I'm doing the interviewing."

"Humor me."

"I'm incredibly stubborn. That's my strength. Your turn. What's your weakness?" Isa asked, taking a square for herself.

"This is a trick interview question."

"It is not!" Isa bit into her chocolate, enjoying the perfect pairing with the fruity red wine.

"Prove it. You go first." Chloe pushed an invisible pair of eyeglasses onto the bridge of her nose. "What's your weakness, Isabella Sawyer?"

Isa placed the wineglass to her lips and smiled against the rim. She had an answer, but it seemed inappropriate to admit that her weakness lately was a tall, dark-haired, blue-eyed Marine with a husky laugh and a talented tongue.

"Why, I'm a perfectionist of course," Isa said instead.

"Ha! And a phoned-in answer! Told you it was a trick." Chloe broke off another piece of chocolate and Isa continued the interview, glad she had someone under her employ who was capable and smart and believed in Sable Concierge as much as she did.

No matter what happened with Eli or the Cranes, at least she had Chloe.

* * *

"You are kinkier than I imagined, Isabella Sawyer."

Isa looked away from her laptop at Eli, his lazy smile and hooded eyes the signature of an insanely satisfied man. As well he should be after what they just did.

She'd admit, when she went back into the dining room to grab her laptop, she'd done so with an extra spring in her step.

"Working from bed and wearing nothing at all." He stretched one tatted arm behind his head, showing off biceps and muscles leading to a chest that was downright drool-worthy.

"Don't you find sex invigorating?" She tapped the keyboard of her laptop again. She'd also grabbed a sleeve of crackers and two cups of coffee on the trip for her laptop. Eli's mug was steaming away on the nightstand. Hers was half gone, its handle in one hand while she typed with the other.

"Intense, yes. Amazing, absolutely. Invigorating, not quite. All I want to do is nap." He reached over and cupped her thigh with one hand, his eyes sliding shut. She liked how comfortable this was. How their worlds had intersected, finding a happy medium they both could live with.

Who knew sex was such a great equalizer?

"You should."

"Can't," he answered. "Shit to do."

"I hear you. That's why I gave my assistant a promotion."

His eyes opened. "Oh yeah?"

"*Oh*, yeah. Chloe and I discussed a partnership, but we

agreed her taking on the role of senior manager was a better fit. Now we have to hire a new assistant for the office." She pursed her lips as she thought. "Maybe more than one. With two people running the office, there's bound to be twice the workload."

"Yeah." Eli's eyebrows dipped. "So..." His intake of breath stalled his words.

"So...," she prompted.

"I was considering something similar with Refurbs. Hiring someone to run it."

"But?" She could hear his doubt.

"But it's not easy to give up control."

"No, but it's smart. A team can do tenfold what you can do alone. You know this." She nudged him. "Crane Hotels couldn't be what it is without thousands of staff members and a board of directors."

He grunted. For whatever reason, none of the Cranes were fans of the board. Eli had told her that much, but hadn't expounded.

"Without a staff, you're weighed down by the little things. If you found someone, or a few someones, to run the charity—handle the e-mail, flyers, website, scheduling—then you could be free of the duties weighing you down."

He watched her, not saying no, which was as good as a yes from him.

"I can make a few calls. I know a lot of very capable people. Then you could be involved but only do what you want to do." She sipped her coffee. "That sounds like you, don't you think?"

He rolled his eyes when she grinned in triumph.

"What would you do instead?" she asked, because she wondered if he was considering the Crane Hotels COO position. He really would be so great at it. Eli was sharp, swift, and didn't take shit from anyone. His natural air of mystery and intrigue would go a long way for him. And his family would be thrilled.

"Hmm. What would I do instead of work?" He stroked his chin, pretending to consider. "Lie in bed and watch TV? Start a harem?"

"A harem!" she barked. He chuckled, obviously kidding, but when she pictured him with another woman in bed, her hackles shot straight up. She cleared her throat and went back to typing. "Not that it makes any difference to me."

"Hey." It was a gentle call for her attention. "Do you see any women hanging around waiting to join us?" He moved his palm from thigh to her ass and gave her a light squeeze.

"No," she mumbled. But she wondered if there was ever a woman hanging around. If he'd been in love before. It was on the tip of her tongue to ask, but she swallowed the question. She wasn't scared to ask. She was scared of his answer.

Isa didn't know what they had, or what they would have, but she was fairly certain now was the wrong time to dig into his romantic past—if he had one. They hadn't established any boundaries, but she was happy. Happy to work with him, happy he trusted her, and happy they shared the enjoyment of getting naked together.

Really happy about that.

Eli stretched out on his back, both hands behind his head. "It would be nice to let go of the particulars in Refurbs."

She admired the way his long eyelashes shadowed his cheeks.

"But it'd have to be the perfect candidate. I can't let this go to just anyone. It's too important."

"Believe me, I understand putting your passion to work."

His eyes closed. "Maybe you could ask around for me."

"No problem." She leaned over him to set her coffee on the nightstand, opened her e-mail, and started drafting a request. Until they found an assistant, Chloe was pulling double duty.

"Not *now*." He opened his eyes.

"Why not?"

"Because we have other things to do."

"Like what?"

He answered by setting her laptop on the nightstand next to their coffee mugs. Then he pulled her down next to him and tucked her against his side.

"Like sleeping." He pressed a kiss to her forehead. "Or"—he stroked his fingers over her arm—"resting."

"Resting?"

"You've heard of it, right?" he asked, his voice heavy with impending sleep. "It's when you lie still and listen as your heart rate slows."

Isa rested her head on Eli's chest, taking a deep breath and listening as his heart rate did just that. And then she listened as his breathing shifted into a contented snore. He was three things she'd never imagined he'd be: warm, snuggly, and in this moment, all hers.

* * *

Eli woke from his nap refreshed, but alone.

Wearing nothing but a pair of boxers, he walked out of

his bedroom to find Isa dressed, her hair tied into a pony-tail at the back of her head. She glanced up, then took an even longer gander, her eyes wandering down his form as a cat-got-the-cream smile stole her mouth.

She made him feel capable. He liked that. It'd been a while since he'd felt like a hero, arguably wasn't feeling quite that way now, but this was a step in the right direction.

"You're terrible at resting." He lowered his face to hers and she tipped her chin to place a kiss on his lips.

That move, he liked a hell of a lot.

The way her eyes fluttered closed, the way her hair swung behind her when she lifted her mouth to his. The way she was here, in his space. He didn't think he liked anyone in his space, but like everything else he'd experienced with her, Isa was the exception.

"While you were sleeping, I found two candidates perfect for running Refurbs," she said. "They have past charity experience and one of them is a personal friend of mine. I put together a sort of fact sheet on each of them." She clicked a button and the printer purred to life in his office and started spitting sheets.

"You like lists," he observed, his eyes wandering over her open planner and notebook filled with to-dos. Nearly every item had a line through it.

"I do. Nothing gets done unless I write it down first."

"Have you always been like that?" He eased into the chair next to her, genuinely curious. About what she preferred, what she liked. What made her tick.

She watched him for a second before lifting her shoulder into a cute shrug. "I...yeah. I have. Organized. Neat. Ready to help."

"But it didn't sit well with your parents when you didn't want to run their empire," he said, grateful his parents hadn't been that way. Reese was always the one. He knew it, Mom and Dad knew it, and Tag and Eli had aspirations separate from running a corporation.

"I wanted to pave my own way." She dropped her chin on her fist. "What about you? What is it about Crane Hotels that makes you run and hide?"

"I'm not hiding." He felt the jerk in his shoulders when he pulled them back, ready to argue. He'd do anything for his family...like stay out of the way when he couldn't add value. "I've been busy."

"Not anymore." She pointed at her computer screen. "You can do Crane work once we have Refurbs handed off to a responsible manager. Then you can park in a big, plush office and get an assistant who answers your ringing phone."

"I have an office." He grabbed the back of Isa's chair and yanked her closer. "I have an assistant."

Another kiss left them both breathless.

"You smell good, Sable."

"So do you."

They shared a moment of silent appreciation, one that he ended with another kiss he couldn't resist stealing.

"I don't expect you to stay forever," he told her, suspecting her mind went down that same path.

"No?"

"No. Stay until I wrap up Refurbs. Finish my unfinished business." His thoughts jetted to Benji's widow. Michelle was unfinished business, and until he'd checked her off his mental to-do list, he wasn't willing to let Isa go. Her being here in any capacity gave him the strength and courage to do what needed to be done.

What an odd realization. But nonetheless true. Isa made him better in every way.

"Is that a demand?" Isa raised an eyebrow. "I didn't hear a question mark at the end of that statement."

He released her chair and sat back in his. "Not a demand."

It wasn't fair to keep her longer than she preferred. God knew he wasn't one to sink his hooks into anyone. As a man who'd made most of his life about fighting for freedom, he would never restrict Isa from spreading her wings.

"A request," he said.

"In that case, I'm glad to stay." She fiddled with her ink pen and avoided his eyes. "And if you need me to help with your transition to COO, I'll stay a little longer."

"You'd do that?" He hadn't meant to ask, but her offering to stay when he knew she had more to do than answer to his whims was humbling.

"Of course." Whiskey-brown eyes hit his and held, as if there was no question she'd continue showing up simply because he wanted her to be here.

He liked how she was willing to stay. With him. To see things through. He wondered how long it would last as much as he wondered why he wanted it to so badly. He'd long lived a temporary lifestyle where relationships were concerned.

His ex had lived with him, but his commitment hadn't extended further than companionship. With Isa, he felt the low hum of possibility in the center of his chest. That hum enthralled him.

And Eli Crane wasn't easily enthralled.

"Whatever you think is best." He stood up from the

192   *Jessica Lemmon*

chair and kissed the top of her head and swaggered toward his bedroom—How about that? A *swagger*—to grab a shower and dress for dinner.

He paused in the hall and turned back to Isa, who was jotting something else into her open planner.

"Sable."

She blinked up at him.

"Do you have plans for dinner?"

CHAPTER 12

Isa agreed to dinner, but she insisted on going home first to change. Not because she needed to dress fancy—not in the casual atmosphere of Eli's house—but because she was about to sit down with his family. She'd met Tag, Rachel, Merina, and of course Reese, but this would be the first time she'd spend time with them outside of work.

After making love with Eli today, she'd *radiated* sexual satisfaction. She'd toned her wardrobe down a bit— changing into a dress that wasn't wrinkled and combing her hair so she didn't look as if she'd been rolling around on Eli's bed all afternoon.

JBF hair, indeed.

She was a little floored he'd invited her tonight, but was trying not to overthink the invitation. Plus, this was rapidly becoming the norm. He'd floored her a lot lately. They'd fit sex into their workday and were able to talk like normal human beings afterward. Call her crazy, but she hadn't pegged him as a guy who was into snuggling after naked time.

Things had changed between them. The only problem was she wasn't sure where to draw the line. Having not been in a relationship for three years had made her rusty. Was it a good sign that she'd been invited to dinner with his family, or was Eli regretting asking her?

"Isa, seriously," she scolded herself as she threw her car into park in Eli's lot. She was starting to remind herself of an unsure teenager. She pulled her purse onto her shoulder and stepped out as Tag slipped into the spot next to hers in the shiniest, sexiest black car she'd ever seen.

Rachel climbed out first.

"Oh, I'm so glad you could make it!" the blonde chirped.

Tag unfolded from the driver's side and Isa watched as he stood. He kept going until he was towering over them both. And Isa was a few inches taller than Rachel. How did *that* work?

"Hey, Cap'n," Tag said with one of his signature lazy grins.

"Are you addressing me?" Isa asked, amused.

"He does that." Rachel rolled her blue eyes, which made her look even cuter. Isa hadn't thought that was possible. "He calls me Dimples." She smiled and poked the divots dotting each side of her face.

"That's because you have two of the cutest ones I've ever seen in my life." Tag leaned down and covered Rachel's lips with a kiss—a kiss that lasted a really long time—and right then, Isa saw exactly how Tag and Rachel "worked." Because they were drop-dead, head-over-heels, hold-my-drink-so-I-can-do-a-cartwheel in love.

Isa's chest filled with hope at the sight. She wanted that. Someday. Today was a little premature for the fantasy, considering she and Eli were...well, she didn't know what they were.

"He does that, too," Rachel said with a breathy sigh when Tag set her on her heels again. Though her grin suggested she didn't mind him grabbing her and kissing her. Isa couldn't blame her. Tag was an attractive guy, and there was no denying his sex appeal. Any girl would feel safe in those tank-sized arms.

But it was Eli who caused Isa's blood to warm significantly. He was the right mix of moody and gruff. He had an honest way about him, unlike Josh who had always been hell-bent to impress. Her ex had laid it on thick in the charm department. Shortly after they'd started dating, Isa had learned the true meaning behind the saying "hook, line, and sinker." He'd totally reeled her in. Eli's bald honesty was one of the reasons she'd been so drawn to him.

Tag, on the other hand...Isa eyed the fun-loving giant who kissed Rachel on the forehead, his arm looped around her neck. Yeah, he was made for the punchy blonde at his side.

"Perfect timing," Tag said as a Porsche growled into a parking space next to his car. "Looks like we won't waste away waiting for sustenance."

The Porsche pulled to a stop and Reese stepped from the car. He was tall, too, but more Eli-tall than skyscraper-sized Tag. Merina climbed out next, her straight, golden hair resting on her shoulders. She smoothed a hand down her slim pencil skirt and gave Isa a smile.

Isa had always admired Merina. The woman was the

epitome of a business matriarch, yet approachable and warm. She was also the reason Isa had received a call from Reese requesting aid from Sable Concierge in the first place. Without Merina, she'd never have met Eli. How about that?

"Well, well, if it isn't Elijah Crane's *personal assistant*," Merina said with a wink as she rounded the vehicle.

"We were surprised to hear we were adding a meal for you," Reese announced, his tone uncharacteristically light. He opened the back door and pulled out several bags from a local sushi restaurant.

"He means 'happy,'" Merina corrected. "We were *happy* to hear you were joining us."

"No, I meant surprised," Reese said. "Eli has a way of pushing people away."

"It's a gift," Tag said, taking one of the bags from Reese.

"You haven't gone anywhere even though he's fired half your staff," Reese said to Isa.

"A third, actually."

Reese's smile warmed his eyes. She'd never seen him out of business mode and in that moment completely understood the gentler side Merina had access to—and had fallen for.

"I can handle Eli," Isa said.

"I'll bet." Tag's voice lilted.

"I meant the workload," Isa quickly corrected when Reese and Tag narrowed their eyes in interest. It was like they could see right through her. She reached for one of the bags of food in Reese's hand. "Here, let me carry one."

"Leave her alone," Rachel said, taking the bag instead. She elbowed Isa. "You should keep your arms free to greet Eli."

Those dimples appeared again. Isa would bet Rachel got away with murder with those things.

After dinner, and clearing the table of takeout containers, the girls moved to the living room with glasses of wine while the men lingered in the kitchen, beers in hand.

"You are missing out not getting to meet Alex Crane," Merina said, elevating her wineglass. "It's easier to understand where those three are coming from when you meet the cloth from which they were cut."

Rachel threw her head back and laughed and Isa smothered a smile. Eli, standing in the kitchen with his brothers, looked over his shoulder and held Isa's gaze a moment before a small smile curved his lips. Isa's heart tommy-gunned her rib cage.

"Holy shit," Merina said, keeping her voice down. "That was some serious eye-fucking."

Rachel laughed again. "I love you."

Merina and Rachel *cheersed* with their glasses. Isa felt a zing of satisfaction that someone other than herself had noticed the way Eli looked at her.

"I presume the *actual* fucking is better." Merina drained her wine and set the glass on the coffee table in front of her. She studied Isa, eyebrows raised, waiting on an answer.

"Uh…"

"This is Merina off the clock," Rachel said. Then she frowned. "Though, I'm pretty sure this is Merina on the clock, too."

"I have no clock-in or clock-out time. It's all the same to me." Merina turned her attention to Isa and leaned one hand on the sofa, stretching closer, to say, "Crane men are difficult, but worth it if you're willing to push."

"And pull," Rachel added.

Oh boy.

"It's a little soon..." They were the only four words Isa said before Merina held up both hands in surrender.

"You're right. I'm sorry. These things take time. I forget not everyone is married instantaneously, then work the hard stuff out after."

"I bet there's a story there," Isa said. There had to be. Merina and Reese's dating and married life had been reported in the local gossip rags numerous times. Photos from their (second) wedding over the summer, even though it was a private backyard affair at Alex Crane's house, had shown up in the *Trib*. At least Isa and Eli weren't subjected to that kind of social pressure.

Merina assessed her carefully before saying, "There is a story. Maybe if things work out with you and Eli, someday I'll tell it to you."

Isa's heart fluttered with nervous excitement. On the outside, she remained calm, lifted her glass, and smiled at the bawdy but refined woman sitting across from her. "Well. Something to look forward to."

Merina grinned. A happily married woman with a secret she loved having.

* * *

"The girls love her," Tag said, leaning one huge shoulder on the dividing wall between the kitchen and dining room.

Eli looked again. He couldn't get enough of Isa in a black dress hugging her curves, her midnight-dark hair rolling over her shoulders. Poised, she sat cross-legged on the chair, holding Merina's and Rachel's full attention as she talked with her hands.

"Apparently, so do you," Reese said.

Eli faced his oldest brother. Reese's eyebrows were raised, his mouth a flat line, but Eli could see approval lurking in his eyes.

"Easy, Cupid." The L-word wasn't a term Eli threw around often or lightly. And with a woman he'd dated— never. "We click."

"Is that a euphemism?" Tag asked with a wry smile. He waggled his beer bottle before Eli could deliver a warning for him to STFU. "I need another."

Reese stopped leaning on the fridge so Tag could pull out a bottle. Eli and Reese both drank theirs and accepted fresh beers.

"Why'd you invite her tonight?" Reese asked, uncapping his bottle.

"Don't be a dick," Tag told him. "You don't have to answer that, E."

"Gee, thanks for the permission slip, Taggart."

There was no easier way to shut his youngest brother up than to use his full name. Tag's lip curled in disgust.

Eli wasn't going to psychoanalyze the way Isa made him feel or why he'd given in to the urge to invite her tonight. Better go with the easy explanation.

"You guys are the ones who wanted me to invite her to a dinner." Now that he and Isa were being divided and conquered by his family, his guard was definitely up. At least Dad wasn't here tonight to add his own brand of parental pressure. Though Eli suspected that Rhona and Isa would get along famously.

"It's good you asked her," Reese said. "Shows you trust your gut."

"She's different," Eli said.

"Than Crystal?" his oldest brother asked.

"Than anyone." Eli had been involved in several short-ish relationships, each more trouble than they were worth in the end. Each with a shelf life of delicate, fresh flowers. It never took long for things to go from full bloom to wilting. Crystal had been the exception to the rule, but then she hadn't worked out either, had she?

"Makes sense that the relationship is different," Tag said. "You're home for the first time permanently. It's a game changer. No chance of you running off to another country to catch a breather in a few weeks." Tag guzzled his beer and when he lowered it, Eli was still staring at him. "What?"

"Nothing." He'd never thought of it in those terms before. Eli knew he wasn't shipping off to war, but he hadn't considered that was the reason the relationship with Isa seemed so much—what was the word?—*heavier* than his other relationships.

"Hey." Isa popped into the room as if on cue. She snagged a bottle of red wine standing on the counter. "We're in need of refills."

No one spoke. Tag pursed his lips. Reese lifted an eyebrow.

"Seems serious in here." Isa sent a glance around the room, her eyes landing on Eli. "You must be discussing Refurbs."

"Re-what?" Tag asked, his face screwing into pleats of confusion.

"Refurbs for Vets. The charity?" she said.

Fuck. Eli scrubbed his jaw and took the hit. Isa didn't know his brothers weren't in the know. It wasn't her fault they were going to lay into him the second she left the room. "Yeah," he told her. "You guessed it."

"I'll...um...go open this in the living room." She grabbed a corkscrew and swished out of the kitchen.

Eli could feel Reese drilling a hole through his head with the power of his mind. "What charity?"

Eli pulled in a breath. "One of the reasons I've been too busy for Crane business is because I started a charity for injured vets...with a focus on amputees."

Reese set aside his beer bottle and folded his arms over his chest.

Tag, all ears, mimicked their brother, folding his arms and leaning on the countertop next to Reese.

Then, Eli told his brothers everything.

* * *

"You *have* to meet Alex," Merina said again, her voice boozy. As if the family patriarch would answer every unanswered Crane men question.

They'd all reconvened at the dining room table, and a third bottle of wine had been opened. The aforementioned Crane men held fast to their beers—but they sipped slowly, letting the girls bottom out the wine. Isa had covertly switched to water a few glasses ago, but Rachel and Merina were set on taking down another bottle.

"What's Alex like?" Isa asked, feeling relaxed and at ease around her new girlfriends.

"He's like..." Merina paused to think, narrowing her eyes at her husband.

"A combo of Reese and Eli." Rachel pointed at one, then the other.

"Yes." Merina raised her hand for a high-five and Rachel slapped her palm.

"Hey." Tag gestured to his wide chest. "What about me?"

"You're more like Mom than Dad," Reese said. "Or, at least, you have her hair."

Tag narrowed his eyes, but as per his usual, his expression was playful. Rachel, who sat next to him, ran her fingers through his long hair and cooed, "*Taggart.*"

He smashed his mouth against hers and Rachel giggled as she kissed him.

"He hates that name." Merina elbowed Isa. "It's too regal for him."

"I can be regal," Tag argued.

"Says the guy in cargo pants," Reese put in.

"At least Rachel calls you by your given name," Isa piped up on the end of a laugh. "Eli doesn't like my name, so he calls me Sable."

"Eli!" Merina clucked her tongue in reprimand.

Eli shifted uncomfortably. He'd grown more withdrawn as the clock ticked on. Isa couldn't have been the only one to notice, which made her wonder if his family was used to him sitting silently while the rest of them chattered. She wanted to check on him, but from across the table, she couldn't casually lean in and ask if he was okay.

"Sable. That's sexy." Rachel rested her head on one of Tag's big shoulders and yawned. It was late, yet no one seemed eager to cut the evening short.

"Eli knows she's sexy," Merina, wineglass in hand, pointed at her brother-in-law. "I can see the glimmer in his eye."

"I'm not glimmering." Eli might not have been smiling, but the glimmer was there all the same. Isa liked being the reason for it.

There was a beat before Rachel filled the gap with, "What are your parents like, Isa?"

"My father is English. My mother is Spanish, but grew up in Greece. I'm a mixed bag." She had her mother's dark features, but her skin was a shade lighter than her mother's deep olive due to her father's fairer coloring. "They own Sawyer Financial Group, which I'm sure you've all heard of." Murmurs and nods confirmed. "My father is professional and intelligent, and my mother works hard at both business and the business of being social."

"Socialite," Merina said, her tone not the least bit judgey.

"She's a master," Isa replied.

"I've met Helena. She's both a socialite and an intelligent businesswoman," Reese said approvingly. "You look like her."

"Beautiful, he means," Eli murmured. From across the table, they shared a heated look. She held his eyes for a few seconds. He looked away first. He was either wrestling with unnamed emotions or good old-fashioned fatigue. Leaning back in his chair, arms folded, eyebrows down, he didn't look up for company any longer. Thinking she was doing him a favor, Isa spoke up.

"You know, it's getting late."

Every pair of eyes at the table landed on her.

"For me, I mean," she quickly corrected. She faked a yawn.

Tag's head turned to Eli, then Isa. "I see."

"No, that's not what I—" Isa started.

"Time to call it a night." Reese interrupted, offering a hand to his wife.

"It's okay, Isa. We've all been there. The infatuation

stage." Merina slipped her palm into Reese's and rose from her chair gracefully—after all that wine, how she did anything gracefully was a mystery.

"We're not used to Eli having anyone—I mean, *anything*—to do," Tag teased. Rachel play-punched his bicep.

Isa wasn't convinced any of them were out of the infatuation stage.

Eli stood, interrupting the banter with an announcement. "I assume everyone knows the way out."

Then he turned on his heel and walked into his bedroom. There was a slight hitch in his step. Maybe the phantom pains had returned—or were about to. Was that why he'd gone quiet?

There was an uncomfortable silence as everyone stood around the table, staring at the closed door at the end of the hall their host had vanished behind.

"I'm sorry. He's..." Isa trailed off when she realized she was addressing a group who knew what Eli was like. Complicated. Moody. Reluctant.

"Don't apologize for him," Merina said. "He can do that for himself." She palmed her empty glass and, along with Rachel and Reese, carried the remaining glassware and bottles to the kitchen.

It was Tag who stayed behind. "It's back?" Tag's face morphed into a mask of concern as he cast a glance to Eli's bedroom door again. "The pain?"

So she wasn't the only one to notice the change in Eli's stride. She sent Tag a shaky smile, unsure how much she should say. First she'd let the Refurbs cat out of the bag, now this. "Um. Sometimes. Rarely. I massaged his foot the other day and it helped a lot."

"He doesn't share stuff like that. Doesn't confide in us." Tag's frown deepened. "Does he tell you things, Cap'n?"

She debated lying, then decided against it. Looking into Tag's intense blue eyes compelled her to be truthful. "He does."

Tag gave an approving nod. "Good. I'm glad he has you."

Rachel appeared at his side a second later. "Everything okay?"

"Yeah, Dimples. We're leaving the Cap'n in charge, and that's not a bad thing."

Reese delivered Merina's, then Rachel's, coats. "Isabella, good to see you."

"Thanks for dinner."

"Anytime." He stole a glance at the bedroom door as well but kept his questions to himself.

"I'm going to check on him before I go," Isa said.

Reese dipped his chin in a silent thank-you.

"You let us know if there's anything we can do," Tag said, Rachel's hand in his. "We're not far." Tag and Rachel filed into the freight elevator with Reese and Merina. By the time the metal door crashed shut and the elevator chugged to the bottom, Isa was on her way to Eli's bedroom.

"Eli?" She rapped her knuckles on the wood and called through the closed door, "Are you okay?"

No answer.

"Eli?"

"Stop knocking, Sable. You want to come in, come in." Well. He didn't sound like he was in pain. When she twisted the knob and stepped into his bedroom, she didn't find him doubled over or in a cold sweat. In fact, he appeared...fine. He stood at his dresser, digging through what sounded like loose change in his top drawer.

"You favored your leg on the way in here. I was worried you were having an attack."

He lifted a decorative pin from the drawer and ran his thumb over it before tossing it back in.

"You became suddenly quiet tonight. Care to tell me why you left me alone with your family?"

"No." More rummaging. When she got closer, she saw not only pins, but also medals. Several of them.

"Wow. Are these yours?"

"All of them except for this one." He handed over a heart-shaped medal. "Dad's. He has more, but that was the one he gave me."

She ran her fingers over the smooth ribbon. She didn't know much about military medals, but she knew what a Purple Heart looked like, and this was definitely one of them.

She handed back Alex Crane's medal and Eli dropped it into the box with the others. "I'm assuming this isn't a military medal." She lifted a gold disc engraved with the words FIRST PLACE.

"Marathon." His lips tipped into a sad smile. He took it from her and rubbed his thumb over the words.

"Will you run one again?" she asked, wondering what was feeding his melancholy.

"Maybe."

Okay. This was getting her nowhere. Time to do what she did best—push him.

"Your brothers didn't know about the charity, did they?" After her visit to the kitchen, she'd left Eli with some explaining to do.

Eli met her gaze wordlessly.

"What did they say?"

"They said they'd feature Refurbs for Vets at future Crane events and help me raise money." Then why did he look upset?

"That's good, right?"

"Yes." After a beat, he added, "I haven't done much to deserve their help."

He was so damn complex. What was he trying to live up to? Why was he in here studying his and his father's medals?

"I don't understand where this is coming from, Eli. I thought we were having a good night. Your family is so great and—"

"And they're here for me. Because *I'm* here. Not everyone gets so lucky." Eli lifted a stack of pictures, handed over the top photo, and closed the drawer. In it was what appeared to be a game of some sort. Eli and another man held men on their shoulders who were fighting with sticks. All of them were grinning. Eli, clean-shaven and head shaved, was almost unrecognizable, save for the grin on his face. She'd seen that expression on him lately. There was a circle of soldiers surrounding them, arms raised like they were cheering.

"You look happy."

"I had my moments."

Had. She didn't like how past tense that sounded.

He sat on his bed like the weight of the entire world was on his back. She joined him. Eli's blunt index finger tapped the man on his shoulders in the picture. "Benji doesn't get to be here."

Benji. One of his friends who died.

"The one who left a wife behind," she said. "Sad." What an understatement. Isa's heart crushed under the weight of knowing the smiling, younger guy in the picture never returned home to the woman who loved him.

"They both left wives behind." Eli's nostrils flared, his voice hardening. "Benji's wife won't talk to me."

Isa remembered him mentioning Benji's wife in the journal entry, but what she didn't understand was: "Why not?"

"Because she knows it's my fault." Eli tossed the photo on the nightstand. "She won't return my calls and she's no longer checking his e-mail. Or if she is, she's not responding. Tonight, I was sitting there with my pain-in-the-ass family and got to thinking that Benji didn't have any more moments with his family. No time with his wife or his brother or his parents. No one bringing him meals because his leg is gone. It's unfair."

This was the kind of grief she wasn't sure how to deal with—that she wasn't equipped to deal with. Isa had never suffered loss at his level. She'd never witnessed the tragedy Eli had lived through.

But she couldn't help trying to comfort him. "Eli, you're allowed to be happy even though he's not here."

"He's not here because I didn't save him," he said, his voice vacant. "I should have saved both of them."

That, she could argue. "I haven't known you for long but I know for a fact if there was any way you could have saved them, you would have—or died trying." She put her hand over his and offered a tender smile. "Am I wrong?"

"No."

She thought she'd reached him until he jerked his arm away.

"But that doesn't change the facts."

"What facts?"

"I'm not good for anyone, Sable."

When he said *anyone*, it sounded like he was including her.

"You don't believe that." She wasn't accepting a brush-off. Not when she had invested in him. She cared about him. Couldn't he see that? She'd stayed instead of filing out the door with everyone else. She was here now, trying to understand him.

"You didn't cause your friends' deaths," she tried again.

If Tag had been here, or Reese, what would they say to Eli to pull him out? How would they reach him? Like a flash, she knew. She didn't miss the flinch of hurt when Reese teased Tag about resembling their mother.

"And you didn't cause your mother's death." She put a hand over his forearm to soften the blow. "You're good for a lot of people."

Like me.

"What the hell do you know?" Rage permeated his features, his eyes going cold. "You, who continue coming back like a kicked dog no matter how I treat you."

"I do not." That wasn't true. Not even a little. She was here because she cared about him. Because of what they'd shared.

Eli got to his feet. "It wouldn't matter what I did, would it? You'd stay."

"Are you trying to make me to leave?" she asked with an incredulous laugh.

"I always knew you were smart." He turned and crossed the room, leaving her sitting on his bed in shock.

Oh. *Hell.* No.

She stood in the center of his bedroom, anger vibrating across her shoulders. It was so like him to wall up and shut down just when she was reaching into a part of him he hid from everyone.

She followed him as far as the hallway before she shouted after him, "You asked me to stick around today! Change your mind?"

Fists balled at his sides, Eli froze, jaw clenched, eyes on his shoes.

"If you're too afraid to deal with your feelings, that's fine. But if you're treating me like shit because you don't want me to see them, that's unacceptable. Not after what I thought we had."

Her heart thudded while she awaited his answer. None came. With a frustrated shake of her head, she decided to call him on his bluff. "You don't have to fire me this time, Beast Crane. I quit. Enjoy being your own assistant."

His fists unclenched, but the final steps he took weren't toward her. He disappeared into his office. A moment later, the sound of papers rustling and the computer firing up came from the room, and Isa had a very important realization.

She cared about him and he had used it against her. He was pushing her away when he should be the one chasing her. She deserved better. She deserved to be pursued. To be swept into his arms the way Tag did Rachel. To be cared for the way Reese cared for Merina.

Merina had said Crane men were worth it, but Isa was worth it, too. That lesson, she'd learned when she walked away from Josh. She mattered. And if Eli didn't see it, then that was his problem.

She collected her coat and purse, chin up and confidence in full force. Eli had retreated, but that was on him. She wasn't in charge of his emotions. She was in charge of his business.

Or was, anyway.

Eli believed he was completely capable of getting along without her.

And so she decided to let him.

* * *

"Just left?" Chloe asked, her mouth agape.

"Yes." Isa bustled by, file folder in hand. The staff with new assignments had already checked in and left for their employers' offices. The second Isa and Chloe were alone at Sable Concierge, Chloe had pressed for an Eli update, and Isa had shared the truth: He was very boyfriend-like when he'd invited her to have dinner with his family, but very one-night-stand-like when he shut her out.

"Are you going back?" Chloe followed Isa to her desk.

"No, I'm not." Isa plunked the file on her desk and sat in her chair, punching in her password on the keyboard. She was determined to get on with her day.

"Ever?" Chloe sounded worried.

"Sable Concierge will survive without him. You said it yourself. If he wants to behave this way, I can tie up loose ends without speaking to him. We are in the twenty-first century, you know—the height of electronic media." If Eli wanted to be left alone, she'd leave him alone. Hell, he might not notice.

But even as she had the thought, part of her called herself on the lie. Of course he'd notice. Eli noticed everything.

"What about you?" Chloe, clearly not done pushing, leaned on Isa's desk, her curly red locks framing her cute, freckled face. "Are you sad?"

Isa looked away from her computer screen into her friend's concerned hazel eyes. Then she blew out a breath and told Chloe the truth about that, too. Isa wasn't like Eli; she couldn't shut people out. She cared about people. She cared about her friends. She cared about him, dammit.

"I'm frustrated." Isa turned in her chair. "I'm also unwilling to be treated the way he's treating me. If he wants to behave like an adult, then together we can *adult*. But if he wants to be a man-child, then he can do that by himself."

"You're smart." Chloe straightened and folded her arms over her chest. "You are smart and strong and one day, I'm going to grow up to be as strong and smart as you."

"Chloe, you're my age."

"True. But if I had a really hot guy who was really good in bed, I'm not sure I could walk away."

Isa let out a weary chuckle. "Well, lucky for you, it doesn't require any smarts to climb into bed with a man who is wrong for you."

"Isn't that the truth?" Chloe turned and strode to the door but before she left, she gave Isa a smile. "You're sure you're okay?"

"I'm fine." Isa wasn't fine, but she would be. She'd have to be.

"Okay. Let me know if you want to delegate any of

your communications with Cranky Crane. I'll be in my *new office*." Chloe swept around the corner and Isa smiled in her wake.

Isa reached for the mug of coffee waiting at her right elbow. It felt good to be back in her office. It felt good to be back in control.

In control of her work and her life.

CHAPTER 13

*B*_{*ing!*}

Really?

Eli had been trying to review and make notes on the report Reese had sent him for the last hour, but his inbox chime had been working overtime. Not just today—he'd been flooded for the last *four* days.

Isabella was no longer sitting at his dining room table intercepting his messages for him. And the reason she wasn't here intercepting his messages for him was because he'd been nothing but impossible to deal with since they'd met.

Friday had been a turning point for her. He didn't blame her for bailing. He didn't know if he would've respected her if she'd continued to take his shit without pushing back. He knew what he wanted from her but couldn't get over the idea that it was completely unfair to keep her close when he was so...unhealed.

You don't deserve her.

Didn't he know it.

His desk phone rang and he lifted it to his ear. "Reese, I'm working on it. I will have it to you as soon as possible."

"You sound chipper," came his brother's droll response.

"Yeah, well, my assistant hasn't showed up for four days, so I'm buried." Reese couldn't see him, but Eli gestured to the pile that had collected on his desk anyway.

"Four days? I wondered why I kept getting e-mails from you instead of Isabella. I also know you're busy with the charity, too. Do you how I know that?"

Smartass. Eli didn't speak.

"Because your girlfriend told me."

"I was there." Eli huffed like a perturbed lion.

"You have my full support, Eli. You should have told me about the charity sooner."

Guilt stabbed his diaphragm. This kind of guilt, he wasn't as familiar with. His brothers and father had been relying on him and he'd proven himself borderline disloyal by keeping secrets. And yet they accepted him.

Eli never should have expected less. Crane men had always been all for one and one for all.

"I appreciate it," he said, his voice low. "Before Isa left, she'd put feelers out for a manager to take over Refurbs." She'd found two qualified candidates, but that was the last he'd heard. He assumed she would let him know if there were further developments, but now...maybe not. Maybe she was legitimately pissed at him and would gladly let him flounder.

That's what he'd been doing without her here: floundering. Not only because he was swamped with work, but also because he'd grown used to sharing lunch with her, and having conversations with her, and listening to her heels click along his floors.

And because you miss the way her laugh echoed down the hall. The smell of her hair when she leaned over you for a kiss hello or goodbye. The way she sighed into your ear when you touched her just right.

Yeah. All of that. And now she wasn't here. Which was his fault, no big surprise there.

"...would appreciate your presence at tonight's board meeting," Reese was saying.

"I suck at dealing with people, Reese," Eli bellowed. "Isn't it obvious? Why do you keep insisting I come back to Crane to be around them?" Silence lingered on the line and Eli knew it wasn't because Reese didn't know how to respond. No, his brother knew what to say. He was debating how to say it.

Finally, he did.

"Because you belong here, Eli." His tone was hard and warm at the same time. "I want you there. Dad wants you there. Tag told me when we left your place Friday that the more he pictures Crane Hotels without you, the more wrong it feels."

Dammit.

"I don't need a guilt trip." But his comment held no venom. It was more of a chagrined mumble. He was behaving petulantly and his family, as always, had his back.

"No, you don't. You seem to have mastered piling it on your shoulders without anyone else's help." Reese waited a few seconds before adding, "Why hasn't Isa been back in four days?"

"Because I pushed her away." Eli sat back in his chair

and tossed his pen onto the desk, feeling the weight of that admission. It was the first time he'd said it aloud. "She came to console me and I acted like an ass."

"Sounds familiar."

Eli could tell by Reese's self-deprecating tone he was referring to himself. His brother had had a few moments of "assery" when it'd come to winning back Merina. Good thing she was a strong woman.

Like Isa.

Was Isa strong enough to accept Eli's apology and forgive him?

"Anyway, I can't attend tonight's board meeting and go to Sable Concierge to get my assistant back, now, can I?" Eli mumbled.

"I guess not." Eli could hear the approval in his brother's voice.

"The least I can do is apologize for behaving badly."

"The very least," Reese said flatly.

When Eli pictured her, he wasn't sure he wouldn't fall into those deep brown eyes or get towed in by her full, plush mouth. He needed her, and as much as he'd like to think he needed her only for business, that wasn't the whole truth. He needed her because she was an amazing person who made him a better one.

"I'd tell you to take flowers," Reese said, "but that was always the kiss goodbye for me."

"I swear I don't know how you talked any woman into going out with you." His brother used to date using a one-and-done rule of thumb. Eli was never able to disconnect enough to be "done" after one night. It normally took several for the fascination to go away—but it always went away.

Except where Isa was concerned. Eli thought of her often, missed her. Wanted her.

"We all fuck up, but there's a way back," Reese said pragmatically. "Look at Tag. Mr. Fast and Loose towed in by a cute, tiny blonde who made him want commitment. He never saw Rachel coming."

"Right, because the Cranes are allergic to long-term relationships." Except someone had found the antidote because here they were—Dad, Reese, and Tag all in long-term relationships.

"It makes sense. Because of Mom."

"You can keep your Freudian theories to yourself. My reasons for not settling down or getting married—*twice*"— Eli added snidely—"or coupling off like the rest of you seem content to do are more deep-seated."

"Uh-huh."

"Anything else?" Eli asked before Reese asked about those more deep-seated reasons.

"Good luck," Reese said, then added, his tone sharper, "I mean with the report I sent over. Getting your assistant back isn't about luck—it'll take a miracle after how many of her PAs you fired. I hope she comes back for my sake. Your typos are horrendous."

"Merina brought out your comedic side," Eli said. "I don't like it."

Reese let out a small laugh and Eli signed off. He took another look at the piles on his desk. When Isabella was here, there were no stacks. She was virtually paperless, which was a skill he hadn't honed.

Were she here, she would've interrupted him by now to refill his coffee, and hers. Three empty mugs sat forlornly on his desk. He liked wandering out of his office, looking over, and seeing her bent over her laptop at his dining room table.

He liked her *here*.

Not because the house was big and empty without her...

But because he was.

With her, he'd caught a glimpse of who he used to be before his life was turned upside down. When he'd become a man and was able to handle the loss of his mother in a healthy way instead of holing up in his bedroom and scribbling his morose thoughts into a notebook. He felt fifteen years old again—lost in the darkness...No, not lost. *Locked*. Like he'd put himself there on purpose. To spare everyone else his coming unhinged.

"Enough," Eli said to himself, closing his hands over his face before sweeping them through his hair. Hands laced at the back of his head, he stared blindly at the e-mail attachment Reese had sent and thought about why he really wanted Isa back here.

Not because of reports or paperwork or coffee refills. He wanted her back because for the first time in his life, he'd found someone with the key. He'd tried to lock himself away but she'd come for him. Literally come for him—into his bedroom, yes, but there was another part of him she'd unlocked.

His heart.

The part of him that had always been partially sealed.

Was he brave enough to give Isa every part of him? Not yet, but maybe he could be in the future. That possibility intrigued and frightened him. That it existed at all was a miracle.

Right now he'd stay in the present. If she was willing to

have him in the here and now, he could find his way out of the emotional prison he'd barred himself into.

If he could convince her to give him one more chance.

* * *

A block from Isa's building, phone to his ear, Eli slowed and slipped into the left lane as Zach relayed details about the latest Refurbs project for a double-amputee soldier who had four kids. Four fucking kids.

Hearing those stories never got easier. It's why Eli created an outlet to provide assistance. He couldn't hear about it and do nothing.

He turned left onto the road where Sable Concierge was located. The report he reviewed for Reese took longer than expected, so Eli had missed his afternoon goal by several hours. Eli settled for driving out here at nearly nine at night instead, hoping that late was better than never.

Either Isa was upstairs in her apartment or downstairs at work, and if she wasn't, he'd turn around and go home. He wasn't going to call. He didn't know how mad she was or how much madder she'd gotten, but he was certain a phone call would equal an ignored call.

"They'll frame it out tomorrow," Zach was saying, after describing the addition to the home.

"Good deal. Hey, I have to go. Call me tomorrow if you need me."

"No, we're good. Just checking in. Later, man."

"Thanks, Zach." Eli ended the call, half amused that at one point he'd been worried about Isa dating the guy. Now that Eli knew her, he knew Zach wasn't the right fit for her.

"Oh, and you are?" he asked himself, shutting off the car and getting out.

He wasn't. But he was trying to be worthy of her. He had a long climb ahead of him.

After knocking a few times on the front door of Sable Concierge and determining she wasn't in the darkened office space, he headed across the lot to her apartment...and confronted a tall staircase.

Looked like his long climb started here.

* * *

Isa was reaching behind her back to unclasp her bra when someone knocked at her door. Frowning, she hastily tucked her silk shirt into her skirt and fluffed her hair. Most likely it was Chloe, but on the off chance another employee had come up here, she wasn't about to answer the door braless and disheveled.

She parted the curtain over her living room window and froze in place. There on her landing stood Eli Crane. He waved, a brief lift of one hand before propping it on his hip again.

He looked sure and strong standing there, and so unexpected, her heart leapt.

Stupid heart.

She fortified herself before opening the door. She couldn't let him know how much she'd missed him. Not until he'd earned it.

"Eli. It's late."

"I know. I got here an hour ago. Damn stairs."

She turned her head to take in each and every step leading up to her apartment.

"That was a joke."

She said nothing, only stood with her hand on the knob.

"A bad one, evidently." Eli palmed the back of his neck and took a deep breath. "I came by to apologize for acting like an ass."

"No need," she said curtly, determined to show her heart who was boss. If she left her heart in charge, she'd have already invited him in, or at least softened at the look of boyish chagrin on his face. If she listened to her heart, she might be reminded that Eli had suffered loss over and over and over again and his mood shifts were understandable and—when he admitted he was in the wrong—forgivable.

"You deserve better," he said, and this time he didn't take his eyes off hers. "Better treatment from a client and better treatment from a lover. I've never been great at this stuff, and as you've recently proven, I've become even worse—"

"Eli," she couldn't help interrupting. What he was saying wasn't solely true. Plus, she wasn't going to make him have this conversation in her doorway. "Do you want to come in?"

"No. I want to go out. With you."

"Now?"

"Please?"

"Please?" Her lips widened into a grin. "You were the last person I expected when I opened this door, Eli Crane. I couldn't imagine you coming here to apologize, let alone beg."

"Desperate times." Half his mouth slid into a cautious smile.

"Do you mind if I change out of my work clothes?"

"Take your time." Eli cast a glance at the staircase. "I'll start heading down the stairs now. Maybe I'll be at the bottom by the time you're ready."

She tsked her disapproval at his joke, but before she could say more, he stepped forward, cupped her nape, and covered her lips with a soft kiss. Her eyes were still closed when he stroked the side of her neck with his thumb.

When she opened them, she met his concerned deep blues.

"I'll make it up to you, Sable. I promise."

She nodded, overcome by the courage it'd taken him to come here. To face the stairs, yes, but also to face her. Not only did he admit to being wrong, but in his own way, he admitted that he didn't want to be without her.

She shut the front door as Eli started down the staircase. His pace was faster than he'd let on, but he was obviously working hard to navigate. As gestures went, his was significant. He'd pushed past his own barriers and comfort zones for her.

"Not bad, Eli Crane," she said to herself as she headed to her bedroom. "Not bad at all."

* * *

Eli reached the bottom of the stairs faster than he'd climbed them, that was for damned sure. Catching his breath at the bottom, he felt better about himself for having tackled them. Maybe he should make climbing part of his training. He could come here and practice a few times a week. He bet he could get faster.

Deep in thought and inspired by the idea of a new

challenge, Eli walked to his car, head down as he pulled his keys from his pocket. He'd parked closer to the entrance of Sable Concierge, so walking to the car took him away from the staircase by about fifty feet.

Which was probably why Sable's voice sounded distant when her scream pierced the air.

Fear wrapped around him like a length of rope, adrenaline dumping into his bloodstream by the gallon as he turned to run back to where she was.

Only he couldn't run. He had the wrong fucking prosthetic on. Not the Gazelle, made for running, but his normal everyday walking foot.

She came into view a few sweaty seconds later and the sight almost stopped his heart. A man wearing a ski mask and gloves, covered head to toe in black, took one look at Eli, who was stalking at top speed toward him, thrust Isa to the side, and raced off at a full run.

Eli, muscles corded and taut, took a few bounding steps before freezing in place, knowing a chase would be futile. He cursed himself for not having a weapon on his person— he hadn't bothered with his concealed carry since he'd returned home—as he watched as the figure grew smaller and smaller in the alleyway before turning right and disappearing altogether.

His heart slammed his chest, his fists balled, his blunt fingernails cutting into his palms. He was reminded that he needed to take a breath when his vision blurred. Isa's delicate voice sliced into his brain a second later.

"Eli."

The rush of adrenaline faded, and with it came a penetrating fear. For Isa. For what could have happened. And God help that asshole if he'd put a scratch on her.

Eli strode back to where she stood, her purse hanging open, the contents of her bag scattered on the ground beside her. She lifted a shaky hand to her hair as she pushed it behind one ear.

"Who was that?" he growled. "Tell me you had some clue." Any description could help the cops.

"I..." Her face crumpled and she shook her head, her hair a mess and hanging in front of her beautiful face.

Shit, he was being insensitive. *At ease, soldier.* As much as he wanted to be able to describe the man who'd attacked her to the police, and as frustrated as he was that he couldn't chase the attacker down on foot and beat him to a bloody pulp, Isa was his priority.

That became clear the second he wrapped her in his arms. Fragile and soft, she folded into him, burying her face in his shirt, her hands wrapped around the lapels of his leather coat. He shushed her, stroked her hair and back, and kissed the top of her head. She was safe now and that's what mattered.

"Sable. I'm here."

Her breaths were shallow, but she didn't cry. After she loosened her hold on him, he felt safe to step away, having calmed down himself. Then he spotted the tear in her sweater along the low, scooped neck, her bra showing and blood dotting down the front.

"What the..." He cradled Isa's face in his hands, and searched the rest of her for injury. No cuts. "Where are you bleeding? What the fuck did he do?" He ran his hands gingerly over her shoulders and down her arms.

"I'm not hurt." Isa sniffed. "He grabbed me and I kneed him in the nuts and then elbowed him in the nose." She showed him her elbow, where another blood spot stained her white sweater. Her arm shook like outdoor chimes on a windy day. "He was a bleeder."

"You were in the process of kicking his ass?" Eli asked, stunned.

"He's lucky you showed up." One half of her mouth lifted into a weak smile. She started to bend over and pick up the items from her purse, but he held her elbow to keep her from it.

"I've got it." He gathered everything that had spilled out, her intact wallet and spare change littering the ground, and put it back into her bag. Then he lifted the other strap onto her shoulder. "Didn't look like he got anything."

"He didn't."

He liked that she was able to get in a few good jabs as much as he hated that he wasn't able to get in a few himself. "Let's get you inside."

He followed her upstairs, a niggling, sickening feeling that the guy attempting to take her purse could have done more than rob her. It heated the blood in Eli's veins to boiling and made him that much more pissed about his inability to hunt down the bastard and smash his face in.

Eli's ascent was slower than hers, which was good because he talked himself down as he walked up. She would benefit more from his calm presence than his unhinged anger. Isa unlocked her door and let herself in, holding it open for him. When he entered her apartment, she took out her phone and dropped her purse on the couch.

She stared at the screen, her fingers hovering before she looked up at him. "I don't know the number for the police."

Shock. He could see it. He had seen it a million times on hundreds of faces, and he had suffered *from* it personally.

"I'll call. You sit." He took her phone and tipped her chin. Her eyes were blank, her teeth worrying her lip. "Sable?"

Her lashes fluttered.

"You're okay now."

"I know." She swallowed, her throat moving as her eyebrows bowed. She looked delicate with her torn shirt, that asshole's blood on her clothes.

"They might want the DNA, so you can't clean up yet. Do you want some water? Tea?"

Her mouth slid to the side. "Do you know how to make tea?"

"Not really." He slipped his hand beneath her hair and around the back of her neck, massaging until she took a breath that lifted her shoulders and filled her lungs.

"Thank God you were here," she told him.

But a sick realization took the place of the pride he didn't deserve feeling. Because the fact of the matter is, this had happened *because* he was here. If he'd never asked her to come out with him tonight—or if he'd waited for her inside her apartment instead of heading down the stairs...

He wasn't a hero. He was to blame.

* * *

Isa sat on the very edge of her couch, uncomfortable, mind whirring. Her knee and elbow throbbed from the physical hit, but her mind replayed it on a loop. Her attacker's arms banded around her, his stale breath and craggy voice.

Don't fight me, you bitch, or I'll gut you.

A shudder streamed through her. Who knew the

defense class she'd taken with her assistants last year would come in handy for her? Isa was lucky Eli had been here. Sure, she'd resisted, but her attacker was much stronger than she was. She wasn't sure if he'd have given up if it'd been just her.

What would have happened if she'd been alone?

Another shudder had her reaching for the blanket on the back of her couch. She pulled it to her chin and stared blindly at the coffee table in front of her. At the fitness magazine promising *Sexy abs in 3 easy moves!*

The older police officer who had questioned her was at the door talking with Eli. He was a big guy with kind green eyes and a thick Chicago accent. He told Eli they'd "be in touch" and the door shut with a click. The next thing she knew, Eli was lowering himself onto the couch next to her, the solid, welcome weight of his arm wrapping around her shoulders.

She was physically fatigued from excitement and fear, yet her mind was overly alert. She had no idea how she was going to sleep tonight.

"I need to shower." *Repeatedly.* She'd already changed and had given her sweater to the police officer for evidence, but even now the feel of her attacker's hands had her skin crawling.

"You can shower at my place." Eli's warm, whiskey-smooth voice rolled through her. But she was already shaking her head.

"You don't have to do that."

"Then I'll stay here."

"I can't run away, Eli. I work downstairs. I live here. I'll have to come home eventually no matter what I do tonight."

"It doesn't mean you can't come to my house. Sleep in my arms. Shower in my bathroom and dry off with one of my towels." His gravel-laden voice was gentle, the rough quality not making her feel any less comforted. His hand on her shoulder, he gave her a light squeeze. "Does it?"

The thought of snuggling into him and feeling safe rather than staring at the ceiling all night and listening for strange noises was definitely a better idea.

"Sable."

She nodded. Just a small nod, but he was already standing and heading into her bedroom. She heard drawers opening, the closet shutting. She curled the blanket around her shoulders and let Eli pack her things without her help.

CHAPTER 14

Eli removed the shower chair and turned on the water and the room began filling with steam. Isa stood in the doorway of the bathroom, looking weary, her arms crossed over her waist.

"Soap and shampoo are in the shower, towel's right here." Eli rested his hand on the fluffy gray towel and watched her, worry eating a hole in his stomach. He wasn't sure how to comfort her. "Do you want my help?"

"No." She gave him a tired smile. "I won't be long."

He thumbed her chin and watched her a moment longer. He understood. Showering was personal. He never wanted help in here either. "I'll be in bed. Join me when you're done."

She gave him a faint nod and he left her alone.

Outside the shut bathroom door, he hesitated, considering going back in there. As tempted as he was, in the end he gave her privacy.

He'd opened a book on his lap but hadn't read a damn word of it. He thought about her instead. How frightened she must be, how he'd failed her—twice now, arguably more.

A short while later, she came into the bedroom, towel wrapped around her body, hair dripping.

Her chin wobbled, and then she started to cry. Eli was off the bed in an instant, peeling the damp towel from her body and hoisting her in his arms. He'd kept his prosthesis on for this very reason. He suspected she might need him to come for her.

He lowered onto the bed, a trembling Isa in his arms. Her dripping hair and leaking eyes made a puddle on his T-shirt.

He held her in his arms and wrapped her in his blanket.

They naturally moved from sitting to lying down, her snuggled deep in his bedding and him facing her, clothes still on, his eyes on hers.

She sniffled again and he swiped under her eyes with his thumb.

"I'm sorry, Sable." It was the first words he'd spoken since before she stepped into the shower, and arguably his apology came late.

"Thank you for letting me stay."

His heart squeezed. The last time they were in this bed, he'd been transfixed by his own grief and hadn't given Isa the consideration she'd deserved.

Tonight, that changed.

"Thank you for coming back," he told her, swiping her drying hair from her face.

"Am I back?" Her eyes, red and puffy, sought his. She was so beautiful it hurt.

"I sure as hell hope so."

When her lips curved, he put a kiss on one corner of her mouth.

"Give me a second." He disentangled himself from her to quickly pull off his clothes and set aside his prosthetic leg. Back in bed next to her, he maneuvered under the covers until she was in his arms once again. Her cool fingers touched his torso and he wrapped her tightly against him. In the dark, Eli took a vow.

If phantom pain attacked his missing limb, or if he suffered a numb arm, or if his back cramped to crippling capacity, he didn't care.

In no way was he letting go of Isa until sunrise.

* * *

The bed bounced, a subtle shift, and Isa pulled in a breath through her nose. Sleep's fingers tickled the edge of her mind, leaving her disoriented, but only for a second. A man cleared his throat behind her, which should've been out of place considering she usually woke alone, but there wasn't a second of hesitation as to who it was.

Elijah Crane.

Eli, who'd come to her house to apologize.

Eli, who'd called the police after she was attacked.

Eli, who'd insisted she come home and stay with him.

Sleep in my arms.

She had. She opened her eyes when he kissed her shoulder. She'd fallen asleep facing him but must have rolled over in the middle of the night. She faced him now. He was propped on his right elbow, hair a mess, eyes hooded and sleepy. Sun poured through the blinds, casting him in yellow light, making his blue eyes shine.

She didn't speak. Neither did he. She wondered if he was also turning over the significance of this being the first night they'd spent together. Waking up to him felt strangely normal. She was comfortable here—comfortable with him.

He lowered his face to hers, slowly, as if testing her reaction. She gave him the kiss he requested.

"How'd you sleep?" he asked, his morning voice rich and deep.

"Better than I would've thought." Hers sounded more like she'd smoked a few cigarettes.

"That's good."

"Thanks for letting me stay last night."

He pushed her hair away from her eyes. She'd slept on it wet, so no doubt she was rocking some serious floppy bed-head. "No thanks needed, Sable."

They shared another quiet moment before Eli leaned forward again. This time when his mouth moved on hers, he opened, an invitation for her to go deeper. She accepted, her tongue tangling with his, warm and wet. He slipped his hand beneath the sheets covering her, palming her breast and thumbing a nipple. Her truncated breaths filled the air as her hand sought his shoulder.

"Eli," she whispered as his fingers brushed over her belly, closer, closer to where she wanted him. He paused, as if he was unsure, so she gave him permission. "Touch me."

He kissed her again, cupping her intimately before he dipped a finger along the seam of her.

"Wet," he said, his voice low and reverent.

"I want you." She gripped his biceps and parted her lips to let loose a gasp when he continued to tease her. Eli watched her as she watched him, his fingers dancing between her folds, unseen beneath the blankets. Each slick glide drawing her closer to the abyss.

Raising one hand, she palmed his beard, stroking her thumb over his bottom lip as she writhed from pleasure that only his attentive, rough touch could deliver.

He moved his fingers faster, faster...until she clutched and came, her eyes squeezing closed as her body bowed off the bed. Heart ratcheting, bloodstream pumping, she lazily opened her eyes to take in the man who'd guided her to the pinnacle with little effort.

He'd known what she needed last night. And he knew what she needed this morning.

"How do you do that?" she asked on a pleased sigh.

He placed a kiss on her nipple, then on her lips. "Do what?"

"Know what I need."

"You seemed tense." His lips tipped, his eyes blinking in that ultraslow way she found enticingly sexy. "Now you don't."

She let out a long hum of satisfaction. He wrapped a hand around her butt, squeezed, then let go to fall to his back.

Isa rolled over and wrapped an arm around his bare chest, admiring the swell of pecs and biceps, the tattoos that swirled over his arm. Flowers and waves, a sunrise, a cross. A plethora of scenery and images that meant enough to him to be immortalized on his skin for as long as he was on this planet.

"Your body is beautiful," she murmured, dropping her chin on his chest.

There was a palpable hesitation in the air, one she didn't ignore.

"I guess guys don't see themselves as 'beautiful.'" She traced a line down his chest and drew a circle around his belly button with the tip of her finger. His abs tightened, each bump standing out from his skin. Her fingers followed to his cotton boxers. He was hard and ready and grunted when she gave him a gentle squeeze.

A rough exhalation tickled her cheek and she wiggled into a comfortable position on the bed. On her side, chin on his ribs, her fist gripping the thick ridge of him.

"You are, though," she said as his eyes sank closed. "Completely beautiful."

* * *

Eli tugged Isa up his body and kissed her, his tongue dancing with hers. Much as he liked her touching him, he wanted her kissing him more. When he pulled away, satisfaction brimmed in her dark eyes. Satisfaction he'd put there. After the scare she'd had last night when he'd insisted she come home with him and lie safe in his arms, in his bed, he considered this happy, sated look a success.

"I was going to return the favor," she murmured against his lips, her hand flat on his stomach and inching lower.

"Were you now?" Her touch was amazing, but it wasn't what she was doing to his body that had him losing his breath; it was what she'd done to his heart. This exotically gorgeous woman draped over his body, drawing a line down the underside of his arm, had sneaked in there without his knowing.

He cared about her. In a way that was different from anyone before her.

She traced the muscles along **his abs. She'd** said he was "beautiful" but he knew what beautiful was, and it was Isa. Still, he couldn't help feeling a modicum of pride that she admired his body.

He'd built muscles because he'd needed them. The more strength he had in the rest of him, the easier it was to maneuver with his new leg. But she hadn't differentiated what parts of him were beautiful. She saw and accepted all of him. It was a sobering realization, and not one he was used to.

"I like you like this." Her hand moved back up to his chest and her full mouth, lush and welcome, smiled at him.

"Like what?" His voice, craggy and low, held a note of lust. Whenever she touched him, it infiltrated the space between them.

"Relaxed." She opened her mouth like she was going to say more, then shut it. Which wasn't like her. Isa said what was on her mind regardless of what Eli wanted or what he thought.

"And?" he found himself asking.

Her eyes screwed to the ceiling, before she admitted, "I was going to say open, but you're not open, are you? You're more like a screen over a window. I can see in, but I can't *get* in."

Isa's honesty made him want to squirm. She wasn't wrong.

"I'm…not skilled at being open," he said, feeling his brows pinch over his nose.

"You're kidding." She gave him a good-natured eye roll.

Open spaces were a threat. As a military man, they were a matter of life and death. As a man who'd lost his mother tragically, they were a matter of internal pain he couldn't escape. Letting someone in—letting himself out—equally dangerous. He knew well the feeling of putting himself on the line and feeling the slap of disappointment, of heartbreak.

His mother had broken his heart into bits when she died.

After a gap of a few breaths, Isa spoke again.

"I'm not sure what we have here." She pushed up on one elbow, not bothering to cover her body with the sheet. Goose bumps prickled her tan skin, her breasts rising when she inhaled. If anyone had practice at being open, it was Isa. In that way she was a hundred times braver than he was.

"I like you, Eli."

He held his breath and waited for the *but*. For her to tell him it was over. Maybe she'd worried as he had after last night that he hadn't been able to keep her safe— that his scaring off a mugger was a little too close for comfort.

His heart hammered an uneven pattern. He worried she'd tell him she couldn't be with him because he wasn't enough. He'd never be enough for the woman who deserved everything.

"But...," she started.

His heart seized like it'd been peppered with buckshot. He didn't want her to go. Not after winning her back.

"...I can't keep guessing what's in your head," she finished.

He was so shocked she wasn't reciting a Dear John letter, he blinked at her in silence. Maybe it was that relief that made him offer her more. "What do you want to know?"

"Do you really believe you're bad luck?"

He blew out a laugh, but it was a desperate attempt to keep her from knowing that she'd hit the nail pretty damn close to the head. "Not exactly."

He chewed on his thoughts another few seconds before committing what to share.

"Good things...don't chase me."

"Life is about *you* chasing good things, Eli, not the other way around."

He thought of last night. Of the position she'd been in. Of his presence there. Of the swamping guilt and seething anger he'd felt at not being able to chase that asshole down. At the very least, Isa deserved someone who could protect her.

"A lot of bad things happen when I'm around."

"Are you afraid you'll screw up?" She shrugged. "We all screw up."

"Some screwups come with a hefty price, Sable. Screwups like letting my two men lead resulted in them losing their lives." He tipped her chin. "Screwups like you being attacked because your attacker didn't believe I could fight him off." Quietly, he added, "And I didn't."

"No." She shook her head, but he ignored her attempt to make him feel better. He knew what happened. He'd been there.

"It's a fact, Isa."

"It's bullshit, Eli." Her gaze sharpened and never left his face. "You came for me after I left, and that was a miracle. If you hadn't showed at all..." She batted her lashes like she was fighting tears. "I don't want to think about it."

He was in awe of her strength. He'd rather take a Taser to the nuts than have this conversation. Especially when fear returned—that prickling spike of adrenaline as he recalled her ear-piercing scream for help. His stomach twisted even though she was here next to him, completely safe in his bed.

"What happened to me is not your fault." She touched his face. "I could have been robbed, raped. He could have climbed those stairs and broken into my house while I was in the shower."

He'd thought about that, too.

"You heard what I told the officer. That guy's eyes were wild like he was high on something. He was twitchy. Strange. He hadn't been lying in wait and carefully plotting. Maybe he saw you in the shadows, maybe he didn't. It could have happened at any time."

He hadn't stopped to consider that. He hadn't considered much of anything other than the fact that he'd failed her.

"But if I wouldn't have shown up at your door, you never would have been outside."

"If you wouldn't have shown up at my door, Eli, I wouldn't be here right now."

He frowned. He was grateful she was here. He valued her safety first, but she wasn't wrong. She was in his arms and in his bed because of last night.

"So...you're moving in with me," he stated, his dark humor hitting its mark when she laughed lightly.

"I have pepper spray. I'll be on alert."

"And have a male employee stay late to walk you up. Finish your work upstairs and never ever head up there after dark unless—"

Her fingers pressed to his lips. "I promise."

Her words made him want to promise her things right back. But he wasn't the man he used to be and fell short of being the man he should be. Crushed beneath that realization, he refused to make Isa a promise and not deliver. He wouldn't fail her again.

Isa fiddled with the edge of the sheet. He admired her raspberry-tipped breasts, bared and beautiful. She was gloriously naked and not hiding from him. That was the crux of who she was—someone who didn't hide.

Meanwhile, Eli had behaved like a hibernating bear.

"Have you ever lived with someone?" she asked suddenly.

He waited for his fight-or-flight response to kick in. When anxiety didn't lodge his throat, he counted it as progress.

"Yes," he answered. "You?"

"Never. Not a romantic interest, anyway. I lived at home and with a friend from college, but I've mostly been on my own. Josh wanted to move in together, but it felt wrong."

"You held back."

"I guess so. I knew we weren't right, but I'm not sure I know what 'right' feels like." She flicked Eli a glance and then looked away, and in that brief exchange, he understood exactly how she felt. He'd spent years not knowing what 'right' felt like and had eventually determined that relationships never felt right. They just *were*.

"Her name was Crystal." Eli slid an arm beneath the pillow under his head. Isa had asked, and dammit, he was going to give her a complete answer for a change. "She and I met through a mutual friend. We dated for three or four months and then she moved in when I deployed. She said it'd make her feel closer to me if she was around my things."

He stole a glance at Isa, who was riveted, yet also

looked like she didn't want to hear any of this. He couldn't blame her. Here he was sharing and he didn't want to talk about it at all. But Isa deserved the truth. If she wanted it, he'd give it to her.

"Do you want me to continue?"

She nodded, and he honored her request.

"Whenever I was back, she'd insist we go house-hunting or talk about financial plans for our future. I would be trying to acclimate to civilian life again, settle into a temporary schedule, and Crystal wanted to play house."

"She loved you." Isa's voice held a truckload of disappointment. He tried to alleviate her fears.

"Maybe." Love wasn't something they'd talked about. Crystal knew what he was like—that he didn't embrace the sentiment of swapping four-letter L-words. If there was one thing he hadn't been successful with at all, it was love. Hell, he didn't even know what it *was* in regard to anyone who wasn't related to him. "She wanted children, a family. A house with a yard. I don't want that."

"Not ever?"

Great question. He didn't feel as opposed to it as he used to. "Now I'm not sure what I want. I've changed in a lot of unexpected ways since I've come back."

Changing had scared him more than anything. He used to know who he was...who he'd been his entire life. After literally losing a part of himself, he wasn't sure who he was anymore. Or who he would become.

Isa snuggled down in the bed next to him, hands in prayer beneath her cheek. Her dark eyes wide with hope as she watched him and he watched her.

"So this...what we have. It's enough for you?" Her tone was careful.

Sometimes it was more than he could handle, but he knew better than to tell her that. Instead, he took one of her hands and laced their fingers together, hoping she'd take what he was about to tell her the right way.

"I'm not sure I can give you more, but I'm not done with us, either."

The light in her eyes dulled. "Okay."

"Okay?"

"That's fair."

It wasn't. He didn't like her heavy acceptance, but he also didn't want her to leave. What he was asking of her made no sense. She should never settle for less than she deserved. Not running her parents' business, not a jackass ex who only wanted to use her as a cog in the wheel of his future. But if she'd stick around long enough for Eli to figure a few things out . . . he'd take it.

"I need you," he admitted. "So if you wouldn't mind staying a little while long—"

She was on top of him in an instant, her wild hair tickling his face, her plush lips crashing into his. Eli wanted to be the man she deserved, but there was a selfish part of him who wanted her any way she'd have him.

He kissed her back, sifting her hair through his fingers and trying not to think about the fact that she, too, could run through his grip like sand.

CHAPTER 15

Things were back to normal.

Kinda.

Isa wasn't at Eli's warehouse, but at her desk dispatching and scheduling. She'd worked on Sable Concierge business more than Crane business, and thank God she had. Business was booming, word getting out about her personal assistants. Partially in thanks to Merina, who had recommended her to a few friends, and mostly in thanks to Chloe, who had taken the new management position and run with it.

Isa had also found a manager for Refurbs for Vets—someone she and Eli had both met with and approved of—so Eli no longer had to handle the day-to-day.

One week ago, he'd rescued her from an attacker, taken her home, and cared for her. Then they'd made love—falling into their routine as a couple as if she'd never left. And while he hadn't made anything clear, she'd received his message loud *and* clear. Eli didn't want to think about how things would go or how long they would last. He wanted to live in the present. After hearing about his ex-girlfriend, Crystal, Isa understood why he felt that way. Sounds like his ex had worked overtime trying to make Eli commit to a future he had no interest in.

After Isa and Josh split, she'd enjoyed being single. She didn't stay single for three years because she had no choice. She'd turned down plenty of men at a time she could've buried her loneliness in someone else. There was enjoyment in being in charge of one's own life and schedule.

She'd stayed alone because she wanted to build her business. Thrive in a way that wasn't attached to her parents or to a man with designs on her parents' business. Losing herself was no longer appealing.

If nothing else, Eli was giving her that same opportunity. He wasn't pressuring her to define what they had or cage her into a routine-riddled relationship. She wanted to be content with the arrangement... She was just having trouble getting her heart on the same page as her brain.

That blame she could place on Eli Crane's gorgeous shoulders. He was the one who'd introduced her to what she'd been missing.

She let out a sigh.

Right or wrong, he was what she wanted. It had to be enough because he wasn't someone she could walk away from.

Her phone trilled with a message and Eli's rudimentary all-caps text read: *DATE TONIGHT.*

She had to smile. He didn't often text, saying he preferred not to mess with it. When he did message her from his office to her office at his kitchen table, he e-mailed instead, which cracked her up. He claimed his fingers were too big for his phone's onscreen keyboard, but she suspected he didn't have the patience to peck out a message.

You have a date? With who? she texted back.

SOME HOT CHICK WHO LICKS ME.

She was still laughing when she swiped the screen and called him instead.

"Shit," he answered.

"Licks you?" She was still laughing.

"*Likes*. I typed *likes*. I hate texting," he grumbled. "I didn't want to interrupt your work with a phone call."

"Well, it wasn't inaccurate." Her laughter faded to a soft hum.

"No," he said warmly. "It's definitely not inaccurate."

He was sweet. She never would have guessed that Eli Crane and "sweet" would go together in her mind.

"So. Our date? When and where?" she asked, not about to turn him down.

"Tag and his buddy Lucas are dragging me out for a beer at Dooley's around eight. I know you're working late tonight, but I figured I could leave and pick you up around nine."

"Don't cut your drinks short on account of me. I can meet you there."

"You want to have drinks with the guys?"

"Sure, why not? There's no sense in you driving to the other side of town when I can easily take a cab."

"A cab? That's not very gentlemanly of me."

"I never accused you of being a gentleman." She could practically hear his smile through the phone. "I'm not sure when I'll be done. It's easier to just cab it there, honestly. And before you ask, yes, I have pepper spray."

"Okay, Sable. Fair enough. See you tonight."

"I'll be there." She ended the call, a smile affixed firmly to her face.

Yeah, she wasn't done with Eli.

It was nice to know he wasn't done with her, either.

* * *

"I can't believe it. Elijah Crane in the flesh."

"Luc, he's not a celebrity. Do not act awestruck." Tag tipped his bottle of beer and drank.

"He's right. I'm a broody loner with a bad attitude." Eli slid his gaze from Tag's best friend, Lucas, and back to his brother. Tag and Luc had been buddies since high school. Back then Eli had considered them a pair of knuckleheads, floating around with zero goals. Eli was proud of Tag, who'd managed to carve out a life that suited him. Guest and Restaurant Services wasn't a department until Tag suggested it; then he ran it his way. Long hair and all.

Eli signaled the waitress for another round, then shouted at the football game on the TV over the bar. "Don't suppose they could win one for me," he griped.

"They never win. You should be used to that by now," Tag said.

"No shit." Eli glanced at his phone: 8:32.

Twenty-eight minutes until Isa gets here.

He'd surprised himself when he'd agreed to come out for beers, then surprised himself further when he'd called Isa to ask her out after. Maybe he was shedding the skin of who he'd been for years. The only problem was he had no idea whether there was a fresh, clean Eli beneath or a scaly monster.

8:33.

"You can't be that much of a loner if you have a lady friend. Is that why you keep checking your phone, then looking toward the door?" A smirk slid onto Lucas's smug face.

"Seriously?" Eli sent a glare at Tag, who, cheeks full of beer, swallowed it down and shrugged.

"What? I mentioned her."

Eli should move out of the state to get some privacy, but he loved his house. He loved this city. And his brothers, the sons of bitches.

"It's a sight to behold—you Cranes toppling like dominoes." Luc crossed his arms over his chest. In a black sweater, black jeans, and boots, he looked a lot like the rock stars he produced instead of an executive. "I always said the right woman changes your world."

"You always said the right woman fucks with your head," Tag corrected.

Lucas let out a loud "Ha!"

Eli shook his head. He wasn't participating in this, though he suspected they were both right. Isa had relocated his center so drastically he'd lost his balance.

"Eli doesn't topple," Tag said. "He's completely in charge of his faculties around women. Isa happened to be the first to crack into his safe, but his security system is fully armed. No way has she taken anything of real value." An elbow shot into Eli's arm. "Isn't that right, bro?"

"Yeah," he agreed, because it was easier to agree with

Tag than engage him. The waitress delivered another round of bottles as Eli drank the last of his.

Ah, right on time. No way was he mulling over Tag's metaphor.

"I'm supposed to bring you a shot of tequila," the waitress said, handing Eli his bottle. "That woman over there said you could pick a different shot if you no longer drink tequila." The waitress pointed to an adjacent table. A brunette he recognized instantly gave him a casual wave, her two friends sitting at the booth across from her studying him over their shoulders.

"Shit," Tag muttered.

Eli felt his frown deepen when her eyes met his. "No. Thanks."

"I'll let her know."

"No, I will."

"Suit yourself." The waitress left with a shrug.

"That's not Isa, is it?" Lucas jerked his glance from the brunette, then back to Eli. "Are you two doing some kinky meet-cute role-play?"

"No, that's not Isa," Tag said. "It's a woman from Eli's past."

"Shiiit," Luc said.

Tag muttered, "They crawl out of the woodwork, don't they?" as Eli stood and excused himself from the table. Chicago was a huge city, but Crystal being at the bar where they'd first met and had often frequented wasn't that big a surprise.

He walked to the booth. When Crystal spotted him, she leaned forward to whisper to her friends, who both scooted out and sidled by him.

"Hi, Crystal." He shoved his hands in his pockets.

"Eli."

"You didn't have to send them away. I won't be long."

"You didn't have to come over." Light blue eyes found his. "You didn't want the shot?"

"If you wanted to talk to me, you could have walked over and said hello."

She pressed her lips together and nodded. "That's true. I guess I was afraid you'd be unkind."

"Sounds like me," he admitted.

"Sit for a second?" She gestured to the empty seat her friends had vacated.

He didn't want to, but he sat.

"How have you been?" Concern etched her face, worry lines deepening her forehead. A typical reaction by anyone who saw him for the first time since he'd been back.

"Recovering," he said. "Working. The usual."

She chewed the side of her cheek, her lips sliding to one side. She'd done that when they were dating. Whenever she was debating saying what was on her mind. Sometimes she said it and other times she'd shake her head and say, "Forget it."

"I was unfair—" she started.

"No." He held up a hand to stop her from recanting or regretting anything. "You don't have to say that."

"I do. If only for me." She inhaled, then looked at her hands when she said, "I should have been there for you. I was..." She shook her head. "I was—"

"Listen, Crystal. We'd already grown apart before I deployed that last time. When I came back, I underwent surgery, rehabilitation. I can't blame you for saying I wasn't what you signed up for." Even though her words had hurt him, he couldn't hold it against her. Losing his leg and not being a soldier any longer wasn't what he'd signed up for either.

"I did say that." Her mouth froze open. "But...it wasn't the whole truth."

Regardless, he wasn't after a rehash. He'd moved on. He had Isa.

He blinked, the thought thunking into his head like a stray tennis ball. *I have Isa.* It was nice to have her, to know she was coming here tonight.

"We had a good run," he said, trying for amicable. "I wasn't the person for you and you weren't the one for me. We were delaying the inevitable."

"That's true."

It was true. But it hurt to think about the time they wasted, the pain they could have spared each other. He lifted an abandoned coaster and tapped the edge on the table. "Did you ever buy the house you wanted?"

"One like it." She leaned back and then he saw her rounded belly. She was pregnant. He blinked several times to test his vision. "And a husband and a dog. A little mutt."

He swallowed thickly, tried to push out a "congratulations" and failed. She'd moved *way* on.

"When I said you weren't what I signed up for, I was only telling you half the truth." Crystal took a breath and then blew out a confession. "I left you because I'd already met Ryan."

Eli stared at her, stonily silent. His eyes went to her stomach again.

"My husband," she needlessly clarified.

Crystal had always wanted the house, husband, dog—and baby—but Eli had been contented to live in the warehouse, to serve his country. She wanted a man to build a home with her and he wouldn't have been able to give her that.

"I should've told you the truth, but I worried it would hurt you more knowing I'd met someone new."

He studied the table, his world fracturing. What he'd believed—that he was too much of a burden, that there was no going back because of his physical changes—was never the truth. Crystal had found someone else—someone to give her the things she wanted.

"Eli. I'm so sorry."

He looked up to find Crystal's expression infused with regret.

"It was wrong of me to lie." Her eyes left his to focus over his shoulder at the same time Eli felt a prickle of awareness at the back of his neck.

"This looks cozy," a whiskey-laced, female voice announced. He knew that voice. Knew the timber of it when she cried out in pleasure and the sound of her husky laugh whenever he was fortunate enough to draw it from her.

He looked up to find Isa wearing a tight, red dress riding high on her thighs and cut low in the front. "You're early."

Isa shot him a black-lashed wink.

"Crystal Billings." His ex introduced herself, chin up, smile polite. Her married name, evidently.

Eli didn't miss his ex's assessing rake down Isa's body. He stood and wrapped an arm around Isa's waist. "Crystal and I used to date."

"Hmm," Isa said, her smile holding a secret. She knew that part because he'd told her. He liked her knowing, and that was an epiphany in and of itself.

"We met here about a million years ago," Eli continued. "Now she's married with a house and a baby on the way."

Crystal's eyes flicked from Eli to Isa. "And a dog."

"Congratulations to you," Isa said kindly. She turned to Eli. "I'll let you two wrap up." Her dark eyes flashed in a way that he knew she was smiling at him from her soul. "I spotted Tag over there."

"Be over in a sec."

"Okay." Isa's voice was a whisper and because he couldn't help himself, he lowered his face and softly brushed her mouth with his. Then she was off and he couldn't help watching her go. She wore that dress like she was doing it a service.

When he refocused on Crystal, her smile was smaller than before. "She's beautiful."

"She's also smart. Driven. Brave." Crystal fell short in that last category. She hadn't been brave enough to tell him the truth. He couldn't decide whether he owed her thanks for that or not.

"I'm glad you said hello." Crystal gripped her glass of what he'd originally assumed was a vodka tonic but now considered was probably a Sprite with lime.

"Are you happy, Crystal?" he asked.

She tipped her chin, her eyebrows closing over her nose.

"With the house, the husband"—he gestured at her stomach—"the whole nine yards?"

She moved her hand over her belly and shot him a beaming smile with absolutely no doubt hiding behind it. "I really am."

"Good." He meant it. She should have what she wanted. What she deserved.

"Are you happy, Eli?" Her gaze snapped from Isa and then back to him.

"I'm getting there."

"It's understandable."

So lost in the idea of getting back to his date, he had to ask her to clarify. "What is?"

"The way you hold back. The distance you force. You're cautious about committing."

Old anger spiked in his chest and he mentally tamped it down. This was an ancient argument. One where Crystal would say he couldn't commit and he would argue that he signed up to potentially die for his country, so how about that for commitment?

It wasn't a road he was willing to repave. Not now. Not ever.

"I'm not trying to insult you," Crystal said, and he could see in her earnest expression that she believed she was being sincere. "I can see the way she looks at you"—his eyes tracked back to Isa, who sat at the table with Tag and Lucas—"and I don't want your hesitation to go 'all in' to ruin your chance at happiness."

Now? Now she cared about his happiness?

His face warmed as his blood pressure shot up. What he wanted to say was, *You accuse me of holding back when you couldn't admit to moving on with the man you're now married to? You didn't think you owed me an ounce of sympathy and a pint of explanation when you e-mailed me back to tell me you didn't "sign up" for a man like me?*

Instead, he forced a smile that probably came off looking like a grimace, and said, "Good luck to you, Crystal."

"You too."

He used the walk away from his ex-girlfriend to calm

himself, not feeling much better for running into her. Not that he should be surprised. Whatever issues he and Crystal had when they split were still there—and he'd be foolish to think they could be put to rest after a two-minute conversation in a bar.

He reached the table, where Tag was delivering a glass of wine to Isa, who was wrapped in conversation with Lucas. Eli's chest tightened at the sight of her, and not in a bad way. In a way that reminded him that as wrong as Crystal was for him, Isa was right.

Right. Had he finally found it?

"Lucas," Eli interrupted, taking the seat next to Isa. "Stop flirting with Sable." Isa put her hand on his and he felt instantly better.

"Sable?" Luc asked. "Is that a stage name or something?"

"Are you suggesting I'm a stripper?" Isa said, feigning insult.

Tag leaned back, arms folded, prepared to watch the show. Eli leaned back, too, his focus on Luc, who futilely attempted to scramble out of the hole.

"No! Not at all. I'm...See, I'm in the music business. So the idea of a stage name applies to my industry as well." Lucas leaned forward and put both hands to his chest. "I'm legit."

"Uh-huh. *Sure.*" Isa lifted her wineglass and her eyebrows, content to give Lucas a hard time. Eli was content to let her.

Lucas continued digging, and Isa continued pretending to be unimpressed. And when Tag caught Eli's eye, he grinned and shook his head. He didn't have to say anything, because Eli could read his younger brother's mind.

Nicely done, E.

Eli couldn't argue that he was damn lucky to have Isa in his life.

Nicely done, indeed.

* * *

"No, no, no. Do not even tell that story." Tag swiped tears from the corners of his lashes, and Isa followed suit. It'd been a long time since she laughed herself to tears, and in unexpected company to boot.

"Senior prom," Lucas started, hand slicing the air like he was telling a serious account.

Impossible. These two were anything but serious.

Before he could continue, Tag elbowed him. "Come on, another time. Isa has heard enough about the Crane boys' adventures." He sent her a golden-lashed wink as Eli's hand slipped around her waist. The simple act of Eli's hand at her back, or hearing his low, subtle chuckle turned her on.

She'd only had one glass of wine, so alcohol wasn't to blame. He inebriated her by being himself. The real him she was starting to uncover. The idea gave her chills.

"Fine. Next time," Lucas said. Everyone at the table stood to say goodbye and Luc pulled her into a friendly hug. "I owe you a story. It was great to meet you."

"You too," she said, meaning it. "Even though you accused me of working the pole."

"Never will I live that down!" He sought help from above before placing a palm on Isa's shoulder and leveling her with a serious look. "You'd get along with my wife."

Whom Luc had brought up repeatedly. What a freaking nice guy. Tag hugged her, a casual, one-armed squeeze. "Later, sis." Her eyes went wide, but Tag only smirked at Eli. "What? Too soon?"

"Get out," Eli said, his dry humor doing nothing to weaken Tag's penetrating smile. When they'd gone, Eli snagged his coat from the back of his chair and held it out for her. "I know, I hate to cover the dress, too," he said when she started to argue. "But it's cold out there and we're walking to the car, so on it goes."

She slid her arms into his coat, leather and Eli overtaking her senses. She hadn't felt this way since high school— the innocence of wearing his coat and laughing with friends. She slid closer when they stepped outside and Eli threaded his fingers with hers as they paced down the sidewalk.

"I like your brother's friend," she said.

"Luc's a good guy. No surprise there. So is Tag."

"So are you." She nudged his arm with hers and he sent her a sideways glance. Her heart zoomed to her feet so fast, she grew light-headed. Focusing on the lamppost beside them, then a flashy black limo that sped by, bass thumping, didn't help reroute her brain. There was no denying what that heart zoom had meant. No more arguing with herself.

She slipped her eyes over Eli. Tracked to the facial hair in need of a trim, to the way his hair curled at his collar. The set of his jaw, the firm purse of his lips, the column of his neck leading to the body she'd kissed over and over...

Yep. She loved him.

The thought inflated her heart and defeated her mind.

Love.

Crap.

"What was that for?" he asked, wiggling their linked hands.

"What?"

"The sigh. Sounded like it came from the depths." One eyebrow hitched in curiosity. "I hope you're not tired. I was going to take you somewhere else."

"Where?" she asked, unable to do anything but ask one-syllable questions, apparently.

"Somewhere deserving of that dress." Blue eyes slid down her body and up again, hunger there.

She stopped walking and faced him, slid a hand into the back of his hair and tugged his mouth to hers. A soft, deep, slow kiss that turned her inside out. A wolf whistle from a passing car caused her to pull back and when she did, Eli promptly tugged her mouth back to his and continued the kiss.

I love you.

"I want to go home with you," she said instead, lust out-lining every word.

His smile was like the sun coming out after a day of rain and clouds. White teeth flashed in the darkness, a wicked promise of what was to come behind his smile.

"Is that okay?" She could see it was more than okay.

"I happen to know the perfect place for that dress," Eli said, then towed her down the block, in more of a hurry than before.

"Don't say your bedroom floor."

"Okay." His eyes reflected that same playfulness when he glanced down at her. "I won't say it."

CHAPTER 16

He'd never been so impatient to have a woman naked in his life. His hands were shaking when he fumbled with the zipper on Isa's dress. She backed toward the bedroom, but he wasn't going in there. He wanted to show her he could take care of her in the way she wanted—in the way she deserved. As good as having her on top on his office chair or in his bed had been, he wanted her a different way.

His way.

He spun her and walked her through the living room instead, stopping at the wall that hid his office. Better a smooth, painted surface than pushing her against the craggy brick wall. Tugging her dress, he put a kiss on one satiny shoulder. Her exhaled sigh filled his ears.

"Sable," he murmured against the soft flesh of her neck.

Her fingers raked into his hair, sending a shock of heat through him. His hips shifted and he ground his pelvis into hers almost desperately.

She reached between them and cupped his erection, giving him a light squeeze. He slammed his lips over hers and yanked her dress so hard, threads popped.

"Fuck. Now I owe you a dress, too."

Her laugh was brief, interrupted by his sharp gasp when she continued to stroke him. Her tongue devoured his mouth anew. Eli didn't want to leave her lips again, but he did for a good reason—to lift the red material over her head. When he tossed the dress to the floor, her breasts were heaving, her hair was everywhere, and her eyes were fiery and honed in on him.

She ripped open the button on his pants and pulled his zipper down, tucking her hand inside at the same time he slipped one hand beneath the lace of her thong. He groaned and not because Isa was massaging his cock with tenderness...well, not *only* because of that. He groaned because her folds were smooth and velvety. She was so ready for him, he hated the idea of a layer of latex between them. What he wouldn't give to skip that part.

"Fuck *me*," he swore out of exasperation.

"Is that a request?" A foxy little smile decorated her red mouth.

"Fuck yeah, it is."

He pushed her hair away from her face and wound it in his fist before laying his lips on hers again. She kissed him, then his beard, then down his neck, all the while her hand working him into a lather.

"Condom in my wallet," he managed. Barely.

"Do not want," she whined before she bit his neck, soothing the mark with her tongue.

"Me neither, but—ahh—" His grunt was because she'd given his cock another squeeze that obliterated the decision-making part of his brain. She moved her hand to redirect his wandering fingers and Eli clamped his jaw tight as he ran them through her slickness.

"Oh!" Her gasp was high and tight as he slipped and slid over her clitoris. To her mantra of, "Eli. There. Yes. There," he continued touching her.

"I have you." He watched her face, enjoying every pleat and crease, the way her beautiful eyes vanished behind smoky eyelids when she closed her eyes and parted her lips, and finally, came.

"Eli. *Eli.*" His name evaporated on a weak gasp as she shuddered. His hands left her body long enough to dig the condom from his wallet and roll it on. Then he was back to her, sliding a hand around her ass and lifting one of her legs to hook around his hip.

"Tilt," he instructed.

"Here?" she panted the word, surprise coloring her face.

"Yeah, honey. Right here." He liked surprising her. He would make love to her here, him in control. No chair or bed needed. He wanted to please her more than anything.

Obeying, she tilted her hips. He positioned himself at her entrance and slid to the hilt in one smooth, mind-mangling thrust.

Hell.

Yes.

"Sable." Her name left his lips like a prayer of thanks when his forehead dropped to hers, their breaths knotting in the air between them.

"You feel so good." Her eyes were open, hooded and filled with leftover lust from her ebbing orgasm.

"Not as good as you feel," he said, sliding deep again.

He stayed in that moment for a while—embedded deep, lingering. Letting her breath waft over his face, the spicy scent of her perfume permeate his every sense.

He took control and she let him, holding on to his shoulders for purchase as he thrust his hips. He drew cries from her throat and when her head fell back, he laid a row of kisses over her neck. Those cries wound into whimpers of delight as he moved. He couldn't hold on to his release much longer.

Hand tight around the back of her neck, his fingers digging into one of her plush ass cheeks, he pumped once, then twice before spilling into the condom with a sound that might qualify as a roar.

That buzz of electricity he always felt with Isa spread like fire through his veins, across his chest, and down to his toes. He dropped his head onto her shoulder and caught his breath, one hand still around her hip, the other flat on the wall behind her. He was spent and not because of the sex or the challenge of standing while doing it, but because Isa spent him in a way he had never experienced.

Heart and soul.

He lifted his face to kiss her. She smelled of spice and citrus. She tasted of oaky, buttery chardonnay. With her scent, flavor, and pussy surrounding him, he couldn't think of anywhere he'd rather be than right here, right now with her.

"Mmm," came her soft hum, a smile following. A shiver shook her.

"Cold, or aftershocks?" He palmed her bare shoulder and rubbed one of her arms to warm her, his chest swelling with undiluted pride. He'd wanted to show this fantastic woman exactly what he could do for her—and he had.

"Would you believe both?" she asked.

"I would." He pushed her hair from her shoulder and smoothed his palms down her arms again, leaving a trail of goose bumps behind. "How about a bath?"

He hadn't made much use of the tub in the master bedroom, but now was a good time to start.

"And candles?"

He thought for a second. "No promises, but maybe."

"Bubbles?"

"For you, anything." He held her eyes as he slipped out of her body. A satisfied groan left both their throats. "Damn, Sable."

There was more to say, but he couldn't find the words. More to say about how different she was, how different she was making him. How differently the time passed whenever they were together.

He offered a hand and she accepted. Side by side they walked to the bedroom at the end of the hall.

* * *

Isa lifted her foot, wrapped her toes around the faucet, and spun the hot water off.

"That is a talent." Eli's lips closed over her ear as his hand slipped through the water—with bubbles—and over her belly. "You have many."

Warm and luxurious, the water slid like silk between them. She'd tied her hair up, so it wasn't in the way when he moved his mouth from her ear to kiss a trail up her neck.

"I didn't know you were hiding this bathtub." A candle flickered at the corner of the tub. "Or a jar candle."

He grunted against her damp skin before tonguing her earlobe. Even though he was turning her brains to mush again, Isa pondered the candle. It obviously wasn't his. It was pink, and "sensual vanilla rose" was an odd scent for a Marine.

"Maybe Crystal left it here," she said.

His lips halted their exploration.

She shouldn't bring up Crystal Billings, but she couldn't help it. Seeing him sitting across from a woman who used to share his bed—his life—had sent Isa's quills standing on end. Oh, she'd maintained her politeness and gave him privacy, but Isa hadn't stopped thinking about the one woman Eli had shared his home with. *This* home.

"Maybe," he said, finding her hand beneath the water and linking their fingers. Soap bubbles slid as she tightened her grip and realized much in the same way he'd found her beneath the suds, Eli had sneaked past her defenses and into her heart.

"You didn't tell me what the two of you talked about."

He hummed.

She wanted to know what that hum meant. "What did you talk about?"

"The past. The present," Eli answered after a deep breath. Isa thought he wasn't going to say any more until he did. "She asked if I was happy."

Isa's heart pounded a hectic beat and she dug deep to find the courage to ask him how he'd answered. But there was no need. He told her anyway.

"*Happy* is an elusive animal for me. But this…I like this." A droplet fell from the faucet and hit the bathwater with a splash. Eli linked his free hand with hers and crossed both her arms over her breasts as he enclosed her in a hug. His voice was deep and reverent, vibrating against the shell of her ear when he said, "I like you, Isa."

I like you. Her heart suffered a tiny fissure at that pronouncement, because while it wasn't bad news, it wasn't the extent of what she felt for him.

"I should hope you like me." After making love to her against the wall...Another thought zapped her brain and this time it tumbled out of her mouth uncensored. "We weren't making *like* in there."

Eli breathed a long, low sigh. Isa kept her arms folded, trying to imagine his facial expression. Dread? Anger?

"No," he finally agreed. "We weren't."

The faucet dripped again. Eli's hands found her shoulders and massaged gently. He was trying to be kind, or maybe he was attempting consolation, but either way it frustrated her. He only gave as much as he wanted; then he retreated. She shrugged his hands away and started to stand, but Eli cupped her breasts and pulled her back against his chest.

His beard brushed her shoulder, lips kissing her shoulder.

"Sable."

"What?" She could absolutely throttle her heart. Didn't it know any better than to fall for a man who was as emotionally inaccessible as Eli Crane?

Eli turned her so she was on her side and facing him. Breasts pressed to his chest, her own arm captive against her body, she surrendered when he dipped his lips to kiss her. By the time their tongues were gently exploring, she was measuring his heartbeats against her own.

Too soon, she lost the heat of his mouth. He studied her

face before speaking, a completely forlorn expression on his own. When he spoke, it was a plea.

"Give me time."

If she wasn't sure she was in love with him before, she was sure now. Because learning he was still holding back all but shattered her.

* * *

They were the only words he could push out of his throat, and saying them made him half sick. It wasn't what Isa wanted to hear. Hell, he was sure it wasn't what any woman wanted to hear. But it was his truth.

She wanted him to open and he'd opened as much as he was capable. Crystal had pointed out tonight that he had a problem with going all in. He hadn't liked hearing it, but she hadn't been wrong. He didn't know how to go all in unless he started chipping away at it bit by bit. Maybe commitment was a lot like relearning to walk—it took practice.

The rest would come, or it wouldn't. And he had no earthly idea if that meant Isa would leave him before he had a chance to clear out the shit in his head and be able to evaluate what they have. But he wanted to try. She deserved a real promise, not one he blurted out to smooth over an awkward moment.

"I'm here," he told her, hoping that explanation sufficed. His fingertips stroked down her cheek and over her full bottom lip.

"I'm here, too," she said.

He nearly collapsed with relief. "Yeah?"

"Yeah."

They didn't make any further promises. There were no accusations, no future plans. The moment was in perfect present tense.

Right now.

He could handle that.

CHAPTER 17

Money, money, moneeeyyyy!" Chloe was singing and waving a fan of envelopes in front of her face. "We have checks, mamasita!"

"This is why I pay you the big bucks." Isa finished stirring the cream into her cup of coffee and took a sip. "I'm not adept in convincing past-dues to pony up."

Chloe frowned.

"What?"

"You okay?" Chloe dropped the envelopes on her desk, then turned back to Isa, hazel eyes assessing.

"Sure, why?" Isa shrugged. She was okay. She felt okay. Kind of okay.

Her assistant wrinkled her nose. "It's the boy, isn't it? Cranky Crane did something horrible over the weekend and it being Monday, I don't know what it is yet. Boys suck."

"He didn't do anything." Isa let out a weak laugh. Wasn't that the truth? She'd fallen in love with him; he'd remained unchanged.

"Isa." Chloe's eyes bled sincerity, *Talk to me*, written in their depths. But then she offered her own theory. "You're in love with him, aren't you?"

"Pfft!" Isa started to lie her way out of that but her smile chipped at the corners. With a sigh, she set aside her coffee mug aside and sagged against the wall by the door. Sable Concierge was empty, the phones turned off for lunch. Might as well spill her guts.

"I'm in love with him," Isa admitted. Saying it out loud made it realer than before. Scarier too.

"Of course you are."

"You're not surprised?"

Chloe shrugged.

"I haven't dated anyone in three years and then the absolutely wrong guy comes along and I fold like an origami goose."

"Since you started working for him, even when he was pissing you off, you have floated around here like you were wearing hover-board high heels. I'm not sure I've ever seen you this happy and I've worked with you closely for most of those three years. You were determined to take Eli on as a client and walk away. The thing is, you never walked away."

"I couldn't." She *could have*, but she sure as hell hadn't wanted to.

"You look..." Chloe tilted her head and studied Isa. "Well, not sad, but definitely not hover-board happy."

"There's a reason for that." A good one. "Only one of us was bitten by the love bug."

"Oh."

"Yeah, *oh*. I didn't tell him how I felt. If I did, he'd...I don't know what he'd do." Isa straightened her posture. "I'm trying to be casual and let things unfold."

"You don't want to pressure him." Chloe's tone was agreeable.

"He's had enough pressure." From Crystal pushing him to build a future with her he wasn't prepared for, to losing the two friends who saved his life, to his family good-naturedly trying to help him at every turn.

"I'm a strong woman," Isa said. "I can have an affair with a man and not build castles in the sky."

"Yes, you can." Again, Chloe's comment was generic.

"But?"

"It's not my place."

"Chloe. I hope you know we're friends."

She smiled. "I know. I just don't want to discourage you when you've found your way."

Isa pursed her lips before saying, "A good manager is able to point out flaws pragmatically and succinctly. A good manager tells the truth. And so do good friends."

"Okay." Chloe looked Isa squarely in the eyes. "You have the right to tell the man you're sharing dinners and evenings and overnights with how you feel, and he has the right to react to it. Don't keep your heart quiet for too long or you'll end up in love alone."

"Wow." Wise words.

"But." Chloe walked over to Isa and gripped her forearms, smiling kindly. "For now, enjoy yourself. Enjoy what the two of you have. You don't have to tell him this second. Pick your timing."

"After sex seems like a good strategy. He'd probably agree to anything," Isa joked.

Chloe chuckled. "You've got this."

She did have this. Maybe she was rushing to make this work out when, like Eli said, all they needed was a little time.

"Lunch at Romano's?" Isa offered, moving to fetch her purse. Amazing how one conversation had left her feeling better.

"Definitely." Chloe struck out for the door and snagged her own purse on the way. "I'll drive."

Isa didn't have everything figured out, but Chloe was right. When the time was right, Isa would tell him how she felt. Until then, she'd have fun with him. She deserved nothing less.

* * *

The soldier's home Zach had been working on was outside of Chicago in a manicured neighborhood. The unique positioning of a double lot gave the crew plenty of room to expand, which was why the addition had gone smoothly.

Eli had made the drive out this morning to meet Brent and his family. Brent was a double amputee having lost both legs to a roadside bomb. He had four smiling kids—three girls and a boy—and a wife who couldn't keep the tears from falling when she thanked both Eli and Zach for acceptance into the program.

Brent and families like his were the reason Eli was doing this—not for the kudos or the way his chest felt so full it might burst, but because without Refurbs, Brent never would have had such a speedy response to his physical needs.

As Eli drove away from the family's newly improved home, a heavy dose of satisfaction swept through him. Many more soldiers like Brent were going to get the help they deserved. He'd done the right thing starting the charity.

There were more projects on the way, and with the details of those projects being handled by his new manager, Allen, Eli was free to pursue the next phase of his life.

Crane Hotels. Back to where he started.

One summer before he'd joined the military, he'd spent fifty hours a week following his father, better known as "Big Crane" by his employees, around at the office.

Crane Hotels, with locations dotted across the nation, was a successful chain that rivaled others like it. Their father had taken it from a few buildings in Chicago to nationwide, and after the Crane name was an established profit machine, Reese had sailed in and run it with ease. Tag had also carved out his place.

It was Eli's turn to step up. He was ready.

He navigated out of the Brent's neighborhood and onto the main road, wondering how he'd arrived at a crossroads with Crane Hotels. Eli had never been a man who ran from hard situations. He ran *into* them. He'd fought for his country. He'd earned medals for bravery. How could suiting up and going to work scare him down to his bones when he'd once heard a bullet whiz by his ear and had *still* managed to pull a search and rescue?

But this wasn't war. This was life.

Wars ended. Life just kept on going.

The same way he'd kept going. When he came home to his old/new life, he didn't want to go back to Crane Hotels. Upper management had always been a forgone conclusion for his brothers but not for Eli. He'd seen a different path for himself—a soldier's path. Now he was buttoning up his past and stepping fully into his present. Crystal had moved on, and as he'd recently learned, had moved on before she'd rejected him. Refurbs was under new management, and other than visiting families or checking in on operations, Eli wasn't pouring hours into the charity the way he used to. And there was Isa...

Ah, Isa.

Talk about being scared down to my bones.

God help him, what he felt for her scared him senseless. He didn't dare label what they had. He didn't dare make a single plan involving promises he wasn't equipped to keep. He didn't dare risk losing her before he'd practiced being there for her—all of him. Not just part of him.

He missed her no longer working with him. Hell, who was he kidding? He missed her and he'd seen her, what? Two days ago?

"Good God," he muttered to himself to stop his back-and-forth thoughts.

Isa was independent, strong, and self-aware. She didn't whine or guilt him. She didn't overload him with pressure. She was there, present in the moment like he was.

So why the questions?

Because she wanted more. He saw it when he'd held her to him in the bathtub and explored the depths of her dark, honest eyes. He'd never evaluated a relationship before. He'd never wondered "what next?" But when it came to Isa, that's exactly what he'd been doing. And "what next?" went beyond dinner plans or getting a soft whimper of satisfaction to exit her lush mouth. This morning in the shower he'd had a passing thought about how the holidays were rapidly approaching.

Would Isa come with him to Thanksgiving dinner? Or spend Christmas morning at his dad's house?

He wasn't sure. After all they'd shared in a short time— the way she'd opened to him and him to her—shouldn't he know?

He pinched the bridge of his nose beneath his sunglasses, his heart thudding and his mind racing. It's like he had fucking PTSD where relationships were concerned. Thinking about someone being around for always and forever was like remembering that dazed, ear-ringing moment when he was on the ground after too close a call with a grenade.

No. That wasn't true.

The grenade had been a different daze altogether—a moment he'd rewound in his head over and over and had tried to rewrite, had tried to make sense of. Whenever he rewound memories of Isa, it wasn't to rewrite their reality, only savor it—to replay her smile or the way she sighed his name.

You want to do right by her, dumbass.

The thought in Eli's head came in the form of his late friend Benji's voice. Eli snapped out of his deep thoughts to find himself at the corner of Lightwood and Sandstone— near Benji's former residence.

"All in," Eli said aloud. He turned right on Sandstone and drove up the neat, tree-lined street. Chicago was cool and crisp as autumn settled over the city, but the sun was bright and bold, damn near blinding as he tried to make out the numbers on the street.

Finally he saw the house. Number 502. And here he sat, no announcement, no warning.

Before his courage failed him, he parked along the curb and climbed out of his car. Michelle Hough, Benji's widow, was inside. She walked past the wide kitchen window, pot in hand—cooking dinner.

He debated calling, and for a second, leaving, but a stronger force propelled him forward. As he walked up the steps that cut into the grass, he spotted a high chair and came to a stunned halt. A baby girl sat in it and Eli smiled in spite of himself when she lifted her chubby hand into the air. At the funeral, there wasn't a baby or a baby bump hinting that Michelle was expecting.

Maybe she was babysitting?

Months had passed and Michelle had refused to talk to him. Perhaps he'd deserved that for approaching her with nothing more than a veiled excuse of wanting her blessing to post Benji's photo. He should've told her the truth. That he wanted her forgiveness over all else.

On the porch, he wiped his hands down his slacks and knocked—three sharp raps.

The door swung aside a moment later and Michelle's mouth dropped open. Her blond hair was tied back in a short ponytail, her blue eyes wide.

"Elijah."

"Hi, Michelle."

"I didn't expect company." She fidgeted, first with the dishtowel in her hand before running that same hand over her ponytail to smooth it.

"I didn't expect to visit. I was in the neighborhood and I decided to try you."

"Oh."

The breeze blew the flowers on a potted mum at his feet. What the hell was he doing here? But before he could excuse himself and chicken out yet again, Michelle spoke.

"Do you want...dinner?" Her face pinched like she wasn't sure she should invite him in.

"That's not necessary." He wouldn't force her to endure his presence. She'd been through enough.

A soft coo in the background drew her attention and when she faced Eli again, she no longer appeared to doubt her invitation.

"You know what? Let me rephrase," Michelle said with a smile. "Eli. You're staying for dinner."

* * *

Dinner was macaroni and cheese, chicken cutlets—which he politely declined—and steamed broccoli. Michelle and Eli sat at the table, glasses of milk in front of them. They ate and caught up on the mundane while her attention was focused on her daughter. That's how Michelle had introduced her.

This is Destiny, my daughter.

Her daughter. He was still wrapping his mind around it, and Michelle had yet to explain.

"Okay, snuggle bug," Michelle told her towheaded daughter as she lifted her out of the high chair. Destiny was yawning and had barely made it through dinner. "She skipped her nap, so I'm going to put her down."

Eli cleared the dishes, looking around at the Hough kitchen as he did. It was tidy and neat, country blue and yellow everywhere. The colors suited Michelle—and Eli knew Benji well enough to know that if his late friend hadn't wanted a giant painting of a rooster crowing in the kitchen, he'd have let Michelle have it if she wanted.

"You didn't have to clean up," Michelle said as Eli loaded the last dish into the dishwasher.

"Your leftovers are in the fridge." He stuffed his hands into his pockets, unsure how to begin to apologize for failing her that scorching, fateful day.

"You must have a million questions," she said.

He returned her half-smile and leaned on the kitchen counter with one hip. "Just one."

Benji had been young and newly married, no children. *We're waiting,* he'd told Eli one day. *Till I get back.* But he'd never returned. That conversation haunted Eli more than any.

"Benji and I were secretly in the adoption process. We wanted two children and thought we'd adopt one and have one of our own and wind up with two children around the same age at the same time. The adoption went through two months ago."

A gurgle came from the baby monitor and Michelle's eyes lit with her smile.

"She's everything, Eli. She healed me. I never thought I'd recover from losing Benji, and well, I haven't recovered. Not completely."

Join the club.

"There are times I wish so much I had been pregnant when he died because then I'd have a piece of him. You know?"

Nothing pained him more than her quiet confession. So, he offered his.

"I'm not here about permission for the photo, Michelle."

She nodded at the floor. "I know."

The heavy fall of her shoulders dragged her into a seat at the dinner table.

"You cleaned off the high chair," she said absently, her eyes filling with tears.

He went to her and sat, leaning an elbow on the small, round table. "I'm sorry, Michelle. I'm so damn sorry."

She watched him long enough that a tear trickled out of one eye. "For a long time, I blamed you."

Blackness coated his soul. She was right to blame him. He blamed himself. How could he not?

"But I'm the one who owes you an apology, Eli," she said.

"What? No." He straightened in the chair, frowning at the woman in front of him who he'd bet never owed an apology to anyone in her sweet, young life.

"Yes," she said, her voice a lot more grown up than she looked. "Benji loved you. Whenever we'd talk, he'd mention you and what an amazing person you are. He talked about the advice you gave him about everything. Fixing up his old Camaro. The best kind of beer for a hot summer evening."

They did talk about those things. And more.

"He loved you, Michelle. I feel like I know you, he mentioned you so damn often. I never should have tried to get your blessing when what I was really seeking was your forgiveness."

Those were the most open, honest words he'd said since he stepped foot inside her home. Raw and real, they left him exposed. He was starting to understand that was how sharing felt. The risk of sharing was rejection. He waited for Michelle to reject him again.

"After Destiny arrived in my life," she started, "I realized things happen for a reason. Generic, right? I was so angry every time someone would console me with that platitude, but it's true. Things happen. What no tells you is that the 'reason' is personal. It's up to you to figure out why you're going through what you are."

She reached across the table and palmed his forearm below his semper fidelis tattoo. "I'm sorry you lost your leg, Eli. And I'm sorry I didn't take your calls. I told myself I was busy, but I was avoiding you. You reminded me of Benji, and having Destiny without Benji hurt at first."

"You have nothing to be sorry about," he told her. "You have to know that I would swap places with—"

"Don't you dare say what I think you're about to say, Elijah Coolidge Crane." Her eyes hardened as her voice wavered. She sniffed, visibly pulled her spine straight, and looked him in the eye. "Benji told me your middle name, too."

He couldn't rustle up a smile, not even when her mouth twitched at the edges.

"Don't you dare tell me you'd rather be in the ground," she said, "because I promise you there are people in your life who would be worse for it. You lost a limb, but you *lived.*"

"I know. That's what has me drowning in guilt every damned day."

"Refurbs for Vets is a good thing. You're giving back in an active way. And yes." She squeezed his arm. "You can use Benji's picture on the website. I'd be honored."

She startled him by wrapping her arms around his neck. "I forgive you. I don't need you to be sorry, but if you need me to say I don't blame you or hold you accountable, believe me when I say I don't."

He hugged Michelle, both arms wrapped around her back as one hand soothed her while she cried. Softly, gently, but she cried. When she pulled back, she smiled through those ebbing tears. A full-fledged smile like the one she'd given Destiny.

"Keep doing what you're doing, Eli. Benji is watching you, and he is proud. I promise. He wouldn't trade places with you. If the situation were reversed, he'd be honored if you'd traded your life for his. Since he traded his for yours, I suggest you live yours to the fullest."

"Yes, ma'am." Eli swallowed hard, his throat full, his heart fuller.

The moment was broken by a shrill cry coming from the baby monitor. Michelle wiped her eyes and shrugged, a busy mom with a routine. "I didn't think I'd get that lucky."

"I have to go anyway." He stood and she walked him to the door, Destiny's loud cries piercing the air.

"Thank you." Michelle squeezed his hand and all he could do was nod. When he was on the porch, the door shut behind him, and he stood observing the sky over the house for a long minute.

"If you're really watching, buddy," he said, hoping Benji could hear him, "fuck you for telling your wife my middle name."

Then with a smile, Eli stepped off the porch, and damn if he didn't feel as if Benji—from wherever he was—smiled back.

* * *

"Dad is going to shit." Tag's smile parted his trimmed beard.

Reese's smile matched their brother's, big and blooming like Eli hadn't seen in a long time. There was the smile he wore whenever Merina was around, and then there was this one. Like he'd come home from battle with the head of his enemy.

Since talking with Michelle, sharing dinner with her daughter, and hearing from her lips that whatever had happened had happened "for a reason," Eli was absolutely, one hundred percent positive he'd done the right thing.

By visiting her, by handing off Refurbs, and by coming home to Crane Hotels.

Eli was the one who'd called this meeting and he'd taken the lead. The second Reese and Tag sat at the conference room table down the hall from Reese's office, Eli had told him the decision he'd made.

He'd be stepping in as chief operations officer, effective immediately.

"Do you need an office?" Reese asked, pulling his phone out to take notes.

"I'll work from home, but I'll be here on occasion," Eli answered.

"Need an assistant?" Tag asked with a wry smile. "Or will Isabella Sawyer be performing that duty among others?"

"Very funny."

"Unless she refuses to let you pay her. Rachel was that way—she didn't want any part of my money." Tag leaned back in his chair and pulled both hands over his broad chest. "Parts of me, however…"

"Moving on," Reese muttered with a peeved glance at

Tag. It bounced off their youngest brother like he was surrounded by a force field. "There are several staff members performing parts of the position in your absence, Eli. I never truly replaced myself when I moved on from COO, so it's up to you how you want to run it. General operations is comprised of several jobs. You can keep the men and women I've appointed in place and oversee them, or you can place them elsewhere and carve out an eighty-hour-a-week grindstone like I did."

"Yeah, but you're a masochist," Tag interjected. "And Eli has a new girlfriend."

"All right. I give." Eli held his hands up in a surrender pose. "I have a girlfriend."

"Duh," Tag said. "She move in yet?"

"I'm not you." The teasing jab had Tag narrowing his eyes. Served him right. "She's not going to move in with me. And I'm not you." He turned to Reese. "If I asked her to marry me, she'd have a heart attack that would immediately precede my own. We're good. We're together and we don't feel the need to define it past that."

The words felt and tasted like stale bread. Eli and Isa weren't "good," and Isa did need to define what they had. He'd known that since the night in the bathtub. But he felt closer than ever to figuring out what a future with a woman might look like, and he needed his brothers off his back.

"Now that we're done with the small talk, can I get to the rest of these bullet points?" Eli tapped the pad of paper in front of him with the end of his pen.

Reese's smile wasn't as big as before, but it was there, suggesting he knew something Eli didn't know.

"Give it time, bro." Tag's grin was as shit-eating as ever.

Hadn't Eli asked the same of Isa? She'd granted him time, but Eli wasn't sure how long she'd given him. Or how long he'd need.

"Next item," Eli said, once again focused on the present and his new position at Crane Hotels.

CHAPTER 18

Isa changed from a black dress to a pink dress. Then to a white dress.

She peeled off the white one and groused at the discarded frocks on her bed before pulling on a pair of slim jeans, a ruffly blue top she'd bought because it matched Eli's eyes, and a pair of black heeled boots.

There.

Whatever he told her tonight, she was ready. He'd phoned earlier in the day and invited her over, saying, "I have dinner handled, Sable. Bring yourself and your appetite. I have big news."

"Business or pleasure?" she'd asked, trying for cheeky while her heart thundered.

"A bit of both."

She had no idea what he'd meant, but she was prepared to hear whatever he had to say. Including a profession of his feelings. Oh, she hoped it was a profession of his feelings. Things had moved fast for her, but she wouldn't second-guess herself. Not when everything felt so undeniably real and right. He'd asked for time, and she'd granted it. Maybe he was as ready as she was to step things up between them.

She regarded her outfit in the mirror on the closet door and bit her lip. Nope. Better go for the dress instead.

She peeled off her boots and started over.

* * *

Isa arrived at Eli's house wearing a skinny black dress and high heels. She wore a coat. As October grew to an end, there was no "showing off the dress" without also "freezing off her ass."

She slid the elevator door aside to reveal a heart-stopping table setting.

Candles.

Flowers.

Eli had never struck her as the flowers and candles type, aside from the time he'd dug one out of the back of the pantry for their shared bath. But there they were: two elegant, slim tapers nested in crystal holders.

"Hello?" She was smiling as she slipped her coat from her shoulders and walked in.

"Have a seat. Out in a sec," he called from the direction of the bedroom.

The flowers were hodgepodge in a glass pitcher. The ends weren't cut, and the iris in the center had a dead petal. Eli hadn't hired a florist. The fork and knife were on the wrong side of the plate for a formal setting, and the napkin was a paper towel.

Her smile grew even wider. He'd done all of it himself. Which meant he'd gone to the trouble to impress her. She gave up trying to calm her excitement as her heart galloped. This was clearly a romantic gesture—and she was ready to hear him out.

"Hey," she heard behind her. Eli strolled out of the bedroom buttoning the sleeves on a white dress shirt, his black slacks and shiny black shoes throwing her off. This was much different from the man in torn jeans and a tight gray T-shirt, yet he was as appealing either way.

"Wow, you look..."

He lifted his face and she lost her breath. Just gone, like a vacuum had sucked it from her. She could see his face. *All of it.*

"You shaved your beard. Completely."

He brought up his tattooed arm and scrubbed his cheek with one hand. "Yeah. Is it weird?"

"Different, not weird."

God, he was gorgeous. The dark angle of his jaw sharp and leading to a strong chin and perfectly firm, kissable lips. His hair was trimmed and neat, a little wavy on top— just the way she liked it.

"Wow."

"You said that already." He grinned as he approached, his steps shortening when he came close. His touch was familiar and welcome, blazing a trail along her waist as he tugged her close. "Want to see how it feels and make your judgment call after?"

"Mmm-hmm." Since she wasn't capable of words at the moment, she went with an affirmative hum. He kissed her and she made the sound again, only it was more of a moan, and turned her knees to jelly. His warm tongue traced hers and instead of feeling the rough texture of his facial hair, she was met with a smooth face, caressing lips, and his ever-present wandering hands.

He smelled like pine and cedar. Tasted like mint.

Felt like heaven.

Every part of her leaned closer and before she knew it, she was standing on her toes absolutely devouring him as she shoved him toward the bedroom. When she went for the buttons on his freshly pressed shirt, he didn't bother stopping her. Good thing. She wasn't in the mood to be dissuaded.

"What about dinner?" he asked between kisses, but he didn't wait for an answer. He palmed her neck and kissed the sensitive spot behind her ear.

"You sound like a good dinner to me." When he raised his head, she kissed then nipped his bottom lip.

With a growl, he took over, deepening their connection, his hands on her face, his tongue stroking hers at a torturous, languid pace. Fingers on the waistband of his slacks, she was hit with a sudden desire—an absolute need. Him, raw and naked and under her.

Button open, zipper drawn, she slipped his pants and boxers down narrow hips. Hard and ready, his cock landed heavy in her hand and she stroked once.

Twice.

A desperate sound left his lips as his fingers trailed into her hair. "Isa."

She shuddered. Hearing her name on his lips was sexier than the nickname he had for her. She bunched his shirt and slid down his body, lifting the material and kissing his flat stomach. He was toned and hard and she explored the many dips with her tongue and teeth. Especially when she drew lower.

She paused to look up at him from her position on her knees—to take in the hunger in his nighttime blue eyes, the muscles in his abs taut as he cradled her head with gentle pressure. Then she took him in. Inch by inch, she slicked her tongue past the head and down the shaft as the most glorious sound of pleasure left Eli's lips.

He rocked, hips tilting forward as he shifted his weight.

Air hissed through his teeth as she bobbed and sucked, licked and kissed.

"Sable." A groan. "I have to…" An exhale, short but powerful. "Sit down."

She let him loose and he swore as he plunked down on the bed, his eyes filled with dark intent, his fists wrapped around the bedding.

She started to lower to the floor and he cupped her elbow.

"I'm not done," she argued.

"No?" His voice was a wheeze.

She shook her head, tugged the skirt of her dress up, and lowered to her knees in front of him. Then she dove in again. This time, she heard his swearing clear as day.

"Fuck, Isa. God. Dammit. Fuck me."

Each word was a rust-covered rumble paired with his hand massaging her head. He bucked his hips, so close now. She could feel him coiling, every muscle in his thighs tightening. She kept going. Kept pleasuring him until he surrendered his release on a shout.

She swallowed him down, every drop, and only then did she let him loose with a soft *pop* before laying a reverent kiss on his shaft. She stood to find Eli had collapsed on the bed, arms overhead, shirt open and revealing his stomach and heaving chest. She admired him for a few seconds: the shadow his lashes cast on his cheeks, the newly shaven jawline she hadn't yet grown accustomed to. Tanned skin and slim waist, thick thighs, and the way his pants were bunched around his ankles.

Knee on the bed, she trailed a hand over his stomach and up to play with one flat nipple.

"You are the most stunningly handsome man." She kissed the corner of his mouth, pleased when he barely had the strength to pucker.

Eyes open and honed in on hers, he gave her a lopsided grin that made her heart flip. "I never imagined someone like you existed."

Her hand froze on his chest as she let the words soak in. The love she felt for him intensified, saturating her very being. She was sure he could see it. *Feel* it. How could he not when she absolutely radiated with it?

"Wait until after dinner." His hand brushed her cheek, pushing her hair away from her face. "I'm going to make you come so hard I'll render you useless."

Her teeth speared her lip and Eli reached up to free the flesh from her bite.

"Do you want that? Me rendering you useless?" His eyes darkened with wicked intent. "At my whim and command? Shaking and pleading with me to stop because you can't take any more pleasure?"

Well. Look who'd found his voice.

"Yes," came her broken whisper. Broken because she wanted all of that. All of *him*.

"Good." He lit her up with a long, wet, warm kiss. "I wasn't going to give you a choice." His slow blink reminded her of a big cat in the sun. Pleased with himself and his kingdom. In control and he knew it.

She wanted to be under Eli's control. She trusted him. Not only with her body—with her heart.

Once upon a time she'd fought for every inch of power and ground she could gain. And now? Now she found herself wanting to sacrifice it for the man she'd fallen for. It was probably why they called it "falling" in love. At some point, she'd let go—an out-of-control tumble in the hopes Eli would catch her.

"Come on, sleepyhead." She pushed off the bed and offered a hand to help him up. "You owe me dinner."

"It's in the oven. Lasagna."

"You made lasagna?"

He sat up and ruffled his shorter hair with one hand. With the clean-shaven jaw and the outfit, he looked so... *businessy*. It wasn't how she was used to seeing him and wasn't a bad look on him at all. He finally looked like a billionaire Crane brother.

He took her hand, but only to kiss it, then stood on his own. He pulled his pants over his legs and tucked his shirt into his waistband.

"I did not make lasagna," he said as he ran his hands into his hair again. "Benicia's Italiano made lasagna. "I heated it in the oven."

"Smart."

"Yeah, well, when you're a bachelor you learn a few tricks." He sent her a wink that beckoned another heart palpitation. Then another when he lowered his lips to hers for a sweet, brief kiss.

* * *

Dinner was *divine*, Benicia's vegetarian lasagna an amazing feat.

"Was that eggplant?" Isa asked after having savored the rich flavors of basil and garlic and robust tomato sauce.

"And portobello mushrooms," Eli answered.

"Why don't you eat meat?" She'd always wondered.

He swiped the napkin over his mouth and watched her for a second. Candlelight flickered on the angles of his face, making him look mysterious and gorgeous.

"Truth?" he asked.

"Always."

"It's not dinner conversation." He reached for the wine bottle and refilled her glass.

"I have a strong stomach."

"You have a strong everything," he said with a smirk of approval. She liked that he saw she was strong, especially since where he was concerned she felt like a kite in the wind.

"After witnessing the mess left behind when I lost my foot and part of my leg…" He shook his head and met her eyes. "Well, without being too morbid, let's say my appetite for flesh went away instantly."

"That makes sense." And had her questioning her own penchant for a juicy hamburger every so often.

"Yeah. Not manly, but there it is."

"Trust me, Eli." She rested her elbow on the table and fed him a line similar to the one he'd delivered on their first date, "No one would ever look at you and see you as 'not manly.'"

She felt like he was dancing around the real reason he'd invited her, and after silence settled between them, it must have become obvious to him, too. The next thing she knew, he brought it up.

"Now for the reason behind this celebration," he said.

Finally.

He refilled his wineglass and Isa lifted her own and took a long drink. Eyes on hers over the candlelight, his smile was at once nervous and sure. Her heart slammed relentlessly against her ribs. She was unable to keep hope from blooming in her chest and spreading down both arms.

"Corporal Benjamin Hough, Junior," he said.

Well, that threw her off. Totally not what she'd expected him to say.

"Known as Benji to me and to his wife, Michelle." Eli's smile faded. "He was the one who shoved me when Christopher dove on the grenade. He shouldn't have died from the blast, but a piece of metal shot out like a dart." Eli pointed at his temple. "Hit him here."

She winced, her skin zapping her like she'd been pricked with a thousand needles. That strong stomach of hers did a somersault.

"If that stray piece hadn't found his head, he would have been lying on the ground next to me missing a leg. Maybe two since he was closer." Eli spun the stem of his glass. "We probably could have bitched our way through rehab together."

His smile didn't last.

"I went to see his wife and met her baby—one she and Benji had planned on adopting."

"You did? That's amazing."

"It was. And it started me thinking about what I was doing with my life, whether I was living it to the fullest. I thought long and hard about what Benji would want. About what *I* would want for him if I was hoeing a row in heaven instead of down here on the pavement."

Eli met her gaze and Isa realized she hadn't taken a full breath in a while. His speech seemed to be leading to something big.

"I don't want to have any regrets," he said, his voice quiet. "I have been holed up alone since I returned. I've challenged everyone I've come in contact with. With the exception of my family, you were the only one who challenged me back. The only one who stayed."

Her breath left between her pursed lips as she mentally talked her blood pressure down to a reasonable level. This was it. He'd had a life epiphany and she was part of it. This was *huge*.

Massive.

Everything was about to change.

Reaching across the table, he took her hand in his. "Isabella Sawyer. You asked me once if I believed I caused people pain. The answer was yes. But you let me off the hook. You said you were fine with me retreating, but you aren't, are you? You want me to live up to the promises I make. You push me to be a better man."

Oh God, here it comes.

She couldn't speak or keep the tears away. She blinked rapidly, hoping the dim light hid her reaction.

Eli squeezed her hand.

Isa gave him a watery smile.

"I'm stepping in as COO at Crane Hotels," he said. "The official announcement is happening at the Royale London event."

With bated breath, she waited for more but he released her hand and sat back, raising his wineglass.

"Good thing you already RSVPd yes for me, right?" he asked with a casual smile.

That was...it? No *I love you, Isa, and can't live without you*? She tried to keep the disappointment at bay, but it crashed into her at warp speed.

"You were right to push me toward Crane Hotels," Eli continued, unaware she was completely devastated. "You were right to encourage me to get involved. I'm working hard to learn to go all in, and this gets me another step closer."

Going all in? Another step closer to *what*?

The rug had been pulled out from under her—no, not pulled. It was like the rug had zoomed hundreds of feet over the city with her on it.

"To you, Isa." He raised his glass in a toast. "Thank you for helping me find where I belong. I couldn't have done it without you."

She didn't raise her glass, too stunned to move. *That* was the big announcement? He didn't notice her shock. He tapped his glass against hers and drank.

"Isa? Are you all right?"

No, she wasn't all right. She'd expected him to confess his feelings for her, not to announce that he'd accepted the position of COO at Crane Hotels.

"Is this your way of being open?" she asked.

He frowned, his brows pulling over his nose.

"When I asked you to be open, I meant with your feelings, Eli, not your business plans."

His chin jerked on his neck. Good. He deserved to feel as stunned as she did.

"You know I don't make it a habit to mince words—or keep my opinions to myself." She dug for the courage to say what she needed to say. "The truth is..."

She swallowed past the lump in her throat—because she had no idea how he would react when she throttled him with this information.

"I'm falling for you, Eli," she blurted. "Hard. The kind of falling where you don't want to be saved."

He went completely still. Eerily quiet. She kept on anyway. What more did she have to lose?

"I want a future with you. I want to see who we can be when you're not holding back. I want to come home to you. Have dinner together and spend holidays together. I want to text and call and see you. I want you. *All of you.* Not just your body. And I definitely don't want you to withhold part of yourself from me."

Silence hovered in the room like an angry spirit. When Eli finally spoke, it was with a heartbreaking, but not surprising, response.

"I asked for time, Sable."

"I know you did. I thought tonight you were ready to tell me how you felt about me. Not that you were going back to work for Crane Hotels."

"I thought you'd be happy," he said, anger eating into his voice.

"I am! It's wonderful," she managed, fighting with her emotions as she tried to be fair. Going back to Crane Hotels was fantastic for Eli, for his whole family. But… "I thought there would be more."

"More," he growled.

"Yes. *More.*"

"There is no 'more.'" With his flared nostrils and flat line of a mouth, Eli looked more like the man who had run off ten of her best assistants. She'd uncovered warm, solid, happy Eli, but that version of him had retreated in an instant.

"Crystal complained I couldn't go all in," he said. "She always said I'm incapable of committing all the way. I *want* to. God knows I've been trying. I've been finishing my unfinished business with Refurbs, with Benji's widow, with Crane Hotels." As he talked, he rose from the table. "Goddamn, Sable, I thought you'd celebrate with me."

"I did! I am!" She stood, too, shaking now. Like a freak flood had hit, everything between them was eroding. "This has nothing to do with Crystal. This has to do with us. Are you incapable of giving yourself to me before everything else in your life is tied in a neat little bow?"

His eyes darkened. "What if I am?"

The words were a slap across the face.

"I asked for time because I need it," he said. "I thought we'd agreed."

"And I thought you'd see what we have." Tears burned her nose but she refused to give in to them. "I have to go."

"Isa, wait."

She heard a pinch of regret in his voice but it didn't matter. He couldn't give her more and she didn't want him to lie and say he was ready just because she was angry.

"Wait! Dammit, Sable."

"It's Isa," she corrected. "You're out of time, Eli."

She slammed the elevator door and rode down to the parking lot. As she marched to her car, a burst of guilt mingled with her own anger and suffocating, heart-rending sadness.

Leaving was the right thing to do.

She loved him and she deserved to be loved in return. She deserved more than half measures from him. She at least wanted the assurance that there was more to come.

She'd given him everything. It was Eli who had held back—or worse.

Maybe the reason he didn't profess his love for her was simple. Maybe he didn't love her.

Maybe he never would.

CHAPTER 19

Okay, he *thought* he'd work from home.

Until his normally comfortable warehouse began crushing him like a trash compactor. Mostly because Isa had left without a goodbye after their argument. The air at home was stale—heavy with the weight of her absence.

On Wednesday, he gave up his home office and stepped into the Crane with—God help him—a leather shoulder bag containing his laptop and other important files.

G.I. Executive.

Eli hadn't been to Reese's office downtown in...he didn't know how long. His older brother was made for this place. Reese had always had a penchant for business, for presentation. For professionalism. Eli preferred some grit in his life. Always had. The most grit inside of the Crane was...well, Eli, at present.

He'd dressed in a suit and tie, face shaved—a sight he hadn't yet grown used to seeing in the mirror.

At the top floor, he stepped out of the elevator and greeted Bobbie, Reese's long-time assistant. Everyone said the woman was a bear to deal with. He didn't get it.

"Good morning, Bobbie," he greeted.

She smiled, but the expression did little to erase the hard lines of her features. "Elijah. You look well."

"How is Derrick?" Her son was military, a few years older than Eli.

"Home for the holidays." Her smile broadened.

"That's good news."

"It's the best news. I'm sorry about your injury, but I'm glad you made it back alive. Derrick has lost friends."

"Comes with the job," Eli commented. The worst part of the job. At least as COO of Crane Hotels, the fallout wouldn't be as traumatic if he fucked up. "Is Reese in?"

"He is." She lifted the handset of her desk phone. "Reese, Elijah is here."

"Seriously?" Reese asked into the speaker.

"I'll send him in." Bobbie pressed a button and Reese's office doors swished open, automated or some fancy shit. Reese stood beyond them, stark surprise on his face.

"What's wrong?" Reese asked.

"See you, Bobbie." Eli touched the woman's shoulder as he passed by and watched as she blushed. Merina and Tag always said the older woman was a hardnose. He didn't see it.

The doors whooshed shut behind him as he stepped into his brother's office. "That's some real *Star Trek* shit."

"She loves you more than any of us," Reese commented, ignoring Eli's observation about the doors.

"Who? Bobbie?"

"I think she has a crush on you."

Eli grunted. "Whatever."

"Yeah. She's married anyway." His brow crinkled. "I think."

Reese's office was regal. A lush leather couch sat under bookshelves packed with spines, and a black block of a desk stood in front of windows that wrapped the room.

"So...?" Reese lifted an eyebrow at the bag slung over Eli's shoulder. "What's wrong?"

"Why does something have to be wrong for me to show up here?"

Reese offered a bland blink.

"As it turns out, I need a space to work that is not at my house," Eli said. He hadn't heard from Isa since she'd walked out. When he texted her on Monday to see if she was okay, she'd replied Tuesday with one word: *Fine*.

Sounded like a bad omen to him.

"Too quiet there." If Eli's options were to overexamine his relationship with Isa or blame the quiet, he'd go with blaming the quiet.

"I thought you liked quiet. You've spent the year trying to get Tag and me to leave you alone."

"I know. I don't understand it either." Eli had changed. And most of the reason for that change had long, dark hair, legs that wouldn't quit, and sincere whiskey-brown eyes that he could fall into and not care if he ever returned... if he could find a way to give her what she wanted without losing his mind in the process.

"Women are complicated," Eli grumbled.

"No kidding." Reese leaned on the corner of his desk and folded his arms. "What happened?"

"Isa and I had a fight." Apparently, they were talking about this. Eli plunked his bag on the guest chair.

Reese shrugged. "Couples fight. What was it about?"

Eli swallowed past his very dry throat, debating on how to collapse what had happened and fit it into a manageable nutshell. "She...expects more from me."

"Hmm."

Eli lifted his chin. His brother wore a smirk of amusement mixed with a dose of *Been there, done that*.

"What's that supposed to mean?"

"If I had to guess, I'd say Isabella Sawyer is under your skin."

All the way under. But admitting it involved him talking about a plethora of other feelings and emotions—none of which he was willing to go into.

"I came in to use an office." Eli jerked his head toward the doors behind him, itching to escape. "Do I have one? If not, I can take the conference room."

"Dad's office is empty. Desk, a stapler, and a wastebasket, but otherwise empty. We saved it for you." Reese smiled. "Just in case."

"I'll take it," Eli said with a nod. Anywhere was better than his warehouse, with his own voice bouncing off the walls.

* * *

At nine o'clock Friday night, Isa was at her desk in her darkened office. She'd given herself time over the week to process. Or, well, she'd given herself the week to get over Eli, but that wasn't happening. She had successfully shelved her tumultuous emotions and arrived at a pragmatic, practical conclusion.

She didn't like the conclusion at which she had arrived.

If Eli wasn't willing to go down Lover's Lane with her, then she'd have to put her heart into reverse and find another highway to travel.

She'd been so busy, her pile of mail had sat in her inbox unopened for the entire week. When she'd finally sorted through it a few minutes ago, she'd come across a crisp, heavy-stock envelope. In it, the invitation to the Royale London event hosted by the Cranes. The event where Eli would be announced as Crane Hotels's COO. As Reese had promised, the function would also serve as a fund-raiser for Refurbs for Vets.

All the top brass from the biggest companies would likely attend the event to make their presence and support known. Sable Concierge, having provided assistants for several of those businesses, would be expected to show as well. She couldn't avoid it for personal reasons.

Plus, being there to hobnob was just plain smart. Isa was a smart businesswoman, and the future of her company depended on her being smart enough to do what was needed rather than what she wanted. Which meant showing up at the event and schmoozing with a chunk of upper-class Chicago.

There was only one problem.

She couldn't do it.

She stroked the vellum over the fancy invitation with one finger, chin resting on her hand, elbow leaning on her desk. As much as she tried to convince herself she didn't need Eli in her future to *have* a future, she wasn't ready to face him again.

Elijah Crane had altered everything in her life. As much as she wanted them to be, a thriving business and shining success were no longer enough for her. She wanted Sable

Concierge to bloom, and she wanted to be in a loving, growing relationship. And not in a generic sense. She wanted a relationship with Eli.

How inconvenient.

Last week, he'd made it clear she was not his priority. He'd made it clearer *this* week when the only contact she'd received from him was a text message. As much as she wanted to vilify him, she couldn't. She understood why she wasn't at the top of his priority list. He had gone back to Crane Hotels and taken on a new role. COO would take most of his time. He'd have to find a new routine, learn the ropes, fall down and pick himself back up.

If she had been navigating a relationship while building her business, one or the other would've collapsed under the weight of long days and longer nights. There simply wasn't enough time to succeed professionally and personally in the beginning.

She set the invitation aside and let out a sigh. This was the hard part. She knew what she had to do and it was the last thing in the world she wanted to do. She'd spent the last week wishing she were the kind of person who could be with Eli and keep her feelings at bay until he was ready.

She wasn't willing to wait. The waiting could last a few weeks—a few months. A few *years*. Being in love alone wasn't an option. When she'd confessed how she felt about him, and he didn't concur, a piece of her shrank. If things continued on that same path, how much longer until she withered away completely?

With Josh, she'd shrunk herself so small that by the time they split, she felt microscopic. She couldn't do that again. She was responsible for a team of people, for running a business that helped very important people. She had to put herself first, which had always been one of her biggest challenges. In this case, that meant she needed to put her needs before Eli's.

Chloe had a date tonight, so she'd already gone home. Isa assured her she would be safe walking from the front door to her apartment. She doubted the mugger would be back for seconds, and if she was by herself, she had to learn how to fend for herself.

She couldn't expect Eli to ride in on his white horse again.

Keys in hand, she pulled her purse over her shoulder and went to the front door. Not for the first time, she considered creating an entrance from the office space to the upstairs apartment. Maybe that was something she would do this year. She had bought a small container of mace to hang from her keychain, so as soon as she had the door locked and was outside, she held it at the ready.

At the foot of her stairs leading to her apartment, headlights shined across the parking lot, causing her to jolt with panic. But the panic was short-lived. The car belonged to her former assistant-slash-new manager.

Chloe stepped out of a grass-green smart car, her auburn curls bouncing. The rest of her, however, wasn't bouncing.

"That was a fast date," Isa said.

"I was stood up." Chloe shrugged, arms out to her sides before dropping them next to her. "My new dress is going to waste. Want to go to Posh for a martini?"

Isa smiled. "Chloe Andrews. Are you asking me out?"

"If you'll have me." She swept an arm toward her car. "Your fuel-efficient, environmentally savvy chariot awaits."

Isa couldn't refuse that offer. Especially after the week she'd had.

Twenty minutes later, Isa and Chloe sat in Posh, a martini bar with a clublike setting.

"I now understand why they have the 'it's complicated' description online for relationships." Isa plucked the cherry out of her Manhattan and pulled the fruit off the stem with her teeth. "You think you know what you're doing," she said as she chewed, "but then sex happens and you have no idea what you're doing."

Chloe nodded sagely and sipped her martini, her reddish hair reflecting the pink bar lights. A DJ hovered from a platform overhead, across from him a shelflike overhang with furniture and a table, a private area for people who'd rather not smash in with the crowd.

Smashing in with the crowd suited Isa just fine.

"Sorry about your date," Isa said to her friend.

"Eh." Chloe shrugged. "Being stood up is better than following a relationship to the bitter end, I guess."

Isa considered that.

Chloe winced. "I didn't mean to imply things were over between you and Eli."

But it felt like things were over, which meant they probably were. Isa hadn't reopened the conversation and neither had Eli.

"It's not like you broke up," Chloe added.

"It's not like we were ever official," Isa amended.

"At least you had a guy."

"You don't want one. Trust me. " Isa lifted her stemmed glass. "I'm the moron who fell in love with him. I have no one to blame but myself."

Chloe patted Isa's hand with sympathy, then sipped her

own cocktail. Isa relinquished her glass to dig the Royale London invitation from her purse. She slid it across the bar to Chloe, who lifted the expensive paper and regarded Isa with confusion.

"What's this?"

"I need you to go on behalf of Sable Concierge." It hurt her heart to say the words. To admit she wasn't going to go to the event herself. Whatever she and Eli had really was over.

"Isa." Chloe shook her head and offered the invitation.

"Please, Chloe." Isa pushed the invitation back into Chloe's hand. "There will be lots of executives from other companies there. Take a date. Take a coworker. Canvas the hotel for potential future clients. One of us should. I can't go. I can't face him."

Partially because she was humiliated and partially because she was heartbroken. She'd been trying to be strong for a week, but right now, miserable and hovering over her martini glass, there was no sense in prolonging the inevitable. Eli had shut her out the moment she'd walked away from him.

Yet, she couldn't regret it. Walking away was, ironically, her way of standing up for herself. It still hurt, though.

"Ladies," a male voice oozed from over her shoulder. Isa turned around to see a man wearing a cowboy hat—a legit cowboy hat. He leaned an elbow on the bar. "Can I buy you two cowgirls a drink?"

"Eww." That came from Chloe.

Isa burst into a fit of liquor-fueled laughter as the man's smile vanished.

"Bitches," he spat, then turned to go find his next prey.

When Isa turned to face her friend, Chloe was giggling.

"I can't even." Chloe swiped tears from her lashes. "I think I'll stay single for a while longer."

"Like until the apocalypse," Isa suggested. "Then if you pair up with someone it will be to save the planet, not get a free drink."

Their laughter ebbed at the same time and Chloe gave Isa a decisive nod. "I'll go to the Crane event for you."

"Yeah?" Isa never knew she could feel relief and regret at the same time. "Thank you." She planned on donating to Refurbs for Vets. Regardless of what she and Eli had been through, the charity was worthy.

"Anything for you. To Sable Concierge." Chloe lifted her drink and Isa tapped the glass with hers and sipped.

Knowing her friend had her back didn't staunch the disappointment settling in her gut. She'd fought for independence a long time ago, but this was the first time she'd felt less than empowered.

Stupid love.

Stupid heart.

* * *

"The Crane brothers, back together." Tag passed a red Solo Cup to Eli and one to Reese and kept one for himself.

Reese took a sniff at the inch of liquid in the bottom. "Tequila?"

"Yeah."

"Not very sophisticated. I like it," Eli said, tapping his brothers' cups with his own before throwing back the shot. Flames lit his throat and he coughed.

"You are out of practice, my friend," Tag said, slapping Eli's back.

This Friday dinner was different from the rest. Eli, Tag, and Reese had worked late, so they came straight from the office. Merina and Rachel had met up for happy hour without them—something called "GNO," whatever the hell that was. The regularly scheduled dinner was on, just later than usual. Even their father and Rhona were planning to attend.

Which left Eli the odd man out. Again.

Fantastic.

"Where is your girl tonight, Eli?" Tag asked.

"Yeah, how are things going with Isabella?" That came from Reese. "You never shared what became of your argument last week."

"First fights suuuck," Tag hissed through his teeth.

No, Eli hadn't shared. Sharing meant admitting he didn't know what the hell he was doing. No sense in being humiliated as well as devastated. His heart and home felt empty. His head was fuzzy. His arms were lonely without Isa in them.

Here he'd thought he was a sorry sack of shit when he'd been discharged. His and Isa's breakup was in the running for first place.

He didn't know if it was the tequila or the rare opportunity to have time alone with his brothers, but one of the two made him say, "She loves me."

There was a distinct pause.

"Like...she can't resist you?" Tag asked. "Or like she literally loves you and you don't know what the fuck to do about it?"

Eli gave him a wry glance. "The last one."

Tag rested both his elbows on the countertop and raised his eyebrows. *Waiting.* Reese, arms folded over his chest, head tilted to the side, waited too.

"Change isn't easy for me," Eli grumbled.

"This comes as a shock to no one," Reese said.

"I have a track record at not giving women what they want—what they really want."

Tag shook his head. "Change isn't easy for any of us, E."

"What is it that Isa really wants?" Reese asked.

I want a future with you. I want to see who we can be when you're not holding back.

"More than I can give her," Eli said. "She needs someone ready. I'm not ready."

Reese mumbled something that sounded like, *Your funeral.*

"You think I was ready to go after Rachel?" Tag asked with an incredulous chuckle. "Lucas's wife had to practically brain me over the head to get me to realize I was being stubborn. I could've lost her altogether." His face contorted as if the possibility made him physically ill. "Don't be that stubborn, E."

"Gwyneth was the one who flushed me out of my hotel suite," Reese put in. "Cranes have a knack for head-up-the-ass mentality."

"Look, I didn't mean for this to turn into an intervention." Eli started to leave the kitchen but then Reese spoke and stopped Eli in his tracks.

"It's not an intervention. If you're not ready, you're not ready. She deserves more than you on the fence. Even if going to her would pull her back in for a short while. She was honest with you, and I assume you were honest back."

"That was the problem," Eli muttered.

"Then maybe it was never meant to be." Reese held Eli's glare, interrupting with a patient blink.

Eli hated when Reese was right. Problem was, he was right a lot. About a lot of things. There was a reason he'd always looked up to his older brother. And now that Eli had manned up in more than just a business sense, it was harder to dismiss Reese or what he knew about life...and love.

"By the way, I proposed to Rachel last night."

Reese and Eli snapped their heads in Tag's direction. Tag folded his hands where he leaned on the counter and smiled.

"No shit?" Reese asked. Then a smile graced his mouth. "Congratulations."

"Sorry, E. Didn't mean to be insensitive. She'll be here any minute wearing a rock the size of your car, so I thought it was better you know before you saw it."

"How'd you do it?" Reese asked.

"Brought back a jar of sand from Maui, from the site of the new Crane hotel. She said the jar wasn't 'pretty enough'"—he mimed air quotes—"to preserve my first new build. We picked out a glass container at an antique shop after dinner one night, and when we arrived home, she insisted in pouring the sand into the new container, and"—he spread his hands—"out came the ring."

Tag's grin widened. A man in love. A man who knew how to love. Eli envied his younger brother more than ever before.

"Damn." Reese frowned. "That was better than my first proposal."

"Yeah, but Merina remarried you, so the second one must have been good."

Reese smiled, his eyes going to one side in thought. "It was."

"Congratulations, Tag," Eli said, meaning it. But the familiar frustration coated him at his brothers' happiness. Frustration he had no right to blame on them. Eli had gotten himself into this mess. He shoved his feelings of inadequacy aside and yanked open a drawer in the kitchen, coming out with a deck of cards. "Can we stop clucking like hens and play poker now?"

"Yes. I'll gladly take your money," Tag said, taking the change of topic in stride.

"You're the worst gambler I know," Reese said.

"Bet you twenty bucks I'm not." Tag grabbed the bottle of tequila and they moved to the table and sat.

"See?" Reese said to Eli, shooting a thumb over his shoulder at Tag.

"Five card draw," Eli announced, shuffling. "Nothing wild."

On cue, Tag drummed the table with his hands and said, "Except for me."

CHAPTER 20

Eli sat, hand wrapped around a bottle of beer. His mood hadn't improved after losing a few hundred bucks to Reese playing cards, followed by the arrival of his brothers' significant others.

"Eli's either doing a complicated mathematical equation," Merina said, "or he has regressed to his formerly grouchy state like when we first started having these dinners."

"He was fine earlier," Tag said. "Maybe the tequila wore off."

Eli flipped Tag off.

Alex let out a gruff laugh. "He seems fine to me."

His family members ringed the table—all of them. Dad and Rhona. Tag sat next to Rachel, who was wearing an incredibly large, sparkling diamond ring Rhona had cooed over for an exhaustingly long time. Reese sat at the table, Merina at his left elbow. Eli sat a seat away from

Reese—beside the seat that was empty. The significance wasn't lost on him.

He was having an unpleasant flashback. Back to one of the earlier dinners where he was thinking about how annoyingly paired off they were. He went around the table again starting with Tag. *Engaged.* Reese. *Married.* His eyes narrowed when he reached his father.

"What's the deal with you two, anyway?" he barked.

Rhona's eyes went wide, but Alex's narrowed. "What do you mean, son?"

"I mean you've been working together for how long now? And you hang out more often than people who work together. You show up here to dinner together; you have your arm around her right now. What are you doing? Are you getting married? Are you living together? I feel like we should know."

Could have heard a pin drop. He'd never thought of that phrase as having any literal meaning until this very moment.

Alex wrapped his hand around Rhona's. They exchanged glances.

"I suppose I've been too careful about this," Alex said. "When you boys lost your mother..." His lips pressed together before he corrected himself. "When *we all* lost your mother, I swore I would never love another woman. I set my sights on work, on raising you three, and on finding pleasure in business rather than in someone of the opposite sex." Alex cleared his throat and Rhona squeezed his hand in support. Eli thought back to the times Isa had touched him. In support. With love. It spiked his misery and sank him lower in his chair.

"I've been too careful," Alex repeated. "I gave you boys

a good example of how to lead." He tipped his chin at Reese. "Of how to grab hold of life and let nothing hold you back." He nodded at Tag. "Of serving your country and never letting anything stand in your way." He gave Eli a warm smile. "What I haven't given you is a good example of a man who gives his heart. Rhona pointed out the other day—"

"Respectfully," she interjected.

"Always respectfully," Alex said to her, his smile warming. "She mentioned that you boys were hurtling your own challenges when it came to love. And how it makes sense because we all lost someone we loved very much. The loss of your mother makes it more frightening to put ourselves on the line, our hearts on the line. Knowing that love could be snatched from you at any moment is a terrifying reality. For years, I closed myself off from the possibility of love. I was protecting my family—or so I thought. In reality, I believe I was protecting myself. But once you find the woman who challenges you, the one who is willing to stick around even though you're a caveman..."

Marina and Rachel cracked smiles. Rhona laughed.

"That's the one you trust with your heart," Alex said. "Even if it means getting hurt again. Even if it means the future is devastating. Because she's worth it. Any heartache you are trying to save yourself from pales in comparison to the love of a woman who gives you her entire self."

No one said a word. Wisdom twinkled in Alex's eyes, his gaze zeroed in on Eli. Reese, predictably, was the first to break the silence.

"It's true."

Six pairs of stunned eyes snapped to the oldest Crane brother.

Reese wrapped his arm around Marina. "Trying to prevent disaster is no way to live life."

"Hear, hear," Tag said, raising his beer.

"So?" Rachel leaned closer to Alex, her smile popping her dimples. "Are you two getting married?"

"I don't know. I haven't had the courage to ask her yet. I'd hate to steal your thunder." Alex thumbed Rachel's chin.

"There's enough thunder for all of us, don't you think?" Rachel asked.

After a brief pause, Alex nodded. "You're right." He turned to Rhona, who wore a slightly dazed but excited expression. "What do you say? Would you like to marry a sixtysomething, retired hotel magnate with three grown boys and possibly grandkids on the way?"

"Alex." Rhona gave him a watery smile. "Do you even have to ask?"

Both hands on his face, she stroked his goatee, then pulled his mouth to hers. The table erupted in cheers, and Eli found himself clapping, a reluctant smile on his own face.

Everything his father had said Eli knew in his gut, and he didn't take it for granted when the man who had been his mentor his entire life spelled it out. Nothing solidified Eli's fucking up more than this moment right now.

"So, it's just me," Eli called over the cheers and good wishes. A quick glance around the table confirmed smiles falling left and right. "My timing sucks for that epiphany. I'm sorry. I just wanted to say you're all smarter than I am."

He pushed away from the table, the chair scraping from rug to floor. "A hell of a lot smarter."

Instead of heading for his bedroom, he walked to the metal set of stairs leading to the loft. The stairs he'd avoided climbing since he came home. Because there was no sense in trying to reclaim who he once was. That was bullshit—like nearly every other belief he'd tried to hang on to since he was discharged. He took each step, rickety metal whining, bracing his upper arms on the railing as he hauled himself up.

When he reached the top, out of breath and sweating a little, he went to the door he hadn't opened since he'd been back home. Time to merge the old him with the new one. God knew they could learn a thing or two from each other.

He flipped the dead bolt and pushed the bar on the door, exiting to the roof. Outside, he shook the leaves off a rusted lawn chair and plopped onto the seat. The air was freezing up here. He crossed his arms tightly as the breeze cooled the damp sweat on his body. Wind blew his hair and chilled his bare face, having a sobering effect.

The city lights were bright, interspersed with porch lights from houses and the glowing sign in front of the cathedral across the street. Somewhere in the city, Isa was without him and doing better for it. That's what he'd tried to make himself believe each day when he'd scrolled back through their texts in his phone. There weren't many. But it hurt to remember how for one fragile moment, he'd had her in the palm of his hand...

Then crushed her without meaning to.

Predictably, the door opened behind him, then shut. He'd expected one of his well-meaning family members to fetch him. The question was, who had drawn the short straw? Tag? Reese? One of the girls?

"You've turned brooding into an art."

Dad.

Of course.

"We each have our talents," Eli said.

"Being a horse's ass seems to be yours."

Eli frowned over his shoulder. His father, weathered skin and white hair, goatee and checkered shirt tucked into dark jeans, looked younger than his sixtysomething years. He was a virile, capable man—an amazing single father. The best Eli could have asked for. And now he was engaged to be married. Because he wasn't a massive coward.

"Why'd you retire, anyway?" Eli asked as Alex located another dilapidated lawn chair that creaked in protest when he opened it and sat down. "This is your fault. If you'd have stayed CEO, Reese would still be COO, and I would be—"

"You'd be what?" Alex interrupted. "You'd be sitting in your warehouse alone and brooding? You never would have met Isabella Sawyer? Yes, your brothers told me about her." A breeze feathered the hair that fell over his forehead. "You're a man who's lost a lot, Eli. Your friends, your leg, your career as a Marine."

Eli gritted his teeth, feeling the pain of those losses like a series of punches to the stomach.

"Your mom," Alex added.

That one was more like a punch to the kidney.

"Like you said, we all lost her," Eli said.

"Yes, but you were the one who held on longer than you should have."

"You're one to talk." Anger vibrated down Eli's arms.

"You worked and kept your head down for years. Hell, you didn't even date. If it hadn't been for Rhona working with you, you may never have..."

Eli quieted. His father's story lined up pretty damn closely with his own.

"Isabella busted through your defenses because she was there every day," Alex stated. "She wiggled her way into your arms and then into your heart."

She had.

"You're the one keeping yourself from her. Why?"

"She loves me," Eli said, the pain of that admission worse than anything else. It was so *fresh*. The wound of losing her hadn't covered with scar tissue—not yet. The ache for her was so acute, Eli wondered if he'd ever heal. Like his unchangeable past—losing friends and his mom and his leg and his career as a Marine—he'd lost Isa, too. "She loved me last Friday, anyway."

Eli rubbed his palm with his thumb, grounding himself to stop the pain in his heart.

Didn't work.

Alex leaned back in his chair, his eyes turning skyward. "I'm sure that's not changed. She's been waiting for you to step up, I imagine."

"I can't give her what she wants. How can I know what the future will bring, Dad? How can I know I won't wake up one day completely different? What if I want to move to Montana to start raising cattle? Where would that leave her?"

"Montana?" His father let out a rough laugh. "Since when are you considering the life of a rancher?"

"I used to know who I was." Eli clasped hands, watching the crunchy leaves scatter over his rooftop. "I was a meat-eating Marine with a live-in girlfriend, buddies I loved like brothers, and both of my legs." He let out a humorless laugh. "I lost it all."

"You're rebuilding it all." His father's blue eyes held wisdom and years and years of pain—pain he'd hurdled.

"How'd you do it? How'd you lose Mom and not curl up and die with her?" Eli had never asked him that question. But he'd always wondered. He used to think it was his father's strength that saved him, but no matter how strong Eli was, he still feared what might go wrong next.

"Because of you. And Tag. And Reese. Without you, I'd have climbed into a bottle of scotch and never come out. Or maybe I would be living on Key West, picking up aluminum cans and muttering to myself. You boys gave me a reason to go on. Family does that. *Women* do that." He raised both eyebrows. "Why do you think I insisted on coming to these dinners? I'm not willing to let you become a loner, Eli. No good lies down that desolate path."

His father was right. They'd gradually pried Eli out of the muck.

"You're retreating. A good soldier knows when he's lost the battle," Alex said. "But, son, your compass is showing false north. You haven't lost. You haven't even tried."

Eli lost his temper, standing and kicking over his lawn chair. "You don't know anything!" He turned for the door, steam from his anger propelling him forward. He wasn't sure where he was going, just that he was going.

"Don't run this time," came his father's calm voice from behind him.

Eli stared at the handle of the metal door leading to his upstairs loft, wanting more than anything to go through it and leave his father's words behind. In the end, he couldn't. Like Reese, Alex was right most of the time, too.

He heard the scrape of the chair and the scuff of his father's leather shoes. A second after that, his father's broad hand landed on his shoulder. "Life doesn't have to be this hard, Eli. You're home now. You're no longer required to fight for a living. So stop fighting, yeah?"

Eli blinked over very scratchy, heated eyes.

"My tough guy. You always were my little soldier." Alex's raspy chuckle ended with pulling Eli into his arms, holding the back of his head while Eli tried to stop the hot tears from burning twin trails down his cheeks.

He held on to his dad, the words his father spoke sinking in. Maybe he could stop fighting—maybe he could let go of the past and the grief that haunted him like ghosts from *A Christmas Carol*.

After a few moments, Alex patted Eli's back, then held him at arm's length. Hands on his cheeks, Alex gave him a pat. "There now. Go get your girl. If you want her. Do you want her?"

Fuck yeah, Eli wanted her. But he also honored her right to leave—her right to walk away when he didn't give her enough.

"She asked for space and I respect that."

His old man's eyes narrowed briefly. "Women are delicate creatures, aren't they?"

Eli pressed his lips together. Isa was both delicate and strong.

"Don't wait too long, yeah?" Alex pulled open the door and gestured for Eli to go in ahead of him.

"Yeah." One trial at a time.

Eli swiped his eyes and sniffed before going in. When he reached the staircase, he began his descent.

CHAPTER 21

For the entire next week, Isa's MO had been work, followed by more work.

Come very early Saturday morning, Isa walked downstairs to Sable Concierge in tall brown boots, a pair of skinny jeans, and a shirt with a long, cream-colored cardigan over the top. She'd left her hair down and put her makeup on, but the reflection in the mirror didn't show her to be the confident, professional woman her clothing should portray.

The hollows beneath her eyes were from lack of sleep and the hole in her heart was because she'd completed a tumultuous first run at a relationship. Eli Crane. What a disastrous choice.

Three hours later, she felt more human than before. At her desk, fingers on her keyboard, it was impossible to not be surrounded by purpose. By blessings. By strength. She'd started this business from nothing, and without the support of her family. She'd built a business from scratch, then nurtured it into being.

A series of knocks came at the glass front door. Isa looked up to find a courier holding a package. She hopped up and jogged to the door, accepting the box before shutting the door again.

She plunked the box onto the nearest flat surface—Chloe's former desk—and grabbed a pair of scissors from the pen cup. Carefully, she sliced the tape as she read the return address.

The Crane Hotel.

Her mind raced to puzzle what might be hiding behind the cardboard. Surely not a delivery from Reese? And surely nothing from Eli.

But when she opened the box, she found a handwritten note on top of the white tissue paper—from Eli.

It read:

Sable,

One thong, one shirt, one red dress. I promised to replace all three while we were together. You deserve this and more.

Eli.

This and more? What was that supposed to mean? She peeled back the paper to reveal the items promised. A black pair of lace thong panties, which made her remember the day in his office when he'd taken a pair of scissors from his lap drawer and joked, *"In case of emergency."*

One red dress—like the one he'd popped the threads on

in his hurry to get her out of it the night after Dooley's bar. The night he'd made love to her against the wall and uttered a request that echoed in her brain: *"Fuck me."*

A cream silk shirt like the one he'd sliced the buttons from before their first kiss, when she made him a promise she'd meant at the time: *"Do it. I won't run."*

But she had run, hadn't she? She'd run and Eli hadn't chased her this time.

Reverently, she stroked the fabric of the shirt, her eyes filling. The door opened, this time letting in Chloe, her auburn curls blowing.

"It's freezing out there." Chloe fluffed her hair, then frowned as she caught sight of Isa. "Oh no, what's wrong?"

Chloe didn't wait for an answer, rushing over to survey the random clothing now spread on her former desk.

"Eli?" she asked after reading the note. "Sent you a random assortment of designer clothes?"

"They're not random." That, she was sure of. What she wasn't sure of was whether this was Eli's way of saying things were over for good between them or something else entirely...

Chloe flipped over the white cardstock. Blank.

"I asked him to give me time and he's giving it to me." Knees weakening, Isa sat in the desk chair. "He asked me for time, but I didn't give it to him. I thought because I was in love with him he had to commit right away." She shook her head, remembering the dinner and how excited he was about the COO position. How she'd selfishly turned a spotlight on what he hadn't given her. "I behaved like a child. No. Worse. I behaved like Josh."

The epiphany hit her so hard it hurt. Josh had once

delivered an ultimatum. Either Isa bend to his will or he'd find someone who would. It wasn't exactly the way things had gone down with Eli, but her terms were now or never.

"Oh, Chloe." Isa put her head in her hands. "I screwed up."

"Isa." Chloe put a palm on Isa's back and rubbed. "Don't beat yourself up. And don't compare yourself to that douchebag ex of yours, okay?"

Isa gave her friend a weak smile. "I made a big mistake."

"So what? People make mistakes. You screwed up."

Isa recalled saying something similar to Eli the day after she was attacked.

"Are you afraid you'll screw up? We all screw up."

"Yeah." Isa blinked and Chloe came back into focus. "We all screw up."

"Which reminds me…" Chloe's supportive smile faded. "I came in because I have bad news." She grimaced and told Isa the rest. "My dad fell off a ladder and broke his leg and he's driving my mom up a wall. I promised to fly to Maryland and help her out. I figured I can go to the Crane event tonight, but then I'll have to be out for a week or so. Is that okay? I'll totally use my vacation time to do it."

"No." Isa shook her head. "No, it's not okay."

"It's not?" Chloe's frown deepened as a smile spread Isa's lips.

"I don't mean you going to Maryland—yes, go. Be with your family. But you can leave tonight if you want to, because I'm going to the Crane event myself."

Eli had reached out, but he still believed she deserved better than him. Isa knew because she knew *him*. He was avoiding her to avoid his heart breaking. The same way he'd avoided Benji's widow.

Isa had delivered the felling blow at Eli's house and until just now, she was sure she'd been right.

"Going is the right thing to do," Isa said. She felt a stab of doubt as she surveyed the clothing on the desk in front of her. "Unless this was his way of evening the scales. Of returning what he took from me."

Chloe's mouth tightened in consideration.

"Except it's not all here," Isa said with a soft laugh.

"No?" Chloe lifted the tissue paper in the box but there was nothing beneath it. "What's missing?"

"I'm afraid Eli still has my heart."

Chloe, arms full of tissue paper, grinned.

"I'm not good at ducking out of my own life."

"I love when you get into Isa-kick-butt mode." Chloe tossed aside the paper and rubbed her palms together. "Give me something to do. What can I help with? Can I help you shop for shoes for tonight? Do you need jewelry? A dress?"

"Actually..." Isa unfolded the gorgeous, bright red dress. The size was spot-on, the neck high and the back cut low. Either Eli knew her style or had help from someone who did. Isa held the dress to her body and smiled at Chloe. "I already have a dress."

* * *

Alex Crane earned a laugh when he made his parting remarks at the fancy-schmancy Royale London dinner. Eli's turn to speak was coming up soon. He was COO now, and the company needed a face, a presence, to go with the name. He'd finally become the man Crane Hotels needed him to be.

Reese, in the emcee position, greeted the mixed crowd again—the board of directors for Crane Holdings were here, and so were several CEOs from other companies. During cocktails at the opening of the evening, Eli had shaken hands with more people than he could remember.

Now he sat at a table off the corner of the stage, in the shadows, feeling a lot like he did before he'd been COO: Alone. With a fire in the hearth and no company but the ticking clock.

Except he'd changed since then. He had...and he hadn't. After his dad talked to him on the rooftop, Eli had nearly bolted out the door to run straight to Isa. Later that next day, he'd nearly called her. And every day thereafter, he'd thought of sending a text message.

It'd all resulted in enough inaction to make a man of action sick. His last-minute idea to ship Isa the items he'd ruined while they were together had come in barely enough time to hire a courier to have it delivered. He'd watched his phone for a call or a text since early this morning. The only one he'd received was one from the courier saying he'd delivered it to a woman with long, dark hair at Sable Concierge.

His assumption was that his gift wasn't well received. He'd known sending it was a risk; he just hadn't anticipated how much it would hurt when she rejected him again.

"Reese is a natural up there. It's disgusting," Tag said, carrying a pair of shot glasses in one hand. He sat at the table next to Eli. Tag never was one for the stage, which blew Eli's mind since the lastborn Crane was a natural showman. Tag shoved a shot glass in front of Eli. "Thought you could use some fortifying before you go up next."

"I'm fine," Eli bit out. Reese was yammering on about the year so far. *Blah blah blah.*

"What's up your ass?" Tag asked under his breath, leaning back in the chair he was dwarfing.

"Currently? Every one of my family members." Eli felt his petulant frown as he recalled what his father had said last week. The reason they'd converged for biweekly dinners was because no one wanted Eli to be alone. Eli was pissed—mostly at himself—but didn't want to disappoint Tag's expectations of Eli being both grouchy and brooding.

"Any one family member in particular?"

"Merina," he grumbled. She'd been the one who'd helped him shop for Isa's clothes. He hadn't told her the details about why he was replacing those specific items, only that he'd promised Isa he would.

When Merina had pushed, he'd brought up the doorknob she and Reese were always joking about and she shut up instantly. Eli didn't want to know the story behind how that particular piece of hardware was intertwined with their love story.

Merina had also encouraged him to deliver the clothes himself. He hadn't, of course. Somehow, with her female superpowers, she'd known. When he'd arrived tonight, Merina stepped directly in his path and asked how Isa was doing. When he'd replied he didn't know, she'd accused him of being too careful. She wasn't wrong, which made him angry.

"Long story short? Merina offered to help me pick out a gift for Isa, only I had it delivered instead of taking it myself. Merina told me I was too careful."

Tag's face pinched. "You didn't take it yourself?"

Eli's next breath sounded more like a growl. "Careful is an insult. She may as well call me a wimp."

"Well. You are." Tag smiled and raised his shot to his lips, knowing that Eli couldn't punch him in the arm for the quip. They may be in the shadows, but the surrounding tables were packed with guests.

A woman peered over her shoulder at them now. Eli sent her a curt smile before turning his attention back to his brother. "I stepped in it with Isa."

"I know that, too."

Eli sighed. "Do you think it's simpler than we make it?"

Tag nodded. "I do. Whatever we're nervous about losing is found in what we have been avoiding."

"Deep," Eli said, but Tag nailed it. Eli had attempted to avoid the pain of losing Isa and then lost her anyway.

"Catch twenty-two," Tag murmured.

"I never went to her, and I should have. I held back." God, that phrase fucking *haunted* him.

"Why didn't you go to her, E? Did you decide she wasn't worth it?"

"No. Fuck no." He scrubbed his forehead, wanting to explain but not knowing how. Tag continued waiting, so Eli gave it a try. "It's like...my head is muddy whenever I try and think about what she means to me. When she's gone, my arms and heart are empty—cavernous. Whenever she was around, my breathing went shallow and my chest caved in."

"I know the feeling." Tag smirked.

"I wanted to be certain—completely certain—about how I felt about her before I made promises. I don't want her to have less than she deserves." Eli dropped his hands in his lap and blew out a frustrated breath.

"You're in love," Tag stated with such certainty that Eli's heart skipped a beat, then kicked his chest with twice the force.

"I don't know what love is," Eli said numbly.

Tag let out one of his heartier laughs. "What you described is *exactly* what love is, E." He shook his head. "The not knowing, the uncertainty. The nausea. That feeling of fullness and lightness at the same time."

"So you're saying it's a lot like public speaking," Eli quipped.

Tag looked nauseous at the mention of it. "Kind of."

"...my brother, Eli Crane," Reese introduced, and everyone in the room began clapping.

"Well, that's inconvenient," Eli said, standing and buttoning his tuxedo jacket.

"You're up." Tag slapped him on the back. "Give your acceptance speech and try not to cry."

* * *

After a brief speech, Eli stood with his brothers and father sipping scotch. He'd thanked his family and his country and assured everyone he had big plans for running operations at Crane Hotels. When he told the crowd to hang on because they *ain't seen nothin' yet,* everyone erupted in whistles and applause.

Once they quieted down, he thanked Christopher and Benji, too, and asked everyone in attendance to consider donating to Refurbs for Vets. Then he stepped down, accepted a glass of scotch from his father, and mingled with the fray.

Eli didn't love scotch, but now that he was a corporate man in charge, it felt right to hold a drink poured into a sturdy rocks glass.

"It isn't so bad, is it?" his father asked with a smug

smile beneath his mustache. His dad's goatee reminded Eli of his own beard. He'd missed it and started growing it back. Eli smoothed his facial hair now, taking in his father's bright red tie. The color reminded him of the dress he'd sent to Isa. He wondered if she'd bothered opening the box.

He missed her so damned much.

"Elijah Crane." A short, round man with graying hair and a wide smile approached with a hand extended. "Dave Dillon. I was talking with your contractor, Zach." He shot a thumb over his shoulder at the tall, blond man walking their way. "My company designs kitchens and we'd love to get involved with Refurbs for Vets. Can we talk more? I liked everything you said about rehabilitation not stopping in the hospital. About how real contribution was meaningful contribution."

"Sounds more regal coming from you." Eli shook the older man's hand.

"Thank you for your service," Dave said, and then turned to Alex. "And yours, sir. I hear you are a Marine as well."

"I am that." Alex put a hand on the man's shoulder. "I'm curious to hear more about your company. Have a drink with me?"

"Dave has deep pockets," Zach muttered against the mouth of his beer bottle as Alex Crane walked the other man to the bar.

"Dad will find the bottom," Eli told him.

Zach was dressed in black pants, the collar of his white button-down shirt open. No tie for him.

"Appreciate the intro," Eli told him. "We'll take all the contributions we can get."

"How about another?" Reese asked. At first Eli thought

Reese was offering him a refill on his empty scotch, but then he looked up to find a beautiful blonde in a white dress, her bright blue eyes shrewd and assessing. "Penelope Brand, my brother, Eli."

"Nice to meet you, Mr. Crane." She extended her hand and when he shook it, her grip was a hell of a lot stronger than Eli had expected.

"Ms. Brand is the PR specialist I used a few years back when I was vying for CEO," Reese said. "Now that you've accepted the limelight, she's a great ally to have. If you or any of your staff at Refurbs need public spin, Penelope is your woman."

"Zachary Ferguson," came a syrupy introduction.

Eli watched as Zach put on his I'm-a-harmless-country-boy act. Penelope's eyes narrowed, her jaw set.

"Nice to meet you, Mr. Ferguson. You stay out of trouble so that Mr. Crane doesn't have to call me in, okay?" Her smile was as sharp as her assessment of Zach.

"Yeah, that'd be awful," Zach said, his dimpled smile not budging.

"Excuse me for a moment." Eli couldn't take another second of other people flirting around him. He dropped his empty glass onto a tray, strolling toward the bar as he checked out the room. Mostly employees of Crane Hotels were in attendance, though they'd taken their drinks and coffee to the tables, one by one loosening their ties and kicking back to shoot the shit about work.

"What can I get you, sir?" the bartender asked.

Eli opened his mouth to say scotch, but a smoky, sensual female voice ordered for him.

"Two Stella Artois. Bottles."

He turned to find Isa behind him, dressed in a body-hugging, thigh-baring, short red dress. The very dress Merina had promised would be "perfect for her." Merina was right.

As gorgeous as Isa was with her hair in waves around her shoulders and her gold jewelry understated and winking in the lighting, it was her presence that floored Eli the most.

"Isa." His voice was a dry croak. "You're here."

"Hey, soldier. You didn't think I'd let your big night pass by without coming to congratulate you, did you?" Her smile shook for a second, giving him a spike of hope that she was here for more than business reasons.

"Nice dress." He took a step closer to her and her smile vanished. She fiddled with the ring on her right hand in a nervous gesture.

"Did you pick it out yourself?" she asked.

"Merina."

"She has good taste."

He kept his eyes on hers, that feeling of falling into them not as scary as it was twenty-four hours ago.

Tag was right. Eli was in love. He knew because he wasn't sure he'd be able to hold himself upright if Isa rejected him again—and she might.

"Why did you really come here tonight, Sable?" His heart was in his throat, half scared of her answer. She had the power to break him—he was hers through and through. No wonder he'd never wanted to admit as much. Not knowing if she felt anything for him was terrifying.

"You know me. I don't run away from uncomfortable situations." She thrust her chin out, but he noticed her pulse flutter to life in her neck. Nerves?

God. He hoped so. He hoped she was nervous for the same reasons he was—because she was uncertain about where he stood. But she didn't have to worry.

"I do know you." He took a step closer. "You tend to step into the lion's den boldly, don't you?"

Her gaze flitted to the side, but she held her ground. He loved her for it. This strong, beautiful, brave woman. She was everything he wasn't—and some of what he was finding his way back to.

"Your beers, sir," the bartender announced. Eli held up a hand signaling him to hang on.

"Tell me why you came, Sable." He hadn't dreamed she'd show up tonight, and until this very moment hadn't realized how much he had needed her to. "Professional courtesy? Networking?"

Her nod was shaky.

"Or for personal reasons?" He lifted his hand to her face and cupped her jaw.

"Your note wasn't clear." Her breathy whisper was more of a plea. "What more do I deserve Eli?"

He caught the tail end of her sentence with his mouth, moving his lips softly, firmly over hers. She gave and gave, until their tongues tangled. Soon, his hands were spearing upward into her hair as he held her close—as Isa's fists curled around his lapels and she anchored herself to him.

When her hand flattened over his heart, he felt every aching ounce of loss that had compounded over the last two weeks. When it hit him, the ferocity stopped his heart and throttled his brain. He pulled his mouth from hers.

"Isabella." He swallowed thickly, feeling weak in the

knees—not good for a guy who'd lost everything below one of them. "It's a beautiful name."

She shook her head on a soft laugh.

"You deserve better than a man like me," he said. "That's what I meant in the note."

"So you lied," she said, one eyebrow arched. He shook his head to argue, but she continued. "I gave you an ultimatum and I shouldn't have. You asked for time and I didn't honor that request. I should have."

"No. You shouldn't have."

She blanched.

"I've had all the time I need, Sable." She'd come to him. She'd sought him out, bravely and surely. She was here and he knew the reason why even if she hadn't voiced it. She loved him. She had to. No way would she have poured herself into the dress he'd sent and stood before him like this unless she did.

He reached behind him for the nearest empty chair and collapsed into it, the weight of what this woman had done for him pushing him down. Hands on his knees, he struggled for air.

He loved her. She loved him. They were going to make this work.

Everything he'd been fighting had come to pass. She was exactly what he needed.

Isa came into view, concern in her whiskey-colored eyes as she knelt before him on the carpet, dress be damned.

"Eli." Her hands covered his. "Are you in pain?"

He looked up, a smile on his face when he tipped her chin and told her the truth. "Not anymore."

* * *

Eli's face...

Isa's heart slammed into her chest at full force. The lightness in his eyes, the tender grip he had on her jaw told her he was telling the truth. Eli wasn't in pain.

Not anymore.

"I love you, Sable."

She stared, mute, shaking her head. She'd come here to apologize, to get back on track with Eli—to give him the time he'd requested. She'd never expected a profession. He'd completely flipped that script.

"I wasn't ready before," he said. "The truth is I don't want to be ready." He brushed her cheek with his fingers. "I've never built something to last. I've never bothered trying. But with you...I want to build a future with you, Isa. Because any moment of the present where you're not here is a dark, dark day."

She blinked, hoping her twenty-dollar mascara held up and didn't streak down her cheeks.

"I should have been braver." He fingered the sleeve of the dress. "I should have brought this to you in person."

"Eli Crane," she said when she found her voice. "You're the bravest man I know."

"You're the bravest woman I know." He delivered the sweetest kiss to the center of her lips. "Do you still love me, Sable?"

His jaw tightened as he watched for her answer. The background and the din of chatter faded as she looked into his soulful, dark blue eyes.

"I fell in love with you a long time ago," she told him. Worry ate into his eyes, and he swallowed thickly, but he had no reason to worry. "I haven't had the good sense to fall back out."

"No?"

She loved the hope that filtered into his eyes. She loved *him*.

"Not even a little," she said.

He offered his palms and she accepted, sliding her hands into his. He helped her to her feet, standing with her, their clothes brushing as they stood close. Isa pushed her hands into his shorter hair and tipped her head back to study the scruff currently residing on his jaw.

"I prefer the beard."

A flash of white teeth when he grinned swelled her heart and lifted her chest.

"I prefer you," he said. "Always."

"Always is a big commitment."

"Always might not be long enough."

Her eyes dipped as his lips came over hers and then...

They were rudely interrupted.

"He can handle it."

Isa, lips still puckered, opened her eyes to find Tag standing next to them, his arm around Rachel's shoulders.

"Making out in the middle of a company dinner isn't professional," Reese said as he joined their cozy circle.

"Yeah," Merina told Eli. "PDA is more your brother's forte." She tipped her head to admire her husband.

"I only did that for the paparazzi," Reese told her.

"I think the Cranes have a penchant for public attention," Rachel said. "Tag never minded making a spectacle of himself."

"Look at him," Merina quipped. "He *is* a spectacle."

"Don't you guys have anywhere else to be?" Eli asked through his teeth. But he held fast to Isa, his hand warming her lower back.

"We don't," Rachel said, her wide eyes innocent—which Isa was quickly gleaning she was not.

Eli turned to Isa. "They come with the package. You don't get one Crane without getting them all."

"I like them all." Isa stroked her fingertip over his scruff and along his full bottom lip. She belonged here in the circle of his arms. "But I only love one of you."

"Me, I hope," Eli said.

"It's always been you."

His lips lowered to hers, but she couldn't keep her smile away when whoops and cheers came from Eli's brothers and the women who had tamed the other Crane men. Isa tucked their cheers, and Alex's raspy "ooh-rah" of approval, into her heart.

She was finally falling in love—with a man who had confiscated her heart and upended her life. And she knew Eli, sure and strong on his own two feet, would keep a tight hold of her as she did.

Playboy Reese Crane will do anything to become CEO of Crane Hotels...even propose a marriage of convenience to Merina Van Heusen...

Merina will do anything to get her parents' boutique hotel back—even marry cold-as-ice-but-sexy-as-hell Reese Crane.

It's a simple business contract: six months of marriage, total secrecy, and they both get what they want. But when the sparks fly between them, suddenly this façade of a marriage starts to feel very, very real...

An excerpt from
The Billionaire Bachelor follows.

CHAPTER 1

The Van Heusen Hotel was the love of Merina Van Heusen's life. The historical building dominated the corner of Rush and East Chicago Avenue, regal and beautiful, a living work of art.

Her parents' hotel had once been the Bell Terrace, home away from home to celebrities such as Audrey Hepburn, Sammy Davis Jr., and, more recently, Lady Gaga and the late Robin Williams. The original structure had perished in the Great Chicago Fire of 1871, only to be resurrected bigger, better, and more beautiful.

There was a life lesson in there.

Latte in hand, Merina breathed in the air in the lobby, a mix of vanilla and cinnamon. Faint but reminiscent of the famed dessert invented in the hotel's kitchen: the snickerdoodle. On her way past Arnold, who stood checking a guest into the hotel, she snagged one of the fresh-baked cookies off a plate and winked at him.

The dark-skinned older man slid her a smile and winked back. Having practically grown up here, Merina thought of the VH as a second home. Arnold had started out as a bell-man and had worked here for as long she could remember. He was as good as family.

She dumped her purse in her office and finished her cookie, holding on to the latte while she meandered down the hallways, checking to make sure there were no trays outside the doors that needed collecting. At the end of the corridor on the first floor, she saw a man outside one of the rooms, drill whirring away.

"Excuse me," she called. Then had to call again to be heard over the sound. When she came into view, he paused the drilling and looked up at her.

He wore a tool belt and navy uniform, and an antique doorknob was sitting on the floor at his feet along with a small pile of sawdust.

"What are you doing?" she asked, bending to pick up the heavy brass. Her parents had done away with "real keys" the moment they took over, installing the popular keycard entry hotels now used, but the antique doorknobs remained.

"Installing the fingerprint entry." From his pocket, the uniformed man pulled out a small silver pad with a black opening, then went back to drilling.

"No, no, no." She placed the doorknob back on the ground and dusted her hand on her skirt. "We're not doing any fingerprint entry." She offered a patient smile. "You need to double-check your work order."

He gave her a confused look. "Ma'am?" He was looking at Merina, but his voice was raised.

Merina's mother, Jolie, appeared from behind the hotel

room door, her eyebrows raising into hair that used to be the same honeyed shade of blond as Merina's but now was more blond to hide the gray.

"Oh, Merina!" Her mother smiled, but her expression looked a little pained.

"Can you give me a minute with my daughter, Gary?" Like she was Gary's mother, Jolie fished a five-dollar bill from her pocket and pressed it into his palm. "Go to the restaurant and have Sharon make you a caramel macchiato. You won't be sorry."

Gary frowned but took the cash. Merina shook her head as he walked away.

"Sweetheart." Jolie offered another smile. A tight-lipped one meaning there was bad news. Like when Merina's cat, Sherwood, had been hit by a car and Jolie had to break it to her. "Come in. Sit." She popped open the door and Merina entered the guest room.

White duvets and molded woodwork, modern flat-screen televisions and artwork. Red, gold, and deep orange accents added to the richness of the palette and were meant to show that a fire may have taken down the original building but couldn't keep it down.

Jolie gestured to the chair by the desk. Merina refused to sit.

"Mom. What's going on?"

On the end of a sigh that didn't make Merina feel any better, her mother spoke.

"Several changes have been ordered for the Van Heusen in order to modernize it. Fingerprint entry is just one of them. Also, the elevators will be replaced."

"Why?" Merina pictured the gold decorative doors with a Phoenix, the mythical bird that arose from the ashes of its predecessor, emblazoned on them. If there was a beating heart in the Van Heusen, it was that symbol. Her stomach turned.

Instead of answering, Jolie continued. "Then there's the carpeting. The tapestry design won't fit in with the new scheme. And probably the molding and ceiling medallions will all be replaced." She sighed again. "It's a new era."

"When did you take to day-drinking?" Merina asked, only half kidding.

Her mother laughed, but it was brief and faded almost instantly. She touched Merina's arm gently. "Sweetheart. We were going to tell you, but we wanted to make sure there really was no going back. I didn't expect the locksmith to arrive today." Her eyes strayed to the door.

Merina's patience fizzled. "Tell me what?"

"Your father and I sold the Van Heusen to Alexander Crane six months ago. At the time, he had no plans on making any changes at all, but now that he's retiring, the hotel has fallen to his oldest son. Evidently, Reese had different ideas."

At that pronouncement, Jolie's normally sunny attitude clouded over. Merina knew the Cranes. Crane Hotels was the biggest corporate hotel outfit in the city, the second biggest in the nation. Alexander (better known as "Big Crane") and his sons ran it, local celebrities of sorts. She'd also read about Big Crane's retirement and Reese's likely ascension to CEO.

But none of that mattered. There was only one newly learned fact bouncing around in her brain. "You sold the Van Heusen?"

She needed that chair after all. She sank into it, mind blanking of everything except for one name: Reese Crane.

"Why didn't you tell me?" Merina stood up again. She couldn't sit. She could not remain still while this was happening. Correction: This *had* happened. "Why didn't you talk to me first?"

"You know we'd never include you in our financial difficulties, Merina." Jolie clucked her tongue.

Financial difficulties?

"Bankruptcy was not an option," her mom said. "Plus, selling gave us the best of both worlds. No financial responsibility and we keep our jobs."

"With Reese Crane as your boss!" Her mind spun after she said it aloud. My God. They would be answering to that arrogant, idiotic . . . "No." Merina shook her head as she strode past her mother. "This is a mistake."

And there had to be a way to undo it.

"Merina!" her mother called after her as Merina bent and collected the discarded doorknob off the ground. She strode through the lobby, dumping the remainder of her latte in the wastebasket by the front desk, and then stomped outside.

As luck would have it, the light drizzle turned into steady rain the second she marched through the crosswalk. Angry as she was, she'd bet that steam rose off her body where the raindrops pelted her.

"That stupid, smarmy jackass!" she said as she pushed through a small crowd of people hustling through the crosswalk. Because seriously, who in their right mind would reconstruct the Van Heusen? Fingerprint entry? This wasn't a James Bond movie! She caught a few sideways glances, but it was hard to tell if they were because she was muttering to herself like a loopy homeless person or because she was carrying a disembodied doorknob around with her.

Could be both.

Her parents had sold the Van Heusen to the biggest, most ostentatious hotel chain in the world. And without telling their own daughter, who also happened to be the hotel's manager! How close to bankruptcy had they been? Couldn't Merina have helped? She'd never know now that they'd sneaked behind her back.

How could they do this to me?

Merina was as much a part of that hotel as they were. Her mother acted as if selling it was nothing more than an inconvenience.

Focus. You're pissed at Crane.

Right. Big Crane may have done her parents a favor buying it, but now that he was about to "peace out," it sounded like Reese had decided to flex his corporate muscle.

"Shit!" She didn't just do that. She did *not* just drown her Louboutin pumps in a deep puddle by the curb. She didn't splurge on much, but her shoes were an indulgence. She shook the rainwater from one pump as best she could and sloshed up Rush Street to Superior, her sights set squarely on the Crane Hotel.

Seventy floors of mirrored glass and as invasive as a visit to the ob-gyn. Given the choice between this monstrosity and the Van Heusen, with its warm cookies and cozy design, she couldn't believe anyone would set foot in the clinical, whitewashed Crane Hotels let alone sleep there.

At the top of that ivory tower, Reese Crane perched like

an evil overlord. The oldest Crane son wasn't royalty, but according to the social media and newspaper attention he sure as hell thought he was.

Halfway down Superior, she folded her arms over her shirt, shuddering against the intensifying wind. She really should have grabbed her coat on her way out, but there hadn't been a lot of decision-making going into her process. She'd made it this far, fists balled and steam billowing out of her ears, her ire having kept her warm for the relatively short walk. She should have known better. In Chicago, spring didn't show up until summer.

Finally, she stood face-to-face with the gargantuan, seventy-floor home base. The Crane was not only the premier hotel for the visiting wealthy (and possibly uncultured, given that they stayed *here*), but it was also where Reese slept, in his very own suite on the top floor, instead of his sprawling Lake Shore Drive mansion. She wouldn't be surprised if he slept right at his desk, snuggling his cell phone in one hand and a wad of money in the other.

Stupid billionaires.

Inside, she sucked in a generous breath and shook off her chill. At least there was no wind, and despite the chilling whitewash of furniture, rugs, and modern lighting, it was warm. But only in temperature. The Crane represented everything she hated about modern hotels. And she should know, because she'd worked diligently alongside her parents to keep the integrity of their boutique hotel since she started running it. Her hotel was a place of rich history, beauty, and passion. This place was a tower of glass, made so that the lower echelon of the city could see in but never touch.

Perfect for the likes of Reese Crane.

She walked through the lobby, filled to overflowing with businesspeople of every color, shape, and size. Flashes of suits—black, gray, white—passed in a monochrome blur, as if the Crane Hotel had a dress code and each and every guest here had received the memo. Merina, in her plum silk shirt and dark gray pencil skirt and nude heels, didn't stand out...except for the fact that she resembled a drowned rat.

A few surly glances and cocked brows were her reward for rushing out into the storm. Well. Whatever.

She spotted the elevator leading to Crane's office, catching the door as an older woman was reaching for the button. The woman with coiffed gray hair widened her eyes in alarm, a tiny dog held snugly in her arms. Merina skated a hand down her skirt and over her hair, wiping the hollows below her eyes to ensure she didn't go to Reese's office with panda eyes.

"Good morning," she greeted.

The older woman frowned. Here was the other problem with the Crane. Its guests were as snooty as the building.

Attitude reflects leadership.

The doors opened only once, to deliver the woman and her dog to the forty-second floor, and then Merina rode the car to the top floor without interruption. She used the time to straighten herself in the blurry, reflective gold doors. No keys or security codes were needed to reach the top of the building. Reese Crane was probably far too smug to believe anyone would dare come up here without an appointment. She'd heard his secretary was more like a bulldog that guarded his office.

The elevator doors slid aside to reveal a woman wearing

all black, her grim expression better suited for a funeral home than a hotel.

"May I help you?" the woman asked, her words measured, curt, and not the least bit friendly.

"You can't," Merina said, pleased the rain hadn't completely drowned out her rage. "I need to speak with Mr. Crane."

"Do you have an appoin—"

"No." She supposed she could have made an appointment, could have called ahead, but no sense in robbing Reese Crane of the full effect of her face-to-face fury.

The phone rang and the woman slid her acerbic glare away from Merina. She waited as the other woman answered a call, spoke as slowly as humanly possible, and then returned the receiver to the cradle. The woman folded her hands, waiting.

Even with her nostrils flared, Merina forced a smile. There was only one way past this gatekeeper. She called up an ounce of poise—an ounce being the most she could access at the moment. "Merina Van Heusen to see Reese Crane."

"Ms. Van Heusen," the woman said, her tone flat, her eyes going to the doorknob in Merina's hand. "You're here regarding the changes to the hotel, I presume."

"You got it," Merina said, barely harnessing her anger. How come everyone was so damn calm about dismantling a town landmark?

"Have a seat." Crane's bulldog gestured one manicured hand at a group of cushy white chairs, her mouth frowning in disgust as she took in Merina's dishevelment. "Perhaps I could fetch you a towel first."

"I won't be sitting." She wasn't about to be put in her

place by Reese's underling. Then her prayers were answered as the set of gleaming wooden doors behind the secretary's desk parted like the Red Sea.

Jackpot.

Merina barreled forward as the woman at the desk barked, "Excuse me!"

Merina ignored her. She wouldn't be delayed another second...or so she thought. She stopped short when a woman in a very tight red dress, the neckline plunging into plentiful cleavage, her heels even higher and potentially more expensive than Merina's Louboutins, swept out of the office and gave her a slow, mascaraed blink back. Then she sashayed around Merina, past the bulldog, and left behind a plume of perfume.

Interesting.

Reese's latest date? An escort? If Merina believed the local tabloids, one and the same. Paying for dates certainly wasn't above his pay grade.

Before the doors closed, she slipped into Reese's office.

"Ms. Van Heusen!" came a bark behind her, but Reese, who stood facing the windows and looking out upon downtown, said three words that instantly silenced his secretary.

"She's fine, Bobbie."

Merina smirked back at the sour-faced, coal-eyed woman as Reese's office doors whooshed shut.

"Merina, I presume." Reese still hadn't turned. His posture was straight, jacket and slacks impeccably tailored to his muscular, perfectly proportioned body. Shark or not, the man could wear a suit. She'd seen the photos of him in the *Trib* as well as *Luxury Stays*, the hotel industry's leading trade magazine, and like every other woman in

Chicago, she hadn't missed the gossip about him online. Like in his more professional photos, his hands were sunk into his pant pockets, and his wavy, dark hair was styled and perfect.

Clearly the woman who had just left was here on other business...or past business. If something more clandestine was going on, Reese would appear more mussed. Then again, he probably didn't muss his hair during sex. From what she gleaned about him via the media, Reese probably didn't *allow* his hair to muss.

The snarky thought paired with a vision of him out of that suit, stalking naked and primed, golden muscles shifting with each long-legged step. Sharp, navy eyes focused only on her...

He turned to face her and she snapped out of her imaginings and blinked at the stubble covering a perfectly angled jaw. What was it about that hint of dishevelment on his otherwise perfect visage that made her breath catch?

Thick, dark brows jumped slightly as his eyes zoomed in on her chest.

She sneered before venturing a glance down at her sodden silk shirt. Where she saw the perfect outline of both nipples. A tinge of heat lit her cheeks, and she crossed her arms haughtily, glaring at him as best she could while battling embarrassment.

"Seems this April morning is colder than you anticipated," he drawled.

And that was when any wayward attraction she might have felt toward him died a quick death. The moment he opened his mouth, her hormones pulled the emergency brake.

"Cut the horseshit, Crane," she snapped.

The edge of Reese's mouth moved sideways, sliding the stubble into an even more appealing pattern. But she wasn't here to be insulted or patronized.

"I heard some news," she said.

He didn't bite.

"Your father purchased the Van Heusen," she continued.

"He added it to the family portfolio, yes," he responded coolly.

Portfolio. She felt her lip curl. To him, the VH was a number on a spreadsheet. Nothing more. Which could also mean he didn't care enough about it to continue with these ridiculous changes.

"There's been an error. My mother is under the impression that many of the nostalgic and antique fixtures in the building will be replaced." She plunked down the heavy doorknob on his desk. A pool of rainwater gathered on his leather blotter.

Reese sucked in a breath through his nose and moved to his desk—a block of black wood the color of his heart—and rested one hand on the back of a shiny leather chair.

"Have a seat." He had manly hands for a guy who spent his days in an office and spare time eating souls, and they were about as disturbingly masculine as the scruff lining his jaw.

She didn't want to sit. She wanted to march over there and slap the pompous smirk off his face. Then she remembered her compromised top, refolded her arms over her breasts, and sat as requested.

You win this round, Crane.

Reese lowered himself into his chair and pressed a button on his phone. "Bobbie, Ms. Van Heusen will need a car in fifteen minutes."

"Yes, sir."

So he'd deigned to carve out fifteen minutes for Merina. Lucky her.

"I don't want a car."

"No? You're planning on walking back?" Even sitting, he exuded power. Broad, strong shoulders filled out his dark jacket, and a gray tie with a silver sheen arrowed down a crisp white shirt.

"Yes." She wondered what time of day he finally gave up and yanked the perfect knot out of that tie. When he surrendered the top button. Another flare of heat shot through her. She hated the way he affected her. She was just so damn aware of him.

It was unfair. She frowned.

"You were saying something about horseshit," he said smoothly, and she realized she had been sitting there glaring at him in silence for a long while.

She cleared her throat and plowed through what she needed to tell him.

"You can't redesign the Van Heusen Hotel. It's a landmark. Did you know the hotel was the first to install elevators? The hotel's chef created the snickerdoodle. That building is an integral thread woven into the fabric of this city."

She pressed her lips together. Perhaps she was being a tad theatrical, but the Van Heusen did have historical importance to the city, and beyond that, a personal history to her. She'd gone to college straight from high school and graduated with her business degree, her dream to run the Van Heusen. A dream she'd realized and was currently living until this little snafu.

"Born and raised in Chicago, Ms. Van Heusen. You're

not telling me anything I don't know," he said, sounding bored.

"Then you know remodeling the Van Heusen makes no sense," she continued, using her best ally: reason. "Our hotel is known for its style. Guests come there to experience a living, breathing piece of Chicago." She stopped short of going into a monologue about how even the fires couldn't destroy the dream but opted against it.

"My hotel, Ms. Van Heusen," he corrected.

His. A fact she'd gleaned only a few minutes ago. A dart of pain shot through the center of her chest. She should have demanded to see the contract her parents signed before sloshing over here in a downpour and parading her nipples for Mr. Suit & Beard. She was almost as pissed at them for keeping this from her as she was for Crane thinking he could strut in and take over.

"No matter who owns the building, you have to know that robbing the Van Heusen of its style will make it just another whitewashed, dull hotel," she said.

Her stomach churned. If she had to bear witness to them ripping up the carpeting and replacing it with white shining tile or see a Dumpster filled with antique doorknobs, she might just lose her mind. The hand-carved moldings, the ceiling medallions...each piece of the VH had been preserved to keep the integrity of the past. And now Reese wanted to erase it.

She heard the sadness creep into her voice when she ventured, "Surely there's another way."

He didn't respond to this. Instead he pointed out, "Your parents have been in the red for nearly two years."

She felt her eyes go wide. Two *years*?

"I gather this is news to you," he added, then continued. "Your father's hospital bills put them further in debt."

He was referring to her dad's heart attack last year. Merina had no idea the bills had buried them. She lived in the same house. How had they hidden this from her?

"They came to us to buy the building and we did," Reese said. "I could have fired them, but I didn't. I offered a generous pension plan if they stayed on through the remodel."

A shake worked up her arms and branched over her shoulders. Pension?

"I take it you didn't know that either."

"They didn't want to worry me," she said flatly, but it didn't take the sting from the truth. They'd kept everything from her.

Her pie-in-the-sky parents who loved that building arguably as much as they loved each other had to have gone to Big Crane as a last resort. They'd overlooked he had Satan for a son.

"They trusted your father to take care of them," she said, her anger blooming anew. "Then you waltz in and wipe them out."

"My father likes your parents, but this isn't about what nice people they are," Satan continued. "He mentioned how well they'd maintained the local landmark with what funds they had available."

Merina's nostrils flared as she inhaled some much-needed oxygen. Her parents had cared for and upgraded the Van Heusen as best they could, but face it, her family didn't have the billion-dollar bankroll the Cranes had.

"Your father is a wise man," she said, pitting the two men against each other. Sure enough, a flicker of challenge shone in Reese's navy eyes. "I doubt his intention when he purchased the Van Heusen was to turn it into a mini-me of the Crane."

"My father is retiring in a few months. He's made it clear the future of the Van Heusen is in my hands." Reese shrugged, which made him look relaxed and made her pulse skyrocket. "I fail to see the charm in the funky, run-down boutique hotel, and I assume most visitors do as well."

Funky? Just who did this jerk-off think he was?

"Do you know how many Hollywood actors have dined in our restaurant?" she blurted. "Hemingway wrote part of his memoir sitting on the velvet chair in the lobby!"

"I thought he mostly wrote in Key West."

"Rumors," she hissed.

A smirk slid over his lips in a look that likely melted his fan club's collective underpants, but it had no effect on her. Not now that she knew how far he was taking this.

"You have outdated heating and air," he said, "elevators that are so close to violating safety codes, you may as well install ladders for the guests on the upper floors, and the wood putty isn't fooling anyone, Merina."

At the cool pronouncement of her name, she sat straighter. She'd been told last month that the building inspector had come by for a reassessment for property value, not that he'd be feeding information to the vulture sitting across from her now.

She'd clearly been left out of a lot of discussions.

"The elevators are original to the building."

"It shows." He offered a slow blink. "The Van Heusen is stodgy and outdated, and revenue is falling more each quarter. I'm doing your parents a favor by offering them a way out of what will be nothing but a future of headaches." Reese folded his hands on the desk blotter, expertly avoiding the water gathered there. A large-faced watch peeked out from the edge of his shirt, the sleeves adorned with a pair of onyx and platinum cuff links. "The Crane branding is strong, our business plan seamless. If you love the building as much as you claim to, you'd support the efforts to increase the traffic. We'll see profits double with an upgrade." He shook his head. "But not with your parents there. And not with you there."

A shiver climbed her spine, the rain and Reese's words having sunk right into her bone marrow. Wait. Was he suggesting...

"You're...firing...me?"

He remained stoically silent.

"My family's goddamn name is on the marquee, Crane!" She shot out of her seat and pressed her fingertips onto his desk. Shining, perfect, unscarred. No character. No soul. No history.

Like Reese Crane himself.

"Your family's name will remain on the building," he stated calmly. And while those words tumbled around her brain and set fire to the fury that he'd put on to sear, he added, "Your parents are getting close to retirement age. Are you sure you swam over here on their behalf? Or is this about you?"

"Of course I'm sure," she said too quickly. She wasn't sure at all. Her world had been upended. Like when she'd learned there was no Santa Claus and that her dad had been sneaking downstairs to eat the Oreos all those years.

She thought back to her mom telling her about the sale of the Van Heusen and recalled the dash of hope in Jolie's expression.

Did they want out?

"Think about it, Merina. What I'm offering is more than retirement, and at their age I'm sure they don't want to find work," Reese stated. "Running the Van Heusen is all they've known."

If she had said that, the sentence would have been infused with passion hinting at the fairy tale by which they came to own the Van Heusen. When Reese said it, he made the hotel sound like it was a lame, deaf, blind dog needing to be put down.

No. She would not accept this. Not from Reese. Not from her parents. It was possible they'd forgotten how much the hotel meant to them. Not having money created desperate feelings. Her father wasn't as spry as he once was given his heart condition. Maybe they needed her intrusion.

Reese's phone buzzed and Bobbie stated, "Ms. Van Heusen's town car is here, sir."

"I don't want it," Merina bit out, still leaning over his desk.

He angled his eyes up to her and they stayed locked in a heated staring contest until "Very well" came from the phone's speaker, then clicked off again.

Merina straightened. Outside, the rain started coming down in sheets. Didn't it figure? An involuntary shiver racked her spine, and possibly her lips were turning blue from her wet hair, but she kept her knees locked and her arms folded securely over her peek-a-boo breasts.

"I have an appointment I can't miss, but I won't leave

you in suspense." Reese stood, deftly unbuttoned his jacket, and shrugged out of it. Those shoulders. My God. He was a mountain of a man. Tall and broad and the absolute opposite of what anyone might expect a hotel owner-slash-billionaire to look like.

"Suspense?" she repeated, her voice dipping low when he came out from behind the desk. Her eyes screwed up to meet his as he draped his suit jacket over her shoulders.

"I'm not going to put you out on your fantastic ass, Merina." His lips tipped—lush lips. His was a mouth made for sin. But then, Satan. So it made sense.

She gripped the jacket when he let go. She should be throwing it at him, but it was warm and she was freezing. And it smelled of leather and money and power. Three things she wished didn't make her feel safe. What was it about this man? She'd seen pictures of him before, and yes, noticed he was attractive, but in the flesh there was something about him that made her feel utterly feminine. Even at the worst possible times. Like when he was dangling her job over a lava-filled pit and daring her to grab for it.

"I appreciate your reconsidering. I belong at the Van Heusen." Until she figured out a way to get the hotel back, at least she could be there. She would come up with a way to delay the remodel.

"No, you misunderstand me. I can't keep you there," he said, a frown marring his otherwise perfect brow. "But I can offer you almost any position you'd like at Crane Hotels. We have openings in Wisconsin, Virginia, and Ohio. I know it's not Chicago, but chances are you can stay in the Midwest."

He slid past her while she stared at the sheeting rain, her fingers going numb around the lapels of his jacket. Not only was he firing her, but he expected her to work for him? Expected her to leave Chicago? This was her city, dammit! He didn't reserve the right to boot her out.

When she turned, Reese was pressing a button on the wall. His office doors whispered open.

A balding, smiling man appeared in the doorway and gave Reese a wave of greeting. He noticed her next and offered a nod.

Well. Merina didn't care who he was; he was about to get an earful. She wouldn't allow Reese Crane to dismiss her after dropping that bomb on her feet.

She stomped over to the doorway between him and his guest.

"You listen to me, you suited sewer rat." Disregarding their current third party, she seethed up at Reese. "I'm going to find a way around your machinations and when I do, I'm going to march back in here with the contract my parents signed and shove it straight up your ass."

Reese's eyebrows rose, his lips with them. Instead of apologizing to his guest, he grinned over at the balding man, who to his testament was appropriately shocked, and said, "You'll have to forgive Ms. Van Heusen. She doesn't like when she doesn't get her way."

The balding man laughed, though it sounded a tad uneasy.

Reese tilted his head at Merina. "Will there be anything else?"

"Your head on a pike." With that parting blow, she left, holding fast to the suit jacket. She wore it on the ride down the elevator, through the bland lobby, and out onto

Superior Street, where she wadded it up and threw it into a mud puddle gathering near the curb.

She walked back to the Van Heusen in the rain, telling herself she'd won this round. But Merina didn't feel victorious.

She felt lost.

Fall in Love with Forever Romance

STARLIGHT BRIDGE
By Debbie Mason

Hidden in Graystone Manor is a book containing *all* the dark little secrets of Harmony Harbor...including Ava DiRossi's. No one—especially her ex-husband, Griffin Gallagher—can ever discover the truth about what tore their life apart years ago. Only now Griffin is back in town. Still handsome. Still hating her for leaving him. And still not aware that Ava never stopped loving him...

Fall in Love with Forever Romance

HOMETOWN COWBOY
By Sara Richardson

In the *New York Times* bestselling tradition of Jennifer Ryan and Maisey Yates comes the first book in Sara Richardson's Rocky Mountain Riders series featuring three bull-riding brothers. What would a big-time rodeo star like Lance Cortez see in Jessa Mae Love, a small-town veterinarian who wears glasses? Turns out, *plenty*.

THE BASTARD BILLIONAIRE
By Jessica Lemmon

Since returning from the war, Eli Crane has shut everybody out. That is, until Isabella Sawyer starts as his personal assistant with her sassy attitude and her curves for days. But will the secret she hides shatter the fragile trust they've built? Fans of Jill Shalvis and Jennifer Probst will love Jessica Lemmon's Billionaire Bad Boys series.

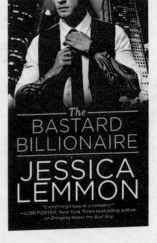

Fall in Love with Forever Romance

CHAIN REACTION
By Tara Wyatt

Alexa Fairfax is practically Hollywood royalty, but after she discovers a plot more deadly than any movie script, Alexa desperately needs a bodyguard. So she accepts the help of Zack De Luca, a true friend with a protective nature—and chiseled muscles to back it up. Zack is training to be an MMA fighter, but his biggest battle will be to resist his feelings for the woman who is way out of his league...

IF THE DUKE DEMANDS
By Anna Harrington

In the *New York Times* bestselling tradition of Elizabeth Hoyt, Grace Burrowes, and Madeline Hunter comes the first in a sexy new series from Anna Harrington. Sebastian Carlisle, the new Duke of Trent, needs a respectable wife befitting his station. But when he begins to fall for the reckless, flighty Miranda Hodgkins, he must decide between his title and his heart.

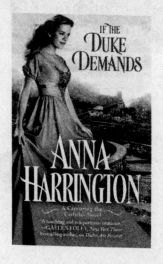

READ MORE FROM
JESSICA LEMMON

THE LOST BOYS SERIES
BOOK 1

MEET THE ULTIMATE BAD BOY...
AND A LOVE THAT CROSSES
ALL BOUNDARIES